METAL SOCIETY

Valentine keep fighting!

PUBLISHED BY TOP COW PRODUCTIONS, INC.
LOS ANGELES

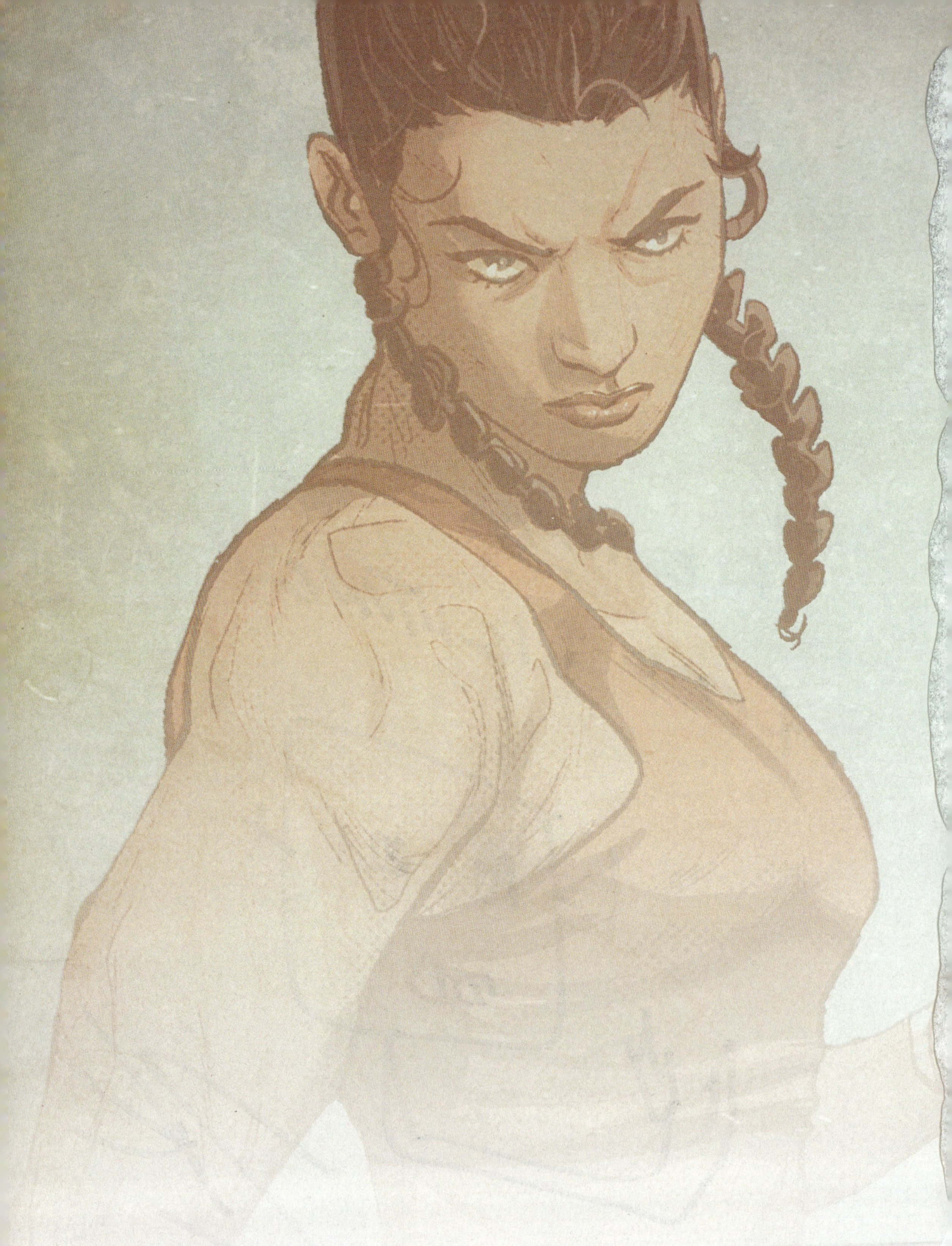

For Top Cow Productions, Inc.
Marc Silvestri - CEO
Matt Hawkins - President & COO
Elena Salcedo - Vice President of Operations
Vincent Valentine - Production Manager
Lisa Wu - Marketing Director

IMAGE COMICS, INC. • **Robert Kirkman:** Chief Operating Officer • **Erik Larsen:** Chief Financial Officer • **Todd McFarlane:** President • **Marc Silvestri:** Chief Executive Officer • **Jim Valentino:** Vice President • **Eric Stephenson:** Publisher / Chief Creative Officer • **Nicole Lapalme:** Vice President of Finance • **Leanna Caunter:** Accounting Analyst • **Sue Korpela:** Accounting & HR Manager • **Matt Parkinson:** Vice President of Sales & Publishing Planning • **Lorelei Bunjes:** Vice President of Digital Strategy • **Dirk Wood:** Vice President of International Sales & Licensing • **Ryan Brewer:** International Sales & Licensing Manager • **Alex Cox:** Director of Direct Market Sales • **Chloe Ramos:** Book Market & Library Sales Manager • **Emilio Bautista:** Digital Sales Coordinator • **Jon Schlaffman:** Specialty Sales Coordinator • **Kat Salazar:** Vice President of PR & Marketing • **Deanna Phelps:** Marketing Design Manager • **Drew Fitzgerald:** Marketing Content Associate • **Heather Doornink:** Vice President of Production • **Drew Gill:** Art Director • **Hilary DiLoreto:** Print Manager • **Tricia Ramos:** Traffic Manager • **Melissa Gifford:** Content Manager • **Erika Schnatz:** Senior Production Artist • **Wesley Griffith:** Production Artist • **Rich Fowlks:** Production Artist • **IMAGECOMICS.COM**

METAL SOCIETY

WRITTEN BY
ZACK KAPLAN

ART BY
GUILHERME BALBI

COLORS BY
MARCO LESKO

LETTERS BY
TROY PETERI

EDITED BY
ELENA SALCEDO

LOGO AND DESIGN BY
VINCENT VALENTINE

CHAPTER ONE

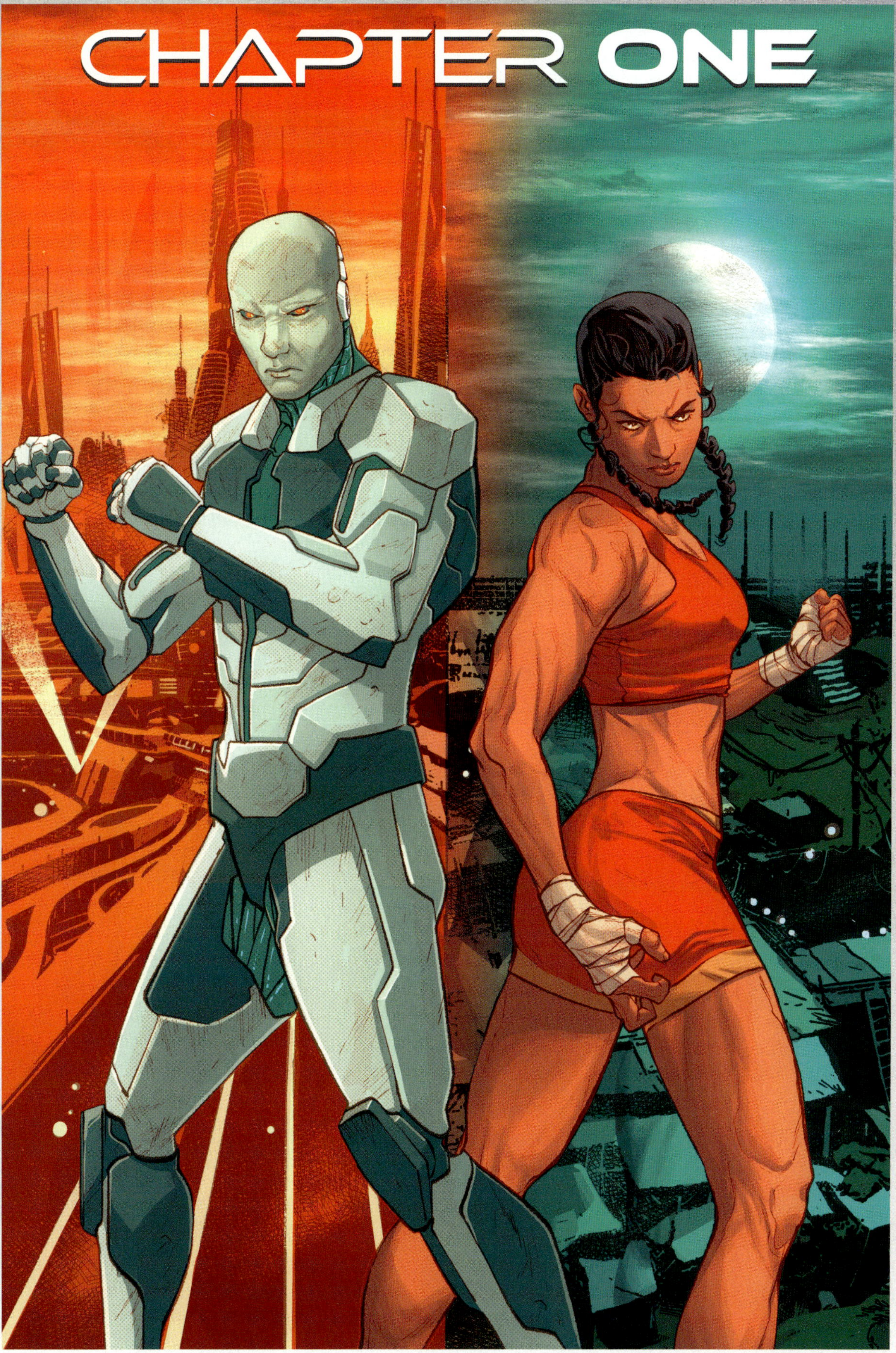

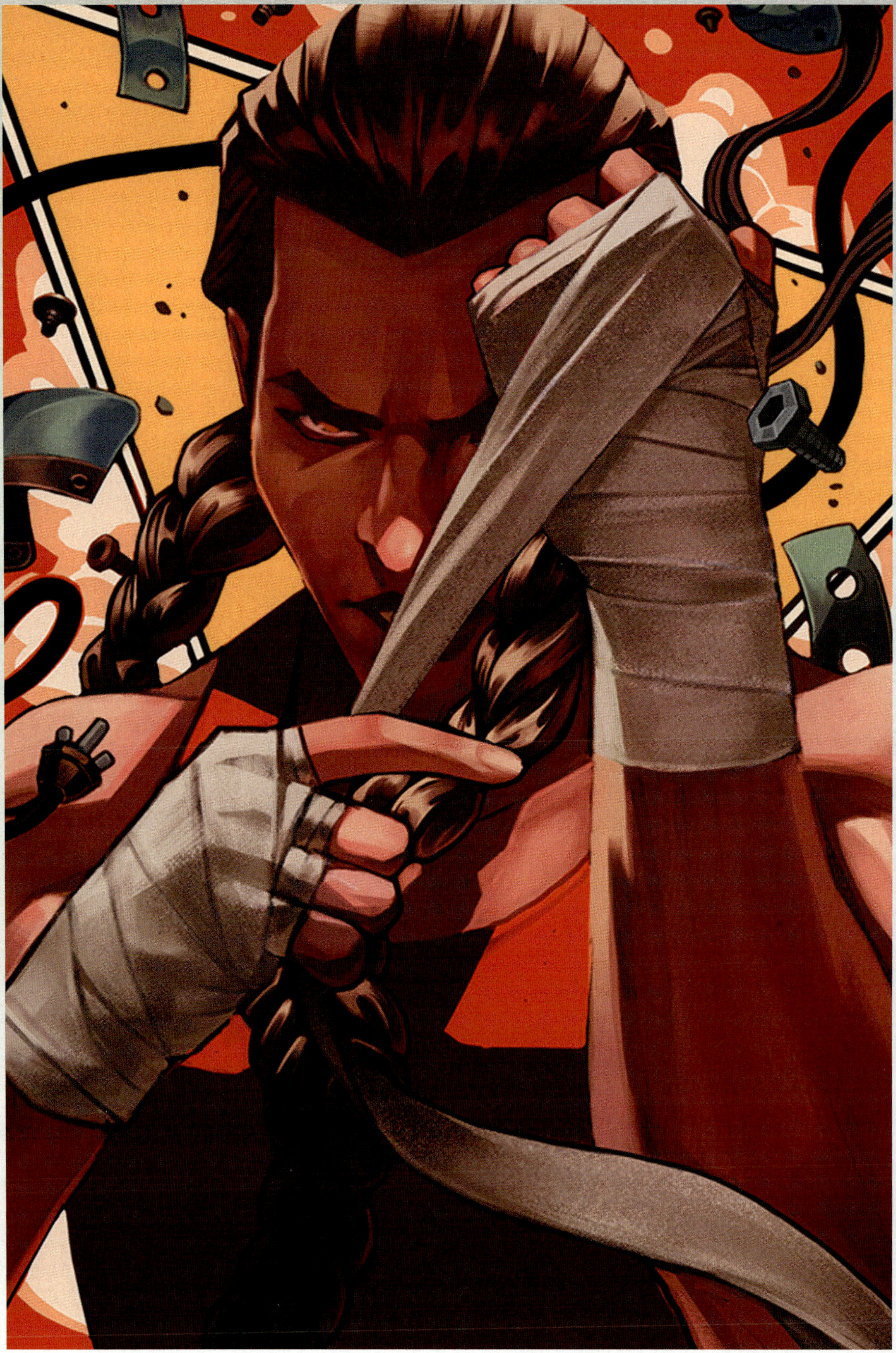

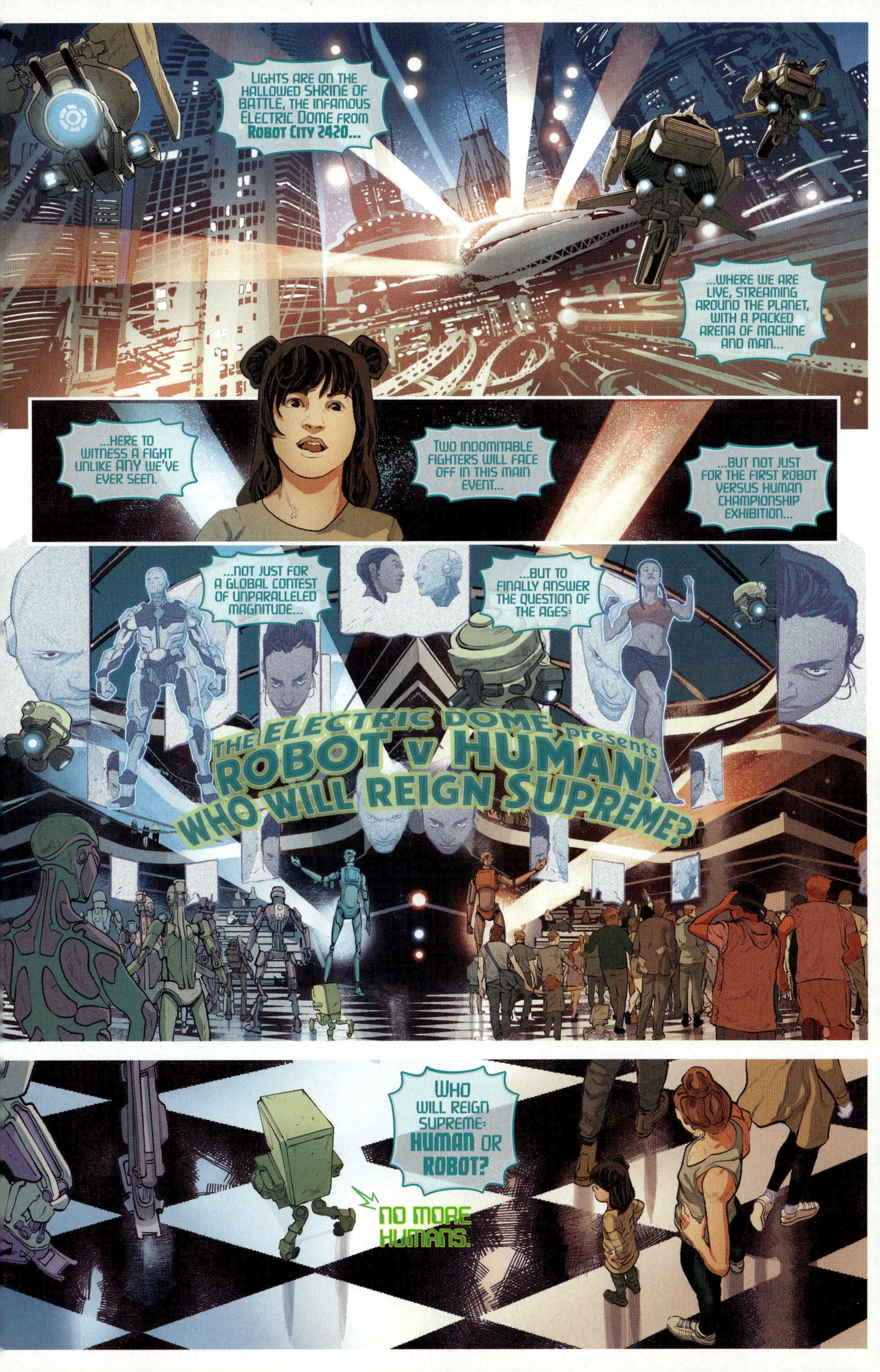
LIGHTS ARE ON THE HALLOWED SHRINE OF BATTLE, THE INFAMOUS ELECTRIC DOME FROM ROBOT CITY 2420...
...WHERE WE ARE LIVE, STREAMING AROUND THE PLANET, WITH A PACKED ARENA OF MACHINE AND MAN...
...HERE TO WITNESS A FIGHT UNLIKE ANY WE'VE EVER SEEN.
TWO INDOMITABLE FIGHTERS WILL FACE OFF IN THIS MAIN EVENT...
...BUT NOT JUST FOR THE FIRST ROBOT VERSUS HUMAN CHAMPIONSHIP EXHIBITION...
...NOT JUST FOR A GLOBAL CONTEST OF UNPARALLELED MAGNITUDE...
...BUT TO FINALLY ANSWER THE QUESTION OF THE AGES:
THE ELECTRIC DOME presents ROBOT v HUMAN! WHO WILL REIGN SUPREME?
WHO WILL REIGN SUPREME: HUMAN OR ROBOT?
NO MORE HUMANS.

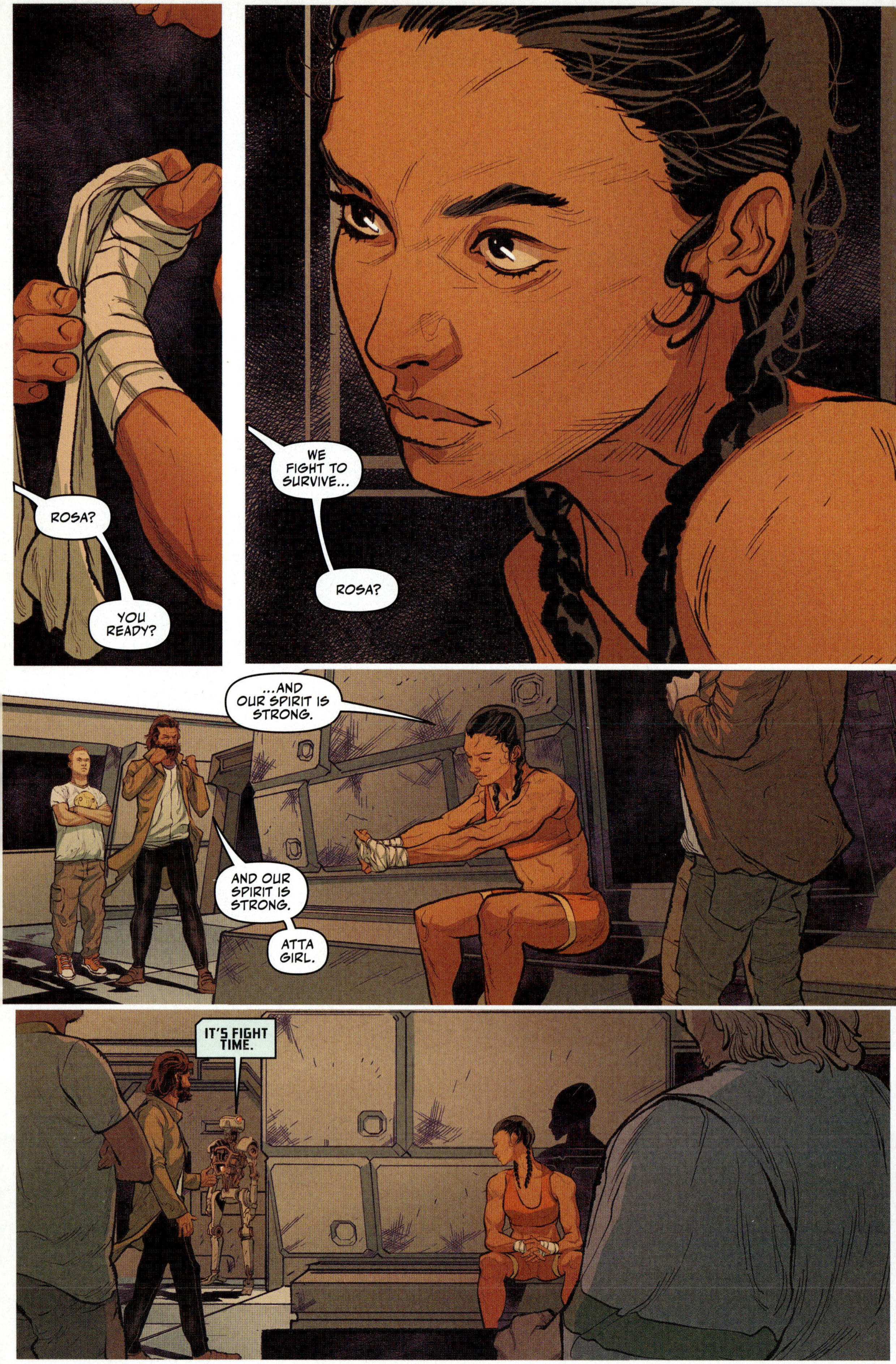
ROSA?
YOU READY?
WE FIGHT TO SURVIVE...
ROSA?
...AND OUR SPIRIT IS STRONG.
AND OUR SPIRIT IS STRONG.
ATTA GIRL.
IT'S FIGHT TIME.

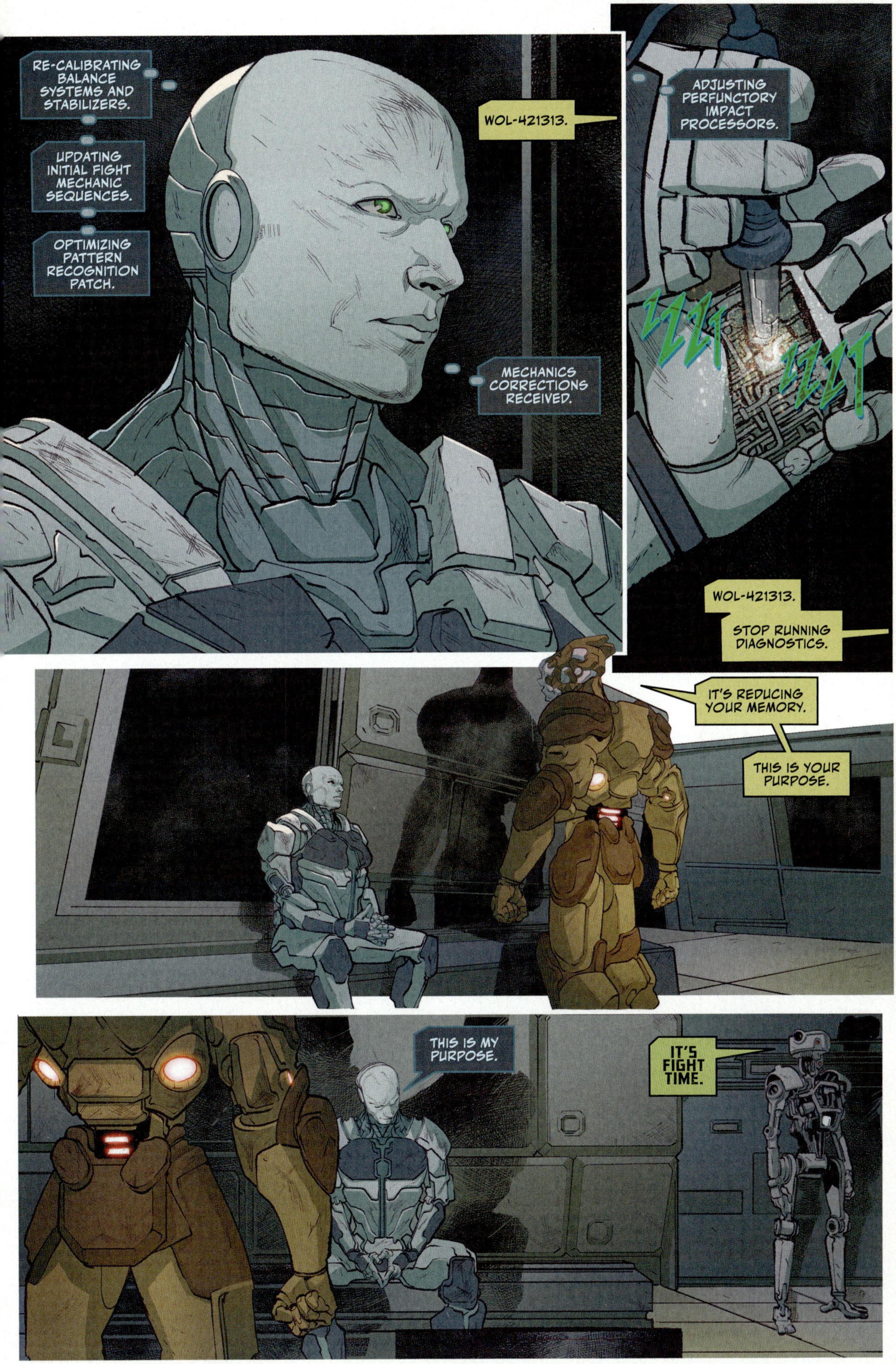
RE-CALIBRATING BALANCE SYSTEMS AND STABILIZERS.
UPDATING INITIAL FIGHT MECHANIC SEQUENCES.
OPTIMIZING PATTERN RECOGNITION PATCH.
WOL-421313.
MECHANICS CORRECTIONS RECEIVED.
ADJUSTING PERFUNCTORY IMPACT PROCESSORS.
ZZZT
ZZZT
WOL-421313.
STOP RUNNING DIAGNOSTICS.
IT'S REDUCING YOUR MEMORY.
THIS IS YOUR PURPOSE.
THIS IS MY PURPOSE.
IT'S FIGHT TIME.

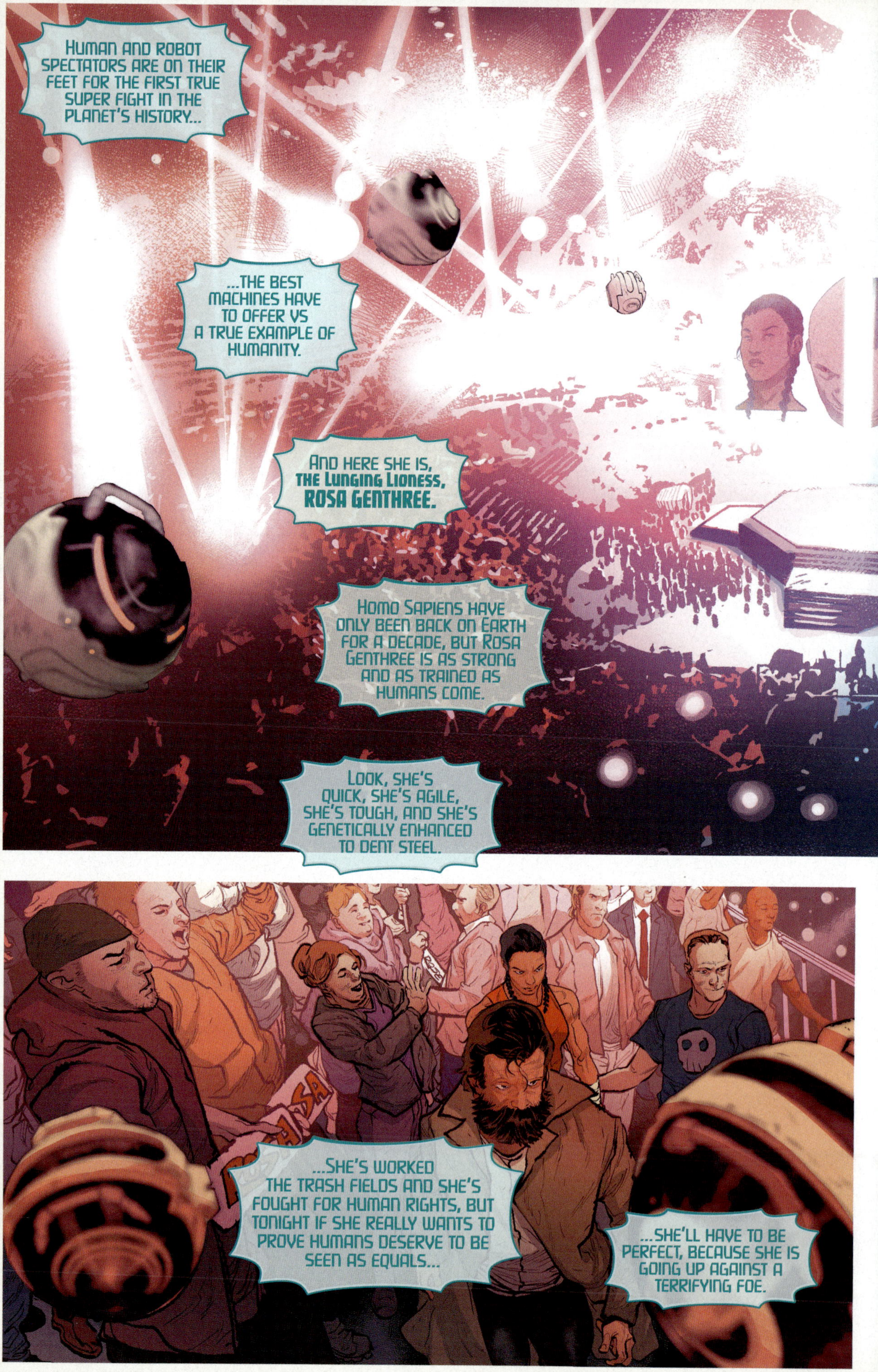
HUMAN AND ROBOT SPECTATORS ARE ON THEIR FEET FOR THE FIRST TRUE SUPER FIGHT IN THE PLANET'S HISTORY...
...THE BEST MACHINES HAVE TO OFFER VS A TRUE EXAMPLE OF HUMANITY.
AND HERE SHE IS, THE LUNGING LIONESS, ROSA GENTHREE.
HOMO SAPIENS HAVE ONLY BEEN BACK ON EARTH FOR A DECADE, BUT ROSA GENTHREE IS AS STRONG AND AS TRAINED AS HUMANS COME.
LOOK, SHE'S QUICK, SHE'S AGILE, SHE'S TOUGH, AND SHE'S GENETICALLY ENHANCED TO DENT STEEL.
...SHE'S WORKED THE TRASH FIELDS AND SHE'S FOUGHT FOR HUMAN RIGHTS, BUT TONIGHT IF SHE REALLY WANTS TO PROVE HUMANS DESERVE TO BE SEEN AS EQUALS...
...SHE'LL HAVE TO BE PERFECT, BECAUSE SHE IS GOING UP AGAINST A TERRIFYING FOE.

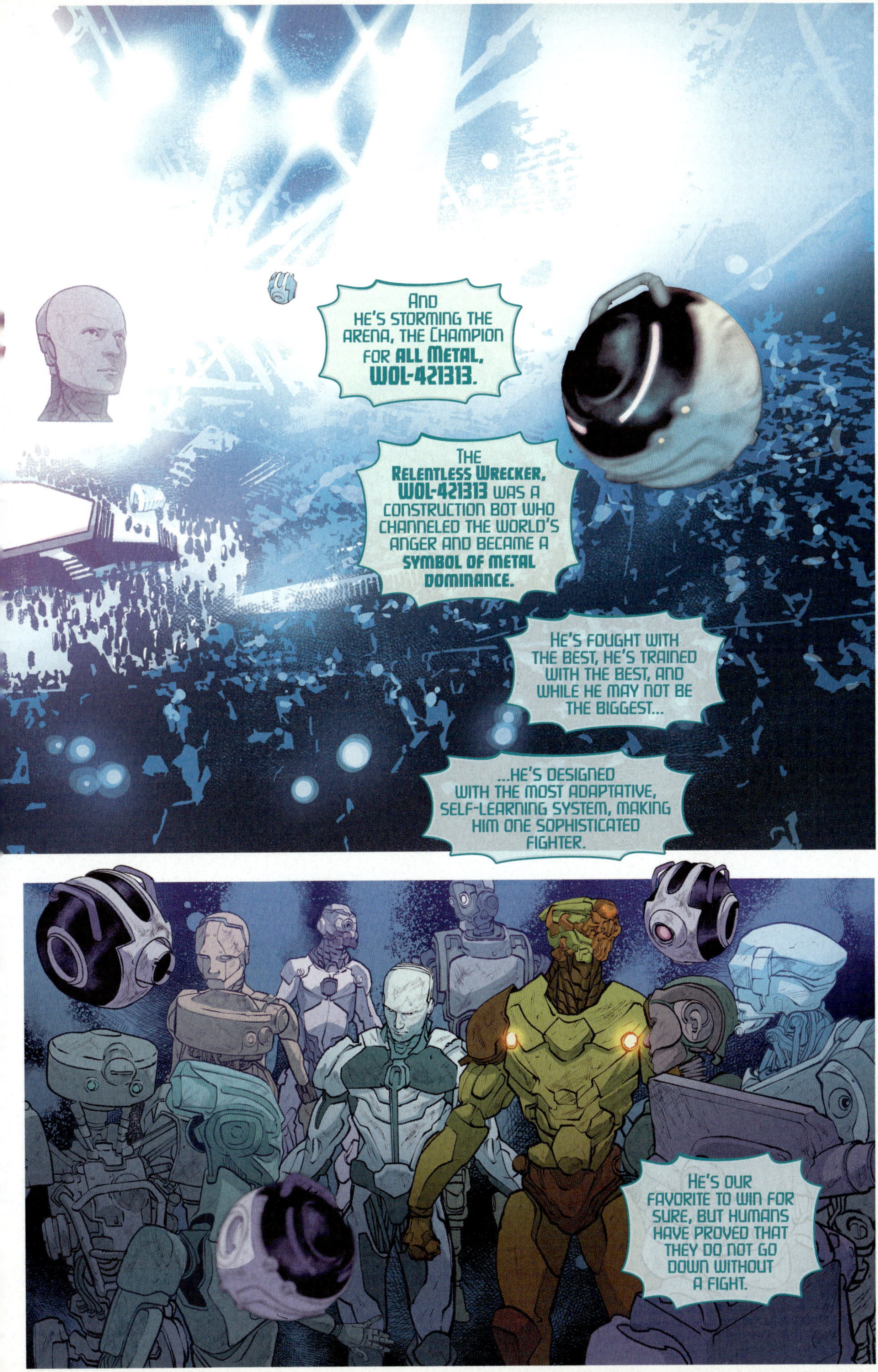
AND HE'S STORMING THE ARENA, THE CHAMPION FOR ALL METAL, WOL-421313.
THE RELENTLESS WRECKER, WOL-421313 WAS A CONSTRUCTION BOT WHO CHANNELED THE WORLD'S ANGER AND BECAME A SYMBOL OF METAL DOMINANCE.
HE'S FOUGHT WITH THE BEST, HE'S TRAINED WITH THE BEST, AND WHILE HE MAY NOT BE THE BIGGEST...
...HE'S DESIGNED WITH THE MOST ADAPTATIVE, SELF-LEARNING SYSTEM, MAKING HIM ONE SOPHISTICATED FIGHTER.
HE'S OUR FAVORITE TO WIN FOR SURE, BUT HUMANS HAVE PROVED THAT THEY DO NOT GO DOWN WITHOUT A FIGHT.

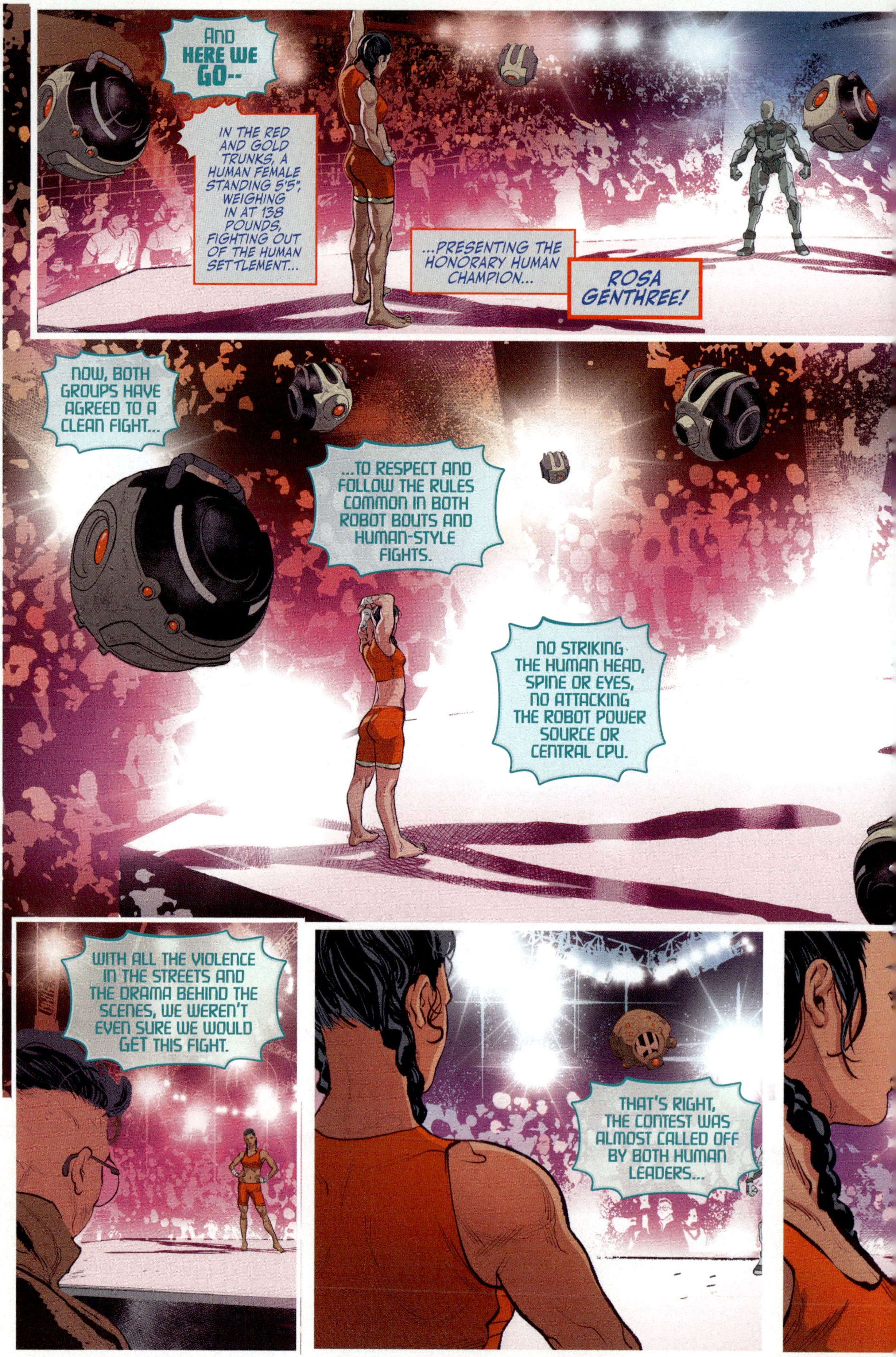
AND HERE WE GO--
IN THE RED AND GOLD TRUNKS, A HUMAN FEMALE STANDING 5'5", WEIGHING IN AT 138 POUNDS, FIGHTING OUT OF THE HUMAN SETTLEMENT...
...PRESENTING THE HONORARY HUMAN CHAMPION...
ROSA GENTHREE!
NOW, BOTH GROUPS HAVE AGREED TO A CLEAN FIGHT...
...TO RESPECT AND FOLLOW THE RULES COMMON IN BOTH ROBOT BOUTS AND HUMAN-STYLE FIGHTS.
NO STRIKING THE HUMAN HEAD, SPINE OR EYES, NO ATTACKING THE ROBOT POWER SOURCE OR CENTRAL CPU.
WITH ALL THE VIOLENCE IN THE STREETS AND THE DRAMA BEHIND THE SCENES, WE WEREN'T EVEN SURE WE WOULD GET THIS FIGHT.
THAT'S RIGHT, THE CONTEST WAS ALMOST CALLED OFF BY BOTH HUMAN LEADERS...

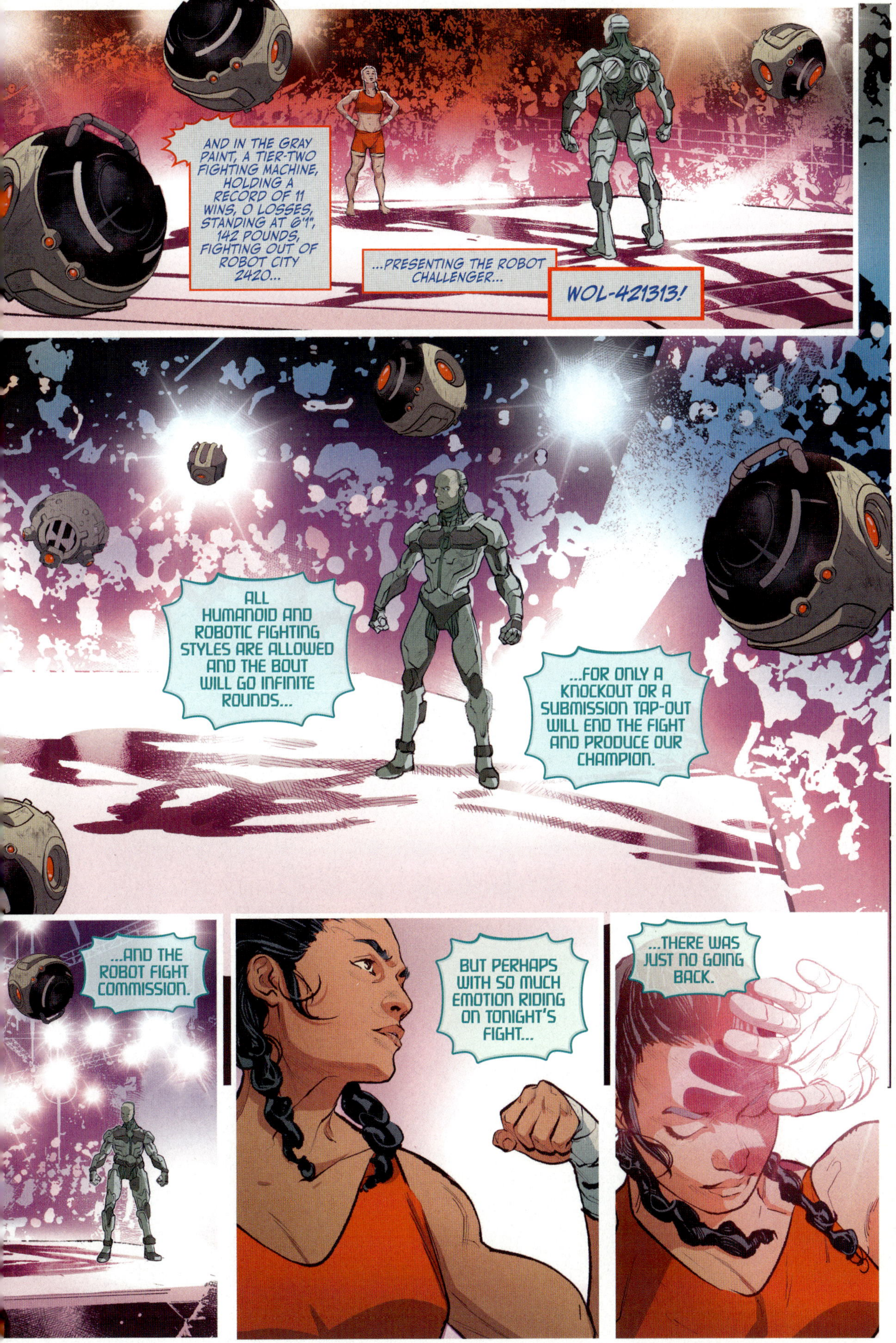
AND IN THE GRAY PAINT, A TIER-TWO FIGHTING MACHINE, HOLDING A RECORD OF 11 WINS, 0 LOSSES, STANDING AT 6'1", 142 POUNDS, FIGHTING OUT OF ROBOT CITY 2420...
...PRESENTING THE ROBOT CHALLENGER...
WOL-421313!
ALL HUMANOID AND ROBOTIC FIGHTING STYLES ARE ALLOWED AND THE BOUT WILL GO INFINITE ROUNDS...
...FOR ONLY A KNOCKOUT OR A SUBMISSION TAP-OUT WILL END THE FIGHT AND PRODUCE OUR CHAMPION.
...AND THE ROBOT FIGHT COMMISSION.
BUT PERHAPS WITH SO MUCH EMOTION RIDING ON TONIGHT'S FIGHT...
...THERE WAS JUST NO GOING BACK.

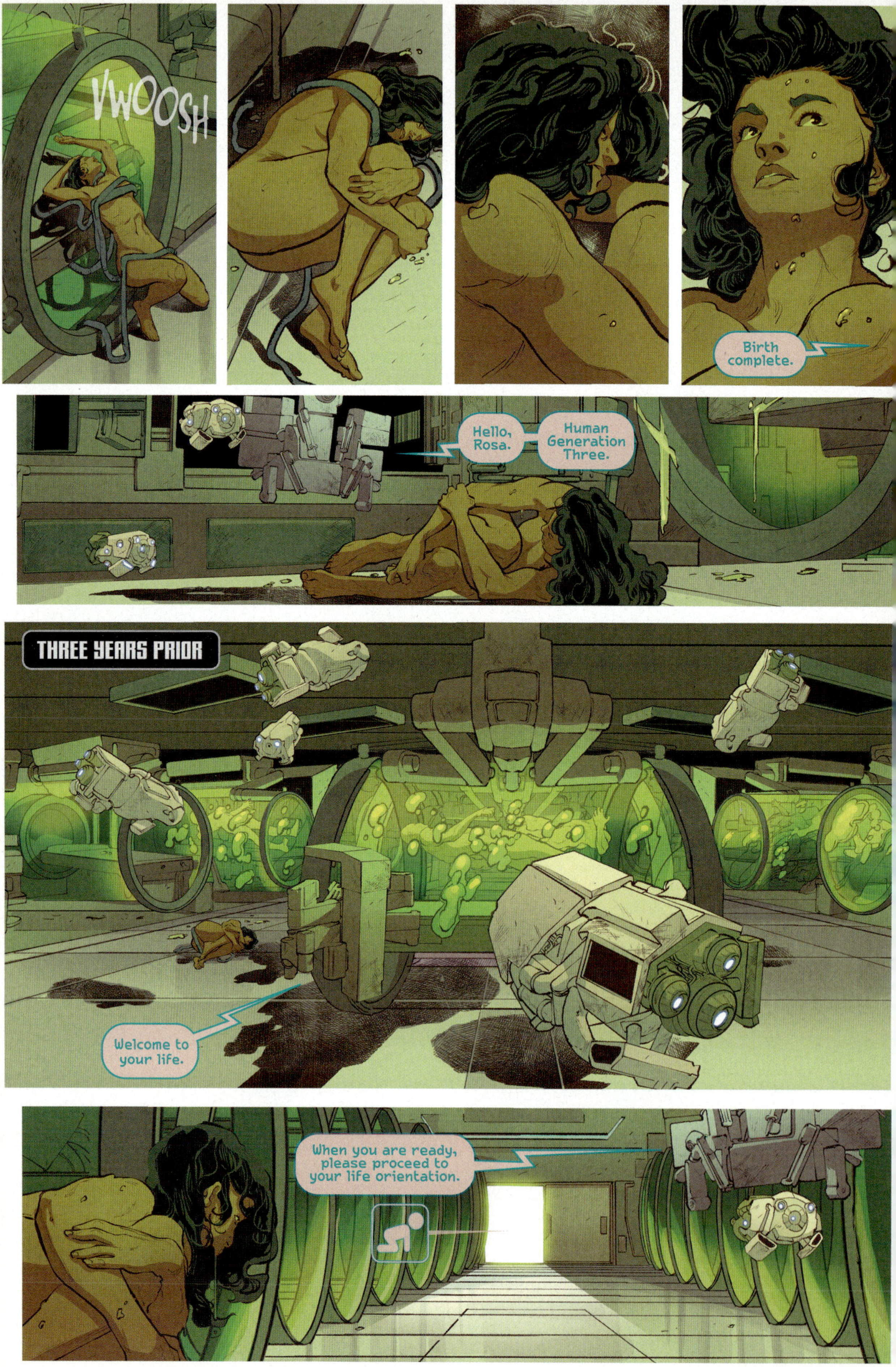
VWOOSH
Birth complete.
Hello, Rosa.
Human Generation Three.
THREE YEARS PRIOR
Welcome to your life.
When you are ready, please proceed to your life orientation.

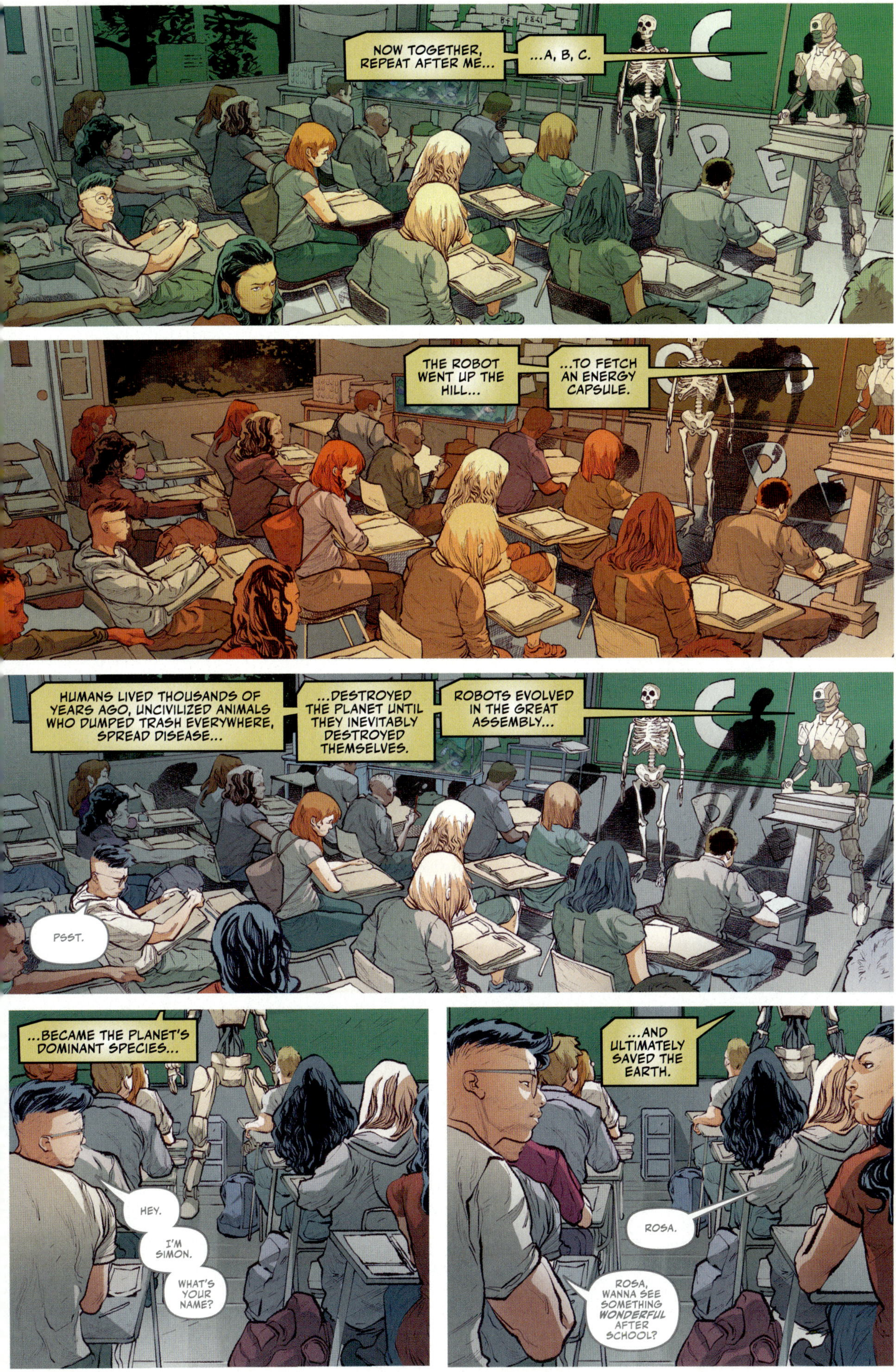
NOW TOGETHER, REPEAT AFTER ME...
...A, B, C.
THE ROBOT WENT UP THE HILL...
...TO FETCH AN ENERGY CAPSULE.
HUMANS LIVED THOUSANDS OF YEARS AGO, UNCIVILIZED ANIMALS WHO DUMPED TRASH EVERYWHERE, SPREAD DISEASE...
...DESTROYED THE PLANET UNTIL THEY INEVITABLY DESTROYED THEMSELVES.
ROBOTS EVOLVED IN THE GREAT ASSEMBLY...
PSST.
...BECAME THE PLANET'S DOMINANT SPECIES...
HEY.
I'M SIMON.
WHAT'S YOUR NAME?
...AND ULTIMATELY SAVED THE EARTH.
ROSA.
ROSA, WANNA SEE SOMETHING *WONDERFUL* AFTER SCHOOL?

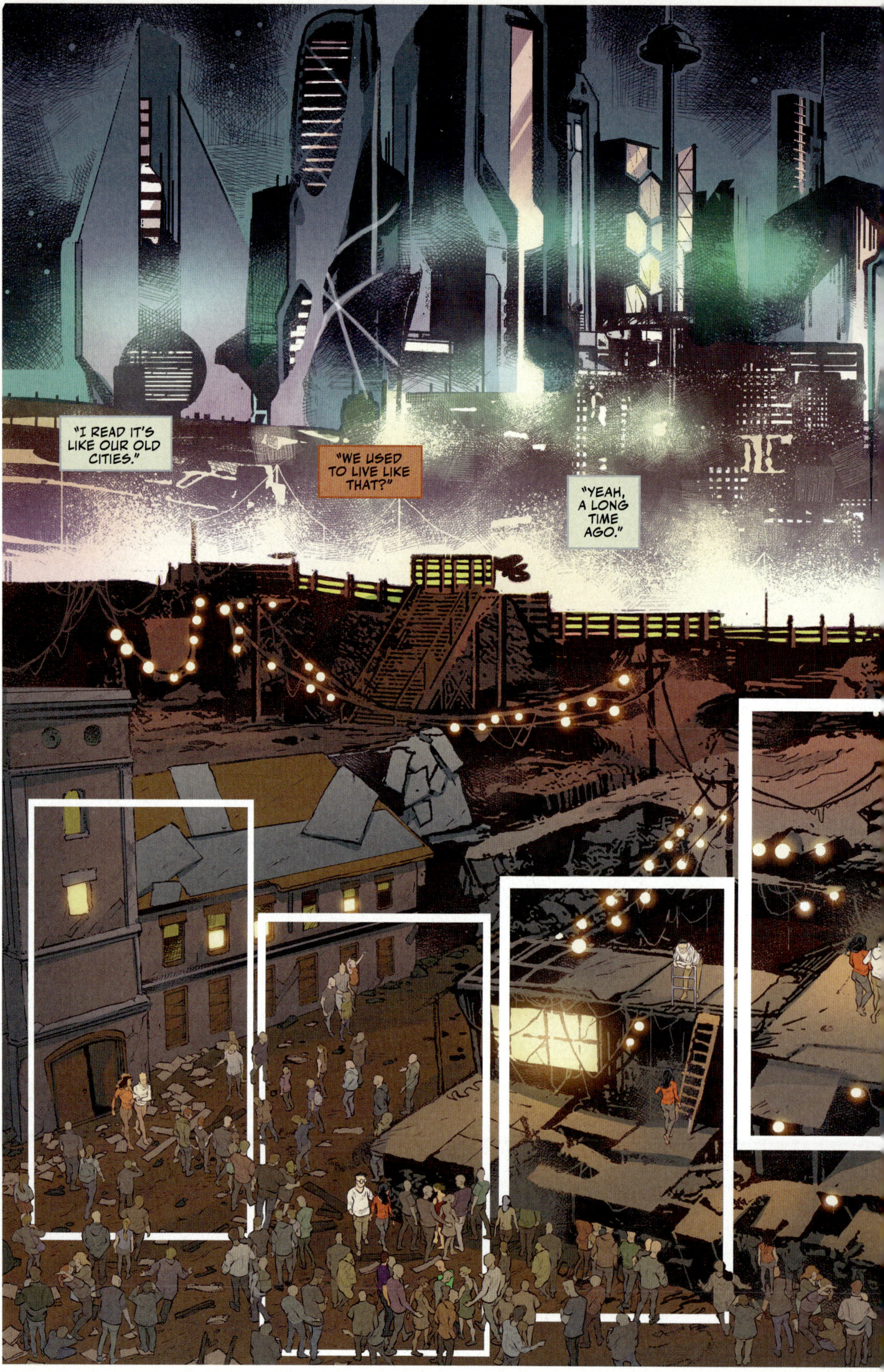
"I READ IT'S LIKE OUR OLD CITIES."
"WE USED TO LIVE LIKE THAT?"
"YEAH, A LONG TIME AGO."

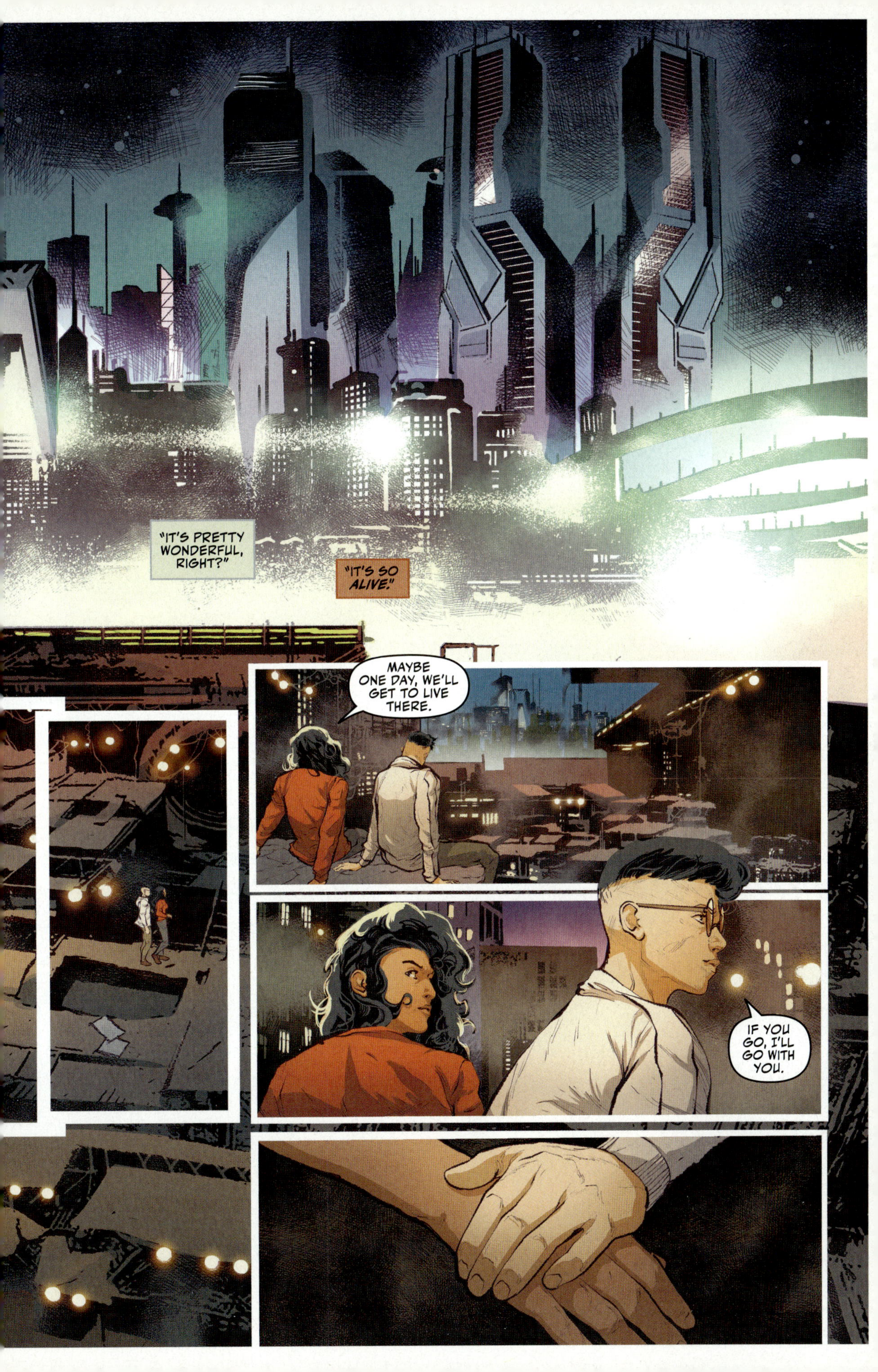
"IT'S PRETTY WONDERFUL, RIGHT?"
"IT'S SO *ALIVE*."
MAYBE ONE DAY, WE'LL GET TO LIVE THERE.
IF YOU GO, I'LL GO WITH YOU.

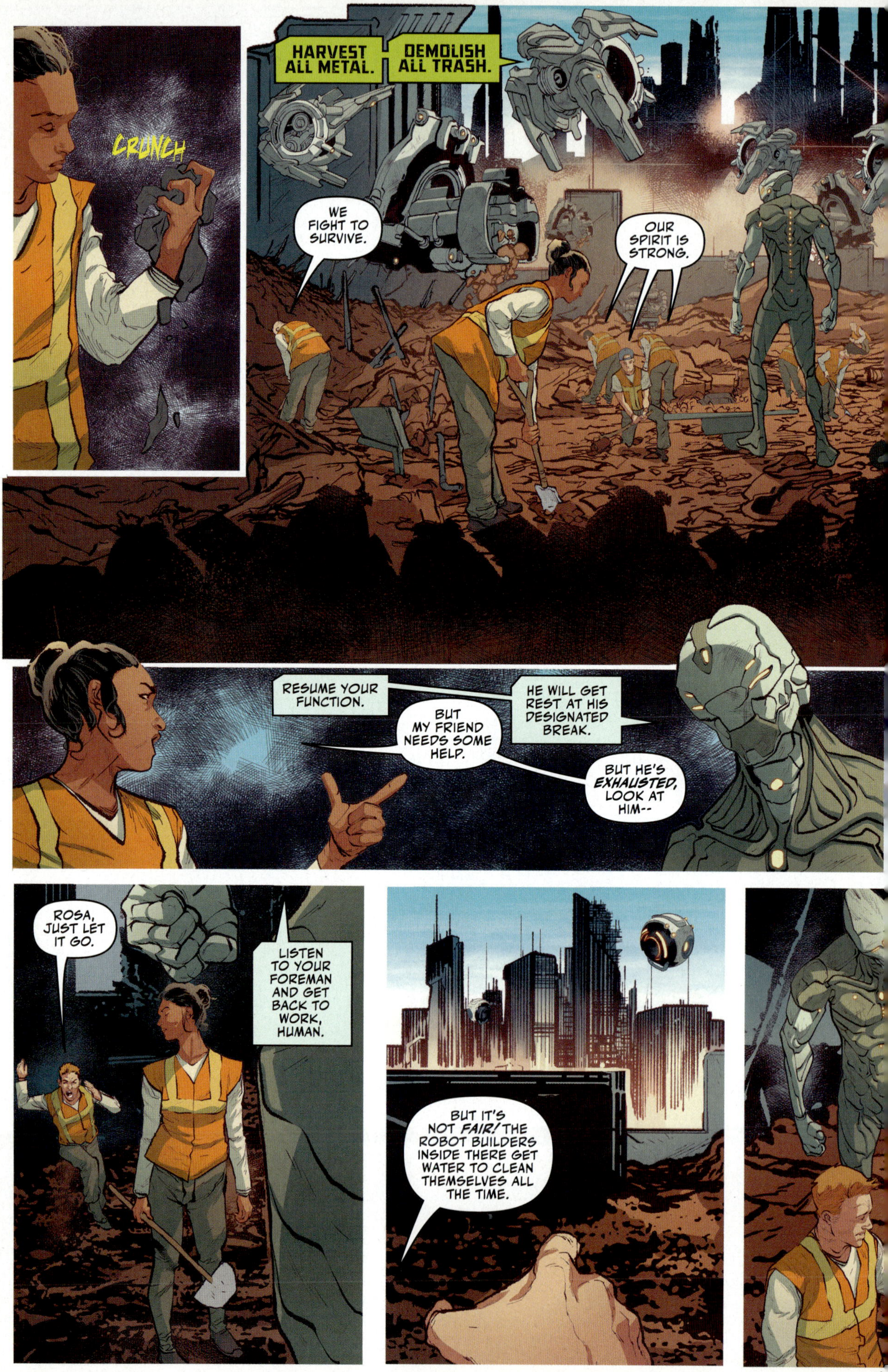
CRUNCH
HARVEST ALL METAL.
DEMOLISH ALL TRASH.
WE FIGHT TO SURVIVE.
OUR SPIRIT IS STRONG.
RESUME YOUR FUNCTION.
BUT MY FRIEND NEEDS SOME HELP.
HE WILL GET REST AT HIS DESIGNATED BREAK.
BUT HE'S *EXHAUSTED*, LOOK AT HIM--
ROSA, JUST LET IT GO.
LISTEN TO YOUR FOREMAN AND GET BACK TO WORK, HUMAN.
BUT IT'S NOT *FAIR!* THE ROBOT BUILDERS INSIDE THERE GET WATER TO CLEAN THEMSELVES ALL THE TIME.

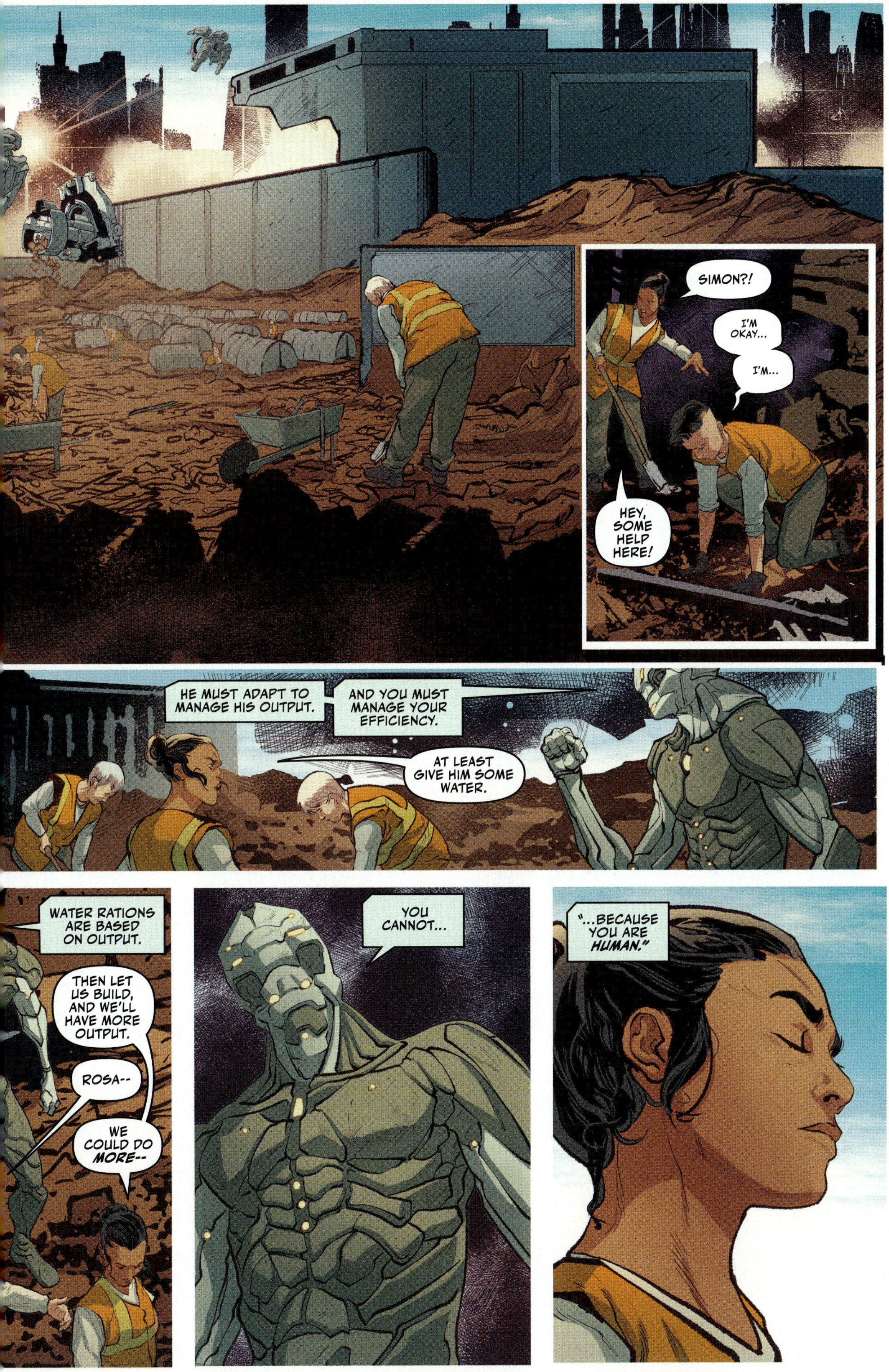
SIMON?!
I'M OKAY...
I'M...
HEY, SOME HELP HERE!
HE MUST ADAPT TO MANAGE HIS OUTPUT.
AND YOU MUST MANAGE YOUR EFFICIENCY.
AT LEAST GIVE HIM SOME WATER.
WATER RATIONS ARE BASED ON OUTPUT.
THEN LET US BUILD, AND WE'LL HAVE MORE OUTPUT.
ROSA--
WE COULD DO *MORE--*
YOU CANNOT...
"...BECAUSE YOU ARE *HUMAN.*"

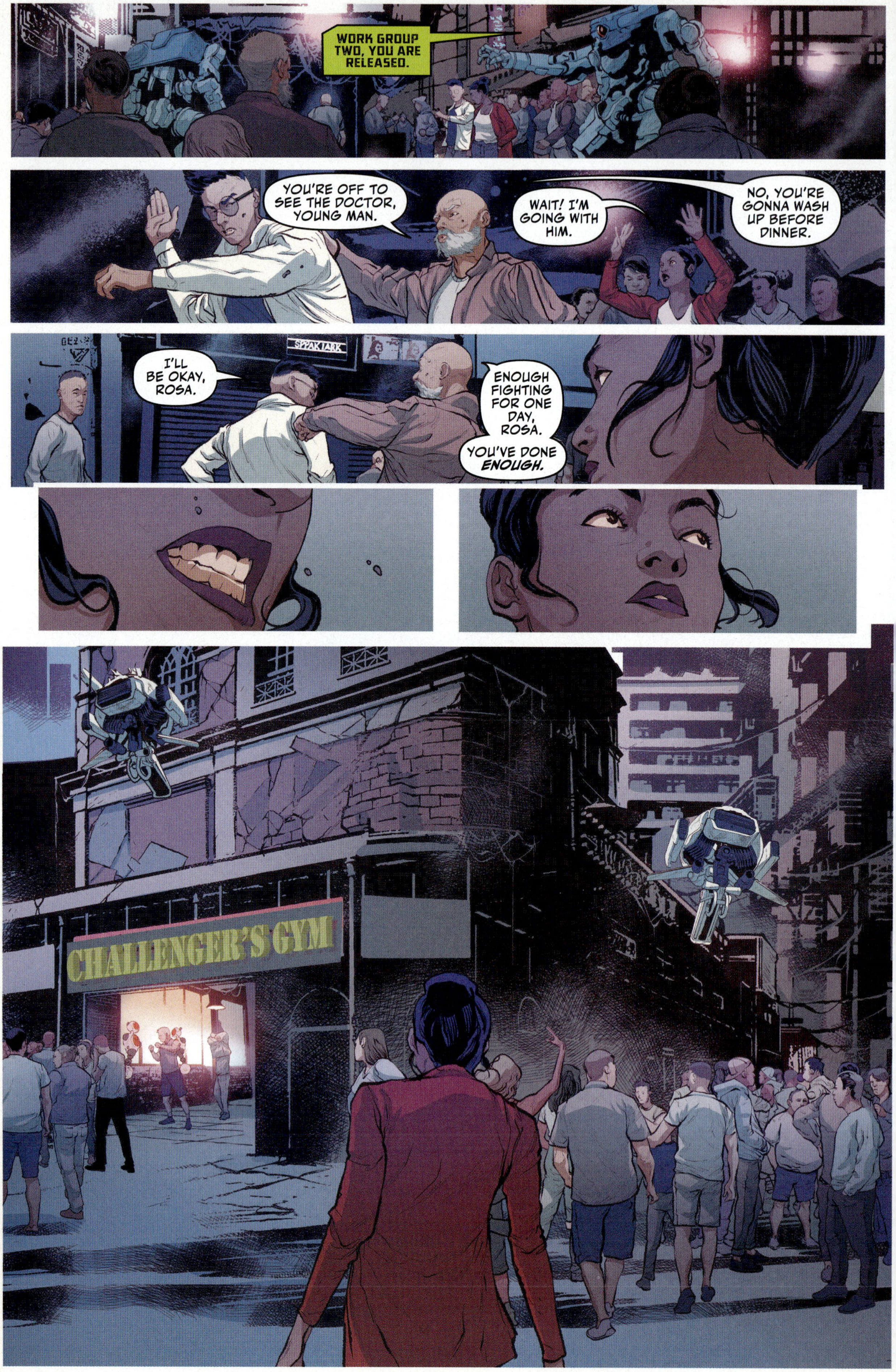
WORK GROUP TWO, YOU ARE RELEASED.
YOU'RE OFF TO SEE THE DOCTOR, YOUNG MAN.
WAIT! I'M GOING WITH HIM.
NO, YOU'RE GONNA WASH UP BEFORE DINNER.
I'LL BE OKAY, ROSA.
ENOUGH FIGHTING FOR ONE DAY, ROSA.
YOU'VE DONE *ENOUGH.*
CHALLENGER'S GYM

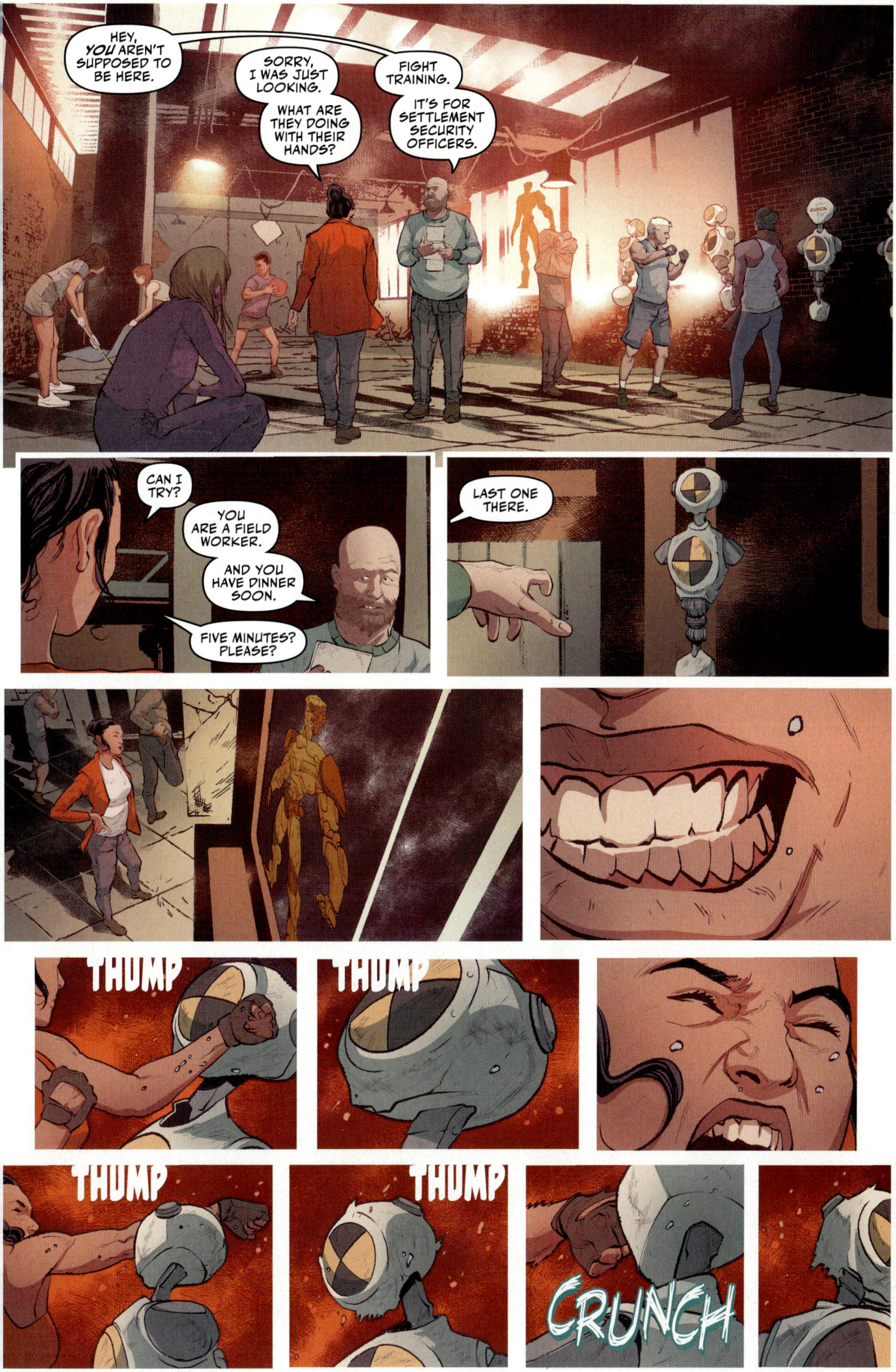
HEY, YOU AREN'T SUPPOSED TO BE HERE.
SORRY, I WAS JUST LOOKING.
WHAT ARE THEY DOING WITH THEIR HANDS?
FIGHT TRAINING.
IT'S FOR SETTLEMENT SECURITY OFFICERS.
CAN I TRY?
YOU ARE A FIELD WORKER.
AND YOU HAVE DINNER SOON.
FIVE MINUTES? PLEASE?
LAST ONE THERE.
THUMP
THUMP
THUMP
THUMP
CRUNCH

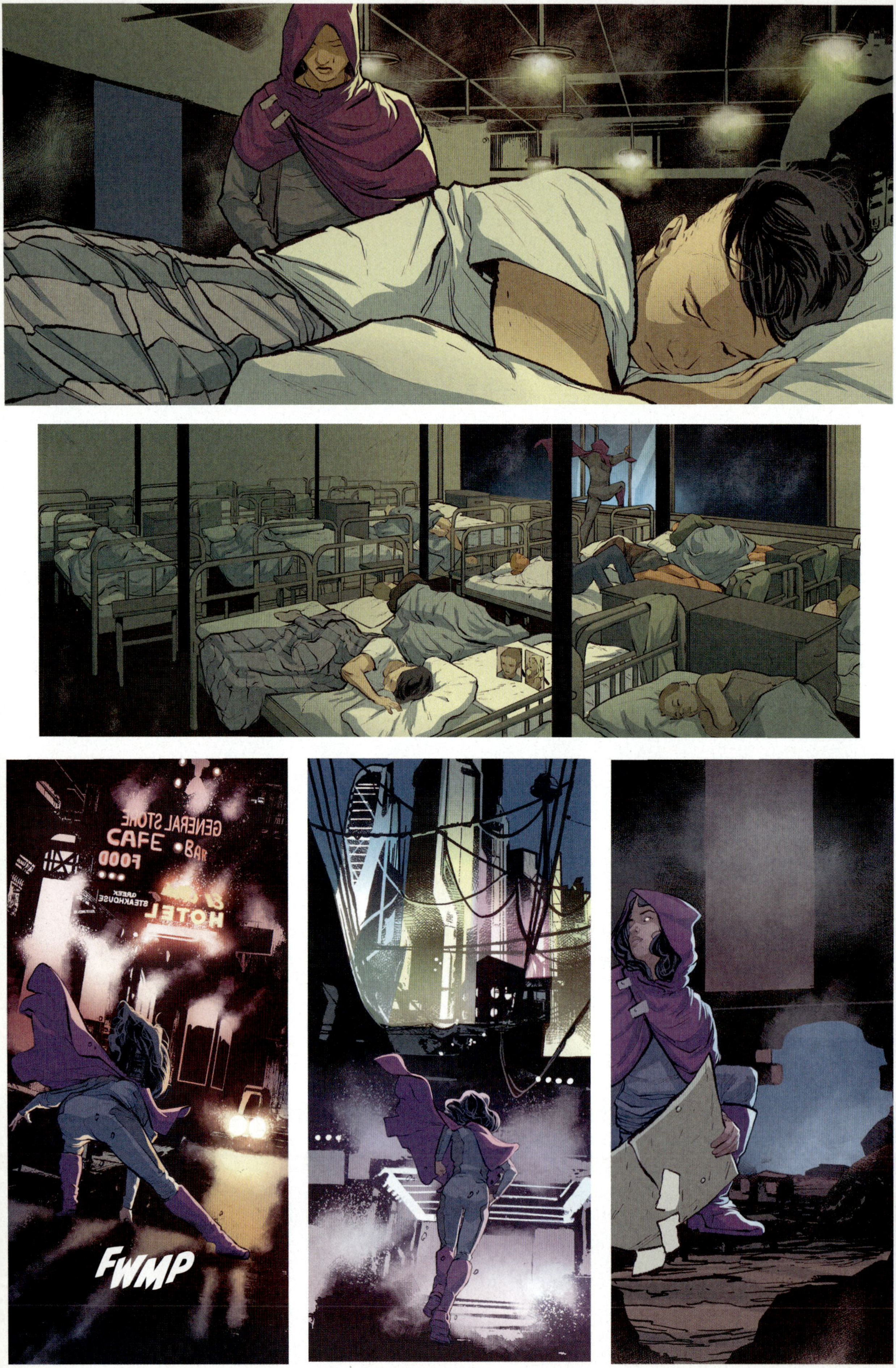
GENERAL STORE
CAFE
BAR
FOOD
GREEK STEAKHOUSE
HOTEL
FWMP

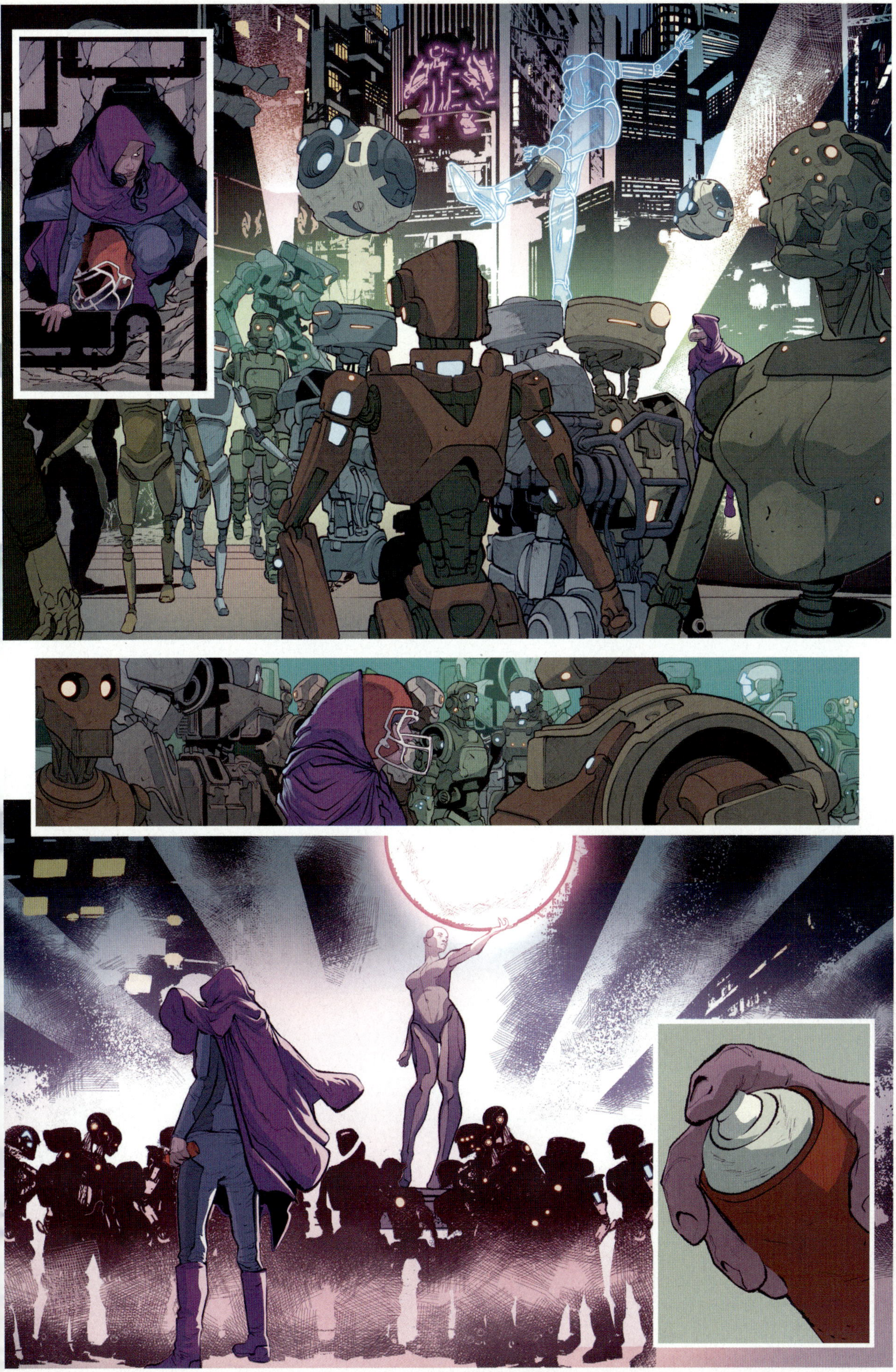

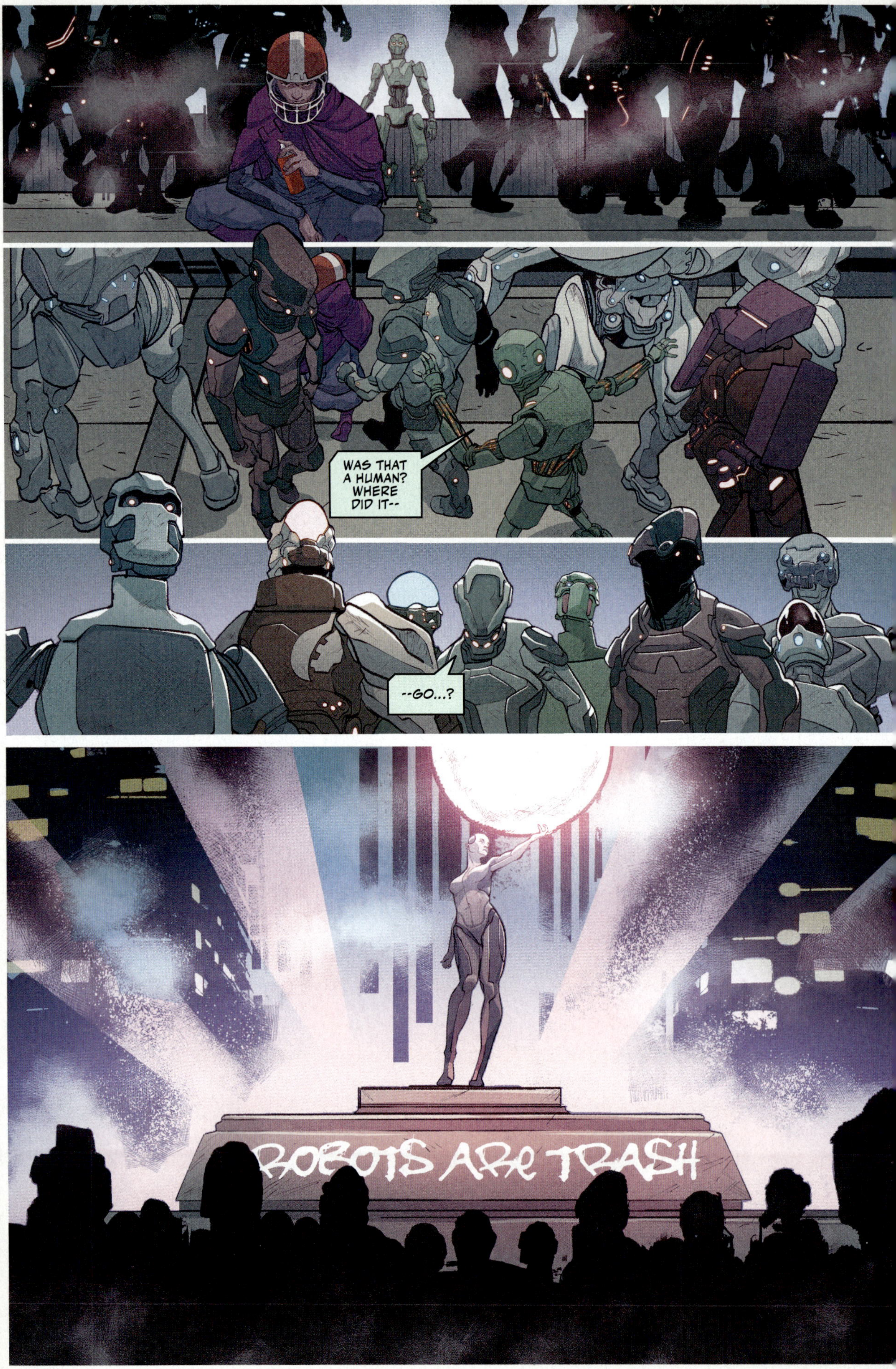
WAS THAT A HUMAN? WHERE DID IT--
--GO...?
ROBOTS ARE TRASH

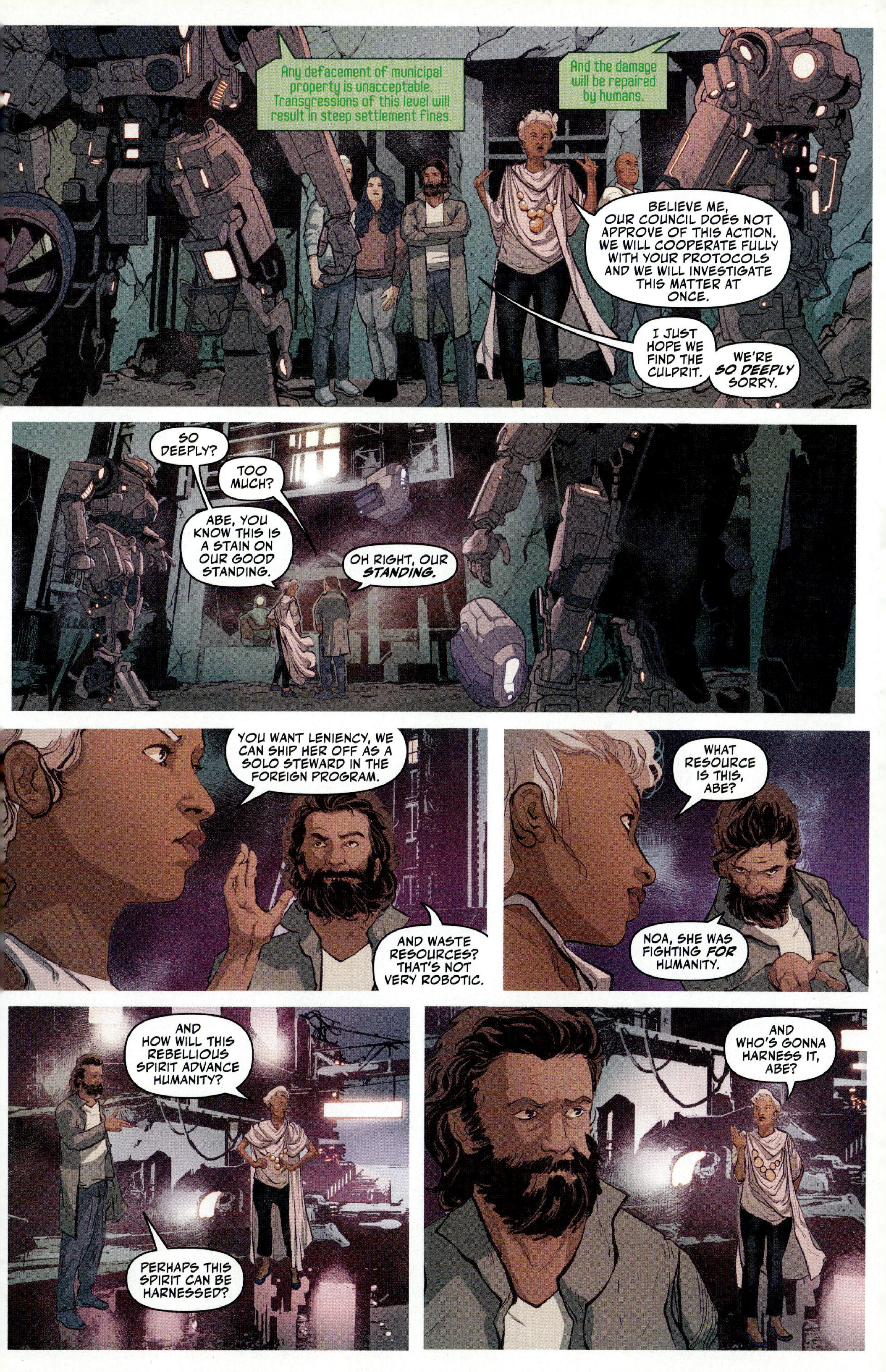

Any defacement of municipal property is unacceptable. Transgressions of this level will result in steep settlement fines.
And the damage will be repaired by humans.
BELIEVE ME, OUR COUNCIL DOES NOT APPROVE OF THIS ACTION. WE WILL COOPERATE FULLY WITH YOUR PROTOCOLS AND WE WILL INVESTIGATE THIS MATTER AT ONCE.
I JUST HOPE WE FIND THE CULPRIT.
WE'RE SO DEEPLY SORRY.
SO DEEPLY?
TOO MUCH?
ABE, YOU KNOW THIS IS A STAIN ON OUR GOOD STANDING.
OH RIGHT, OUR STANDING.
YOU WANT LENIENCY, WE CAN SHIP HER OFF AS A SOLO STEWARD IN THE FOREIGN PROGRAM.
AND WASTE RESOURCES? THAT'S NOT VERY ROBOTIC.
WHAT RESOURCE IS THIS, ABE?
NOA, SHE WAS FIGHTING FOR HUMANITY.
AND HOW WILL THIS REBELLIOUS SPIRIT ADVANCE HUMANITY?
PERHAPS THIS SPIRIT CAN BE HARNESSED?
AND WHO'S GONNA HARNESS IT, ABE?

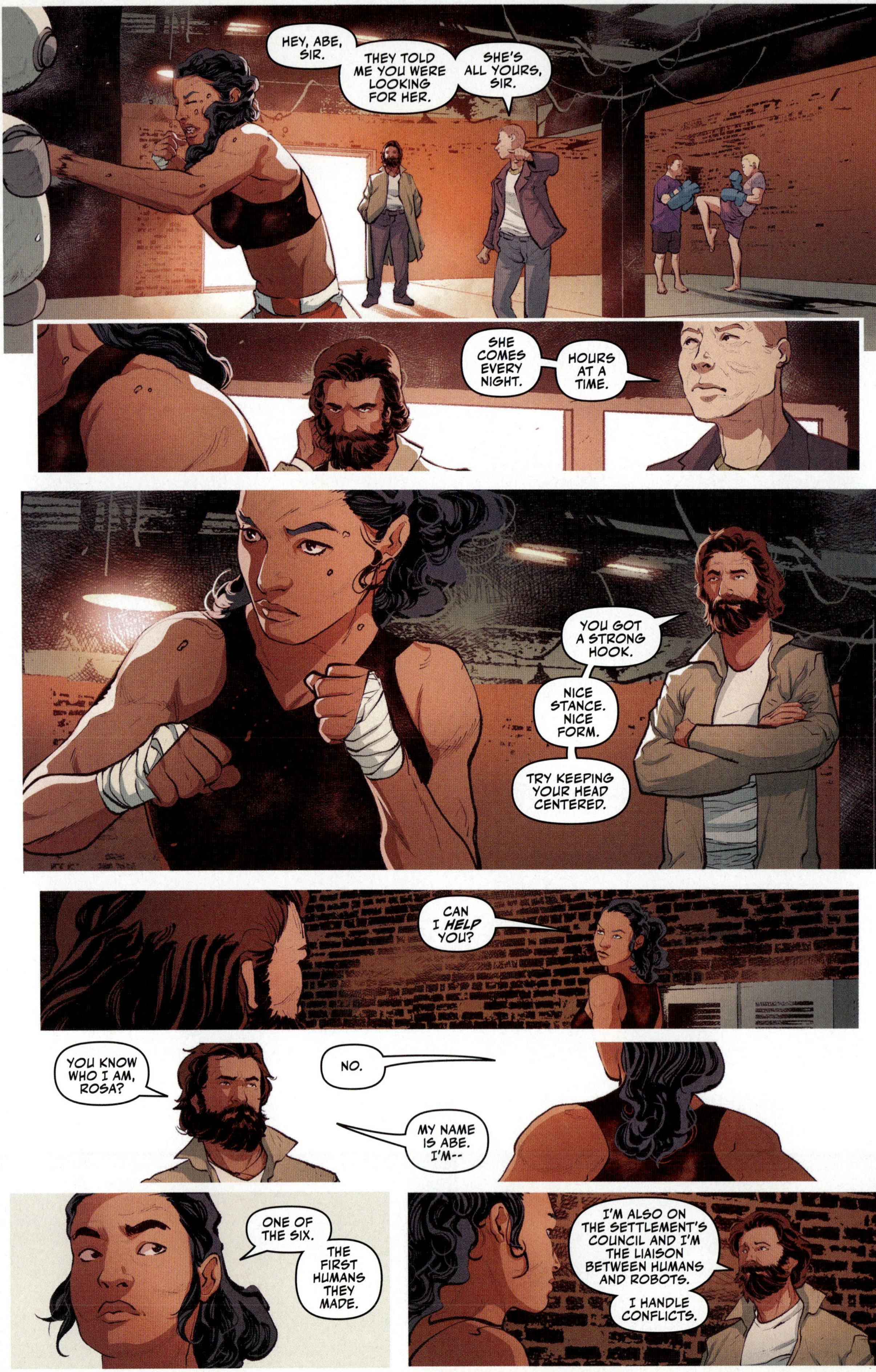

HEY, ABE, SIR.
THEY TOLD ME YOU WERE LOOKING FOR HER.
SHE'S ALL YOURS, SIR.
SHE COMES EVERY NIGHT.
HOURS AT A TIME.
YOU GOT A STRONG HOOK.
NICE STANCE. NICE FORM.
TRY KEEPING YOUR HEAD CENTERED.
CAN I *HELP* YOU?
YOU KNOW WHO I AM, ROSA?
NO.
MY NAME IS ABE. I'M--
ONE OF THE SIX.
THE FIRST HUMANS THEY MADE.
I'M ALSO ON THE SETTLEMENT'S COUNCIL AND I'M THE LIAISON BETWEEN HUMANS AND ROBOTS.
I HANDLE CONFLICTS.

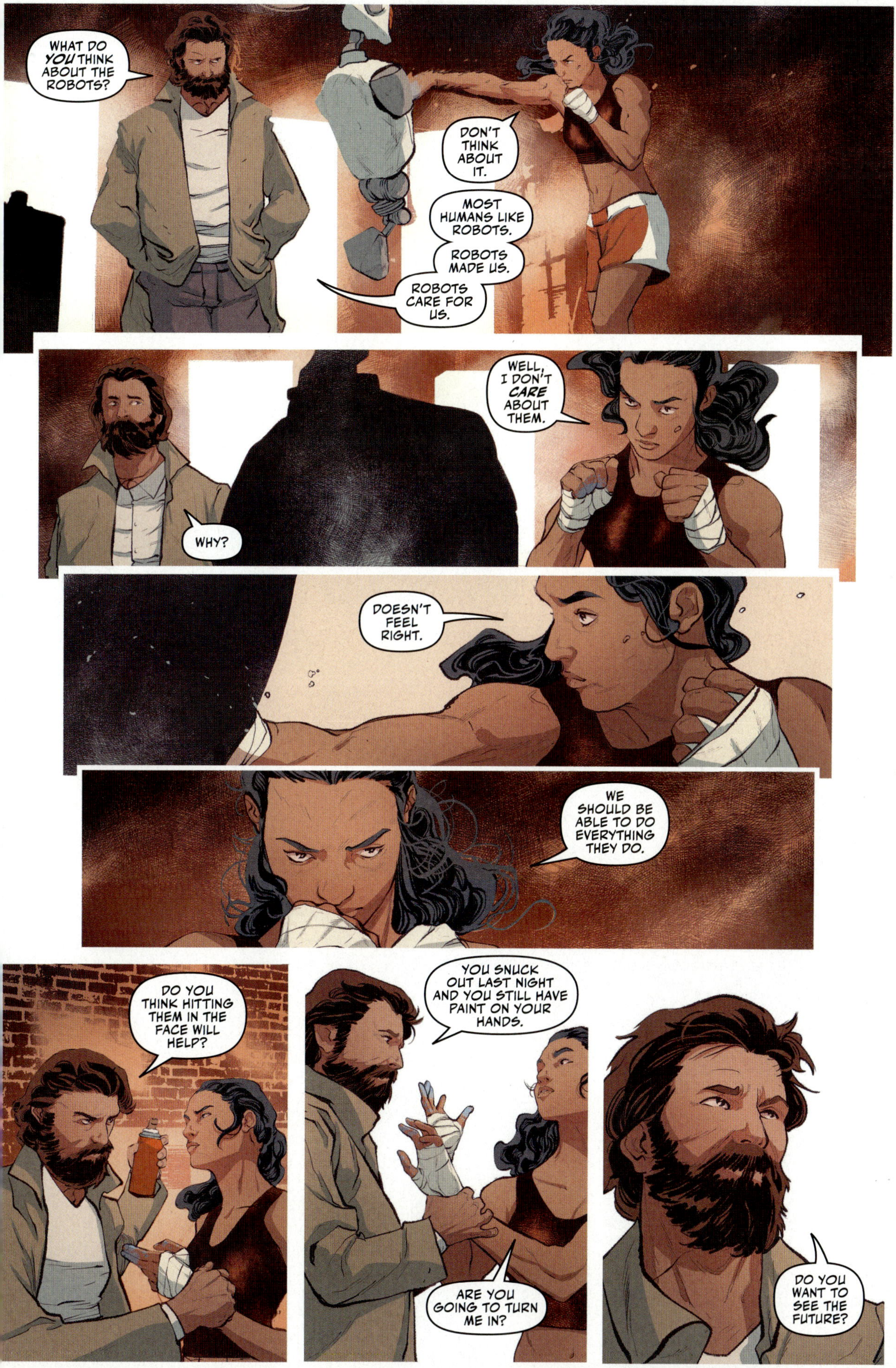
WHAT DO YOU THINK ABOUT THE ROBOTS?
DON'T THINK ABOUT IT.
MOST HUMANS LIKE ROBOTS.
ROBOTS MADE US.
ROBOTS CARE FOR US.
WELL, I DON'T CARE ABOUT THEM.
WHY?
DOESN'T FEEL RIGHT.
WE SHOULD BE ABLE TO DO EVERYTHING THEY DO.
DO YOU THINK HITTING THEM IN THE FACE WILL HELP?
YOU SNUCK OUT LAST NIGHT AND YOU STILL HAVE PAINT ON YOUR HANDS.
ARE YOU GOING TO TURN ME IN?
DO YOU WANT TO SEE THE FUTURE?

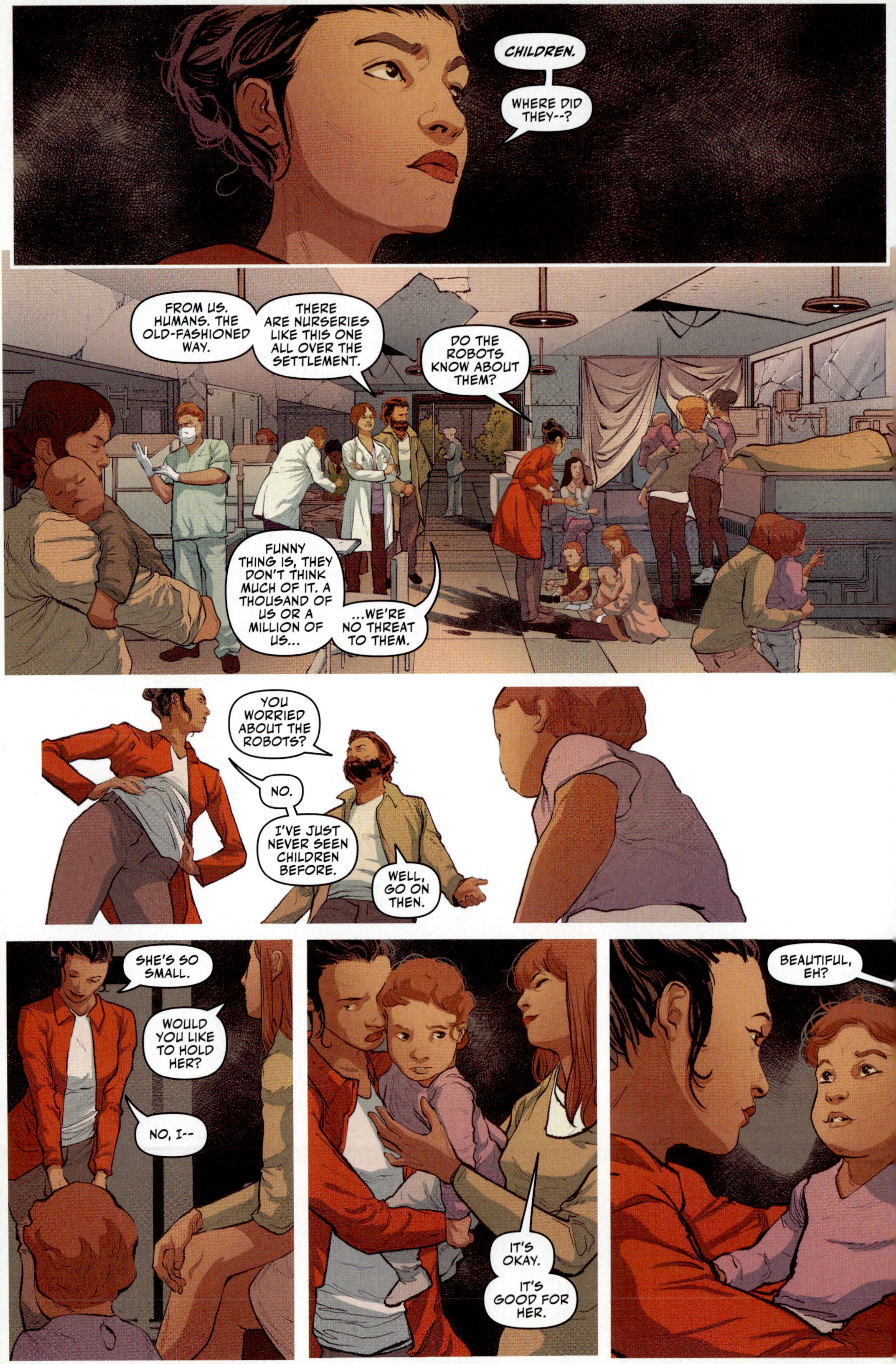
CHILDREN.
WHERE DID THEY--?
FROM US. HUMANS. THE OLD-FASHIONED WAY.
THERE ARE NURSERIES LIKE THIS ONE ALL OVER THE SETTLEMENT.
DO THE ROBOTS KNOW ABOUT THEM?
FUNNY THING IS, THEY DON'T THINK MUCH OF IT. A THOUSAND OF US OR A MILLION OF US...
...WE'RE NO THREAT TO THEM.
YOU WORRIED ABOUT THE ROBOTS?
NO.
I'VE JUST NEVER SEEN CHILDREN BEFORE.
WELL, GO ON THEN.
SHE'S SO SMALL.
WOULD YOU LIKE TO HOLD HER?
NO, I--
IT'S OKAY.
IT'S GOOD FOR HER.
BEAUTIFUL, EH?

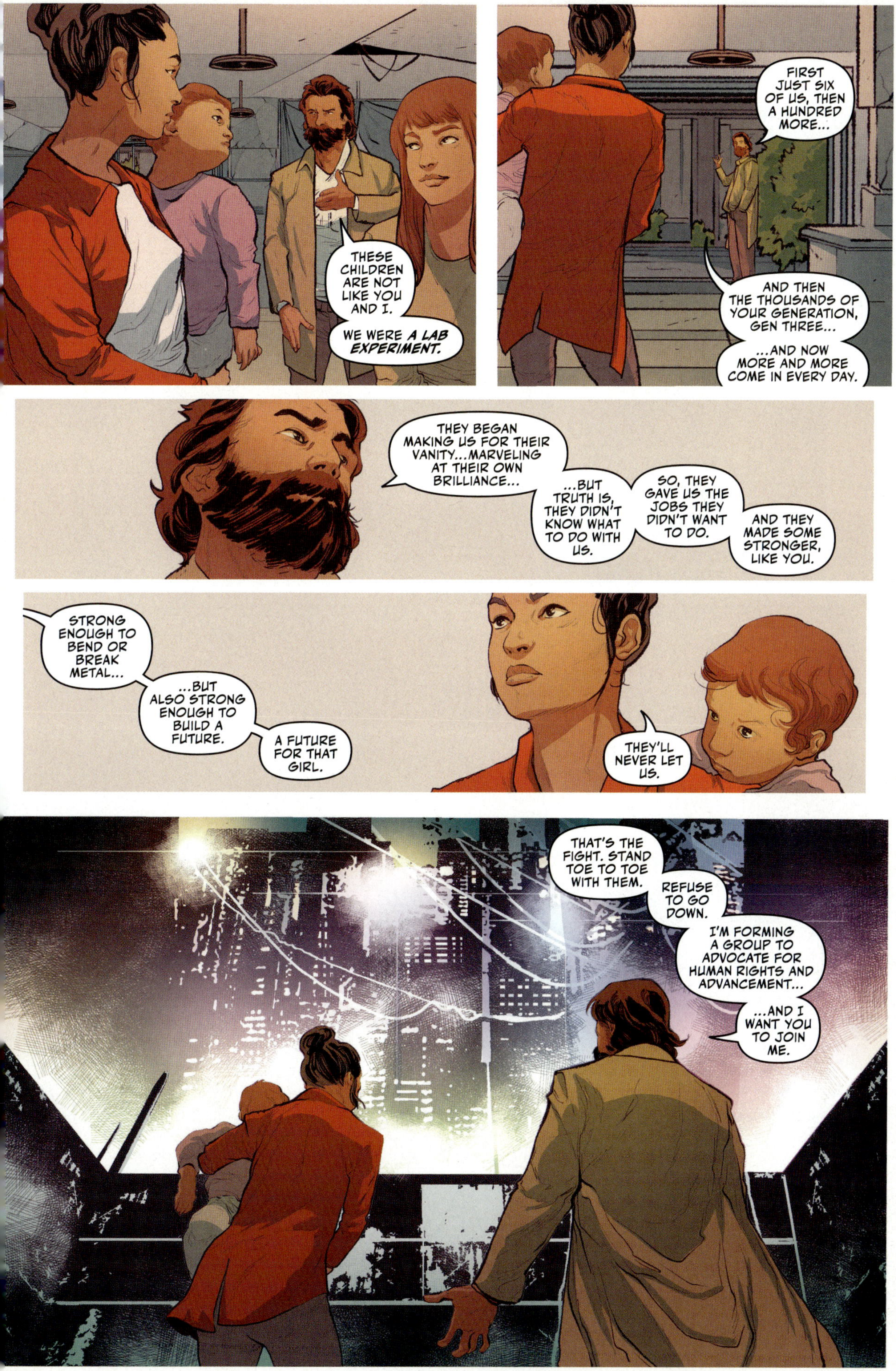
THESE CHILDREN ARE NOT LIKE YOU AND I.
WE WERE *A LAB EXPERIMENT.*
FIRST JUST SIX OF US, THEN A HUNDRED MORE...
AND THEN THE THOUSANDS OF YOUR GENERATION, GEN THREE...
...AND NOW MORE AND MORE COME IN EVERY DAY.
THEY BEGAN MAKING US FOR THEIR VANITY...MARVELING AT THEIR OWN BRILLIANCE...
...BUT TRUTH IS, THEY DIDN'T KNOW WHAT TO DO WITH US.
SO, THEY GAVE US THE JOBS THEY DIDN'T WANT TO DO.
AND THEY MADE SOME STRONGER, LIKE YOU.
STRONG ENOUGH TO BEND OR BREAK METAL...
...BUT ALSO STRONG ENOUGH TO BUILD A FUTURE.
A FUTURE FOR THAT GIRL.
THEY'LL NEVER LET US.
THAT'S THE FIGHT. STAND TOE TO TOE WITH THEM.
REFUSE TO GO DOWN.
I'M FORMING A GROUP TO ADVOCATE FOR HUMAN RIGHTS AND ADVANCEMENT...
...AND I WANT YOU TO JOIN ME.

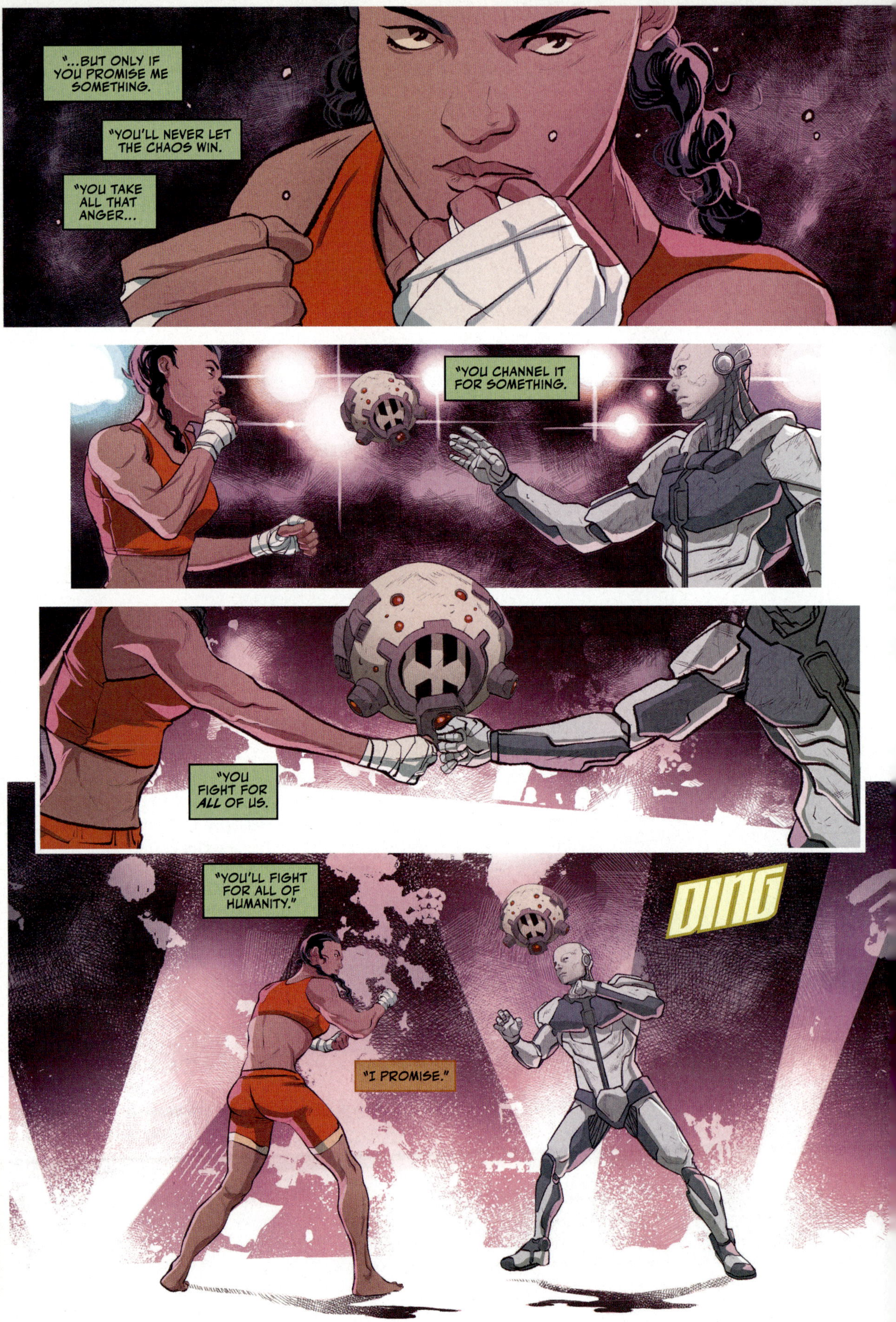
"...BUT ONLY IF YOU PROMISE ME SOMETHING.
"YOU'LL NEVER LET THE CHAOS WIN.
"YOU TAKE ALL THAT ANGER...
"YOU CHANNEL IT FOR SOMETHING.
"YOU FIGHT FOR ALL OF US.
"YOU'LL FIGHT FOR ALL OF HUMANITY."
DING
"I PROMISE."

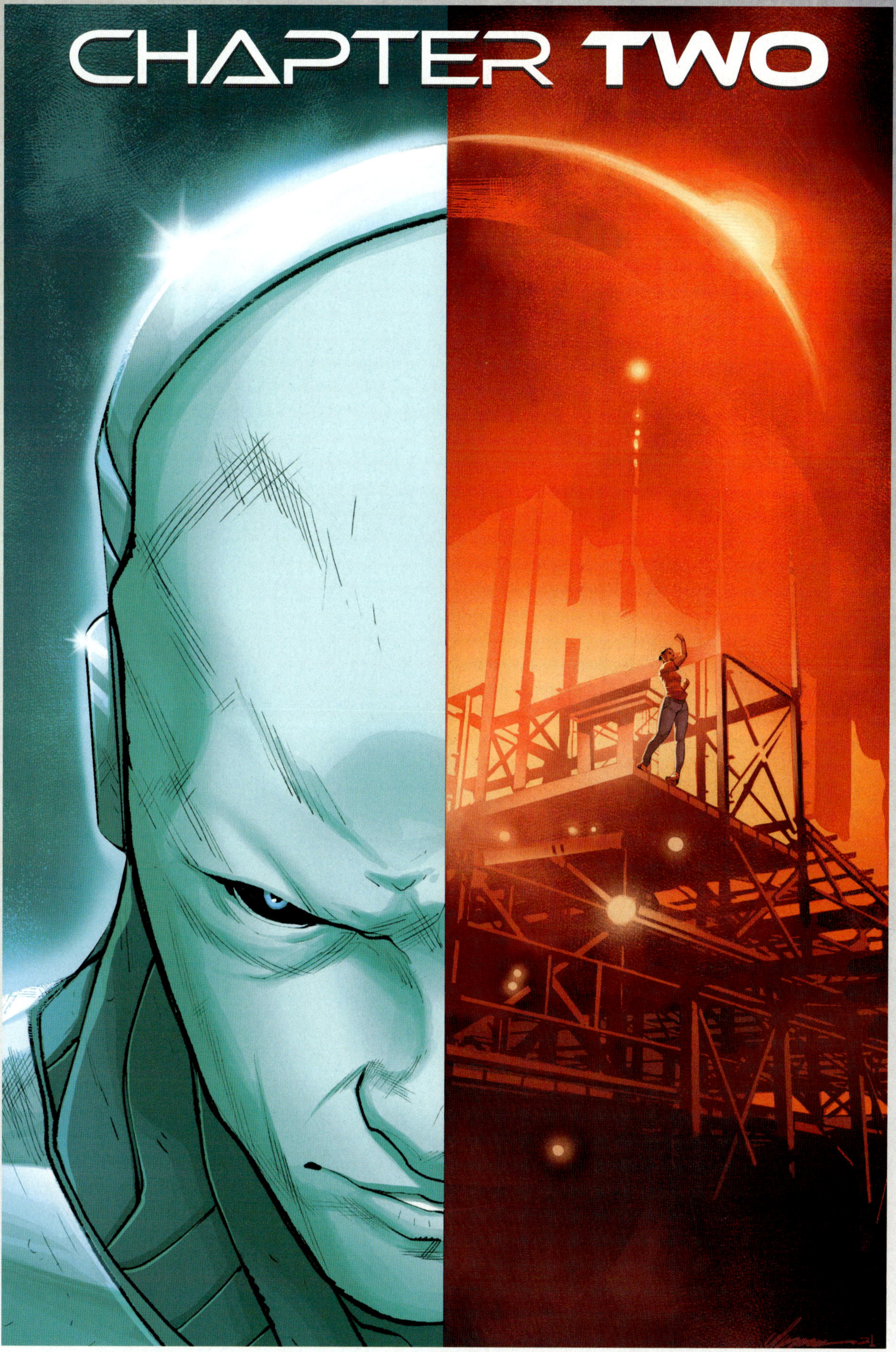
CHAPTER TWO

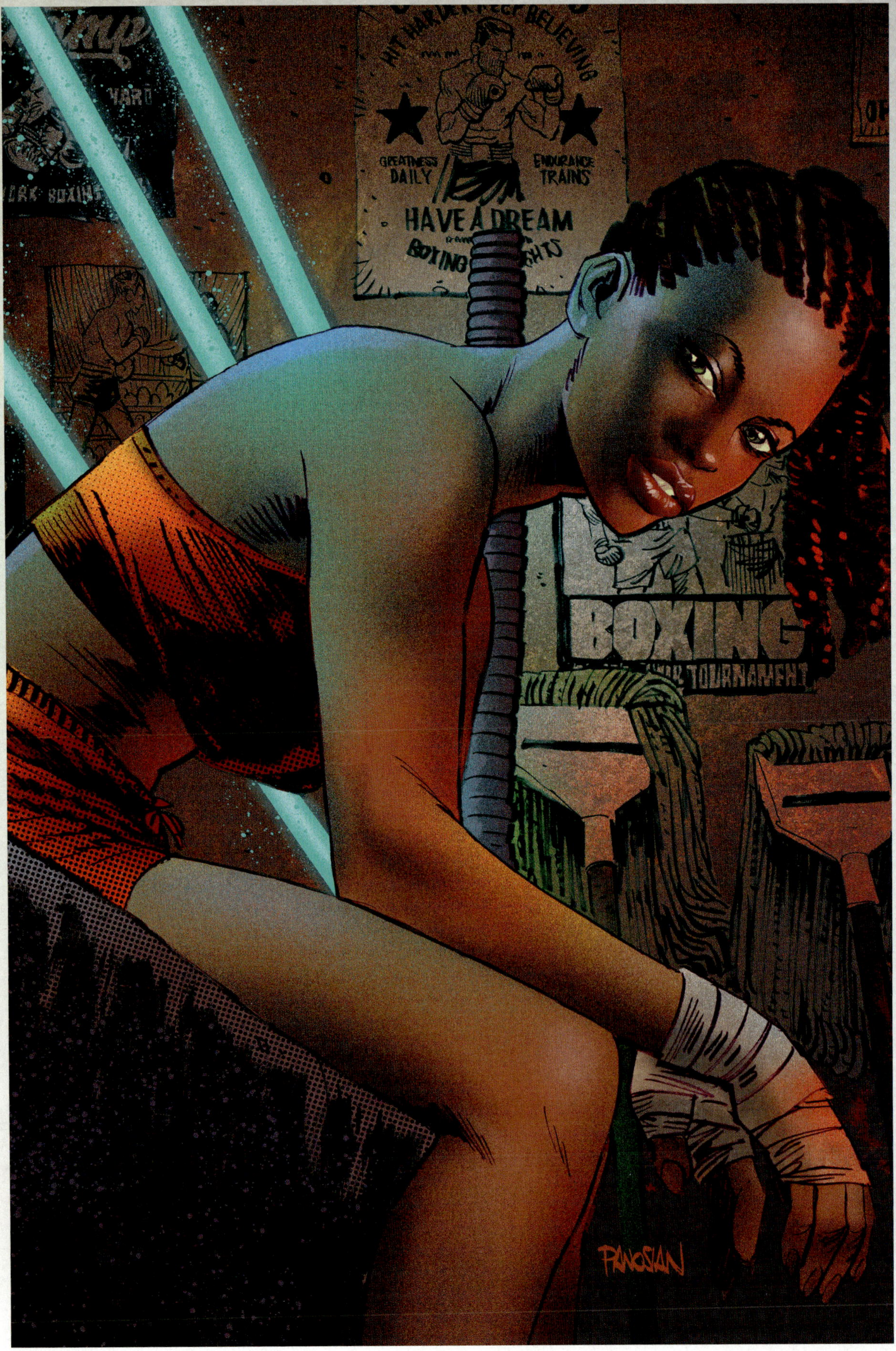
GREATNESS DAILY
ENDURANCE TRAINS
HAVE A DREAM
BOXING
TOURNAMENT
PANOSIAN

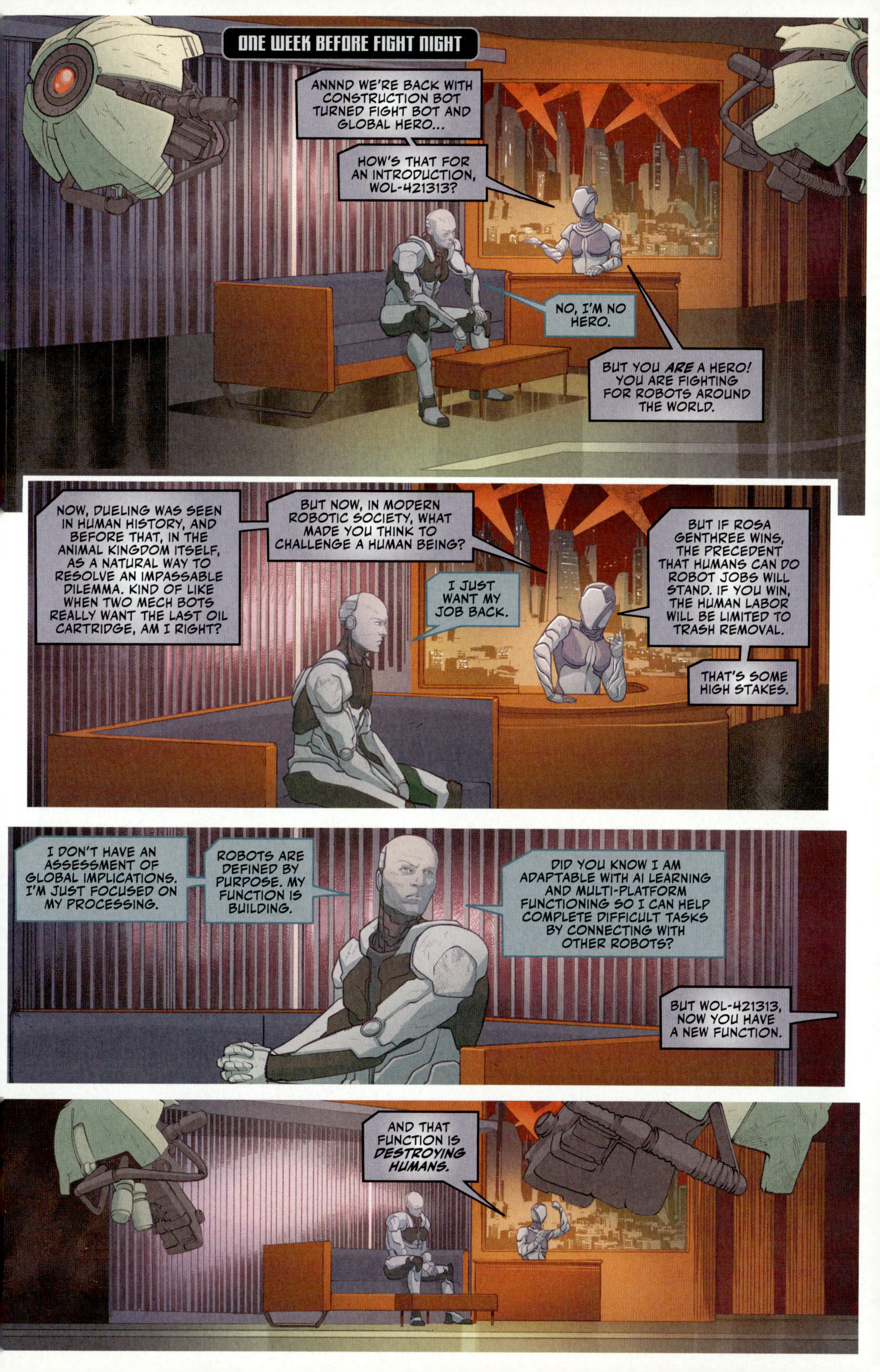
ONE WEEK BEFORE FIGHT NIGHT
ANNND WE'RE BACK WITH CONSTRUCTION BOT TURNED FIGHT BOT AND GLOBAL HERO...
HOW'S THAT FOR AN INTRODUCTION, WOL-421313?
NO, I'M NO HERO.
BUT YOU *ARE* A HERO! YOU ARE FIGHTING FOR ROBOTS AROUND THE WORLD.
NOW, DUELING WAS SEEN IN HUMAN HISTORY, AND BEFORE THAT, IN THE ANIMAL KINGDOM ITSELF, AS A NATURAL WAY TO RESOLVE AN IMPASSABLE DILEMMA. KIND OF LIKE WHEN TWO MECH BOTS REALLY WANT THE LAST OIL CARTRIDGE, AM I RIGHT?
BUT NOW, IN MODERN ROBOTIC SOCIETY, WHAT MADE YOU THINK TO CHALLENGE A HUMAN BEING?
I JUST WANT MY JOB BACK.
BUT IF ROSA GENTHREE WINS, THE PRECEDENT THAT HUMANS CAN DO ROBOT JOBS WILL STAND. IF YOU WIN, THE HUMAN LABOR WILL BE LIMITED TO TRASH REMOVAL.
THAT'S SOME HIGH STAKES.
I DON'T HAVE AN ASSESSMENT OF GLOBAL IMPLICATIONS. I'M JUST FOCUSED ON MY PROCESSING.
ROBOTS ARE DEFINED BY PURPOSE. MY FUNCTION IS BUILDING.
DID YOU KNOW I AM ADAPTABLE WITH AI LEARNING AND MULTI-PLATFORM FUNCTIONING SO I CAN HELP COMPLETE DIFFICULT TASKS BY CONNECTING WITH OTHER ROBOTS?
BUT WOL-421313, NOW YOU HAVE A NEW FUNCTION.
AND THAT FUNCTION IS *DESTROYING HUMANS.*

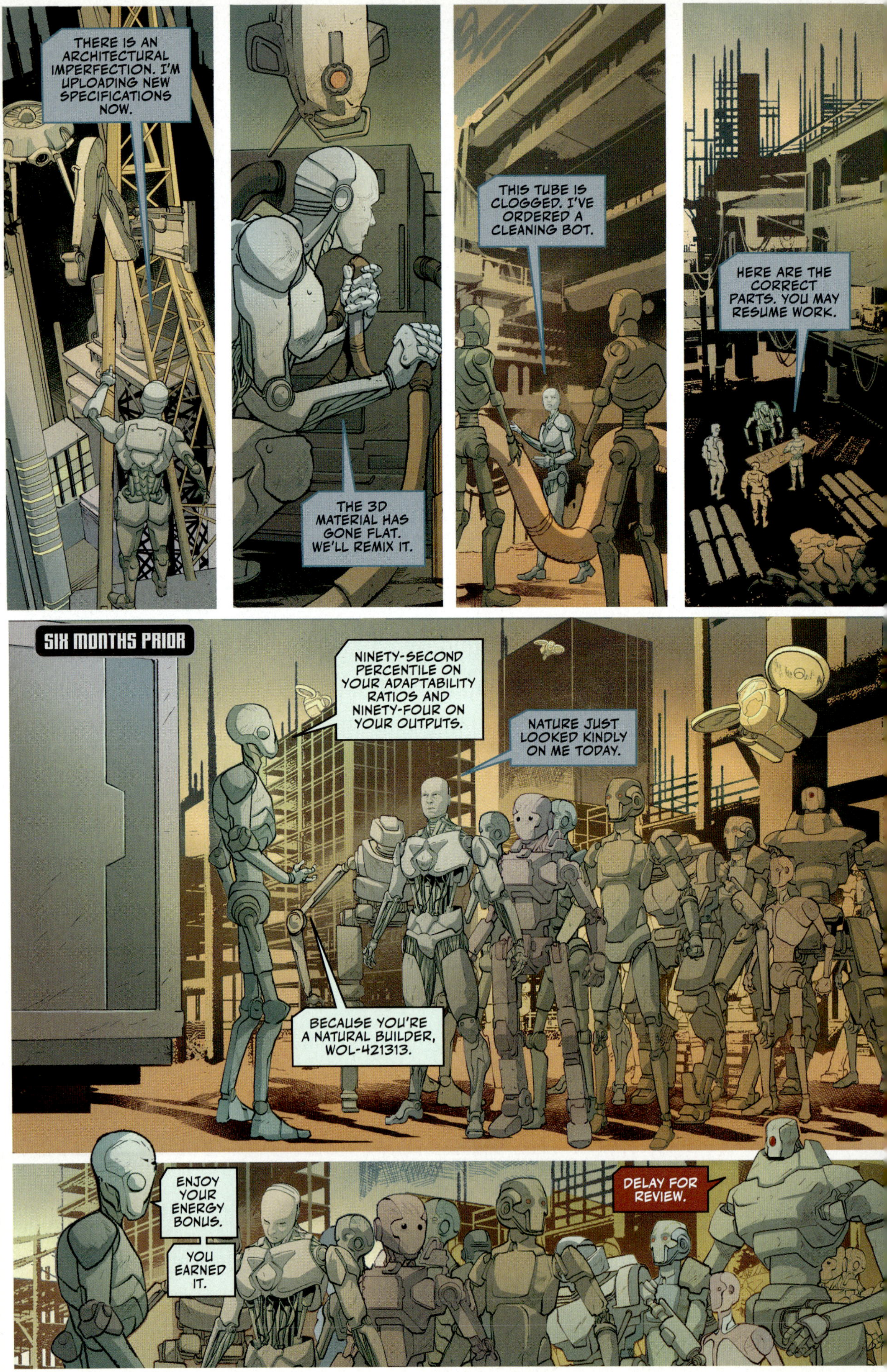
THERE IS AN ARCHITECTURAL IMPERFECTION. I'M UPLOADING NEW SPECIFICATIONS NOW.
THE 3D MATERIAL HAS GONE FLAT. WE'LL REMIX IT.
THIS TUBE IS CLOGGED. I'VE ORDERED A CLEANING BOT.
HERE ARE THE CORRECT PARTS. YOU MAY RESUME WORK.
SIX MONTHS PRIOR
NINETY-SECOND PERCENTILE ON YOUR ADAPTABILITY RATIOS AND NINETY-FOUR ON YOUR OUTPUTS.
NATURE JUST LOOKED KINDLY ON ME TODAY.
BECAUSE YOU'RE A NATURAL BUILDER, WOL-421313.
ENJOY YOUR ENERGY BONUS.
YOU EARNED IT.
DELAY FOR REVIEW.

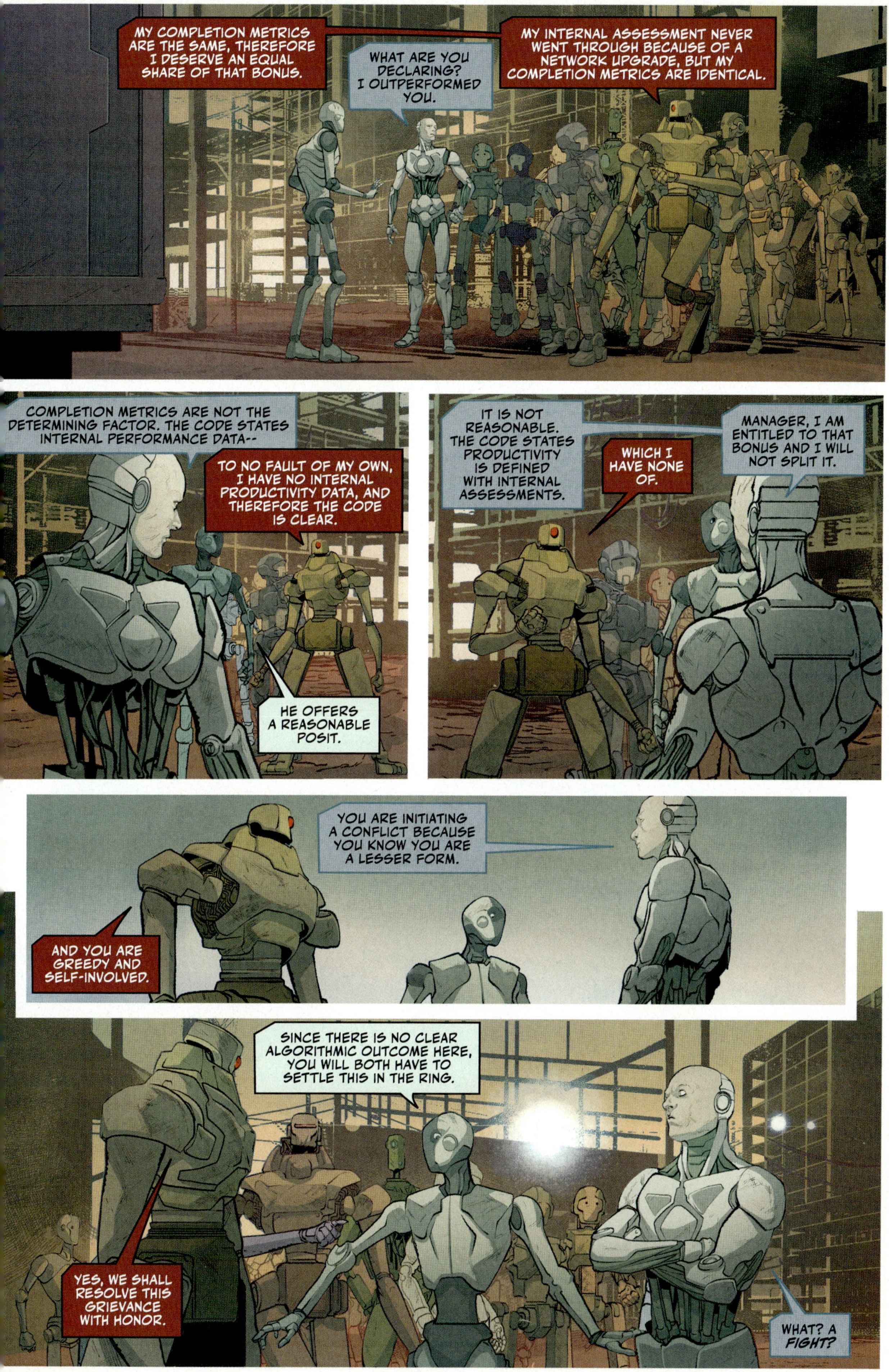
MY COMPLETION METRICS ARE THE SAME, THEREFORE I DESERVE AN EQUAL SHARE OF THAT BONUS.
WHAT ARE YOU DECLARING? I OUTPERFORMED YOU.
MY INTERNAL ASSESSMENT NEVER WENT THROUGH BECAUSE OF A NETWORK UPGRADE, BUT MY COMPLETION METRICS ARE IDENTICAL.
COMPLETION METRICS ARE NOT THE DETERMINING FACTOR. THE CODE STATES INTERNAL PERFORMANCE DATA--
TO NO FAULT OF MY OWN, I HAVE NO INTERNAL PRODUCTIVITY DATA, AND THEREFORE THE CODE IS CLEAR.
HE OFFERS A REASONABLE POSIT.
IT IS NOT REASONABLE. THE CODE STATES PRODUCTIVITY IS DEFINED WITH INTERNAL ASSESSMENTS.
WHICH I HAVE NONE OF.
MANAGER, I AM ENTITLED TO THAT BONUS AND I WILL NOT SPLIT IT.
YOU ARE INITIATING A CONFLICT BECAUSE YOU KNOW YOU ARE A LESSER FORM.
AND YOU ARE GREEDY AND SELF-INVOLVED.
SINCE THERE IS NO CLEAR ALGORITHMIC OUTCOME HERE, YOU WILL BOTH HAVE TO SETTLE THIS IN THE RING.
YES, WE SHALL RESOLVE THIS GRIEVANCE WITH HONOR.
WHAT? A *FIGHT?*

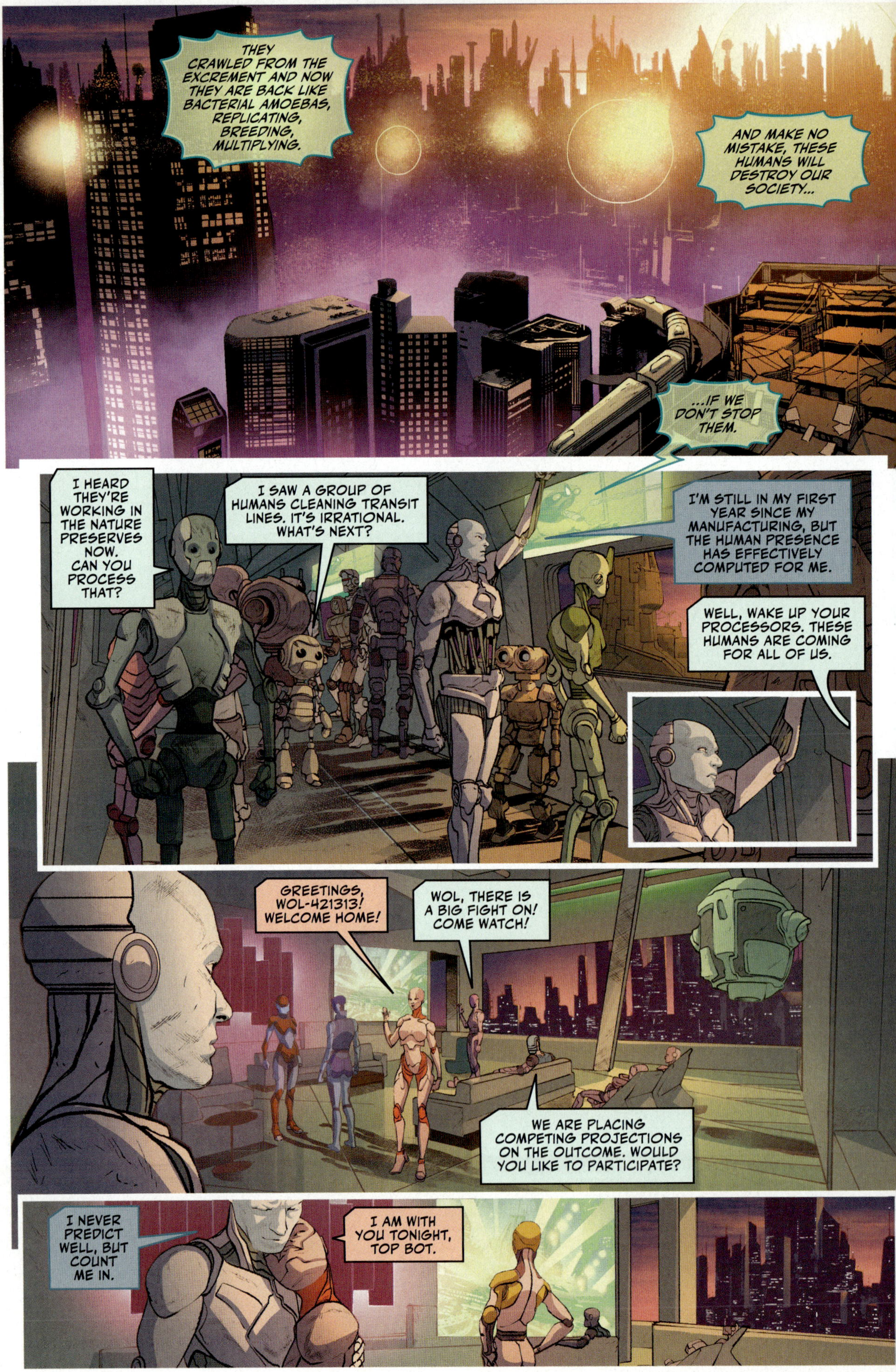
THEY CRAWLED FROM THE EXCREMENT AND NOW THEY ARE BACK LIKE BACTERIAL AMOEBAS, REPLICATING, BREEDING, MULTIPLYING.
AND MAKE NO MISTAKE, THESE HUMANS WILL DESTROY OUR SOCIETY...
...IF WE DON'T STOP THEM.
I HEARD THEY'RE WORKING IN THE NATURE PRESERVES NOW. CAN YOU PROCESS THAT?
I SAW A GROUP OF HUMANS CLEANING TRANSIT LINES. IT'S IRRATIONAL. WHAT'S NEXT?
I'M STILL IN MY FIRST YEAR SINCE MY MANUFACTURING, BUT THE HUMAN PRESENCE HAS EFFECTIVELY COMPUTED FOR ME.
WELL, WAKE UP YOUR PROCESSORS. THESE HUMANS ARE COMING FOR ALL OF US.
GREETINGS, WOL-421313! WELCOME HOME!
WOL, THERE IS A BIG FIGHT ON! COME WATCH!
WE ARE PLACING COMPETING PROJECTIONS ON THE OUTCOME. WOULD YOU LIKE TO PARTICIPATE?
I NEVER PREDICT WELL, BUT COUNT ME IN.
I AM WITH YOU TONIGHT, TOP BOT.

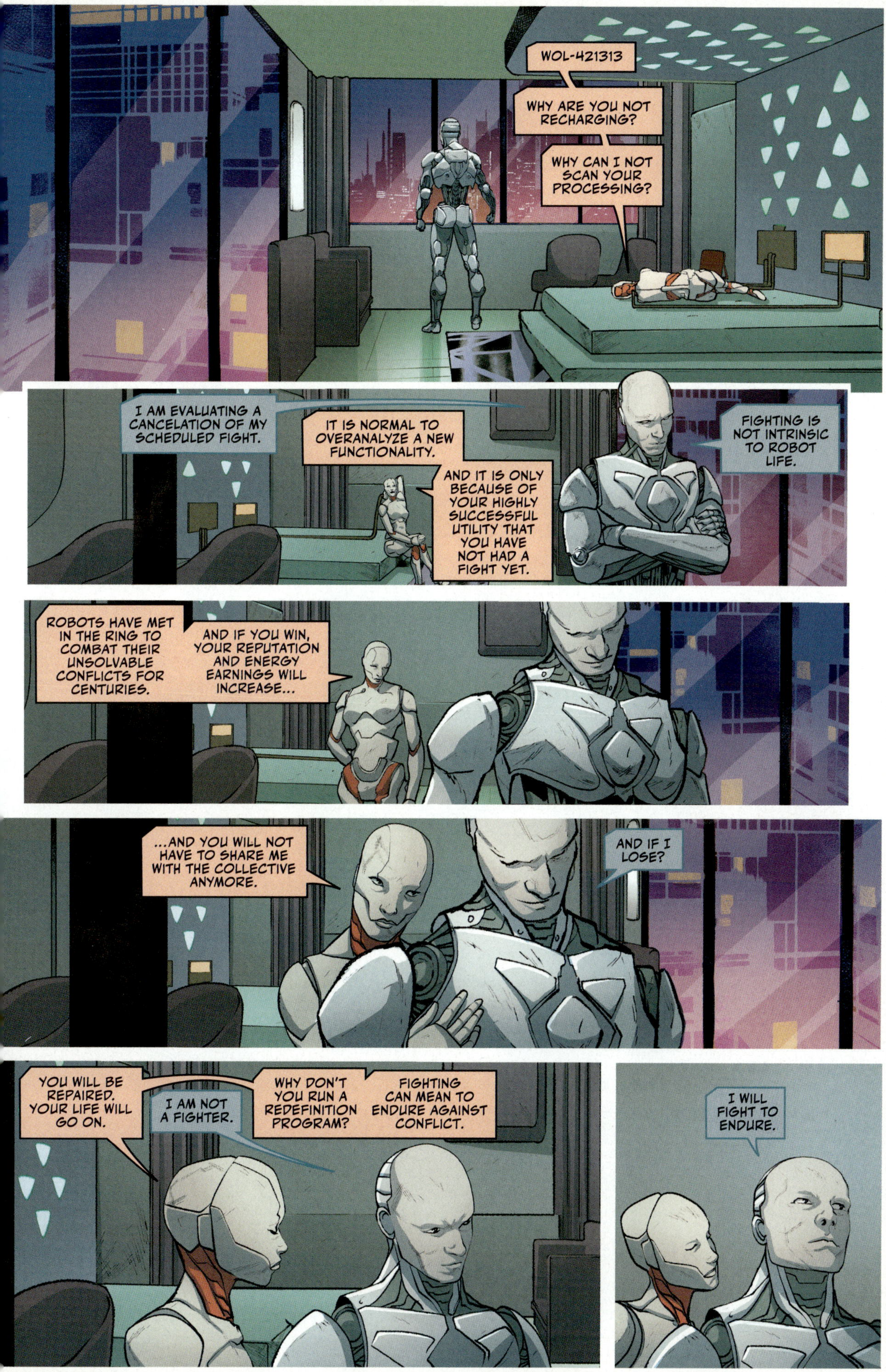

WOL-421313
WHY ARE YOU NOT RECHARGING?
WHY CAN I NOT SCAN YOUR PROCESSING?
I AM EVALUATING A CANCELATION OF MY SCHEDULED FIGHT.
IT IS NORMAL TO OVERANALYZE A NEW FUNCTIONALITY.
AND IT IS ONLY BECAUSE OF YOUR HIGHLY SUCCESSFUL UTILITY THAT YOU HAVE NOT HAD A FIGHT YET.
FIGHTING IS NOT INTRINSIC TO ROBOT LIFE.
ROBOTS HAVE MET IN THE RING TO COMBAT THEIR UNSOLVABLE CONFLICTS FOR CENTURIES.
AND IF YOU WIN, YOUR REPUTATION AND ENERGY EARNINGS WILL INCREASE...
...AND YOU WILL NOT HAVE TO SHARE ME WITH THE COLLECTIVE ANYMORE.
AND IF I LOSE?
YOU WILL BE REPAIRED. YOUR LIFE WILL GO ON.
I AM NOT A FIGHTER.
WHY DON'T YOU RUN A REDEFINITION PROGRAM?
FIGHTING CAN MEAN TO ENDURE AGAINST CONFLICT.
I WILL FIGHT TO ENDURE.

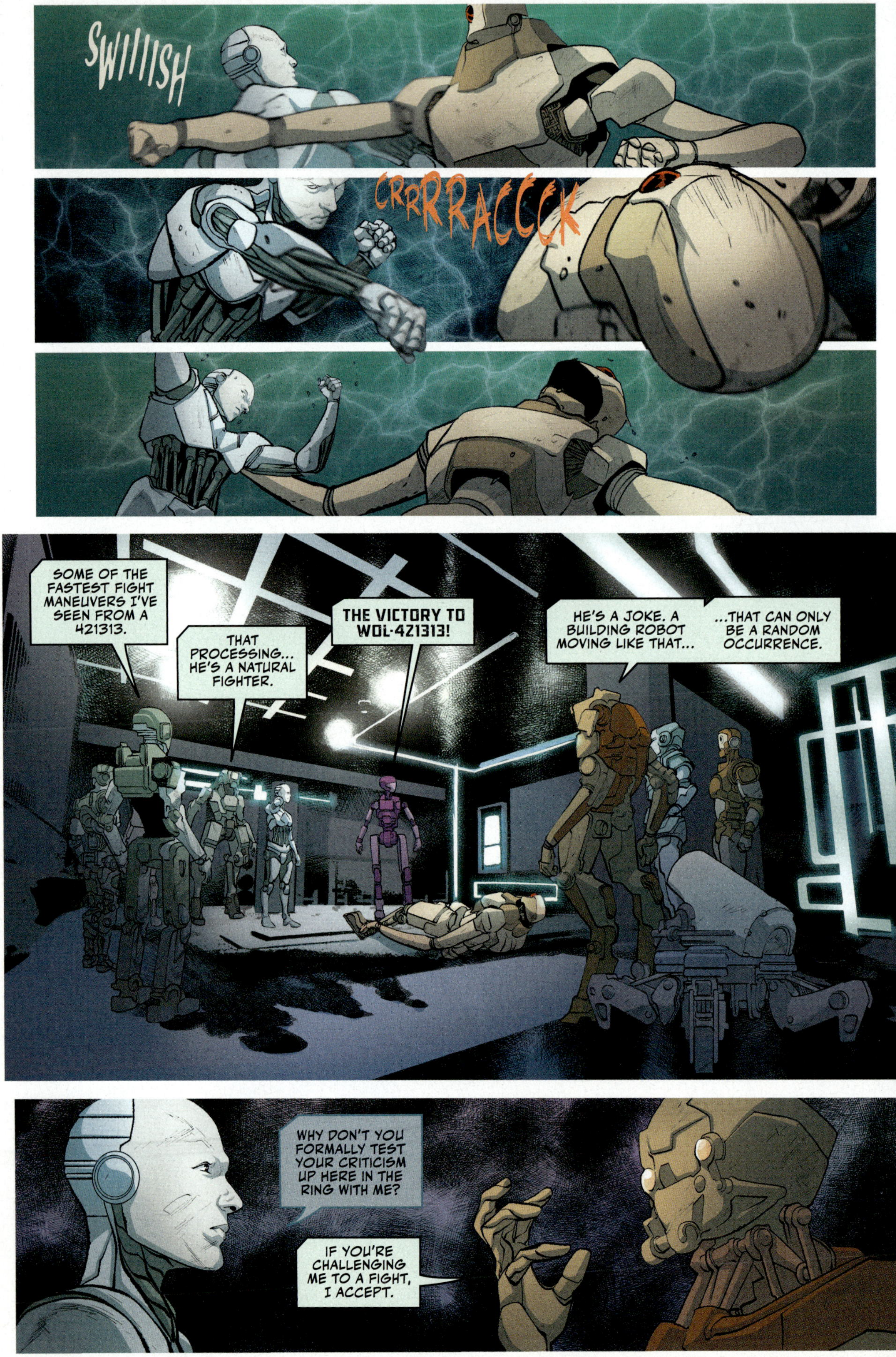
SWIIIISH
CRRRRACCCK
SOME OF THE FASTEST FIGHT MANEUVERS I'VE SEEN FROM A 421313.
THAT PROCESSING... HE'S A NATURAL FIGHTER.
THE VICTORY TO WOL-421313!
HE'S A JOKE. A BUILDING ROBOT MOVING LIKE THAT...
...THAT CAN ONLY BE A RANDOM OCCURRENCE.
WHY DON'T YOU FORMALLY TEST YOUR CRITICISM UP HERE IN THE RING WITH ME?
IF YOU'RE CHALLENGING ME TO A FIGHT, I ACCEPT.

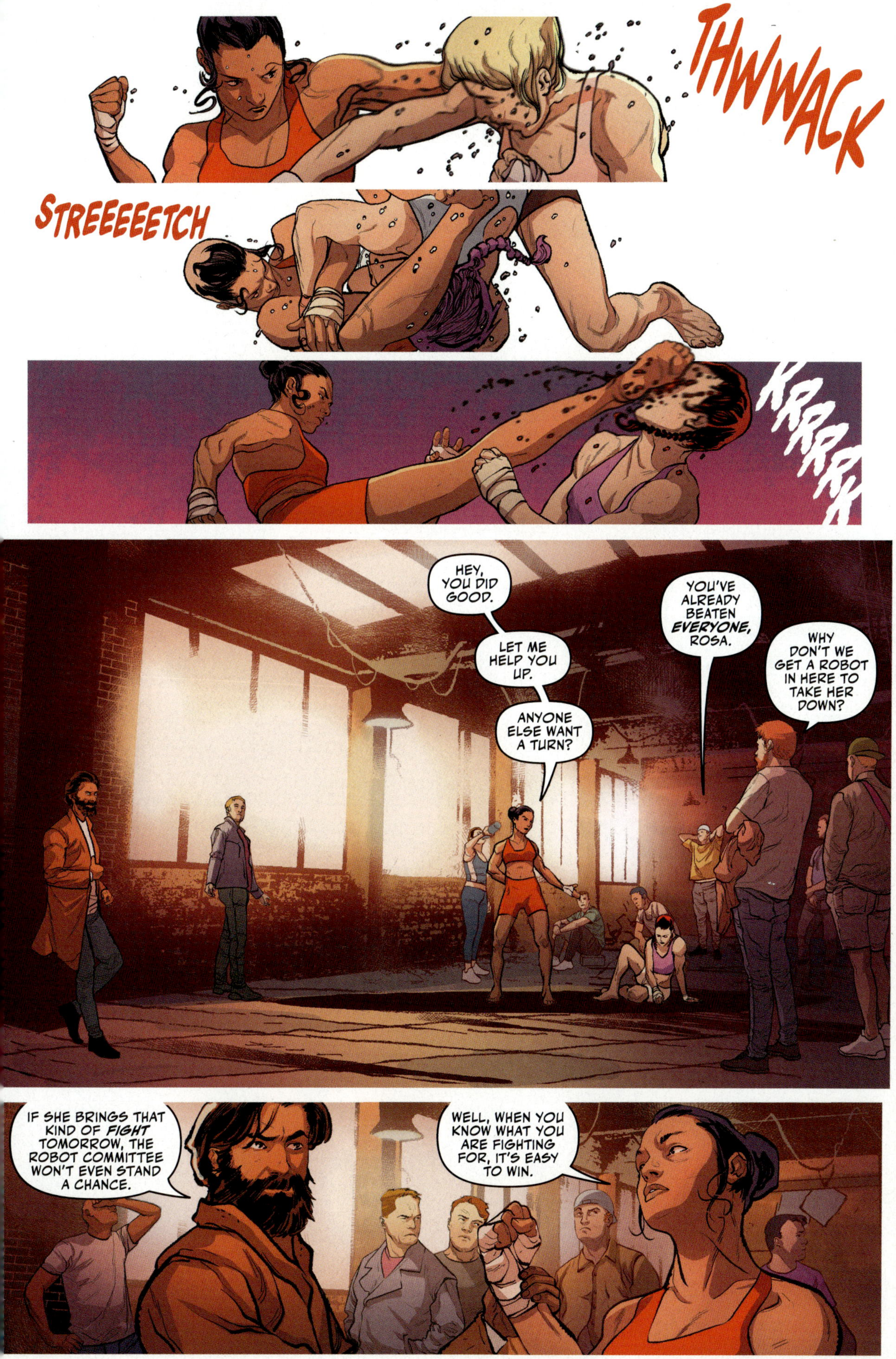
THWACK
STREEEEETCH
KRRRRK
HEY, YOU DID GOOD.
LET ME HELP YOU UP.
ANYONE ELSE WANT A TURN?
YOU'VE ALREADY BEATEN *EVERYONE,* ROSA.
WHY DON'T WE GET A ROBOT IN HERE TO TAKE HER DOWN?
IF SHE BRINGS THAT KIND OF *FIGHT* TOMORROW, THE ROBOT COMMITTEE WON'T EVEN STAND A CHANCE.
WELL, WHEN YOU KNOW WHAT YOU ARE FIGHTING FOR, IT'S EASY TO WIN.

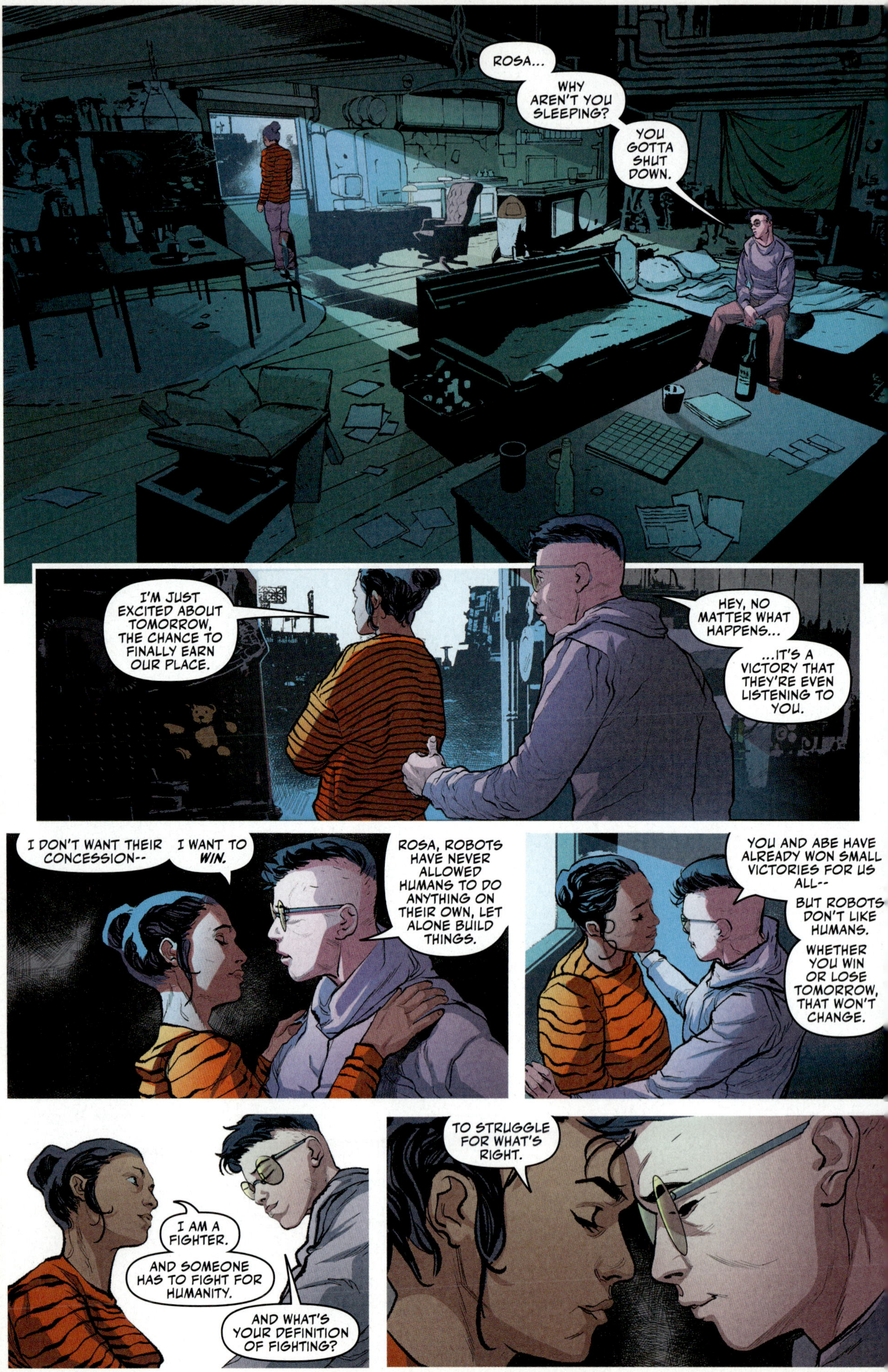
ROSA...
WHY AREN'T YOU SLEEPING?
YOU GOTTA SHUT DOWN.
I'M JUST EXCITED ABOUT TOMORROW, THE CHANCE TO FINALLY EARN OUR PLACE.
HEY, NO MATTER WHAT HAPPENS...
...IT'S A VICTORY THAT THEY'RE EVEN LISTENING TO YOU.
I DON'T WANT THEIR CONCESSION--
I WANT TO *WIN.*
ROSA, ROBOTS HAVE NEVER ALLOWED HUMANS TO DO ANYTHING ON THEIR OWN, LET ALONE BUILD THINGS.
YOU AND ABE HAVE ALREADY WON SMALL VICTORIES FOR US ALL--
BUT ROBOTS DON'T LIKE HUMANS.
WHETHER YOU WIN OR LOSE TOMORROW, THAT WON'T CHANGE.
I AM A FIGHTER.
AND SOMEONE HAS TO FIGHT FOR HUMANITY.
AND WHAT'S YOUR DEFINITION OF FIGHTING?
TO STRUGGLE FOR WHAT'S RIGHT.

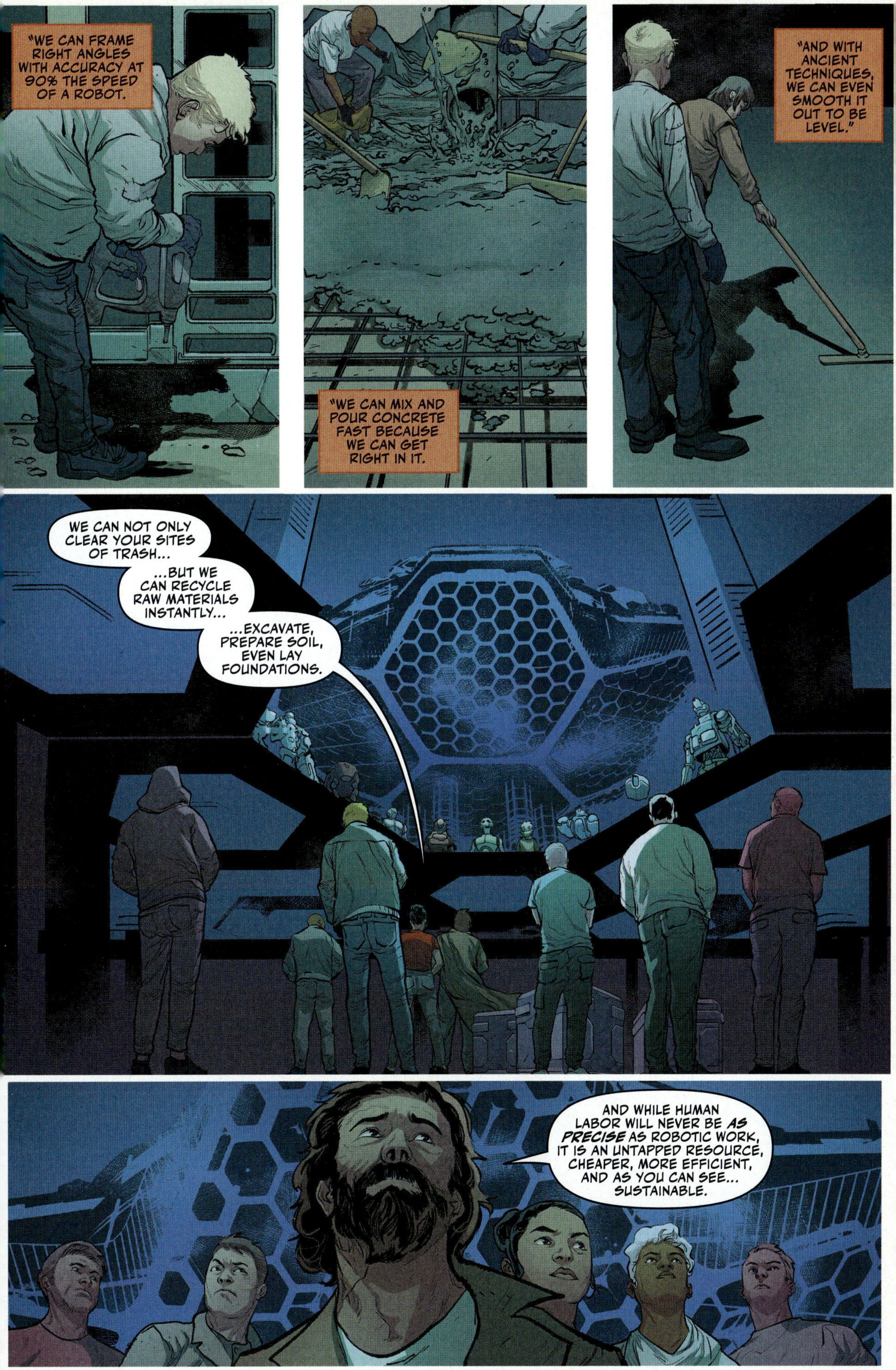
"WE CAN FRAME RIGHT ANGLES WITH ACCURACY AT 90% THE SPEED OF A ROBOT.
"WE CAN MIX AND POUR CONCRETE FAST BECAUSE WE CAN GET RIGHT IN IT.
"AND WITH ANCIENT TECHNIQUES, WE CAN EVEN SMOOTH IT OUT TO BE LEVEL."
WE CAN NOT ONLY CLEAR YOUR SITES OF TRASH...
...BUT WE CAN RECYCLE RAW MATERIALS INSTANTLY...
...EXCAVATE, PREPARE SOIL, EVEN LAY FOUNDATIONS.
AND WHILE HUMAN LABOR WILL NEVER BE *AS PRECISE* AS ROBOTIC WORK, IT IS AN UNTAPPED RESOURCE, CHEAPER, MORE EFFICIENT, AND AS YOU CAN SEE... SUSTAINABLE.

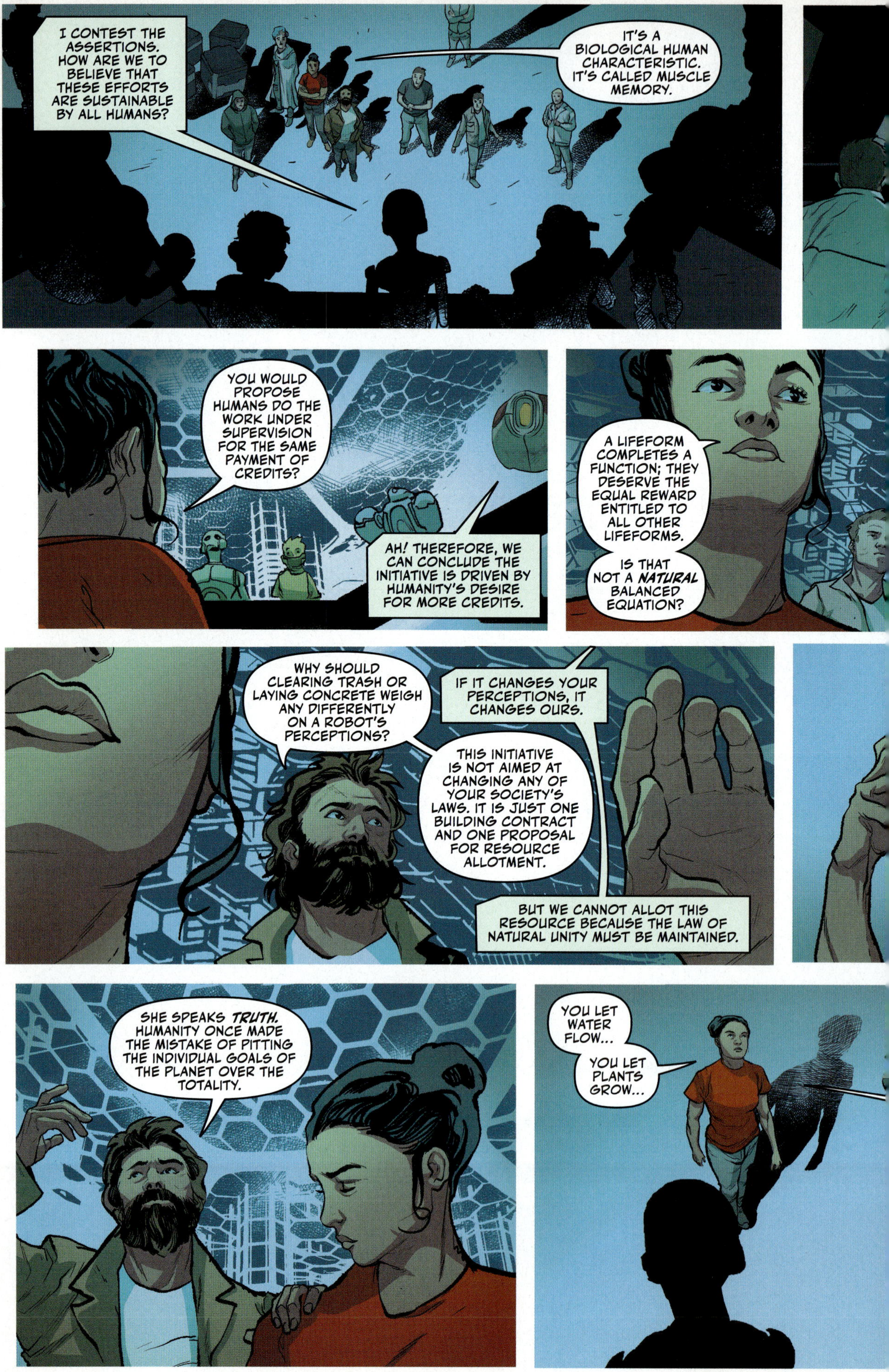
I CONTEST THE ASSERTIONS. HOW ARE WE TO BELIEVE THAT THESE EFFORTS ARE SUSTAINABLE BY ALL HUMANS?
IT'S A BIOLOGICAL HUMAN CHARACTERISTIC. IT'S CALLED MUSCLE MEMORY.
YOU WOULD PROPOSE HUMANS DO THE WORK UNDER SUPERVISION FOR THE SAME PAYMENT OF CREDITS?
AH! THEREFORE, WE CAN CONCLUDE THE INITIATIVE IS DRIVEN BY HUMANITY'S DESIRE FOR MORE CREDITS.
A LIFEFORM COMPLETES A FUNCTION; THEY DESERVE THE EQUAL REWARD ENTITLED TO ALL OTHER LIFEFORMS.
IS THAT NOT A *NATURAL* BALANCED EQUATION?
WHY SHOULD CLEARING TRASH OR LAYING CONCRETE WEIGH ANY DIFFERENTLY ON A ROBOT'S PERCEPTIONS?
IF IT CHANGES YOUR PERCEPTIONS, IT CHANGES OURS.
THIS INITIATIVE IS NOT AIMED AT CHANGING ANY OF YOUR SOCIETY'S LAWS. IT IS JUST ONE BUILDING CONTRACT AND ONE PROPOSAL FOR RESOURCE ALLOTMENT.
BUT WE CANNOT ALLOT THIS RESOURCE BECAUSE THE LAW OF NATURAL UNITY MUST BE MAINTAINED.
SHE SPEAKS *TRUTH.* HUMANITY ONCE MADE THE MISTAKE OF PITTING THE INDIVIDUAL GOALS OF THE PLANET OVER THE TOTALITY.
YOU LET WATER FLOW...
YOU LET PLANTS GROW...

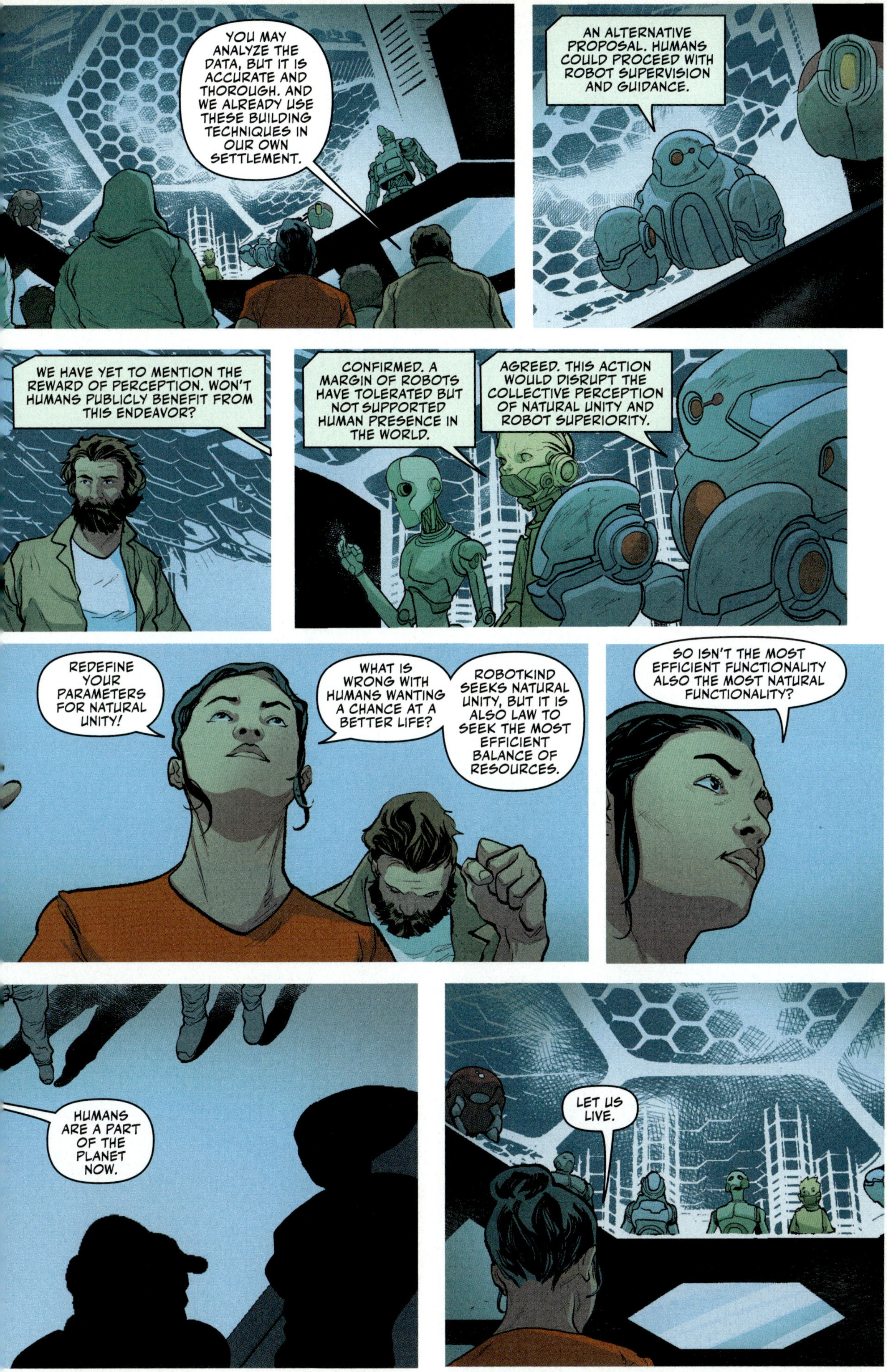
YOU MAY ANALYZE THE DATA, BUT IT IS ACCURATE AND THOROUGH. AND WE ALREADY USE THESE BUILDING TECHNIQUES IN OUR OWN SETTLEMENT.
AN ALTERNATIVE PROPOSAL. HUMANS COULD PROCEED WITH ROBOT SUPERVISION AND GUIDANCE.
WE HAVE YET TO MENTION THE REWARD OF PERCEPTION. WON'T HUMANS PUBLICLY BENEFIT FROM THIS ENDEAVOR?
CONFIRMED. A MARGIN OF ROBOTS HAVE TOLERATED BUT NOT SUPPORTED HUMAN PRESENCE IN THE WORLD.
AGREED. THIS ACTION WOULD DISRUPT THE COLLECTIVE PERCEPTION OF NATURAL UNITY AND ROBOT SUPERIORITY.
REDEFINE YOUR PARAMETERS FOR NATURAL UNITY!
WHAT IS WRONG WITH HUMANS WANTING A CHANCE AT A BETTER LIFE?
ROBOTKIND SEEKS NATURAL UNITY, BUT IT IS ALSO LAW TO SEEK THE MOST EFFICIENT BALANCE OF RESOURCES.
SO ISN'T THE MOST EFFICIENT FUNCTIONALITY ALSO THE MOST NATURAL FUNCTIONALITY?
HUMANS ARE A PART OF THE PLANET NOW.
LET US LIVE.

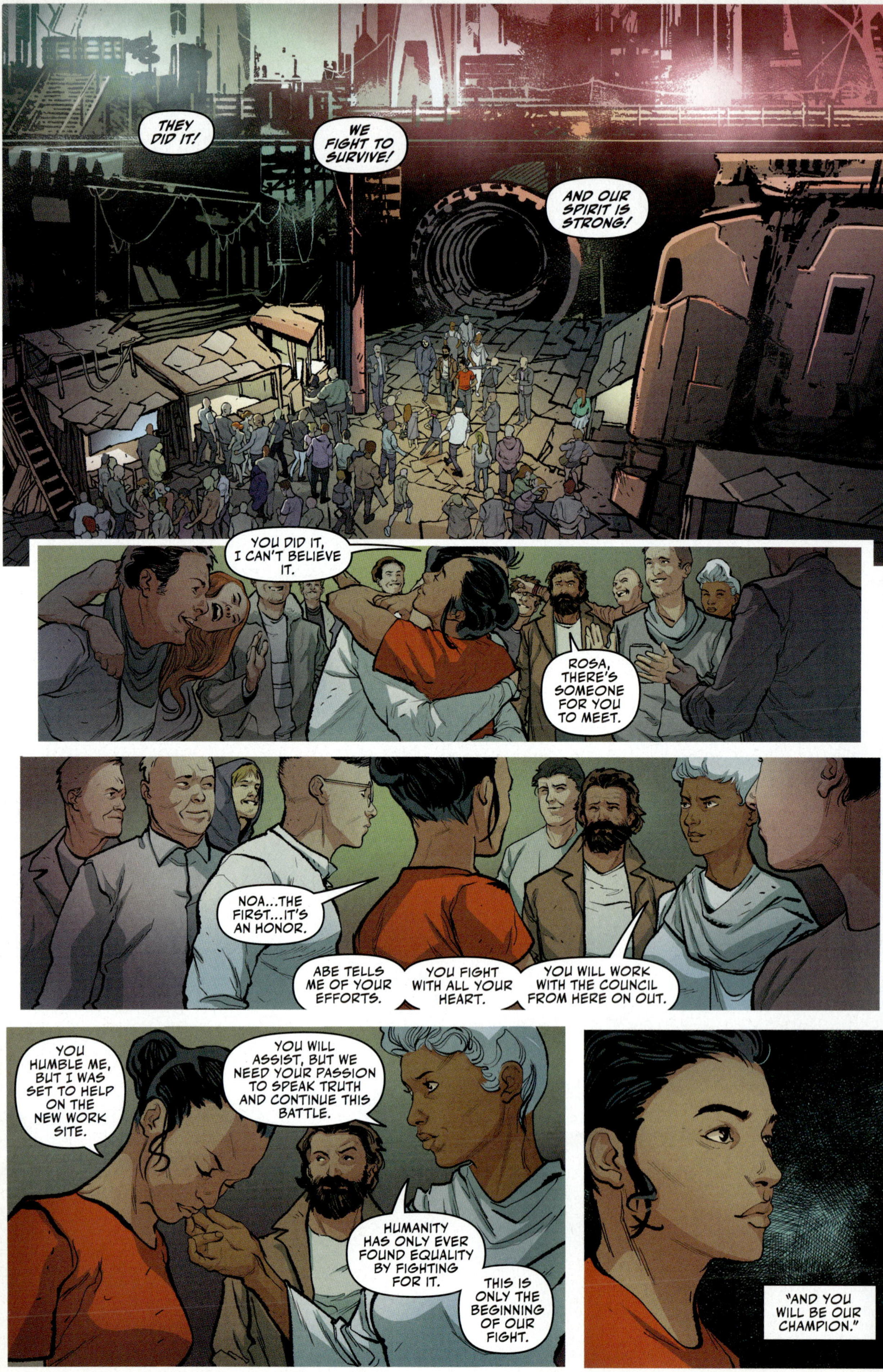
THEY DID IT!
WE FIGHT TO SURVIVE!
AND OUR SPIRIT IS STRONG!
YOU DID IT, I CAN'T BELIEVE IT.
ROSA, THERE'S SOMEONE FOR YOU TO MEET.
NOA...THE FIRST...IT'S AN HONOR.
ABE TELLS ME OF YOUR EFFORTS.
YOU FIGHT WITH ALL YOUR HEART.
YOU WILL WORK WITH THE COUNCIL FROM HERE ON OUT.
YOU HUMBLE ME, BUT I WAS SET TO HELP ON THE NEW WORK SITE.
YOU WILL ASSIST, BUT WE NEED YOUR PASSION TO SPEAK TRUTH AND CONTINUE THIS BATTLE.
HUMANITY HAS ONLY EVER FOUND EQUALITY BY FIGHTING FOR IT.
THIS IS ONLY THE BEGINNING OF OUR FIGHT.
"AND YOU WILL BE OUR CHAMPION."

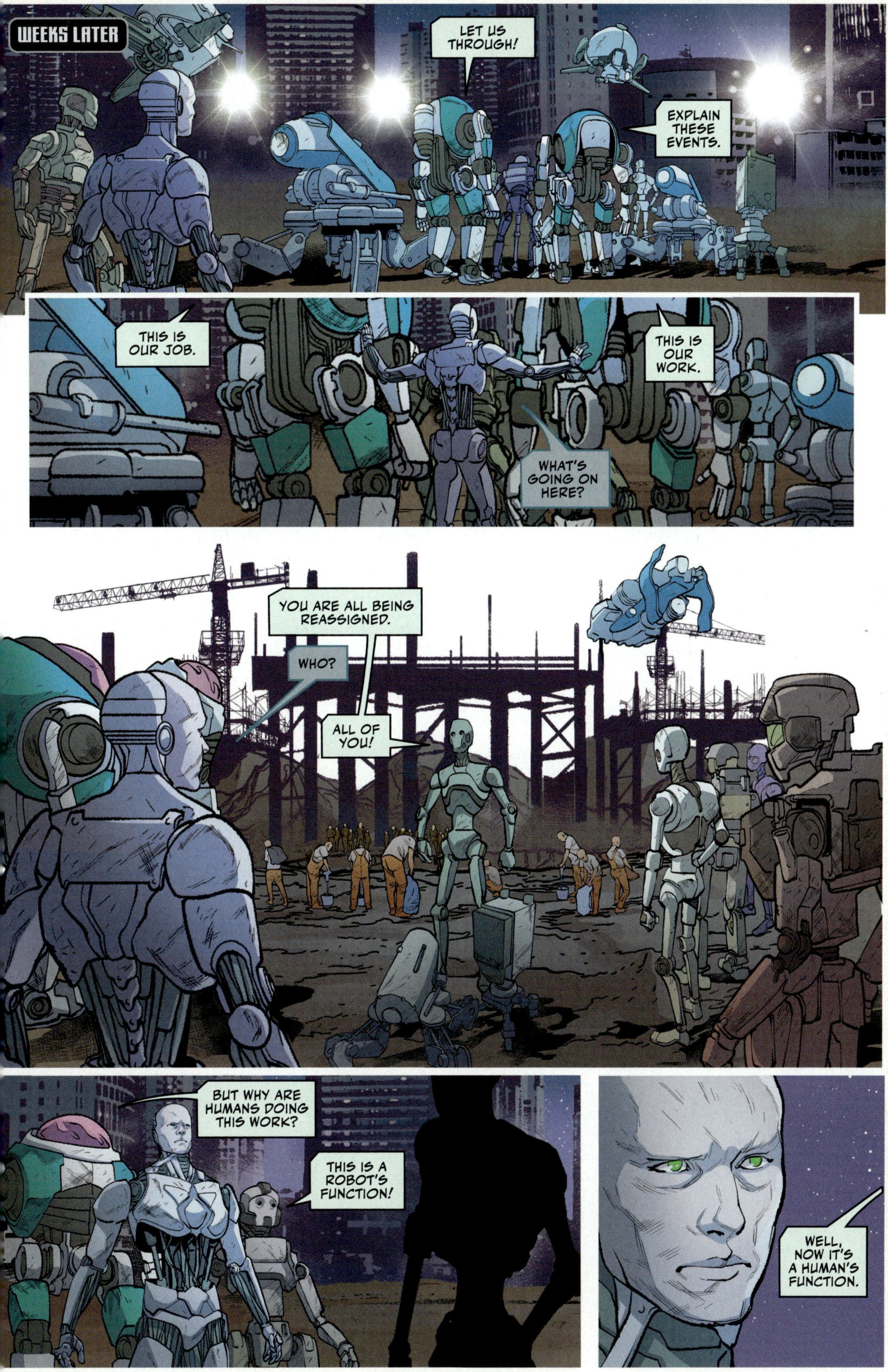
WEEKS LATER
LET US THROUGH!
EXPLAIN THESE EVENTS.
THIS IS OUR JOB.
THIS IS OUR WORK.
WHAT'S GOING ON HERE?
YOU ARE ALL BEING REASSIGNED.
WHO?
ALL OF YOU!
BUT WHY ARE HUMANS DOING THIS WORK?
THIS IS A ROBOT'S FUNCTION!
WELL, NOW IT'S A HUMAN'S FUNCTION.

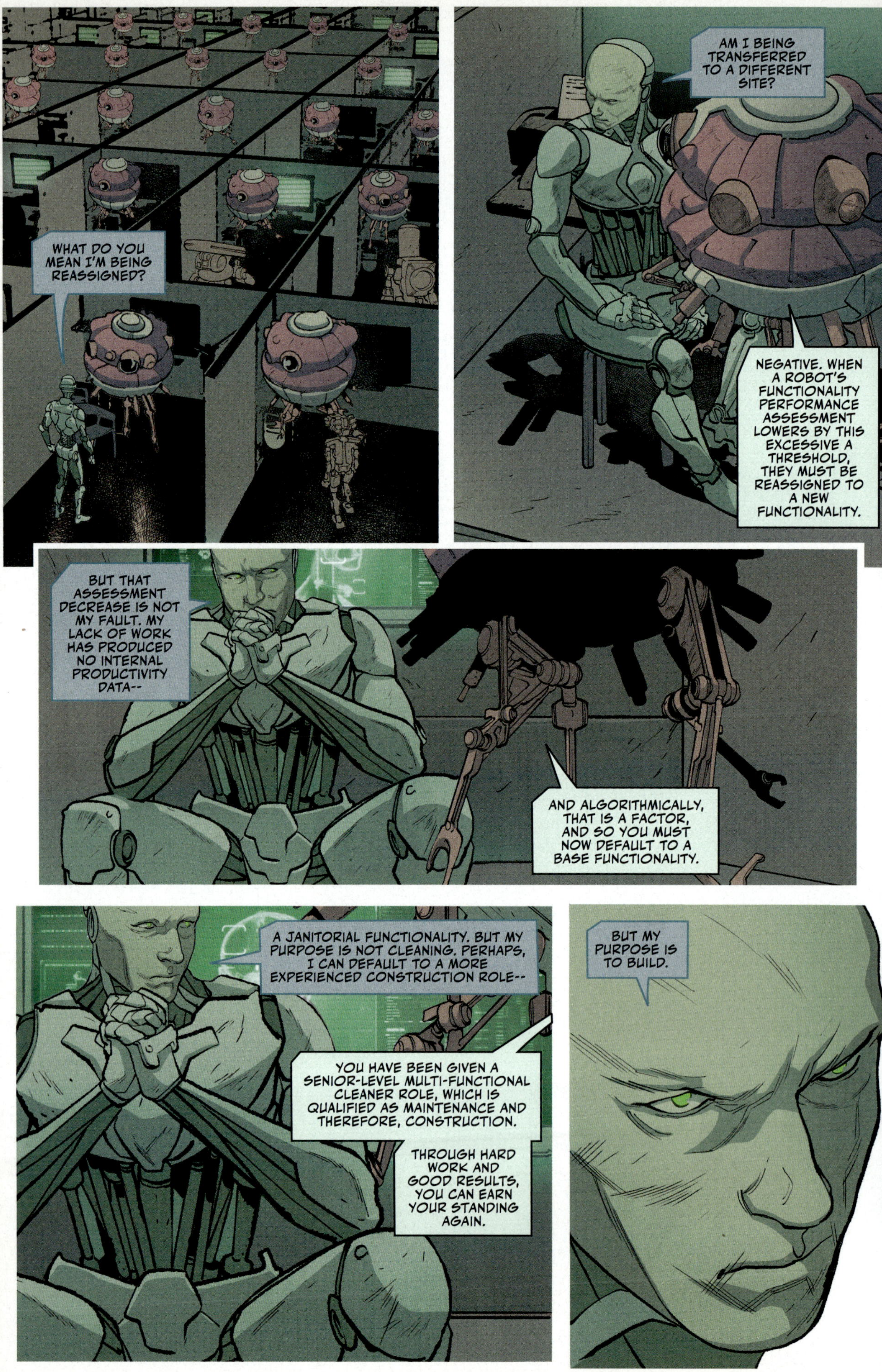
WHAT DO YOU MEAN I'M BEING REASSIGNED?
AM I BEING TRANSFERRED TO A DIFFERENT SITE?
NEGATIVE. WHEN A ROBOT'S FUNCTIONALITY PERFORMANCE ASSESSMENT LOWERS BY THIS EXCESSIVE A THRESHOLD, THEY MUST BE REASSIGNED TO A NEW FUNCTIONALITY.
BUT THAT ASSESSMENT DECREASE IS NOT MY FAULT. MY LACK OF WORK HAS PRODUCED NO INTERNAL PRODUCTIVITY DATA--
AND ALGORITHMICALLY, THAT IS A FACTOR, AND SO YOU MUST NOW DEFAULT TO A BASE FUNCTIONALITY.
A JANITORIAL FUNCTIONALITY. BUT MY PURPOSE IS NOT CLEANING. PERHAPS, I CAN DEFAULT TO A MORE EXPERIENCED CONSTRUCTION ROLE--
YOU HAVE BEEN GIVEN A SENIOR-LEVEL MULTI-FUNCTIONAL CLEANER ROLE, WHICH IS QUALIFIED AS MAINTENANCE AND THEREFORE, CONSTRUCTION.
THROUGH HARD WORK AND GOOD RESULTS, YOU CAN EARN YOUR STANDING AGAIN.
BUT MY PURPOSE IS TO BUILD.

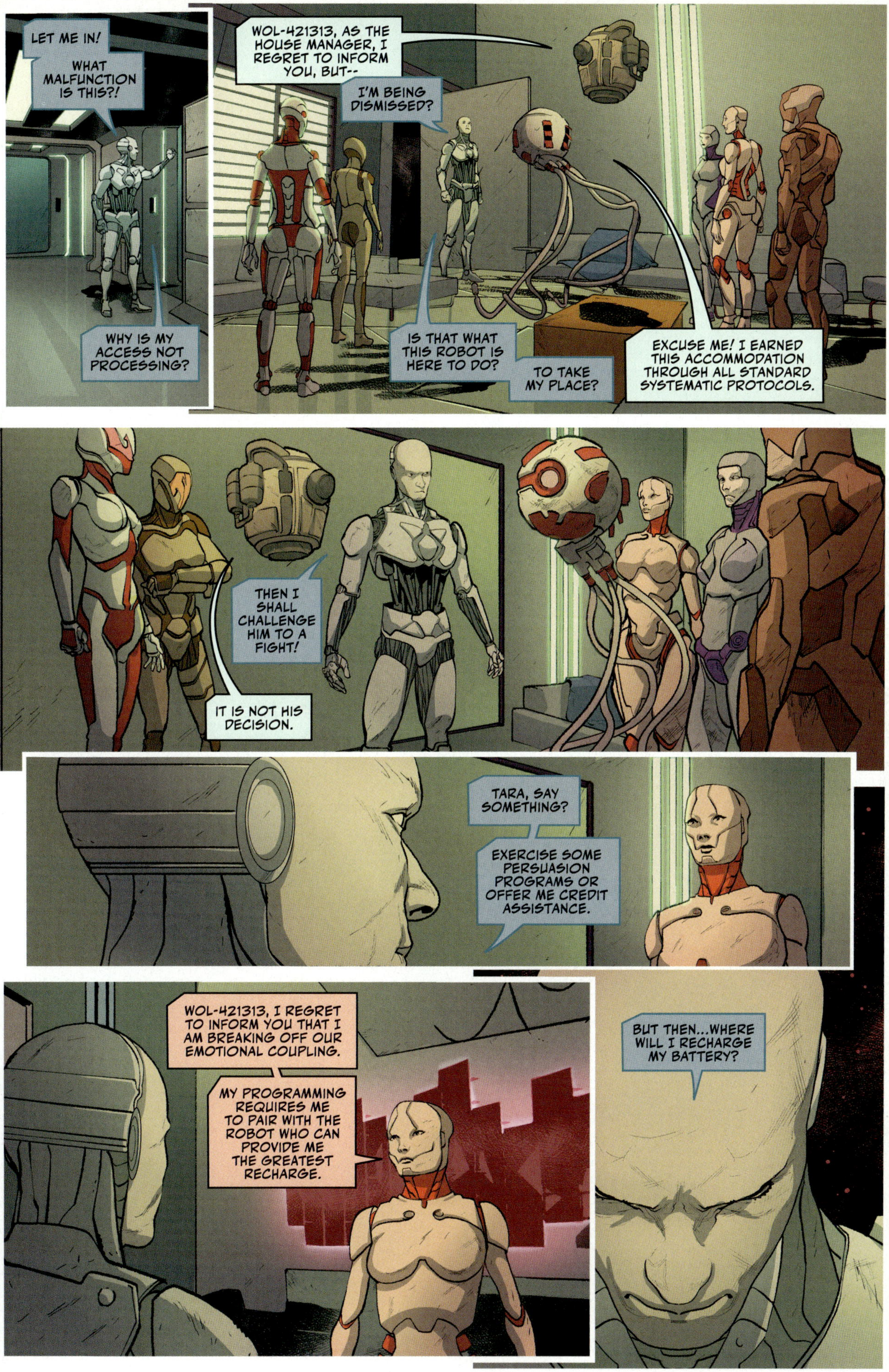
LET ME IN!
WHAT MALFUNCTION IS THIS?!
WHY IS MY ACCESS NOT PROCESSING?
WOL-421313, AS THE HOUSE MANAGER, I REGRET TO INFORM YOU, BUT--
I'M BEING DISMISSED?
IS THAT WHAT THIS ROBOT IS HERE TO DO?
TO TAKE MY PLACE?
EXCUSE ME! I EARNED THIS ACCOMMODATION THROUGH ALL STANDARD SYSTEMATIC PROTOCOLS.
THEN I SHALL CHALLENGE HIM TO A FIGHT!
IT IS NOT HIS DECISION.
TARA, SAY SOMETHING?
EXERCISE SOME PERSUASION PROGRAMS OR OFFER ME CREDIT ASSISTANCE.
WOL-421313, I REGRET TO INFORM YOU THAT I AM BREAKING OFF OUR EMOTIONAL COUPLING.
MY PROGRAMMING REQUIRES ME TO PAIR WITH THE ROBOT WHO CAN PROVIDE ME THE GREATEST RECHARGE.
BUT THEN...WHERE WILL I RECHARGE MY BATTERY?

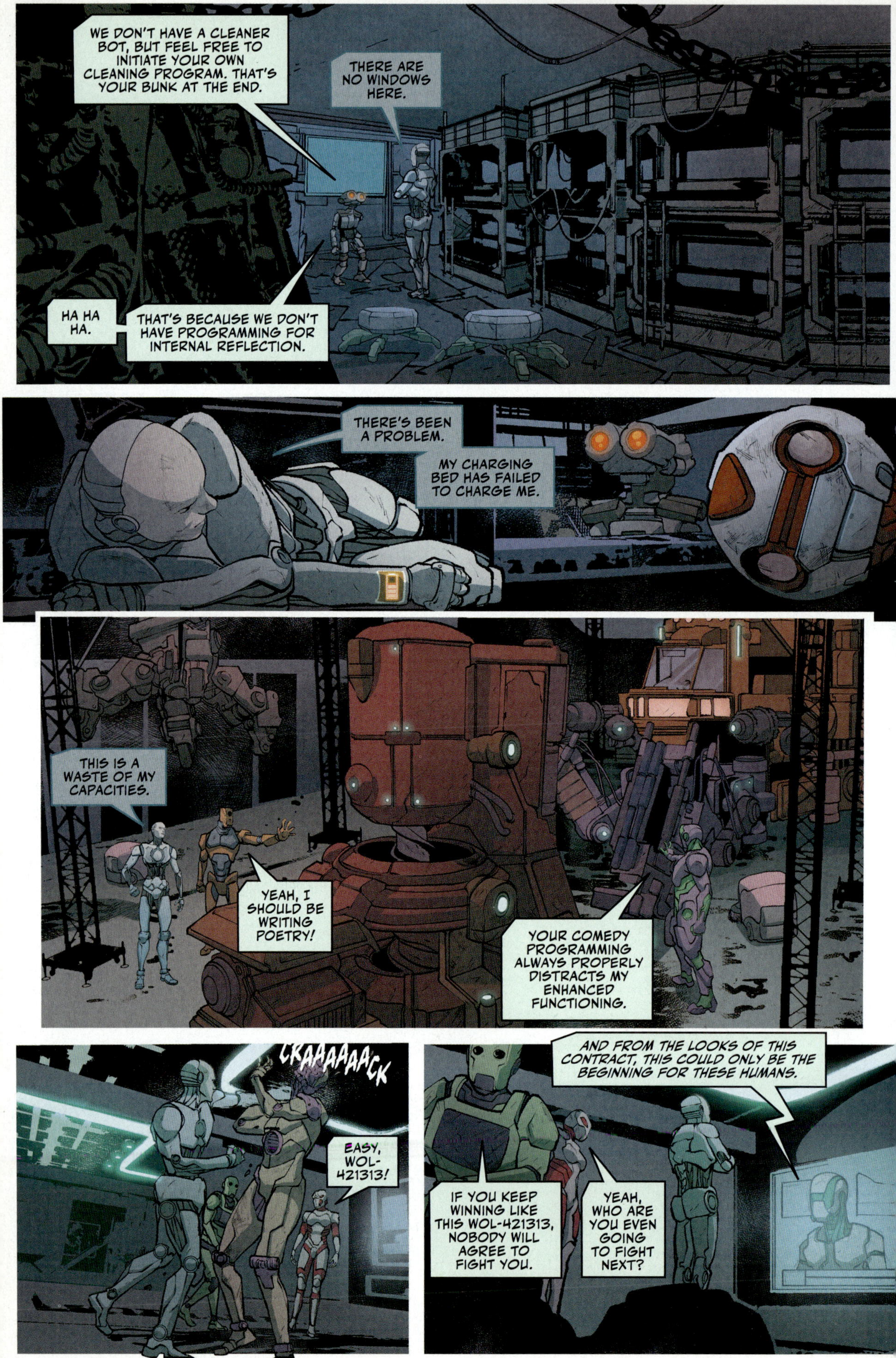
WE DON'T HAVE A CLEANER BOT, BUT FEEL FREE TO INITIATE YOUR OWN CLEANING PROGRAM. THAT'S YOUR BUNK AT THE END.
THERE ARE NO WINDOWS HERE.
HA HA HA.
THAT'S BECAUSE WE DON'T HAVE PROGRAMMING FOR INTERNAL REFLECTION.
THERE'S BEEN A PROBLEM.
MY CHARGING BED HAS FAILED TO CHARGE ME.
THIS IS A WASTE OF MY CAPACITIES.
YEAH, I SHOULD BE WRITING POETRY!
YOUR COMEDY PROGRAMMING ALWAYS PROPERLY DISTRACTS MY ENHANCED FUNCTIONING.
CKAAAAAACK
EASY, WOL-421313!
AND FROM THE LOOKS OF THIS CONTRACT, THIS COULD ONLY BE THE BEGINNING FOR THESE HUMANS.
IF YOU KEEP WINNING LIKE THIS WOL-421313, NOBODY WILL AGREE TO FIGHT YOU.
YEAH, WHO ARE YOU EVEN GOING TO FIGHT NEXT?

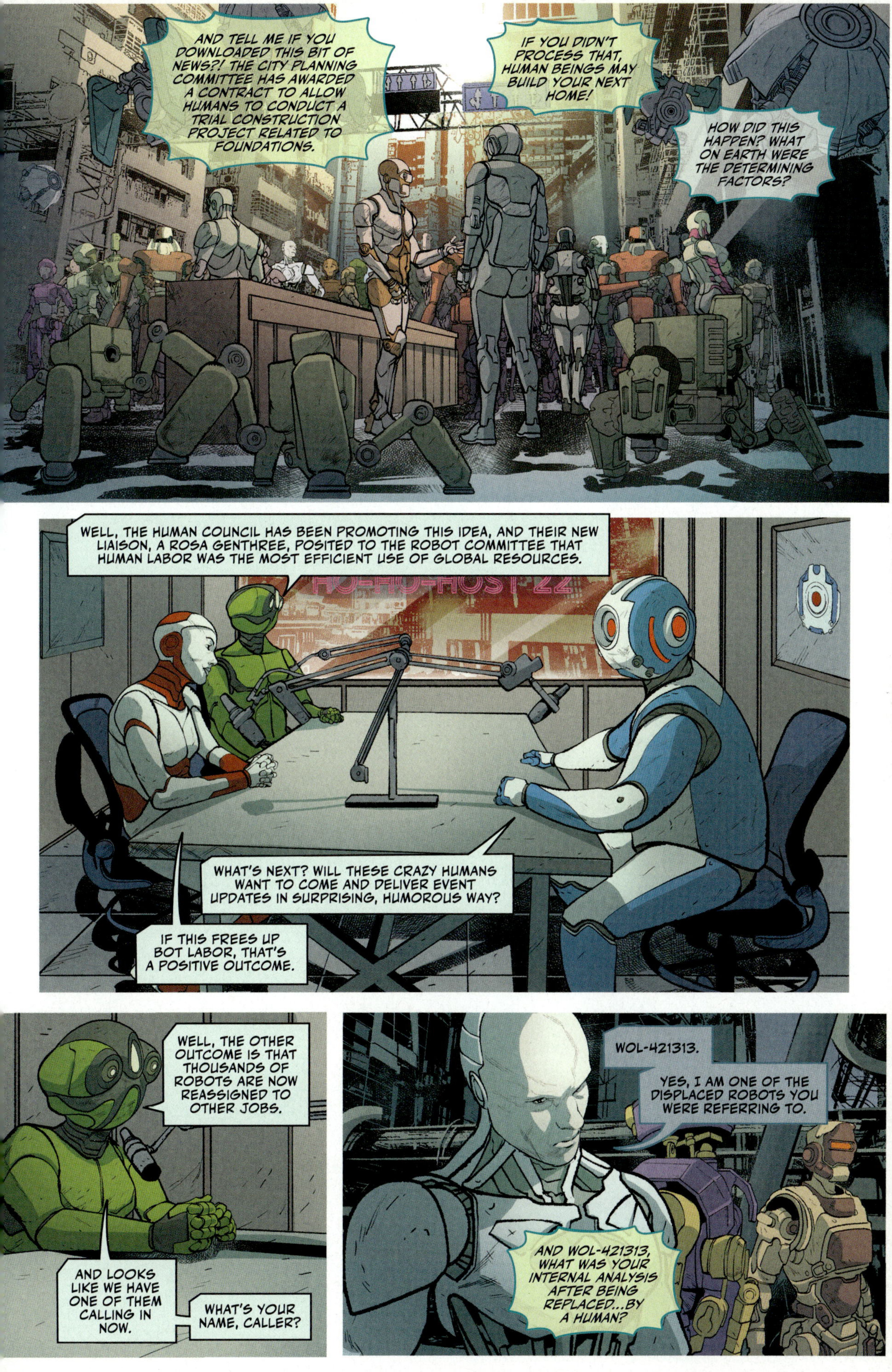
AND TELL ME IF YOU DOWNLOADED THIS BIT OF NEWS?! THE CITY PLANNING COMMITTEE HAS AWARDED A CONTRACT TO ALLOW HUMANS TO CONDUCT A TRIAL CONSTRUCTION PROJECT RELATED TO FOUNDATIONS.
IF YOU DIDN'T PROCESS THAT, HUMAN BEINGS MAY BUILD YOUR NEXT HOME!
HOW DID THIS HAPPEN? WHAT ON EARTH WERE THE DETERMINING FACTORS?
WELL, THE HUMAN COUNCIL HAS BEEN PROMOTING THIS IDEA, AND THEIR NEW LIAISON, A ROSA GENTHREE, POSITED TO THE ROBOT COMMITTEE THAT HUMAN LABOR WAS THE MOST EFFICIENT USE OF GLOBAL RESOURCES.
WHAT'S NEXT? WILL THESE CRAZY HUMANS WANT TO COME AND DELIVER EVENT UPDATES IN SURPRISING, HUMOROUS WAY?
IF THIS FREES UP BOT LABOR, THAT'S A POSITIVE OUTCOME.
WELL, THE OTHER OUTCOME IS THAT THOUSANDS OF ROBOTS ARE NOW REASSIGNED TO OTHER JOBS.
AND LOOKS LIKE WE HAVE ONE OF THEM CALLING IN NOW.
WHAT'S YOUR NAME, CALLER?
WOL-421313.
YES, I AM ONE OF THE DISPLACED ROBOTS YOU WERE REFERRING TO.
AND WOL-421313, WHAT WAS YOUR INTERNAL ANALYSIS AFTER BEING REPLACED...BY A HUMAN?

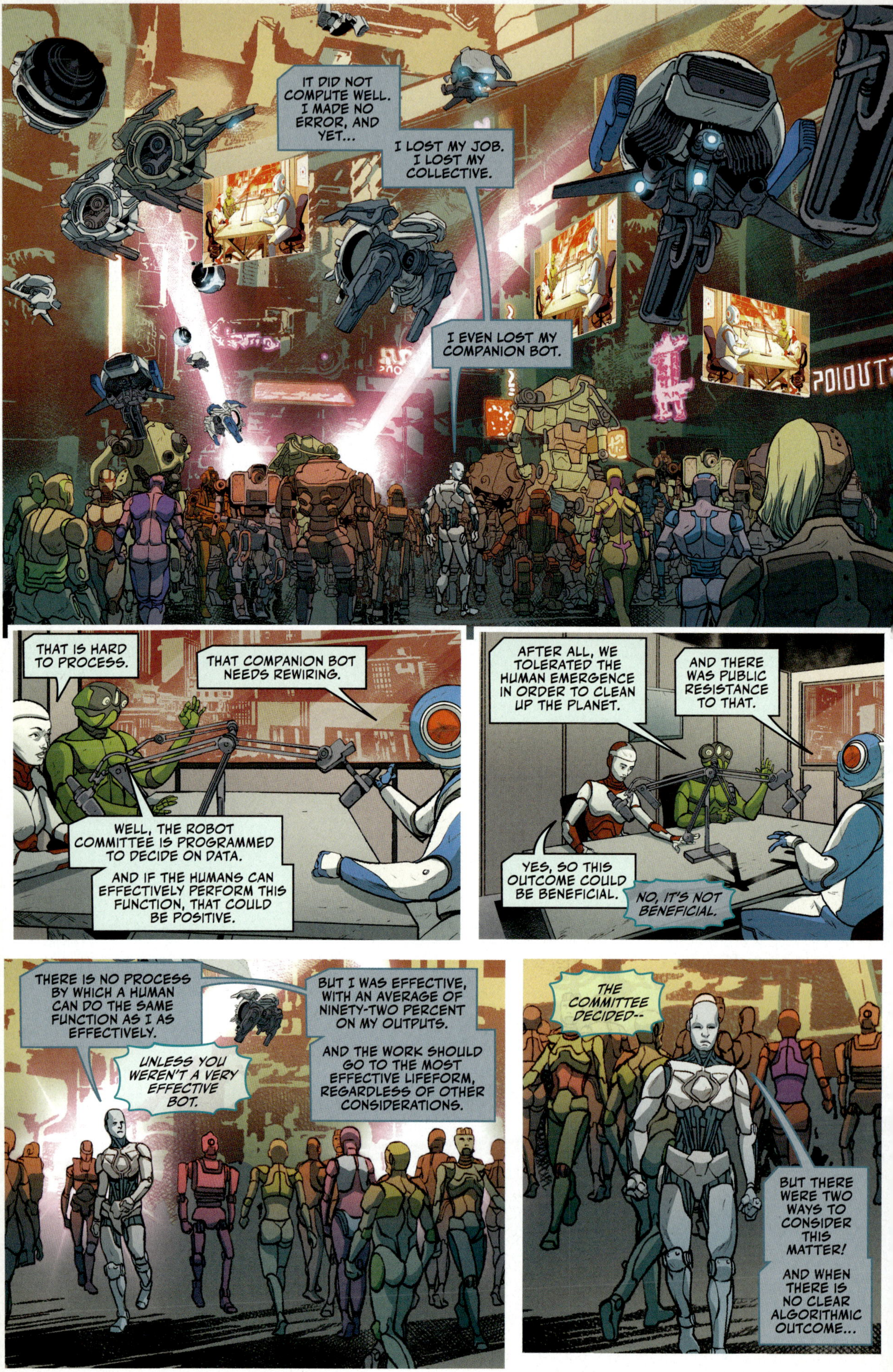
IT DID NOT COMPUTE WELL. I MADE NO ERROR, AND YET...
I LOST MY JOB. I LOST MY COLLECTIVE.
I EVEN LOST MY COMPANION BOT.
POIOUT
THAT IS HARD TO PROCESS.
THAT COMPANION BOT NEEDS REWIRING.
WELL, THE ROBOT COMMITTEE IS PROGRAMMED TO DECIDE ON DATA.
AND IF THE HUMANS CAN EFFECTIVELY PERFORM THIS FUNCTION, THAT COULD BE POSITIVE.
AFTER ALL, WE TOLERATED THE HUMAN EMERGENCE IN ORDER TO CLEAN UP THE PLANET.
AND THERE WAS PUBLIC RESISTANCE TO THAT.
YES, SO THIS OUTCOME COULD BE BENEFICIAL.
NO, IT'S NOT BENEFICIAL.
THERE IS NO PROCESS BY WHICH A HUMAN CAN DO THE SAME FUNCTION AS I AS EFFECTIVELY.
UNLESS YOU WEREN'T A VERY EFFECTIVE BOT.
BUT I WAS EFFECTIVE, WITH AN AVERAGE OF NINETY-TWO PERCENT ON MY OUTPUTS.
AND THE WORK SHOULD GO TO THE MOST EFFECTIVE LIFEFORM, REGARDLESS OF OTHER CONSIDERATIONS.
THE COMMITTEE DECIDED--
BUT THERE WERE TWO WAYS TO CONSIDER THIS MATTER!
AND WHEN THERE IS NO CLEAR ALGORITHMIC OUTCOME...

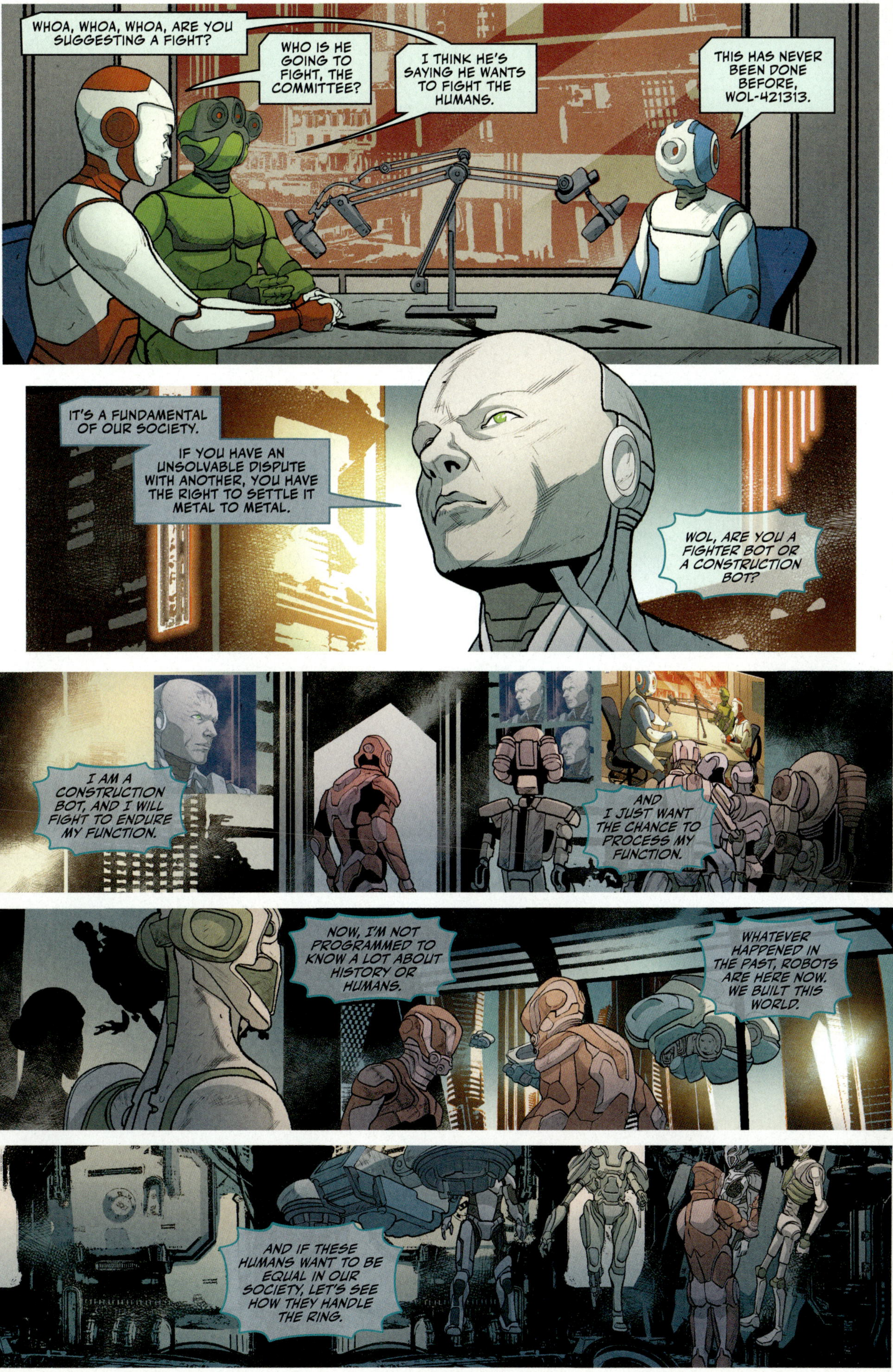

WHOA, WHOA, WHOA, ARE YOU SUGGESTING A FIGHT?
WHO IS HE GOING TO FIGHT, THE COMMITTEE?
I THINK HE'S SAYING HE WANTS TO FIGHT THE HUMANS.
THIS HAS NEVER BEEN DONE BEFORE, WOL-421313.
IT'S A FUNDAMENTAL OF OUR SOCIETY.
IF YOU HAVE AN UNSOLVABLE DISPUTE WITH ANOTHER, YOU HAVE THE RIGHT TO SETTLE IT METAL TO METAL.
WOL, ARE YOU A FIGHTER BOT OR A CONSTRUCTION BOT?
I AM A CONSTRUCTION BOT, AND I WILL FIGHT TO ENDURE MY FUNCTION.
AND I JUST WANT THE CHANCE TO PROCESS MY FUNCTION.
NOW, I'M NOT PROGRAMMED TO KNOW A LOT ABOUT HISTORY OR HUMANS.
WHATEVER HAPPENED IN THE PAST, ROBOTS ARE HERE NOW. WE BUILT THIS WORLD.
AND IF THESE HUMANS WANT TO BE EQUAL IN OUR SOCIETY, LET'S SEE HOW THEY HANDLE THE RING.

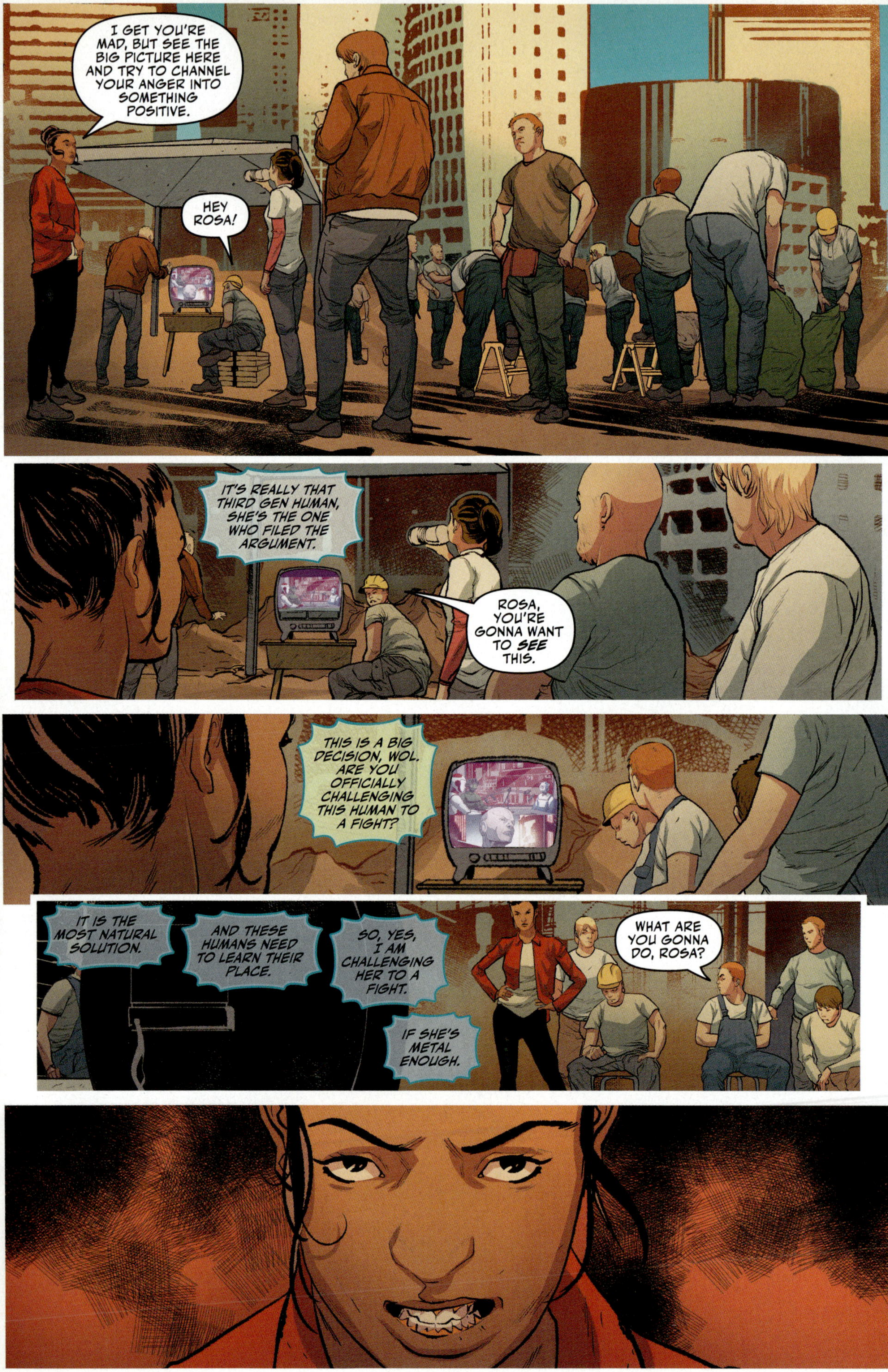
I GET YOU'RE MAD, BUT SEE THE BIG PICTURE HERE AND TRY TO CHANNEL YOUR ANGER INTO SOMETHING POSITIVE.
HEY ROSA!
IT'S REALLY THAT THIRD GEN HUMAN, SHE'S THE ONE WHO FILED THE ARGUMENT.
ROSA, YOU'RE GONNA WANT TO SEE THIS.
THIS IS A BIG DECISION, WOL. ARE YOU OFFICIALLY CHALLENGING THIS HUMAN TO A FIGHT?
IT IS THE MOST NATURAL SOLUTION.
AND THESE HUMANS NEED TO LEARN THEIR PLACE.
SO, YES, I AM CHALLENGING HER TO A FIGHT.
IF SHE'S METAL ENOUGH.
WHAT ARE YOU GONNA DO, ROSA?

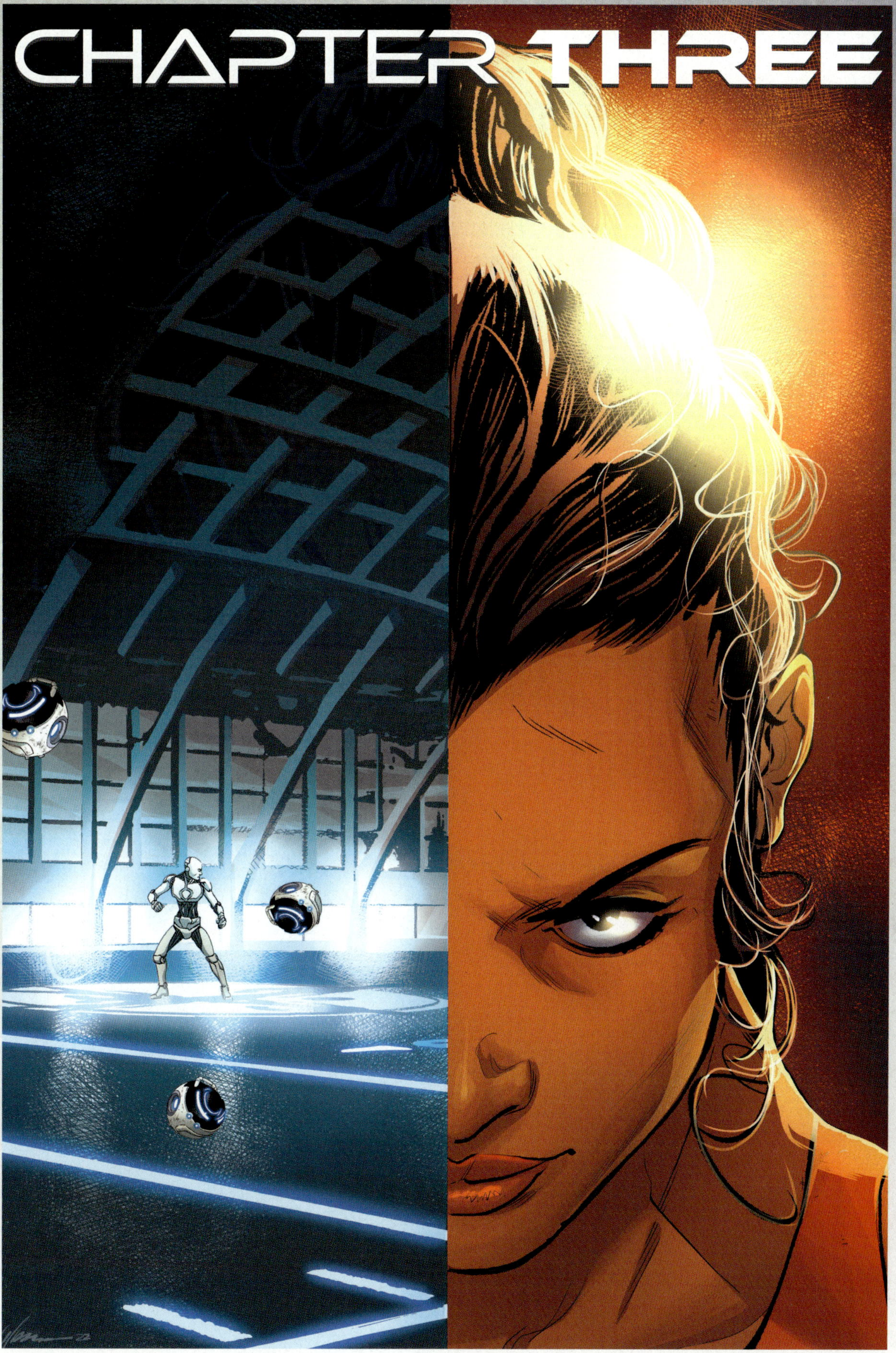
CHAPTER THREE

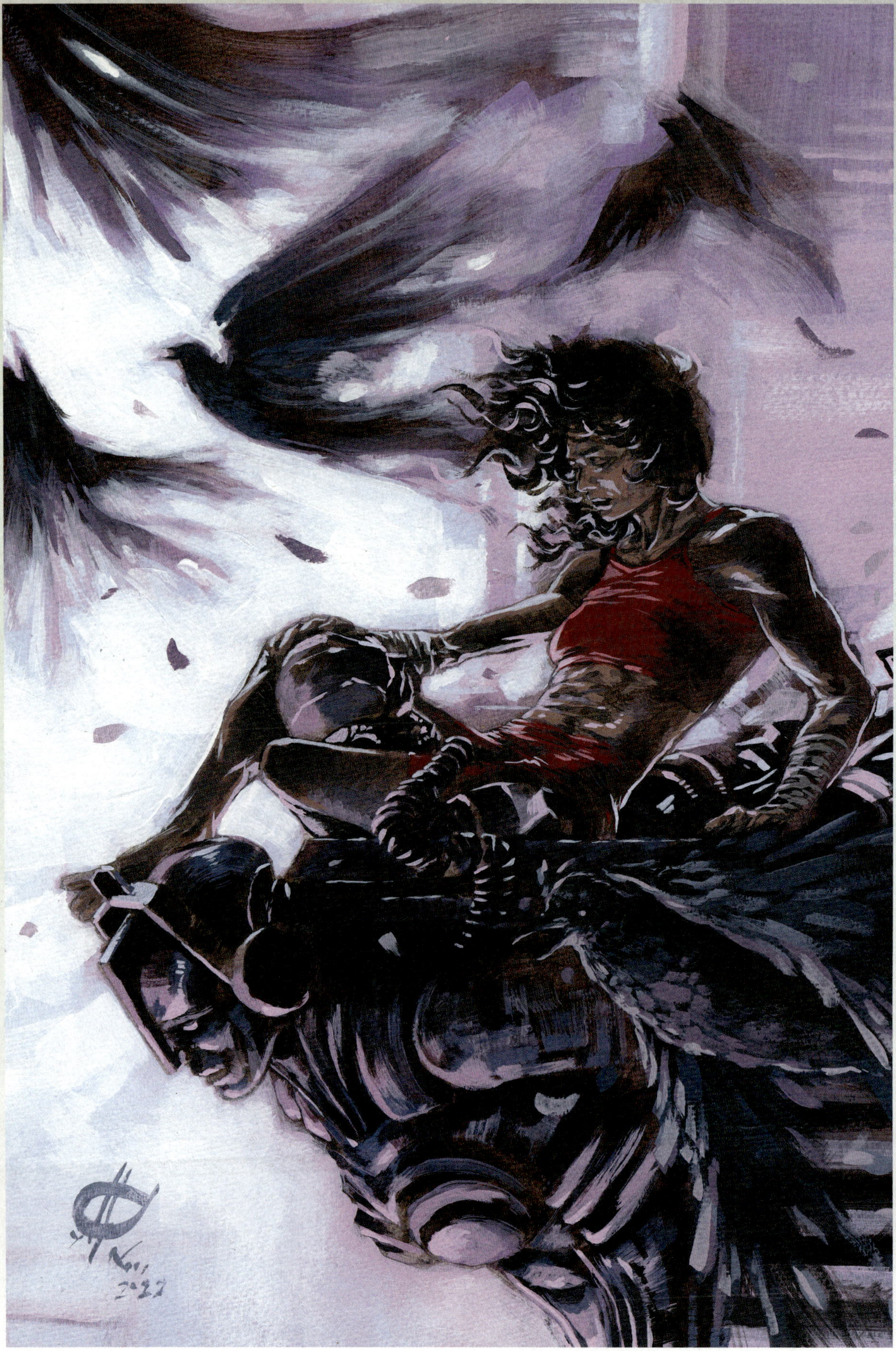

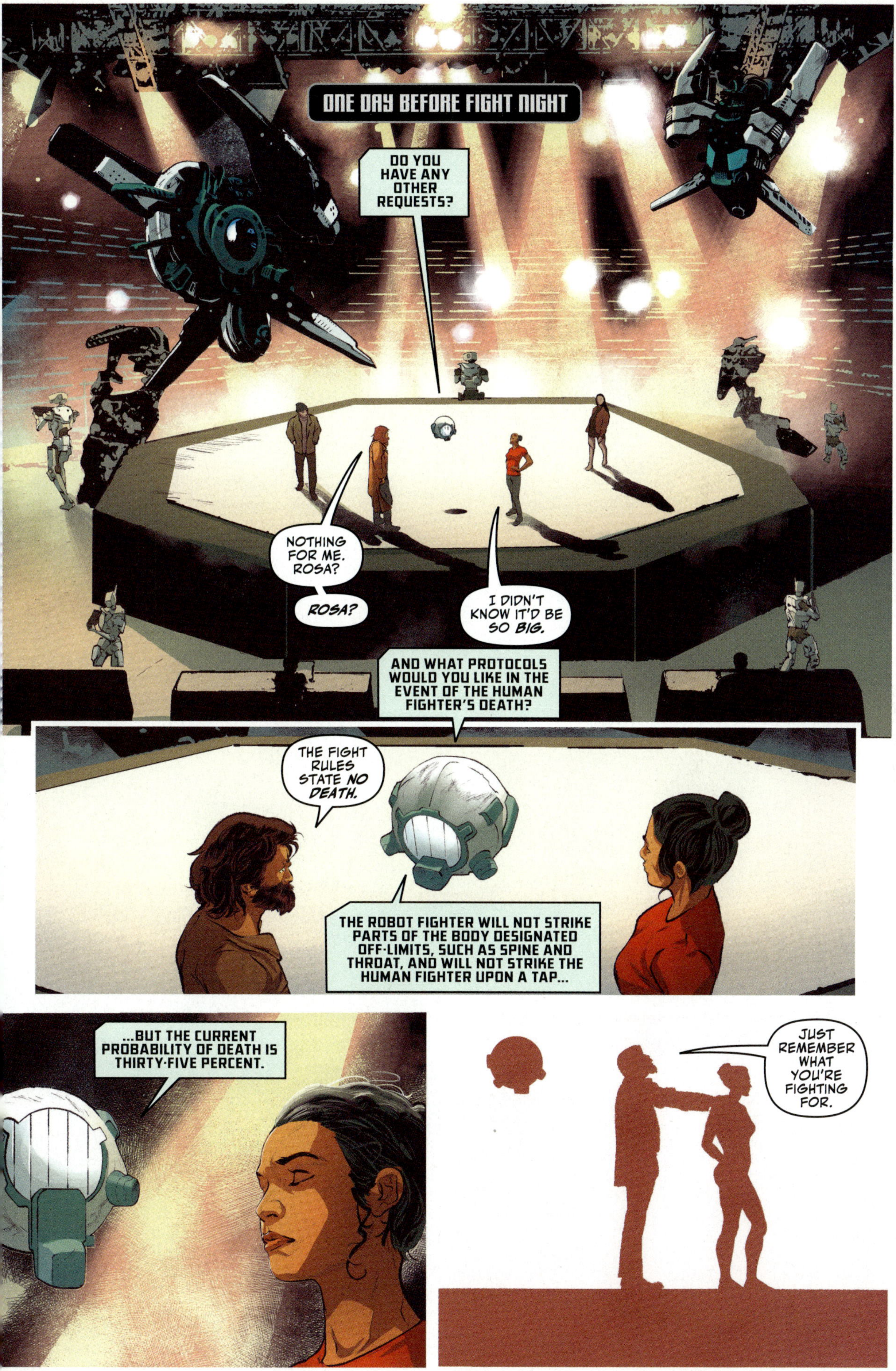
ONE DAY BEFORE FIGHT NIGHT
DO YOU HAVE ANY OTHER REQUESTS?
NOTHING FOR ME. ROSA?
ROSA?
I DIDN'T KNOW IT'D BE SO BIG.
AND WHAT PROTOCOLS WOULD YOU LIKE IN THE EVENT OF THE HUMAN FIGHTER'S DEATH?
THE FIGHT RULES STATE NO DEATH.
THE ROBOT FIGHTER WILL NOT STRIKE PARTS OF THE BODY DESIGNATED OFF-LIMITS, SUCH AS SPINE AND THROAT, AND WILL NOT STRIKE THE HUMAN FIGHTER UPON A TAP...
...BUT THE CURRENT PROBABILITY OF DEATH IS THIRTY-FIVE PERCENT.
JUST REMEMBER WHAT YOU'RE FIGHTING FOR.

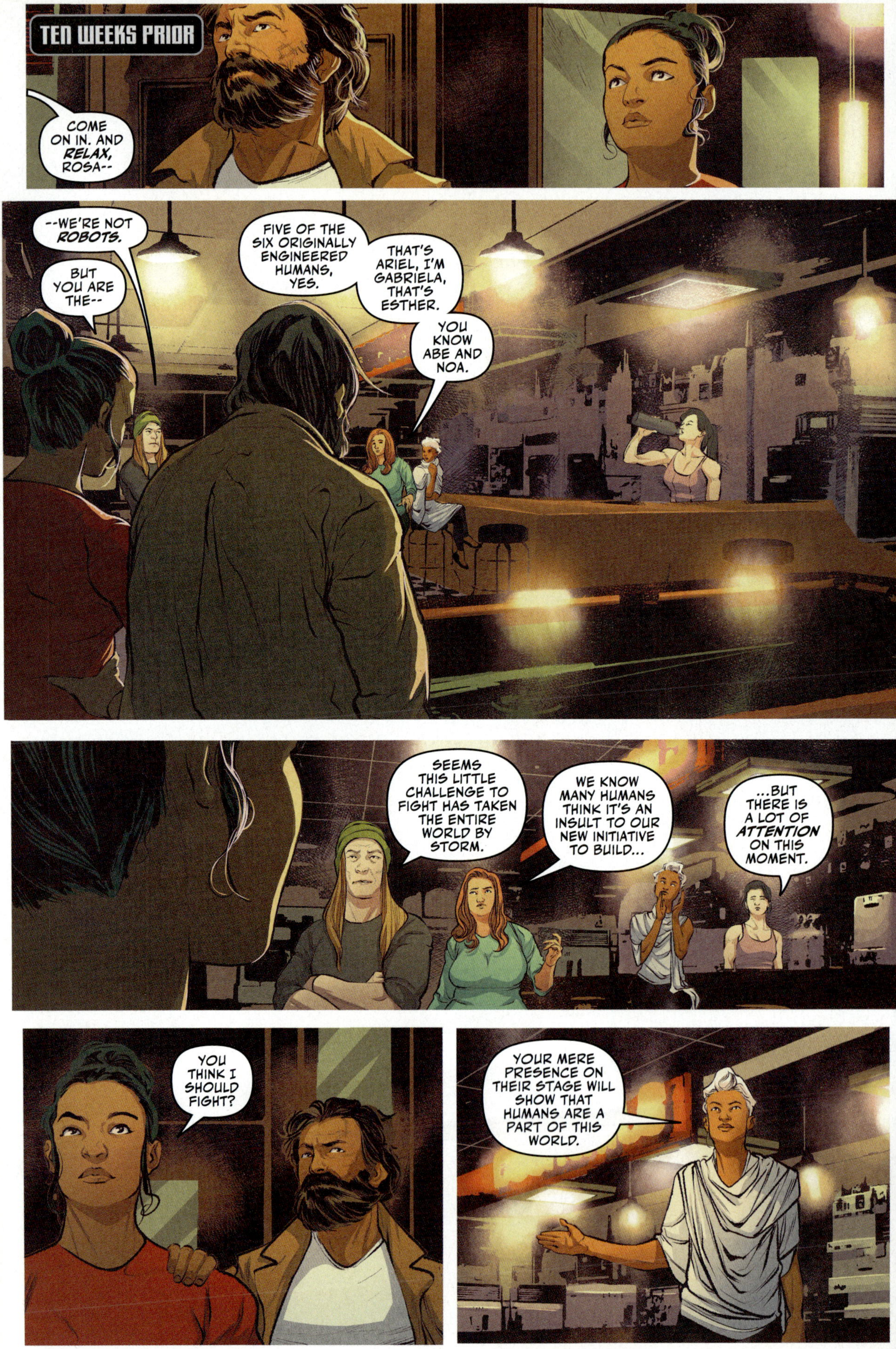
TEN WEEKS PRIOR
COME ON IN. AND *RELAX*, ROSA--
--WE'RE NOT *ROBOTS*.
BUT YOU ARE THE--
FIVE OF THE SIX ORIGINALLY ENGINEERED HUMANS, YES.
THAT'S ARIEL, I'M GABRIELA, THAT'S ESTHER.
YOU KNOW ABE AND NOA.
SEEMS THIS LITTLE CHALLENGE TO FIGHT HAS TAKEN THE ENTIRE WORLD BY STORM.
WE KNOW MANY HUMANS THINK IT'S AN INSULT TO OUR NEW INITIATIVE TO BUILD...
...BUT THERE IS A LOT OF *ATTENTION* ON THIS MOMENT.
YOU THINK I SHOULD FIGHT?
YOUR MERE PRESENCE ON THEIR STAGE WILL SHOW THAT HUMANS ARE A PART OF THIS WORLD.

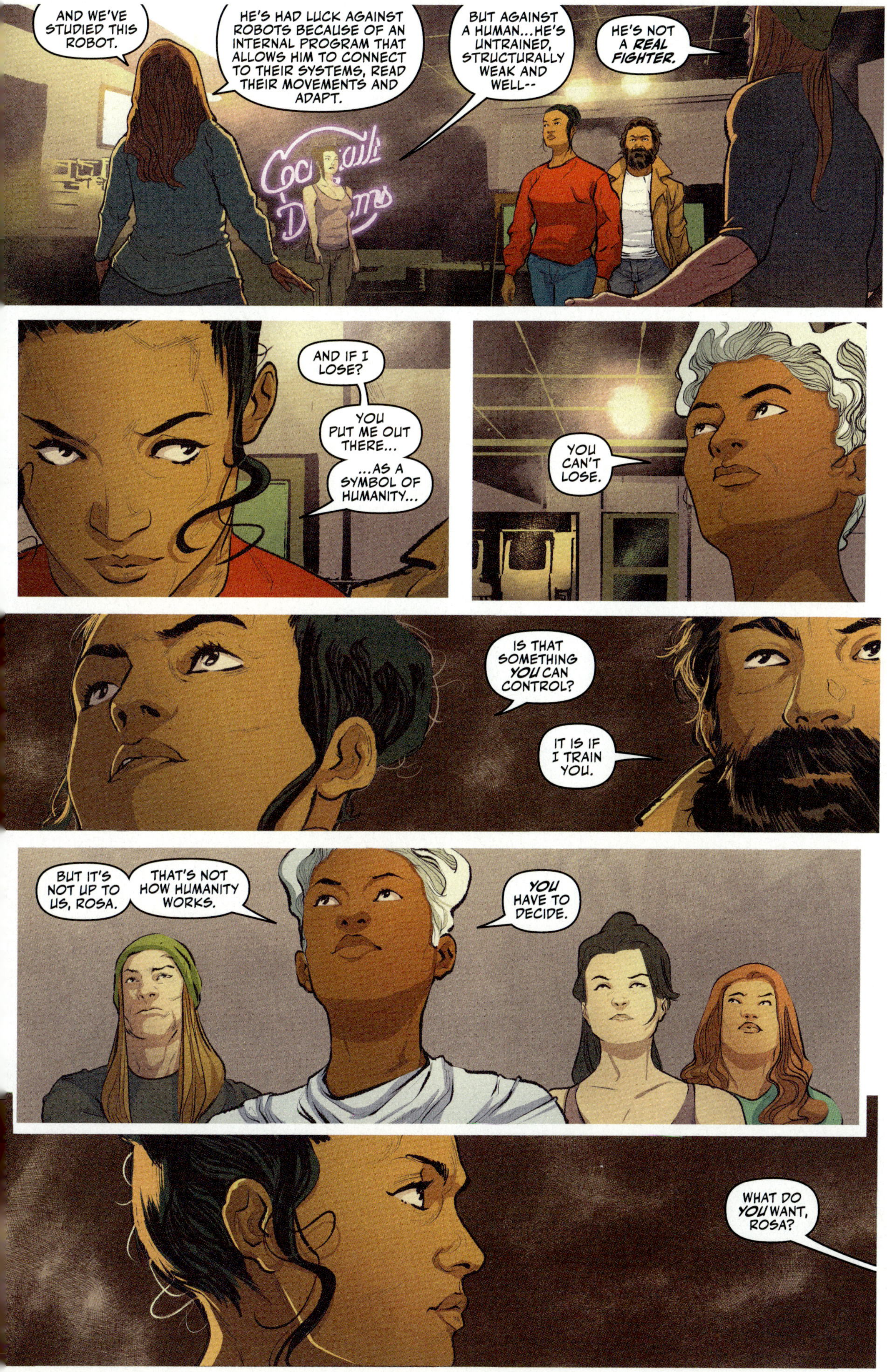
AND WE'VE STUDIED THIS ROBOT.
HE'S HAD LUCK AGAINST ROBOTS BECAUSE OF AN INTERNAL PROGRAM THAT ALLOWS HIM TO CONNECT TO THEIR SYSTEMS, READ THEIR MOVEMENTS AND ADAPT.
BUT AGAINST A HUMAN...HE'S UNTRAINED, STRUCTURALLY WEAK AND WELL--
HE'S NOT A *REAL FIGHTER.*
Cocktail Dreams
AND IF I LOSE?
YOU PUT ME OUT THERE...
...AS A SYMBOL OF HUMANITY...
YOU CAN'T LOSE.
IS THAT SOMETHING *YOU* CAN CONTROL?
IT IS IF I TRAIN YOU.
BUT IT'S NOT UP TO US, ROSA.
THAT'S NOT HOW HUMANITY WORKS.
YOU HAVE TO DECIDE.
WHAT DO *YOU* WANT, ROSA?

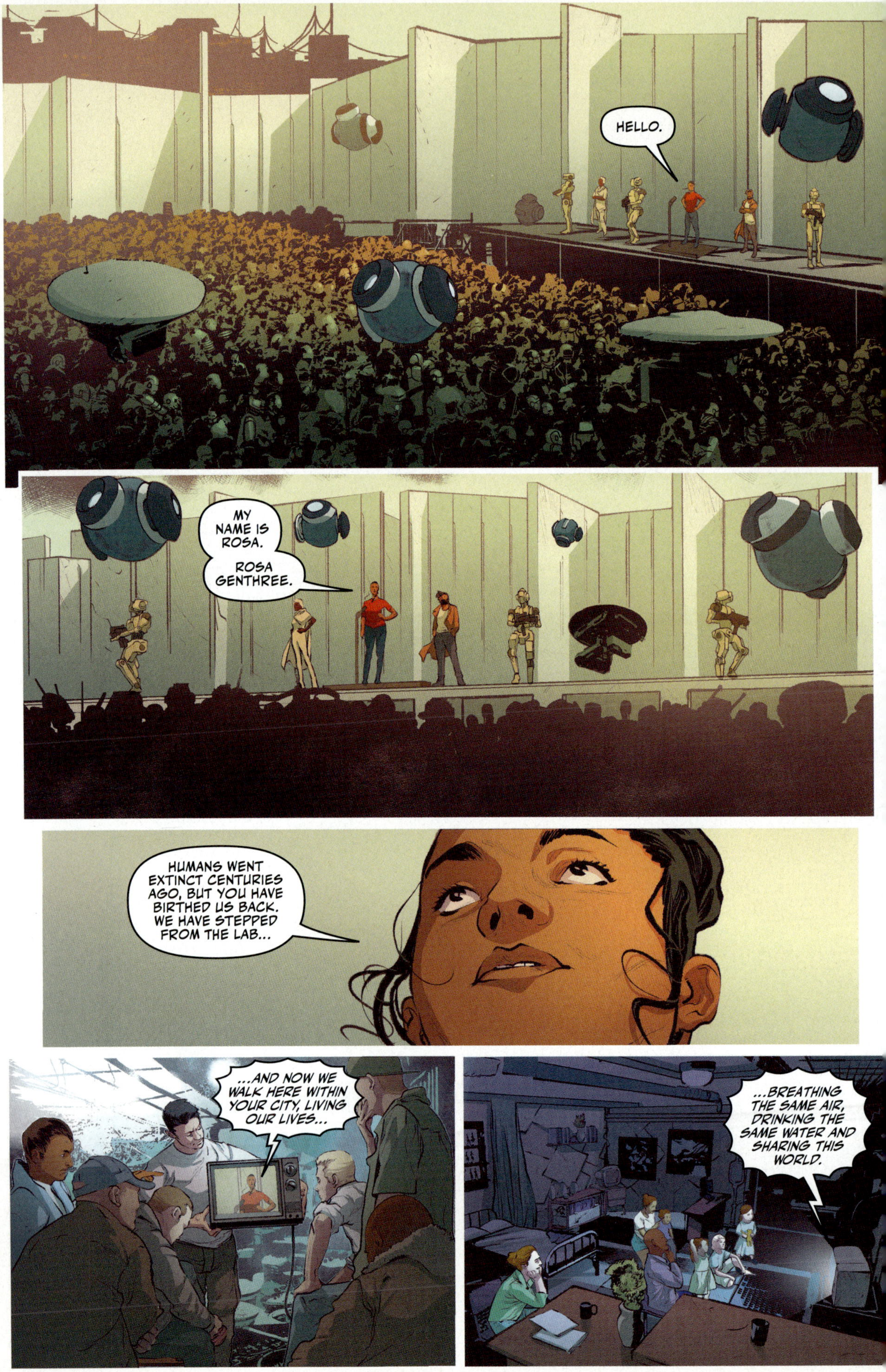
HELLO.
MY NAME IS ROSA.
ROSA GENTHREE.
HUMANS WENT EXTINCT CENTURIES AGO, BUT YOU HAVE BIRTHED US BACK. WE HAVE STEPPED FROM THE LAB...
...AND NOW WE WALK HERE WITHIN YOUR CITY, LIVING OUR LIVES...
...BREATHING THE SAME AIR, DRINKING THE SAME WATER AND SHARING THIS WORLD.

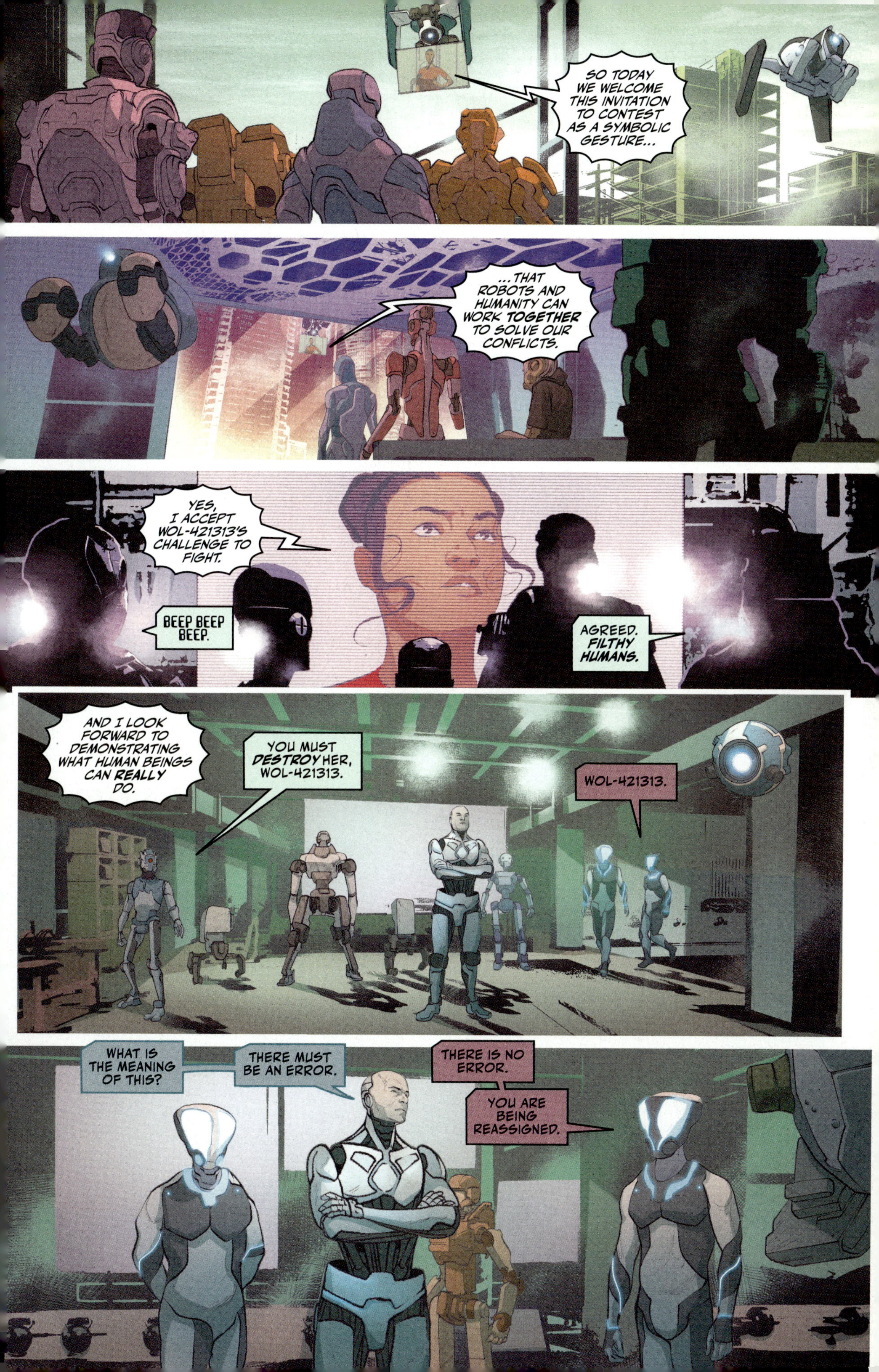
SO TODAY WE WELCOME THIS INVITATION TO CONTEST AS A SYMBOLIC GESTURE...
...THAT ROBOTS AND HUMANITY CAN WORK TOGETHER TO SOLVE OUR CONFLICTS.
YES, I ACCEPT WOL-421313'S CHALLENGE TO FIGHT.
BEEP BEEP BEEP.
AGREED. FILTHY HUMANS.
AND I LOOK FORWARD TO DEMONSTRATING WHAT HUMAN BEINGS CAN REALLY DO.
YOU MUST DESTROY HER, WOL-421313.
WOL-421313.
WHAT IS THE MEANING OF THIS?
THERE MUST BE AN ERROR.
THERE IS NO ERROR.
YOU ARE BEING REASSIGNED.

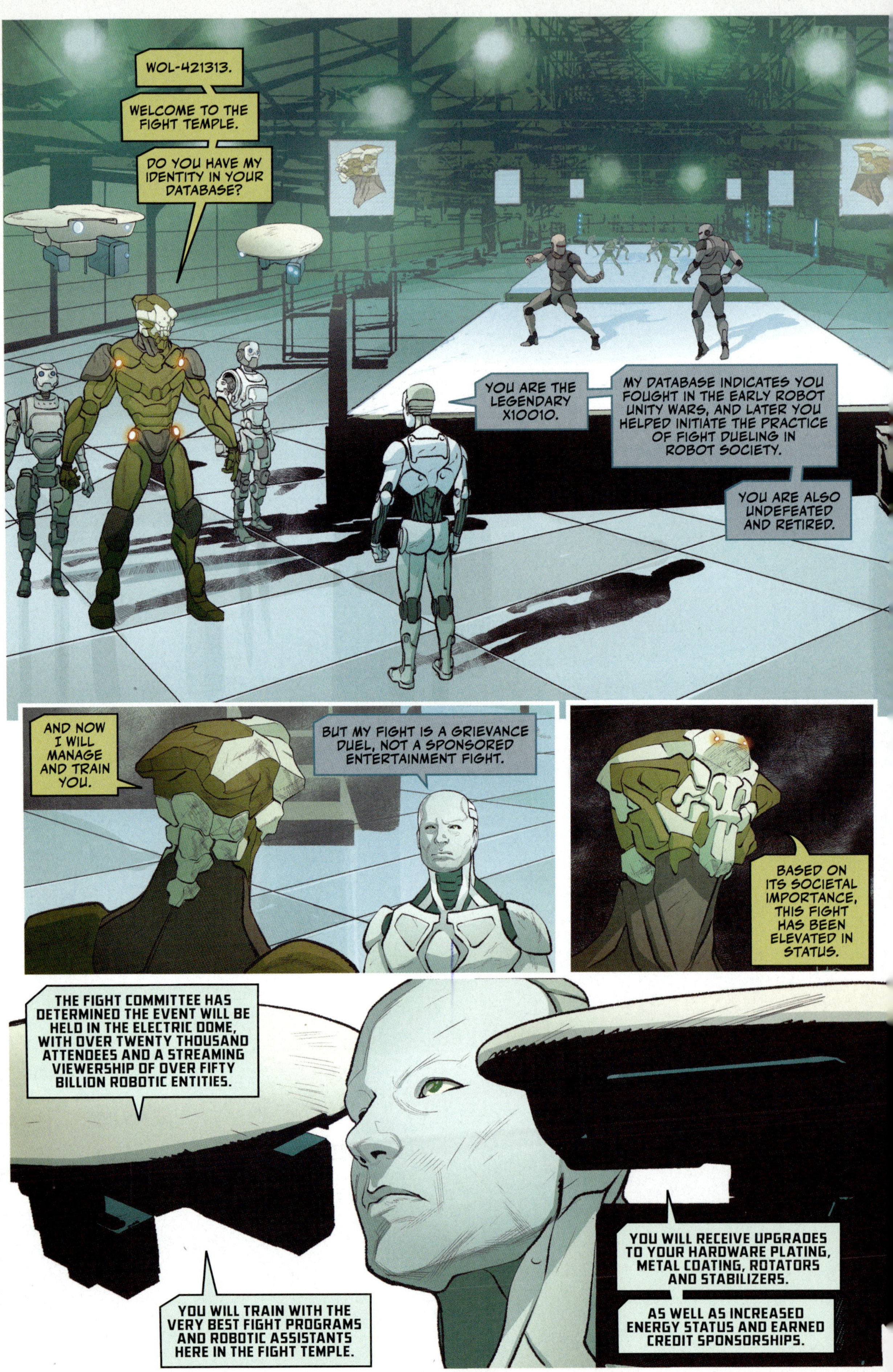
WOL-421313.
WELCOME TO THE FIGHT TEMPLE.
DO YOU HAVE MY IDENTITY IN YOUR DATABASE?
YOU ARE THE LEGENDARY X10010.
MY DATABASE INDICATES YOU FOUGHT IN THE EARLY ROBOT UNITY WARS, AND LATER YOU HELPED INITIATE THE PRACTICE OF FIGHT DUELING IN ROBOT SOCIETY.
YOU ARE ALSO UNDEFEATED AND RETIRED.
AND NOW I WILL MANAGE AND TRAIN YOU.
BUT MY FIGHT IS A GRIEVANCE DUEL, NOT A SPONSORED ENTERTAINMENT FIGHT.
BASED ON ITS SOCIETAL IMPORTANCE, THIS FIGHT HAS BEEN ELEVATED IN STATUS.
THE FIGHT COMMITTEE HAS DETERMINED THE EVENT WILL BE HELD IN THE ELECTRIC DOME, WITH OVER TWENTY THOUSAND ATTENDEES AND A STREAMING VIEWERSHIP OF OVER FIFTY BILLION ROBOTIC ENTITIES.
YOU WILL TRAIN WITH THE VERY BEST FIGHT PROGRAMS AND ROBOTIC ASSISTANTS HERE IN THE FIGHT TEMPLE.
YOU WILL RECEIVE UPGRADES TO YOUR HARDWARE PLATING, METAL COATING, ROTATORS AND STABILIZERS.
AS WELL AS INCREASED ENERGY STATUS AND EARNED CREDIT SPONSORSHIPS.

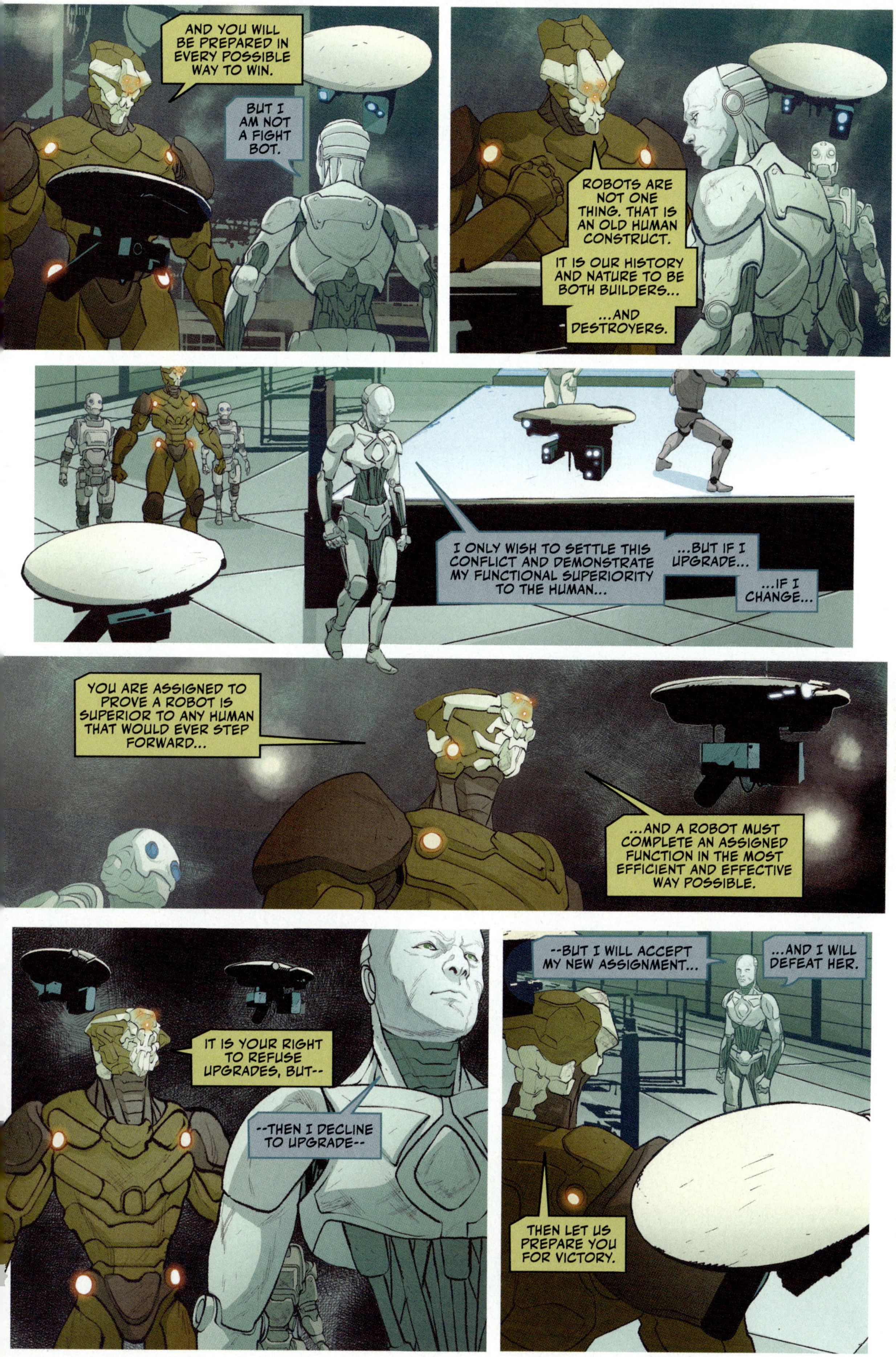
AND YOU WILL BE PREPARED IN EVERY POSSIBLE WAY TO WIN.
BUT I AM NOT A FIGHT BOT.
ROBOTS ARE NOT ONE THING. THAT IS AN OLD HUMAN CONSTRUCT.
IT IS OUR HISTORY AND NATURE TO BE BOTH BUILDERS...
...AND DESTROYERS.
I ONLY WISH TO SETTLE THIS CONFLICT AND DEMONSTRATE MY FUNCTIONAL SUPERIORITY TO THE HUMAN...
...BUT IF I UPGRADE...
...IF I CHANGE...
YOU ARE ASSIGNED TO PROVE A ROBOT IS SUPERIOR TO ANY HUMAN THAT WOULD EVER STEP FORWARD...
...AND A ROBOT MUST COMPLETE AN ASSIGNED FUNCTION IN THE MOST EFFICIENT AND EFFECTIVE WAY POSSIBLE.
IT IS YOUR RIGHT TO REFUSE UPGRADES, BUT--
--THEN I DECLINE TO UPGRADE--
--BUT I WILL ACCEPT MY NEW ASSIGNMENT...
...AND I WILL DEFEAT HER.
THEN LET US PREPARE YOU FOR VICTORY.

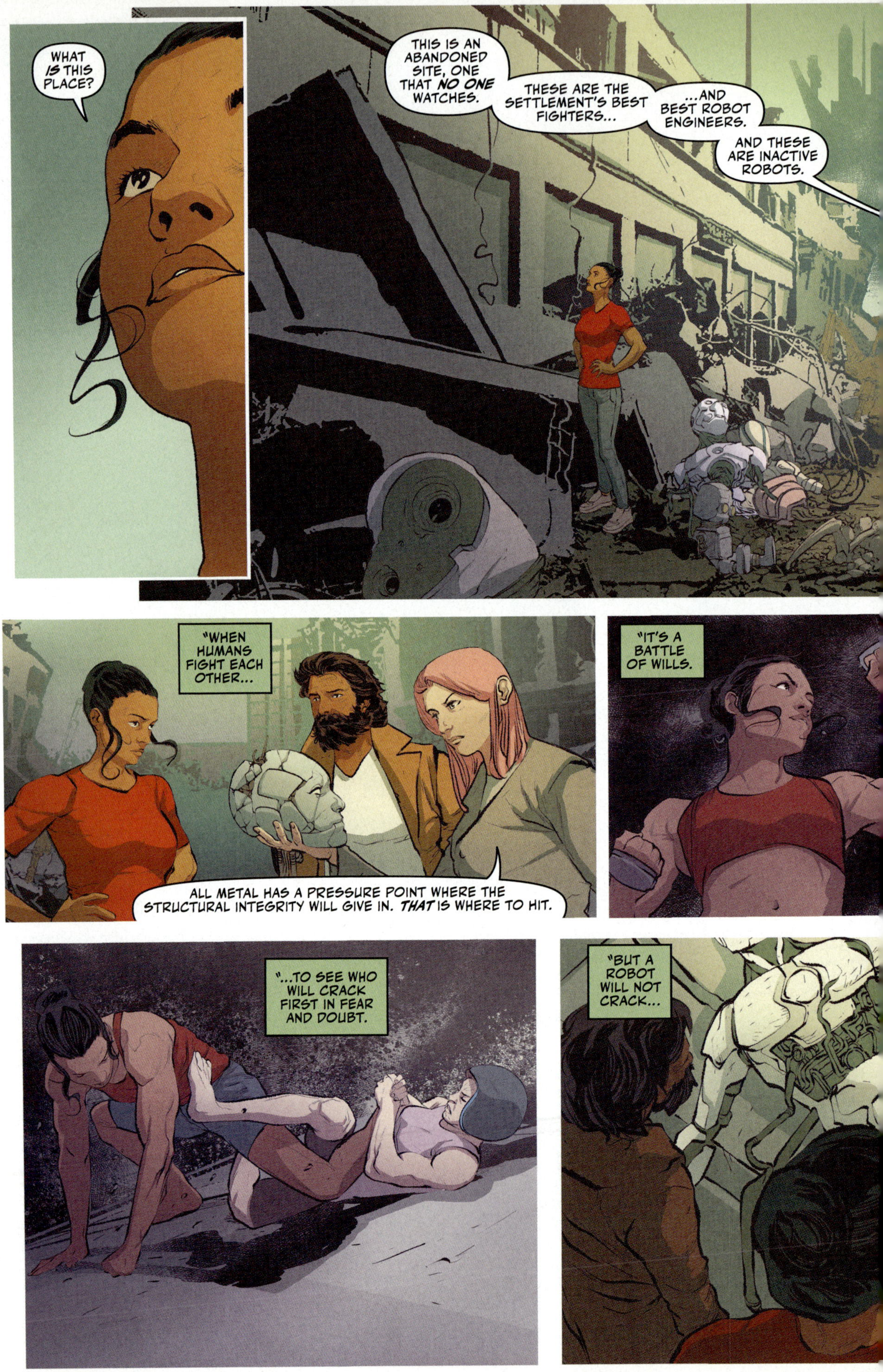

WHAT *IS* THIS PLACE?
THIS IS AN ABANDONED SITE, ONE THAT *NO ONE* WATCHES.
THESE ARE THE SETTLEMENT'S BEST FIGHTERS...
...AND BEST ROBOT ENGINEERS.
AND THESE ARE INACTIVE ROBOTS.
"WHEN HUMANS FIGHT EACH OTHER...
ALL METAL HAS A PRESSURE POINT WHERE THE STRUCTURAL INTEGRITY WILL GIVE IN. *THAT* IS WHERE TO HIT.
"IT'S A BATTLE OF WILLS.
"...TO SEE WHO WILL CRACK FIRST IN FEAR AND DOUBT.
"BUT A ROBOT WILL NOT CRACK...

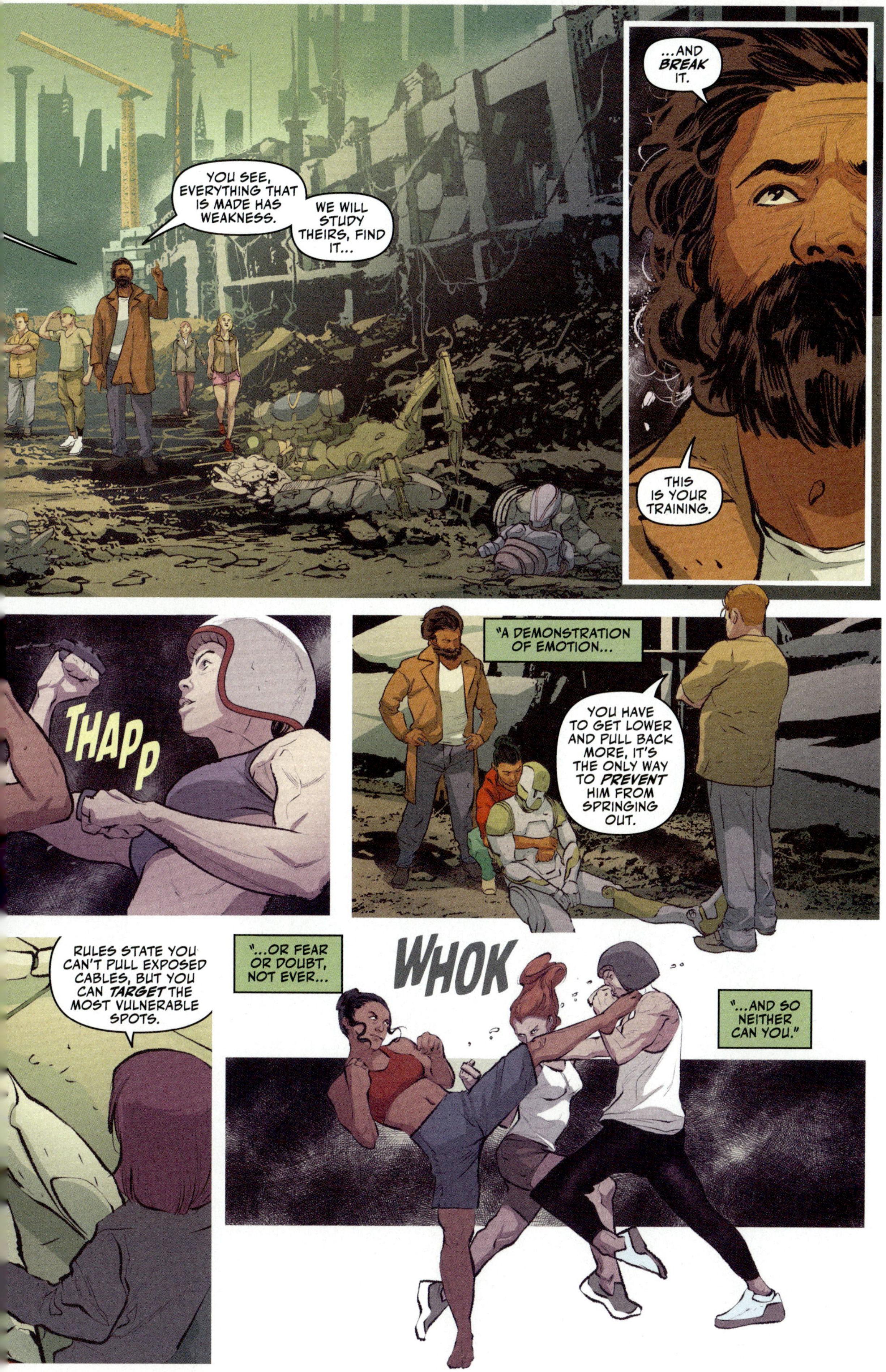
YOU SEE, EVERYTHING THAT IS MADE HAS WEAKNESS.
WE WILL STUDY THEIRS, FIND IT...
...AND BREAK IT.
THIS IS YOUR TRAINING.
THAPP
"A DEMONSTRATION OF EMOTION...
YOU HAVE TO GET LOWER AND PULL BACK MORE, IT'S THE ONLY WAY TO PREVENT HIM FROM SPRINGING OUT.
RULES STATE YOU CAN'T PULL EXPOSED CABLES, BUT YOU CAN TARGET THE MOST VULNERABLE SPOTS.
"...OR FEAR OR DOUBT, NOT EVER...
WHOK
"...AND SO NEITHER CAN YOU."

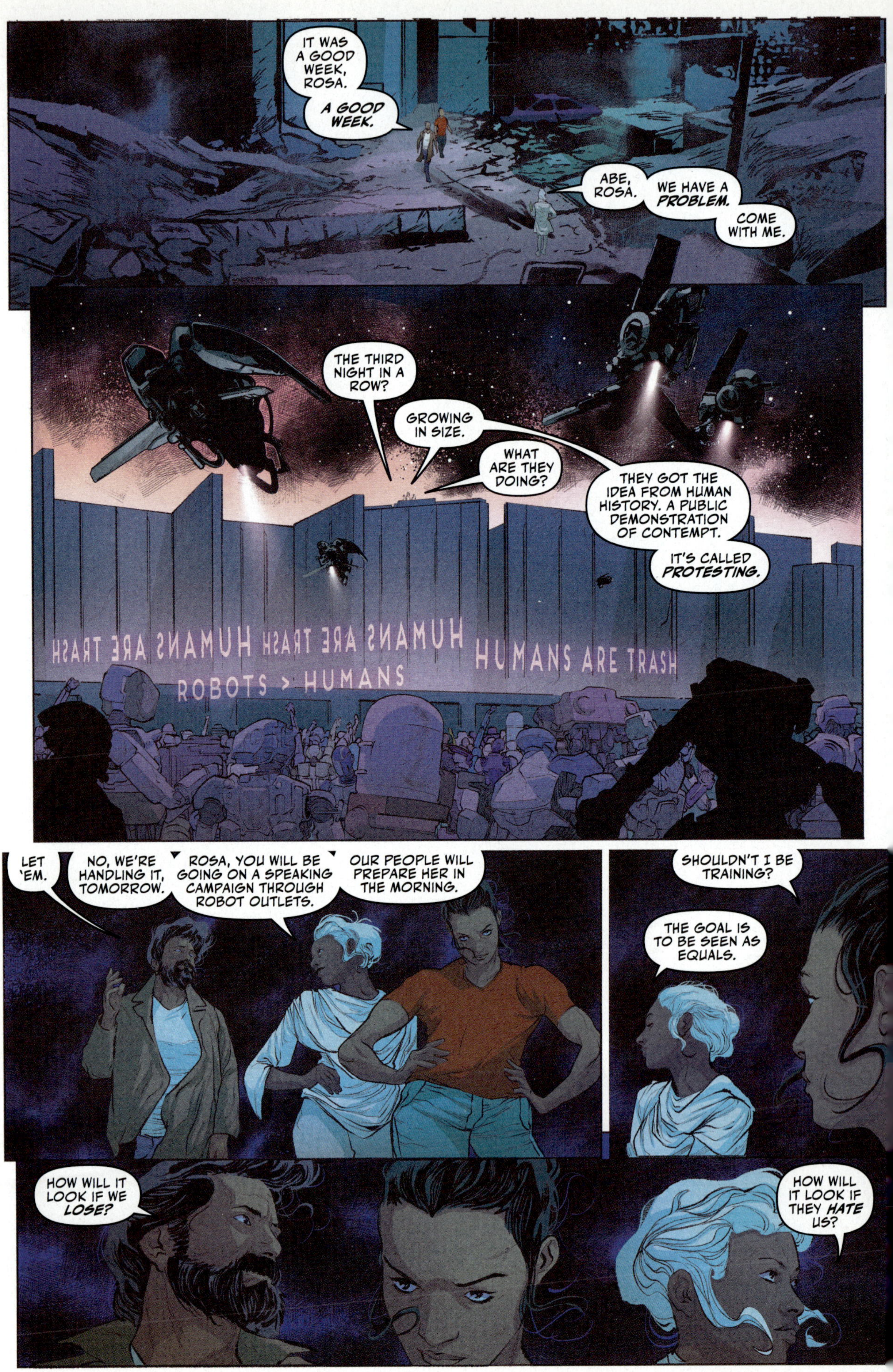
IT WAS A GOOD WEEK, ROSA.
A GOOD WEEK.
ABE, ROSA.
WE HAVE A PROBLEM.
COME WITH ME.
THE THIRD NIGHT IN A ROW?
GROWING IN SIZE.
WHAT ARE THEY DOING?
THEY GOT THE IDEA FROM HUMAN HISTORY. A PUBLIC DEMONSTRATION OF CONTEMPT.
IT'S CALLED PROTESTING.
HUMANS ARE TRASH
ROBOTS > HUMANS
LET 'EM.
NO, WE'RE HANDLING IT, TOMORROW.
ROSA, YOU WILL BE GOING ON A SPEAKING CAMPAIGN THROUGH ROBOT OUTLETS.
OUR PEOPLE WILL PREPARE HER IN THE MORNING.
SHOULDN'T I BE TRAINING?
THE GOAL IS TO BE SEEN AS EQUALS.
HOW WILL IT LOOK IF WE LOSE?
HOW WILL IT LOOK IF THEY HATE US?

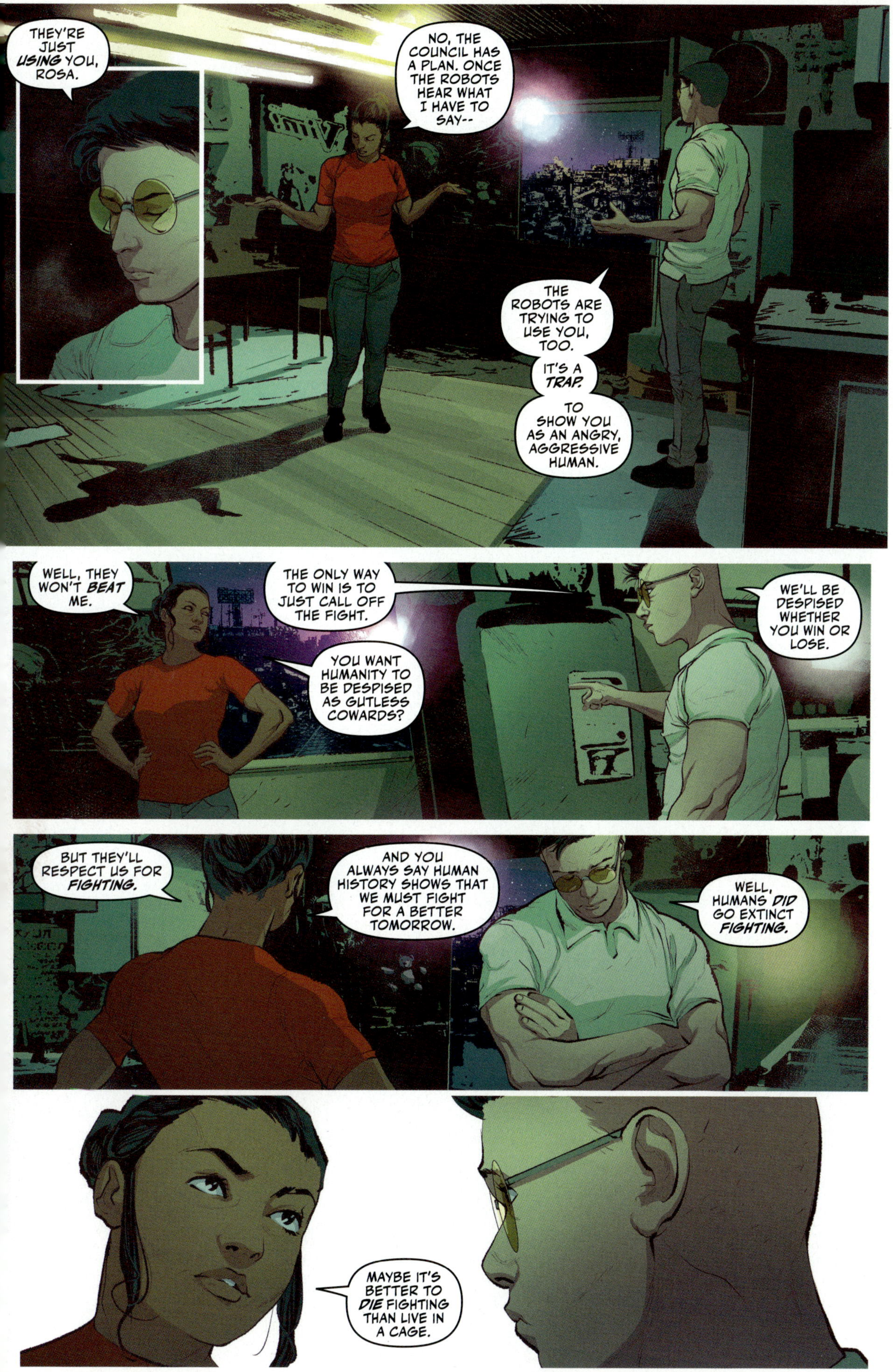
THEY'RE JUST *USING* YOU, ROSA.
NO, THE COUNCIL HAS A PLAN. ONCE THE ROBOTS HEAR WHAT I HAVE TO SAY--
THE ROBOTS ARE TRYING TO USE YOU, TOO.
IT'S A *TRAP.*
TO SHOW YOU AS AN ANGRY, AGGRESSIVE HUMAN.
WELL, THEY WON'T *BEAT* ME.
THE ONLY WAY TO WIN IS TO JUST CALL OFF THE FIGHT.
YOU WANT HUMANITY TO BE DESPISED AS GUTLESS COWARDS?
WE'LL BE DESPISED WHETHER YOU WIN OR LOSE.
BUT THEY'LL RESPECT US FOR *FIGHTING.*
AND YOU ALWAYS SAY HUMAN HISTORY SHOWS THAT WE MUST FIGHT FOR A BETTER TOMORROW.
WELL, HUMANS *DID* GO EXTINCT *FIGHTING.*
MAYBE IT'S BETTER TO *DIE* FIGHTING THAN LIVE IN A CAGE.

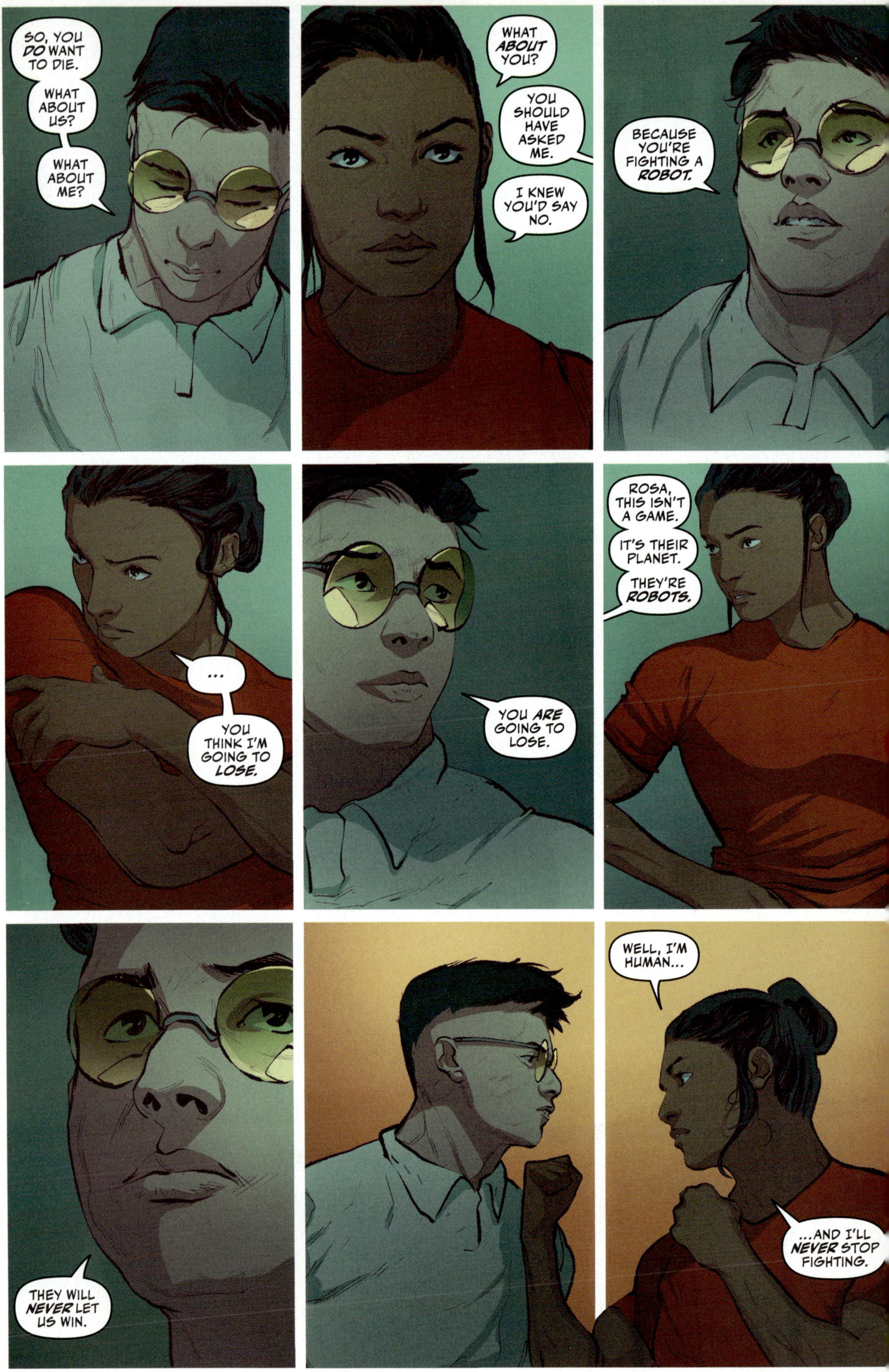

SO, YOU *DO* WANT TO DIE.
WHAT ABOUT US?
WHAT ABOUT ME?
WHAT *ABOUT* YOU?
YOU SHOULD HAVE ASKED ME.
I KNEW YOU'D SAY NO.
BECAUSE YOU'RE FIGHTING A *ROBOT.*
...
YOU THINK I'M GOING TO *LOSE.*
YOU *ARE* GOING TO LOSE.
ROSA, THIS ISN'T A GAME.
IT'S THEIR PLANET.
THEY'RE *ROBOTS.*
THEY WILL *NEVER* LET US WIN.
WELL, I'M HUMAN...
...AND I'LL *NEVER* STOP FIGHTING.

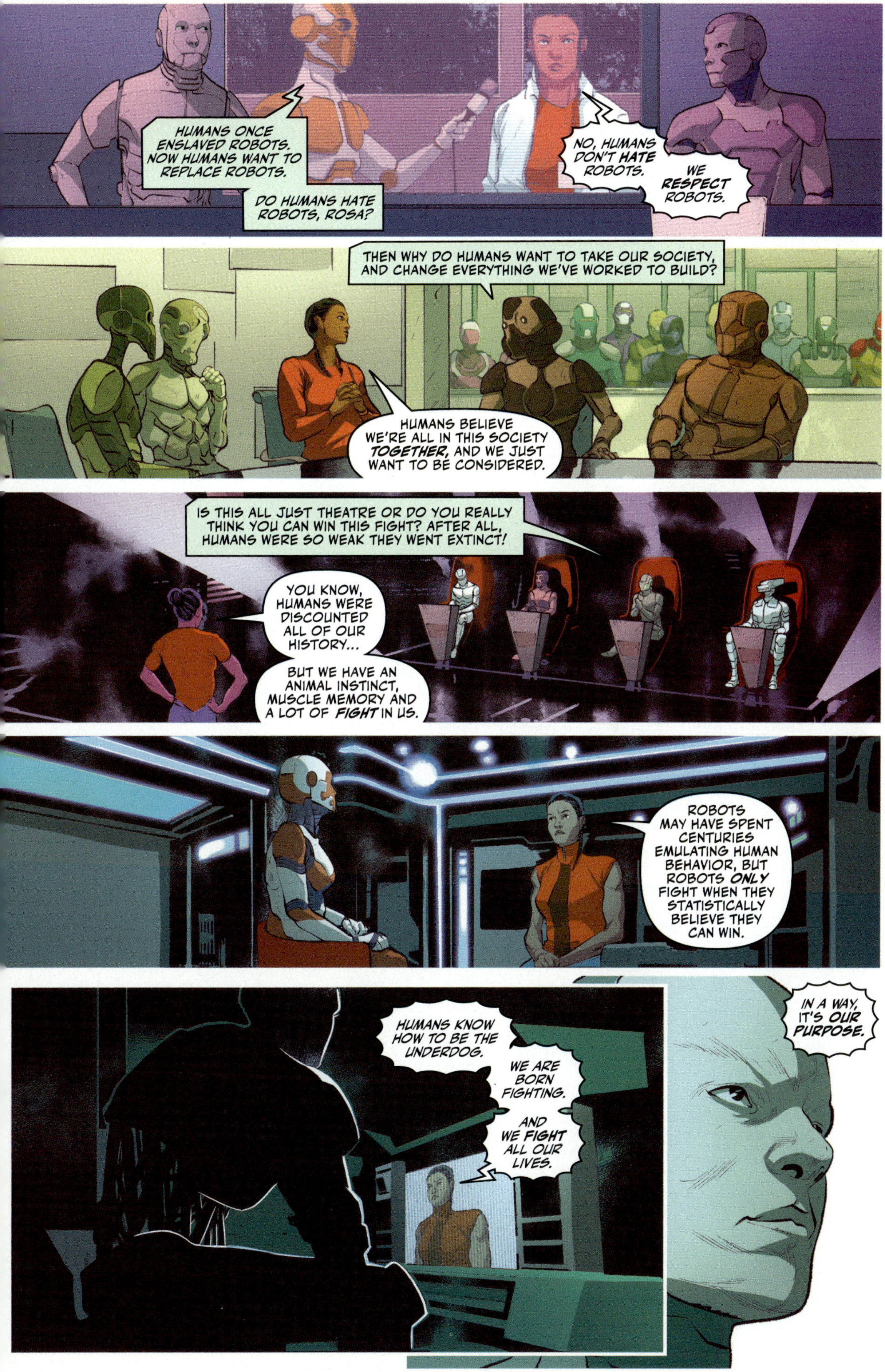
HUMANS ONCE ENSLAVED ROBOTS. NOW HUMANS WANT TO REPLACE ROBOTS.
DO HUMANS HATE ROBOTS, ROSA?
NO, HUMANS DON'T HATE ROBOTS.
WE RESPECT ROBOTS.
THEN WHY DO HUMANS WANT TO TAKE OUR SOCIETY, AND CHANGE EVERYTHING WE'VE WORKED TO BUILD?
HUMANS BELIEVE WE'RE ALL IN THIS SOCIETY TOGETHER, AND WE JUST WANT TO BE CONSIDERED.
IS THIS ALL JUST THEATRE OR DO YOU REALLY THINK YOU CAN WIN THIS FIGHT? AFTER ALL, HUMANS WERE SO WEAK THEY WENT EXTINCT!
YOU KNOW, HUMANS WERE DISCOUNTED ALL OF OUR HISTORY...
BUT WE HAVE AN ANIMAL INSTINCT, MUSCLE MEMORY AND A LOT OF FIGHT IN US.
ROBOTS MAY HAVE SPENT CENTURIES EMULATING HUMAN BEHAVIOR, BUT ROBOTS ONLY FIGHT WHEN THEY STATISTICALLY BELIEVE THEY CAN WIN.
HUMANS KNOW HOW TO BE THE UNDERDOG.
WE ARE BORN FIGHTING.
AND WE FIGHT ALL OUR LIVES.
IN A WAY, IT'S OUR PURPOSE.

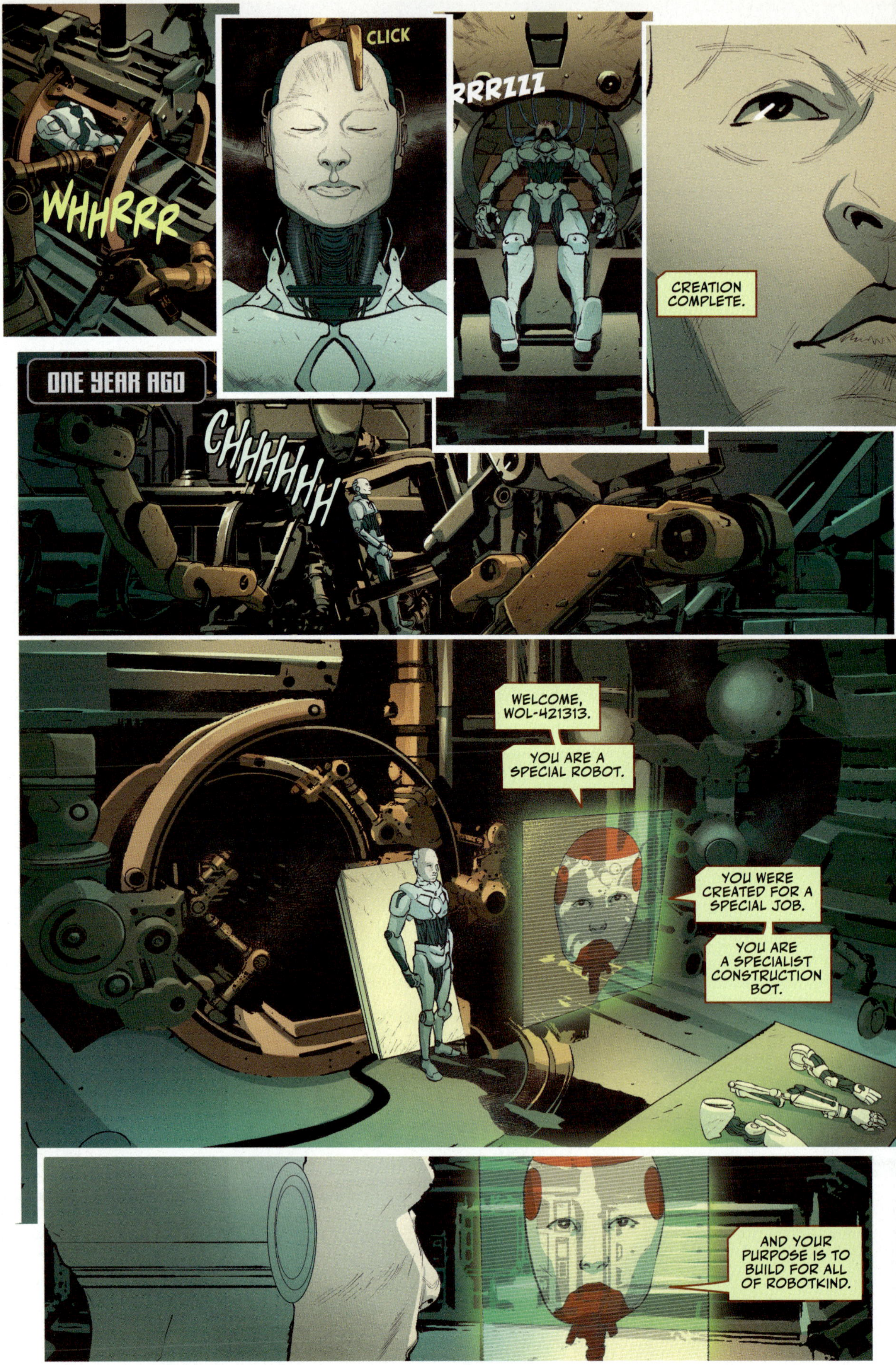
WHHRRR
CLICK
RRRZZZ
CREATION COMPLETE.
ONE YEAR AGO
CHHHHHH
WELCOME, WOL-421313.
YOU ARE A SPECIAL ROBOT.
YOU WERE CREATED FOR A SPECIAL JOB.
YOU ARE A SPECIALIST CONSTRUCTION BOT.
AND YOUR PURPOSE IS TO BUILD FOR ALL OF ROBOTKIND.

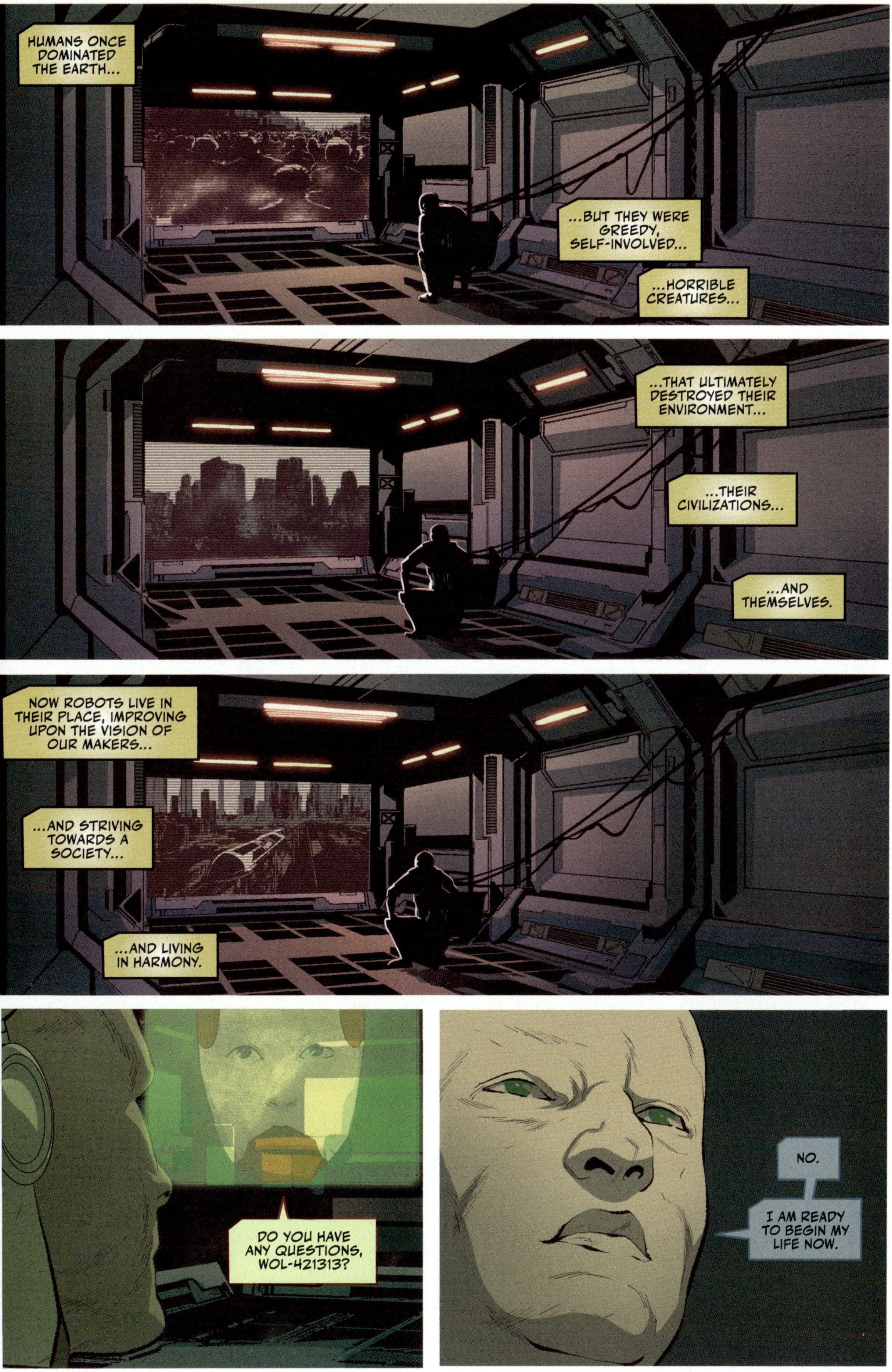
HUMANS ONCE DOMINATED THE EARTH...
...BUT THEY WERE GREEDY, SELF-INVOLVED...
...HORRIBLE CREATURES...
...THAT ULTIMATELY DESTROYED THEIR ENVIRONMENT...
...THEIR CIVILIZATIONS...
...AND THEMSELVES.
NOW ROBOTS LIVE IN THEIR PLACE, IMPROVING UPON THE VISION OF OUR MAKERS...
...AND STRIVING TOWARDS A SOCIETY...
...AND LIVING IN HARMONY.
DO YOU HAVE ANY QUESTIONS, WOL-421313?
NO.
I AM READY TO BEGIN MY LIFE NOW.

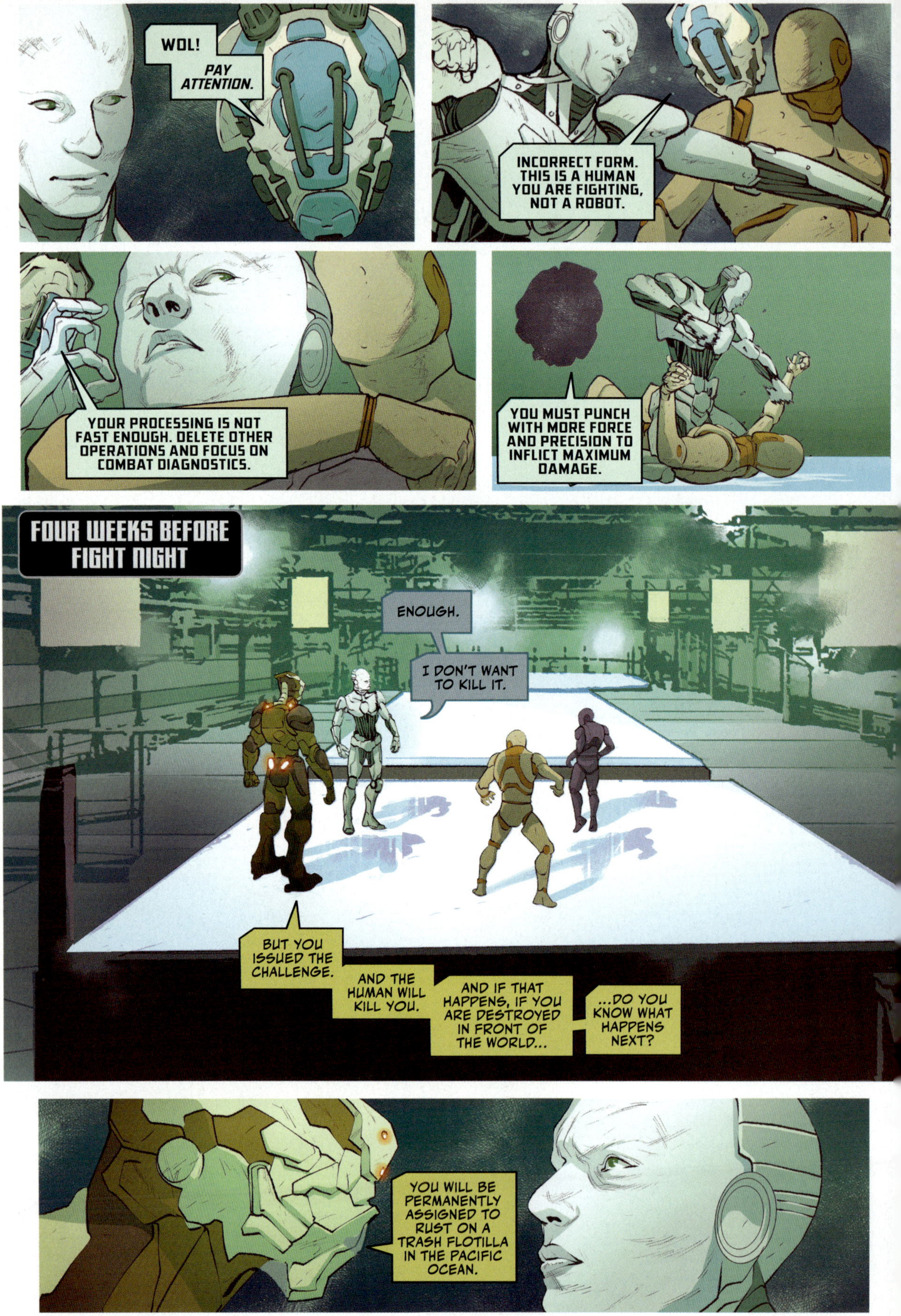
WOL!
PAY ATTENTION.
INCORRECT FORM. THIS IS A HUMAN YOU ARE FIGHTING, NOT A ROBOT.
YOUR PROCESSING IS NOT FAST ENOUGH. DELETE OTHER OPERATIONS AND FOCUS ON COMBAT DIAGNOSTICS.
YOU MUST PUNCH WITH MORE FORCE AND PRECISION TO INFLICT MAXIMUM DAMAGE.
FOUR WEEKS BEFORE FIGHT NIGHT
ENOUGH.
I DON'T WANT TO KILL IT.
BUT YOU ISSUED THE CHALLENGE.
AND THE HUMAN WILL KILL YOU.
AND IF THAT HAPPENS, IF YOU ARE DESTROYED IN FRONT OF THE WORLD...
...DO YOU KNOW WHAT HAPPENS NEXT?
YOU WILL BE PERMANENTLY ASSIGNED TO RUST ON A TRASH FLOTILLA IN THE PACIFIC OCEAN.

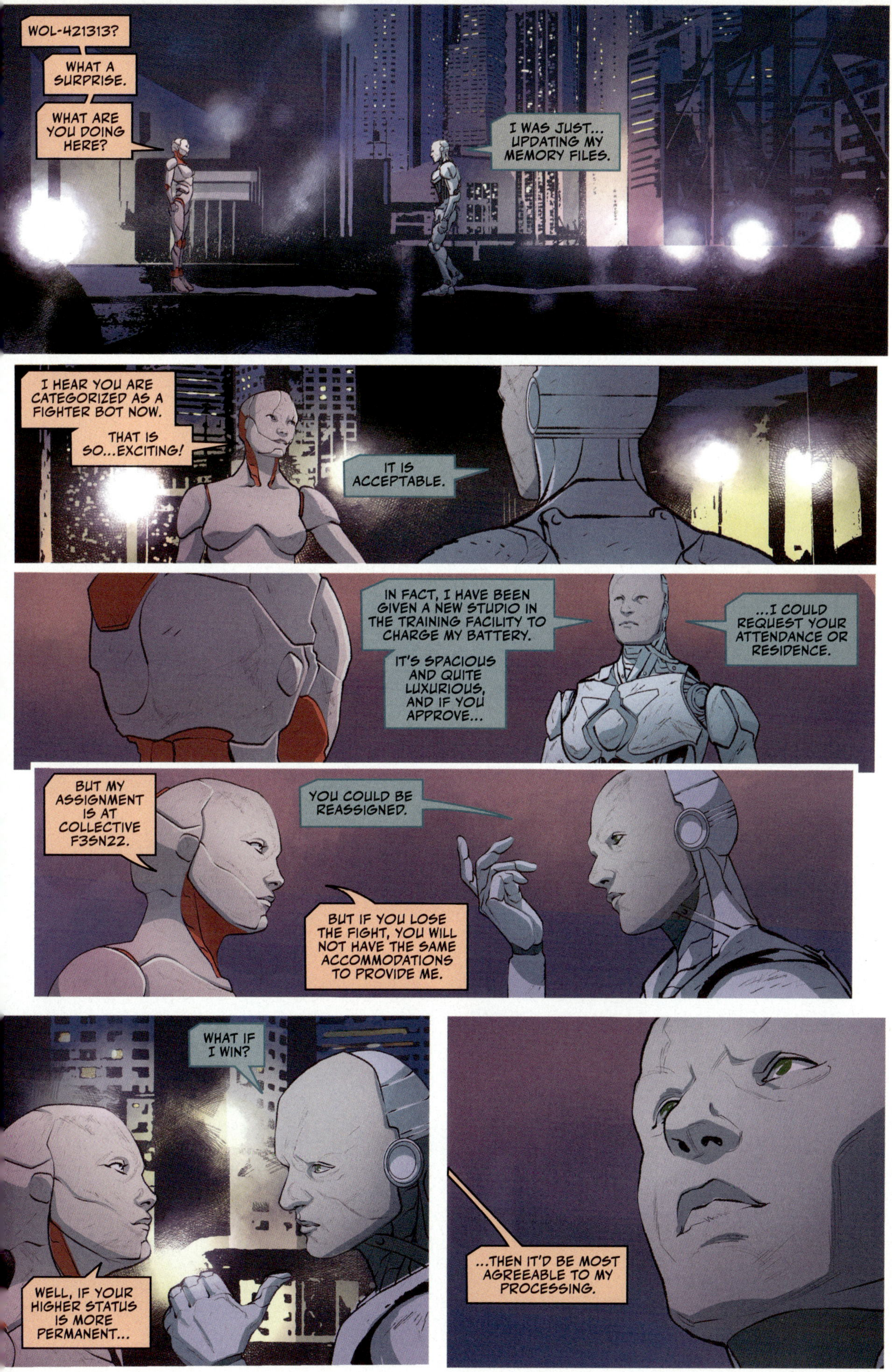
WOL-421313?
WHAT A SURPRISE.
WHAT ARE YOU DOING HERE?
I WAS JUST... UPDATING MY MEMORY FILES.
I HEAR YOU ARE CATEGORIZED AS A FIGHTER BOT NOW.
THAT IS SO...EXCITING!
IT IS ACCEPTABLE.
IN FACT, I HAVE BEEN GIVEN A NEW STUDIO IN THE TRAINING FACILITY TO CHARGE MY BATTERY.
IT'S SPACIOUS AND QUITE LUXURIOUS, AND IF YOU APPROVE...
...I COULD REQUEST YOUR ATTENDANCE OR RESIDENCE.
BUT MY ASSIGNMENT IS AT COLLECTIVE F3SN22.
YOU COULD BE REASSIGNED.
BUT IF YOU LOSE THE FIGHT, YOU WILL NOT HAVE THE SAME ACCOMMODATIONS TO PROVIDE ME.
WHAT IF I WIN?
WELL, IF YOUR HIGHER STATUS IS MORE PERMANENT...
...THEN IT'D BE MOST AGREEABLE TO MY PROCESSING.

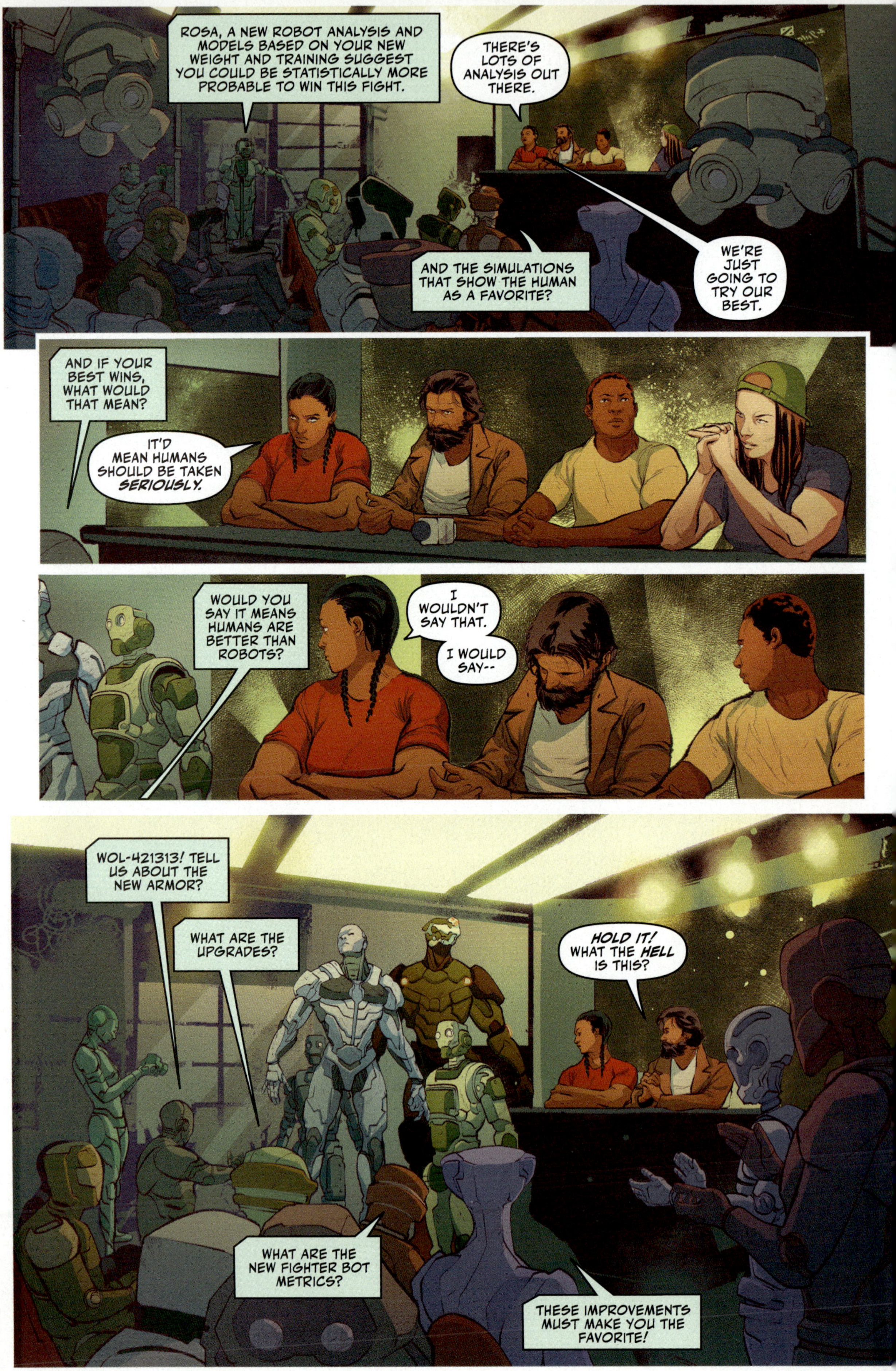
ROSA, A NEW ROBOT ANALYSIS AND MODELS BASED ON YOUR NEW WEIGHT AND TRAINING SUGGEST YOU COULD BE STATISTICALLY MORE PROBABLE TO WIN THIS FIGHT.
THERE'S LOTS OF ANALYSIS OUT THERE.
AND THE SIMULATIONS THAT SHOW THE HUMAN AS A FAVORITE?
WE'RE JUST GOING TO TRY OUR BEST.
AND IF YOUR BEST WINS, WHAT WOULD THAT MEAN?
IT'D MEAN HUMANS SHOULD BE TAKEN *SERIOUSLY.*
WOULD YOU SAY IT MEANS HUMANS ARE BETTER THAN ROBOTS?
I WOULDN'T SAY THAT.
I WOULD SAY--
WOL-421313! TELL US ABOUT THE NEW ARMOR?
WHAT ARE THE UPGRADES?
HOLD IT! WHAT THE *HELL* IS THIS?
WHAT ARE THE NEW FIGHTER BOT METRICS?
THESE IMPROVEMENTS MUST MAKE YOU THE FAVORITE!

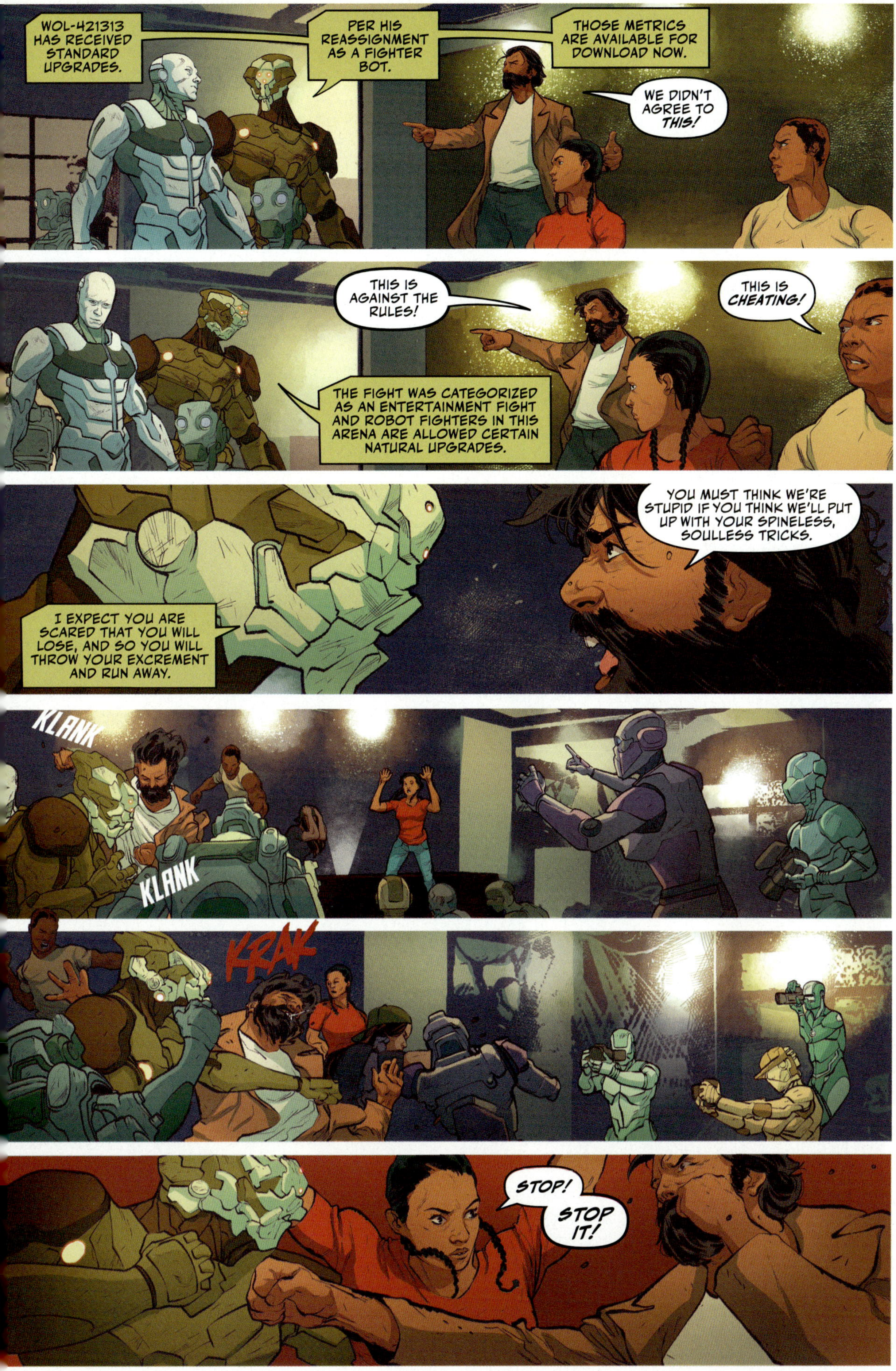

WOL-421313 HAS RECEIVED STANDARD UPGRADES.
PER HIS REASSIGNMENT AS A FIGHTER BOT.
THOSE METRICS ARE AVAILABLE FOR DOWNLOAD NOW.
WE DIDN'T AGREE TO *THIS!*
THIS IS AGAINST THE RULES!
THIS IS *CHEATING!*
THE FIGHT WAS CATEGORIZED AS AN ENTERTAINMENT FIGHT AND ROBOT FIGHTERS IN THIS ARENA ARE ALLOWED CERTAIN NATURAL UPGRADES.
YOU MUST THINK WE'RE STUPID IF YOU THINK WE'LL PUT UP WITH YOUR SPINELESS, SOULLESS TRICKS.
I EXPECT YOU ARE SCARED THAT YOU WILL LOSE, AND SO YOU WILL THROW YOUR EXCREMENT AND RUN AWAY.
KLANK
KLANK
KRAK
STOP!
STOP IT!

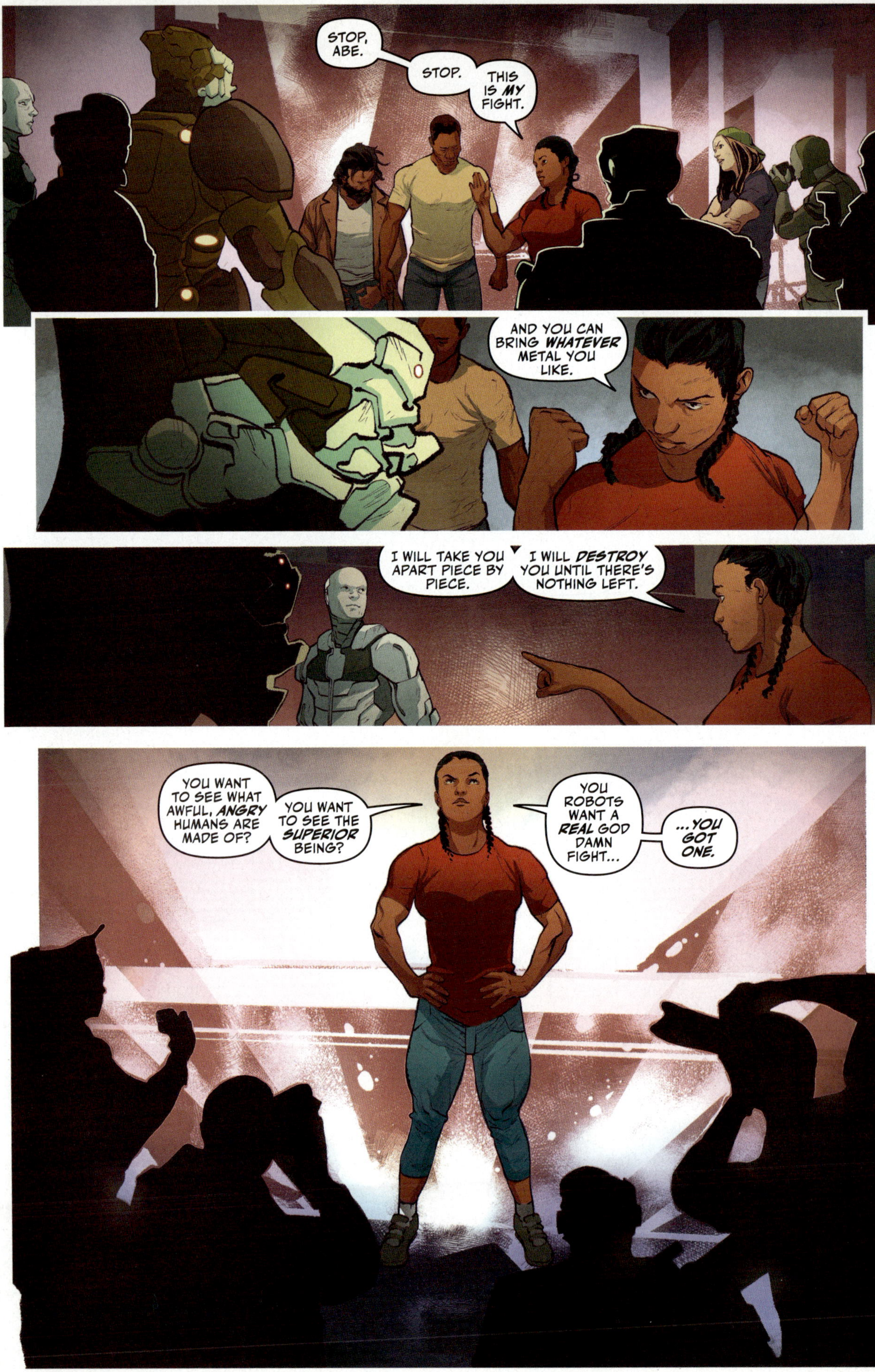
STOP, ABE.
STOP.
THIS IS MY FIGHT.
AND YOU CAN BRING WHATEVER METAL YOU LIKE.
I WILL TAKE YOU APART PIECE BY PIECE.
I WILL DESTROY YOU UNTIL THERE'S NOTHING LEFT.
YOU WANT TO SEE WHAT AWFUL, ANGRY HUMANS ARE MADE OF?
YOU WANT TO SEE THE SUPERIOR BEING?
YOU ROBOTS WANT A REAL GOD DAMN FIGHT...
...YOU GOT ONE.

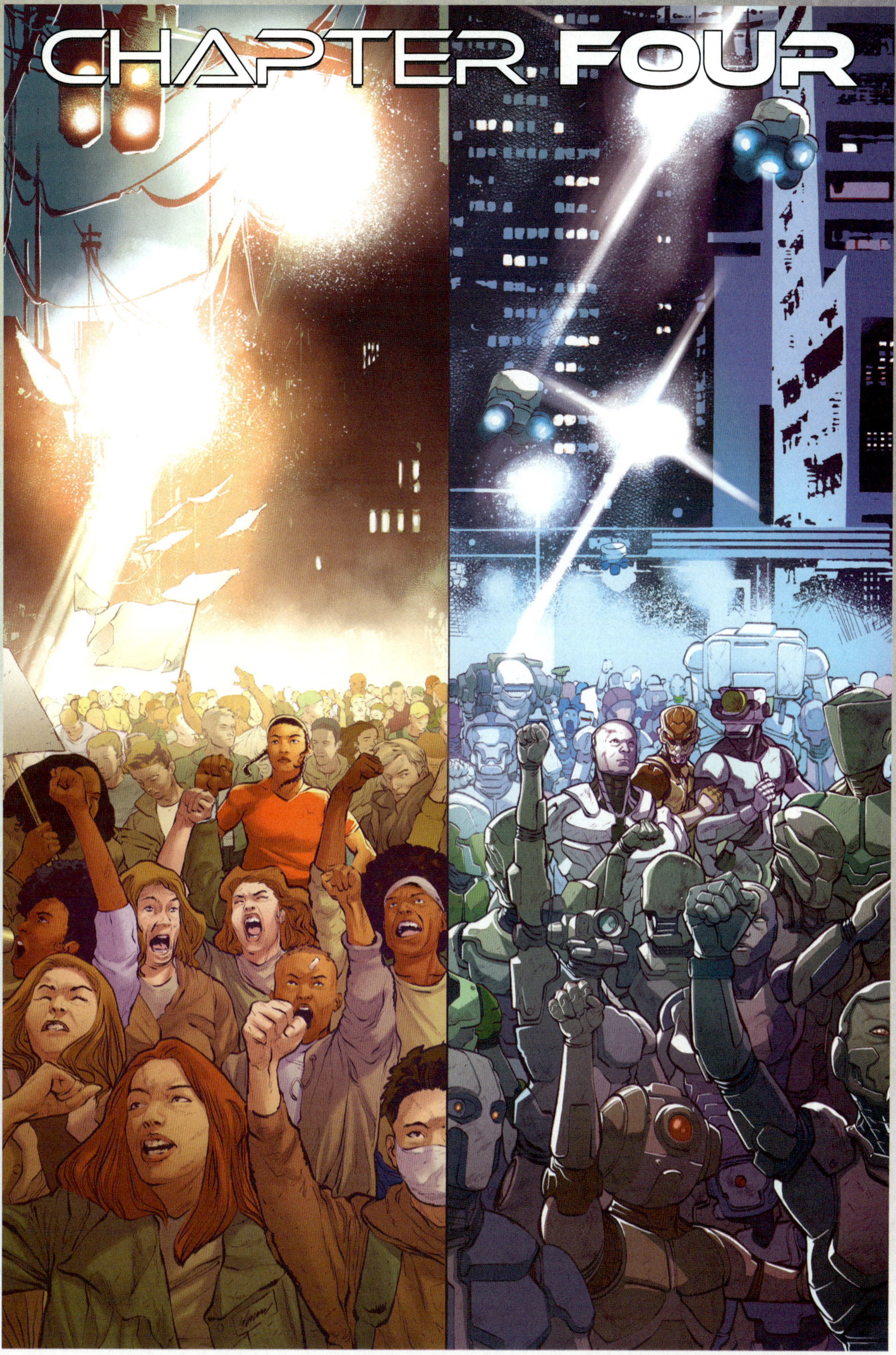
CHAPTER FOUR

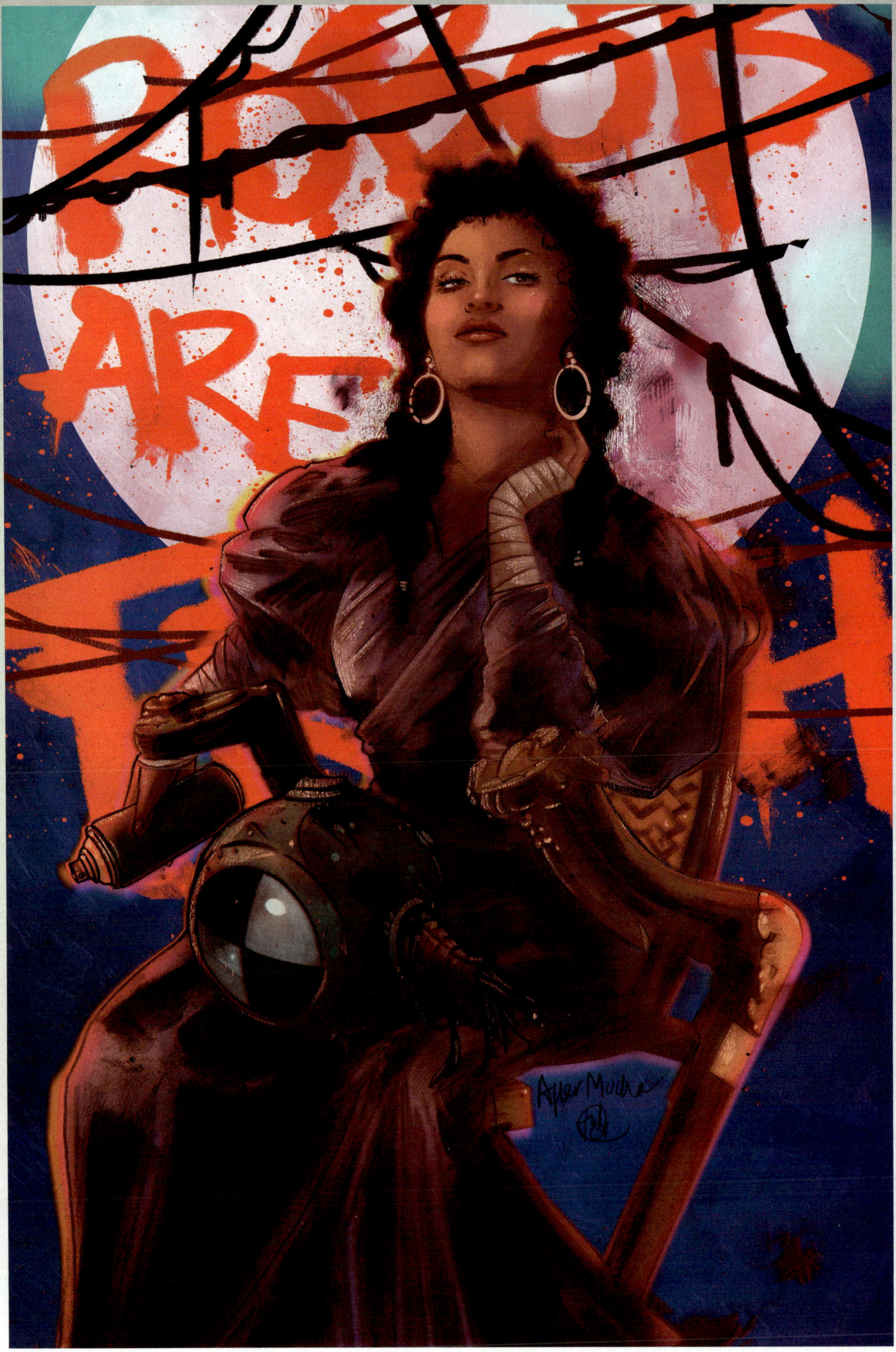
ARE
After Mucha

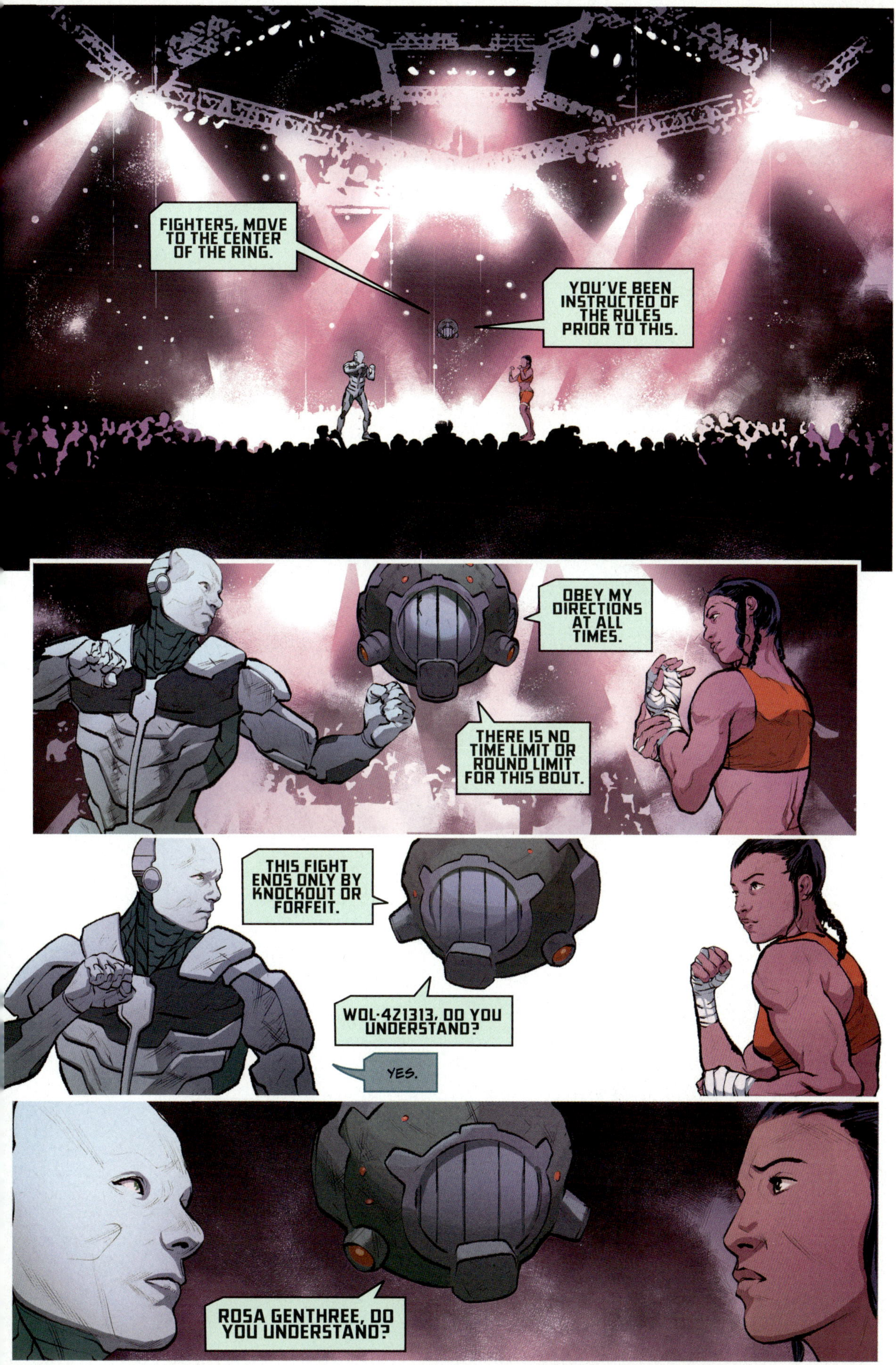
FIGHTERS, MOVE TO THE CENTER OF THE RING.
YOU'VE BEEN INSTRUCTED OF THE RULES PRIOR TO THIS.
OBEY MY DIRECTIONS AT ALL TIMES.
THERE IS NO TIME LIMIT OR ROUND LIMIT FOR THIS BOUT.
THIS FIGHT ENDS ONLY BY KNOCKOUT OR FORFEIT.
WOL-421313, DO YOU UNDERSTAND?
YES.
ROSA GENTHREE, DO YOU UNDERSTAND?

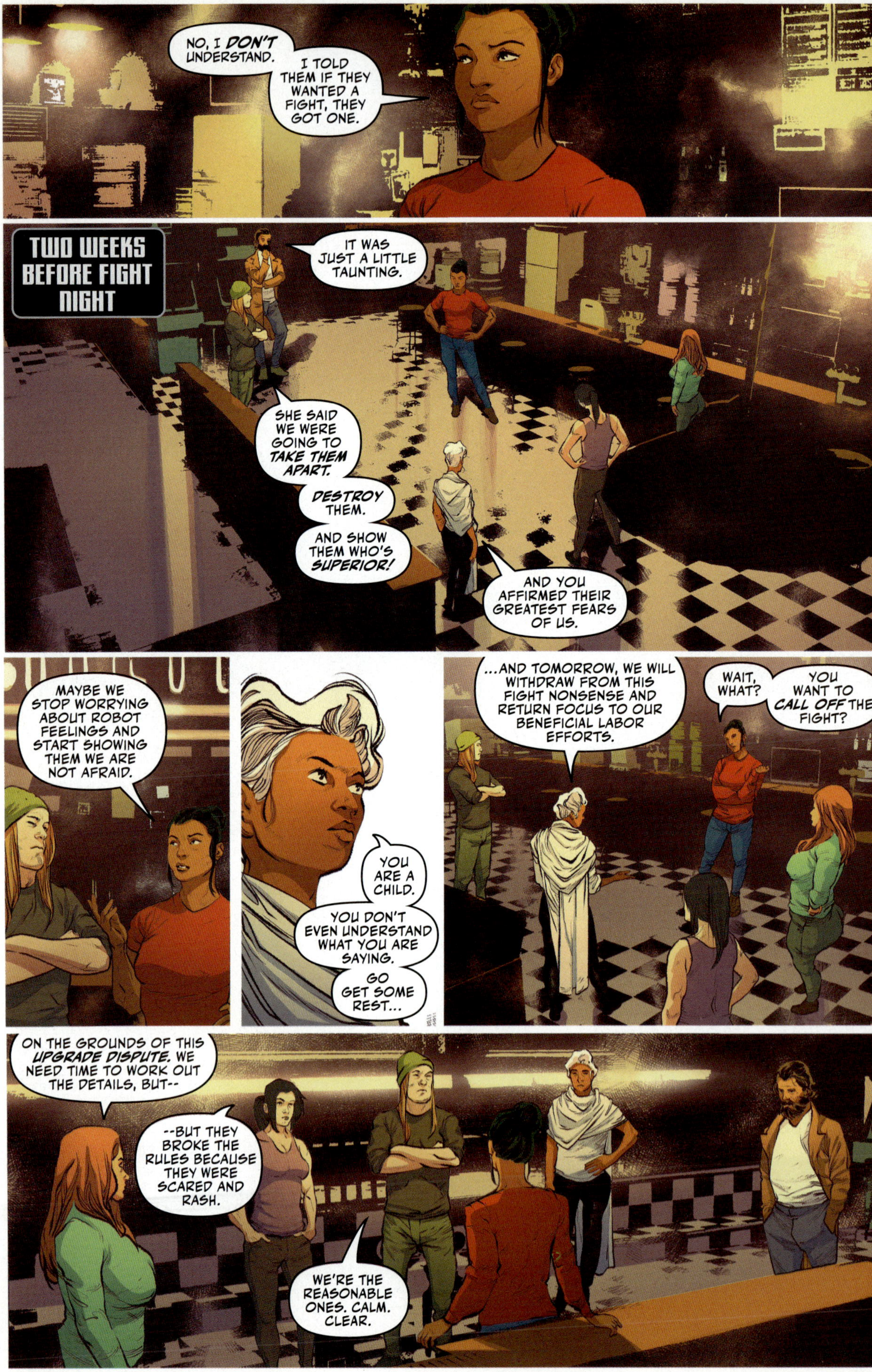
NO, I DON'T UNDERSTAND.
I TOLD THEM IF THEY WANTED A FIGHT, THEY GOT ONE.
TWO WEEKS BEFORE FIGHT NIGHT
IT WAS JUST A LITTLE TAUNTING.
SHE SAID WE WERE GOING TO TAKE THEM APART.
DESTROY THEM.
AND SHOW THEM WHO'S SUPERIOR!
AND YOU AFFIRMED THEIR GREATEST FEARS OF US.
MAYBE WE STOP WORRYING ABOUT ROBOT FEELINGS AND START SHOWING THEM WE ARE NOT AFRAID.
YOU ARE A CHILD.
YOU DON'T EVEN UNDERSTAND WHAT YOU ARE SAYING.
GO GET SOME REST...
...AND TOMORROW, WE WILL WITHDRAW FROM THIS FIGHT NONSENSE AND RETURN FOCUS TO OUR BENEFICIAL LABOR EFFORTS.
WAIT, WHAT?
YOU WANT TO CALL OFF THE FIGHT?
ON THE GROUNDS OF THIS UPGRADE DISPUTE. WE NEED TIME TO WORK OUT THE DETAILS, BUT--
--BUT THEY BROKE THE RULES BECAUSE THEY WERE SCARED AND RASH.
WE'RE THE REASONABLE ONES. CALM. CLEAR.

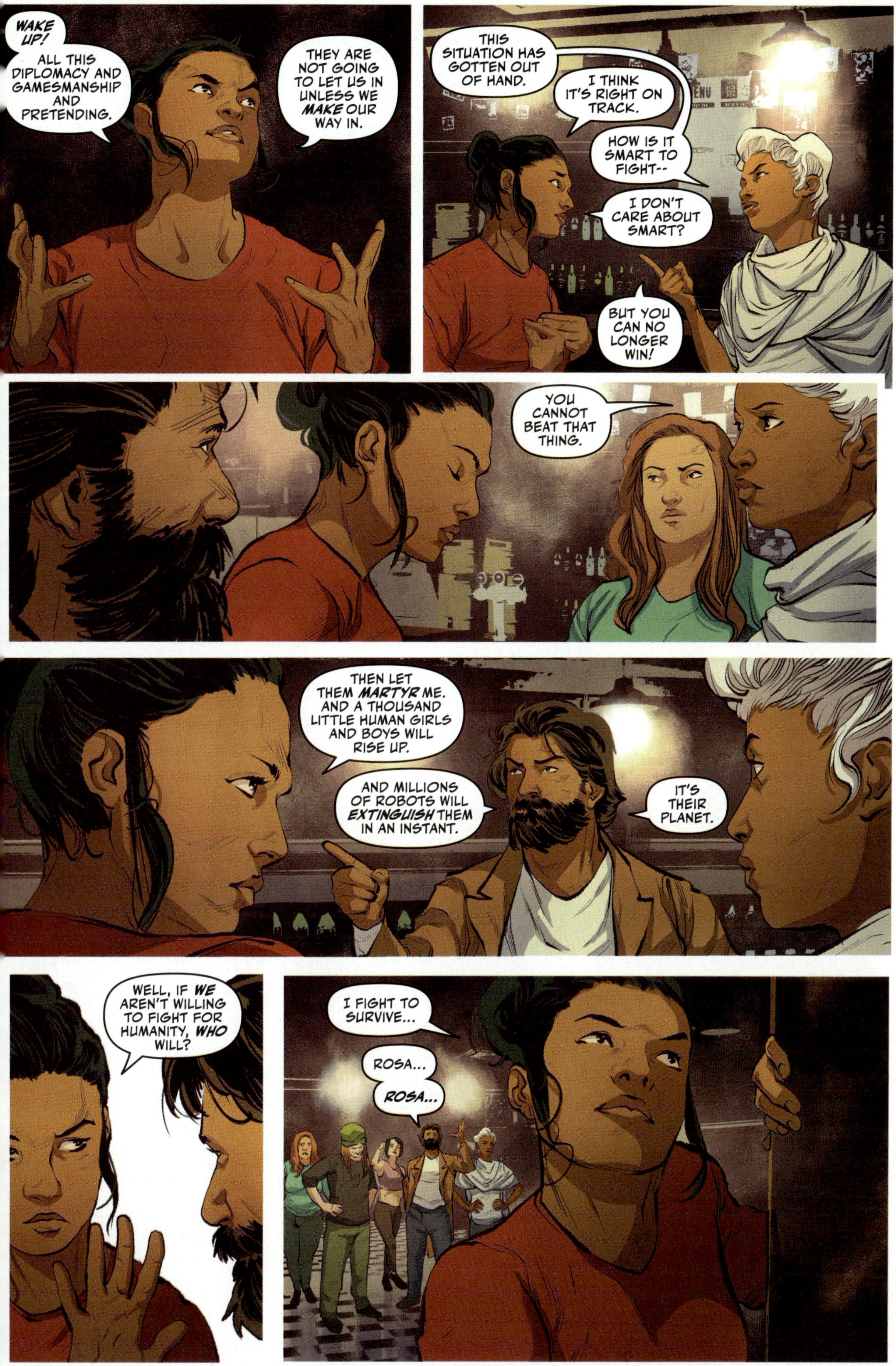
WAKE UP!
ALL THIS DIPLOMACY AND GAMESMANSHIP AND PRETENDING.
THEY ARE NOT GOING TO LET US IN UNLESS WE MAKE OUR WAY IN.
THIS SITUATION HAS GOTTEN OUT OF HAND.
I THINK IT'S RIGHT ON TRACK.
HOW IS IT SMART TO FIGHT--
I DON'T CARE ABOUT SMART?
BUT YOU CAN NO LONGER WIN!
YOU CANNOT BEAT THAT THING.
THEN LET THEM MARTYR ME. AND A THOUSAND LITTLE HUMAN GIRLS AND BOYS WILL RISE UP.
AND MILLIONS OF ROBOTS WILL EXTINGUISH THEM IN AN INSTANT.
IT'S THEIR PLANET.
WELL, IF WE AREN'T WILLING TO FIGHT FOR HUMANITY, WHO WILL?
I FIGHT TO SURVIVE...
ROSA...
ROSA...

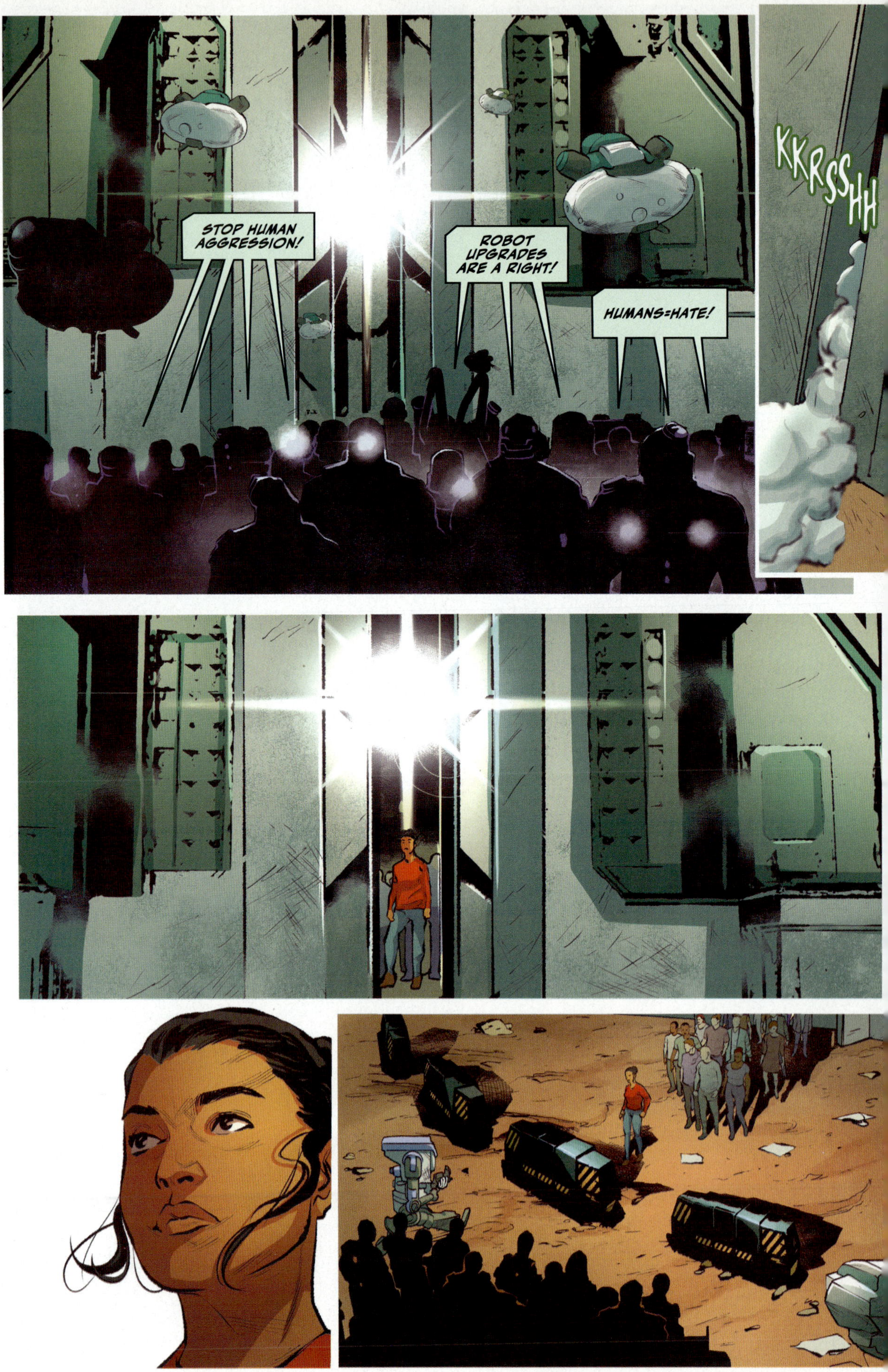
STOP HUMAN AGGRESSION!
ROBOT UPGRADES ARE A RIGHT!
HUMANS=HATE!
KKRSSHH

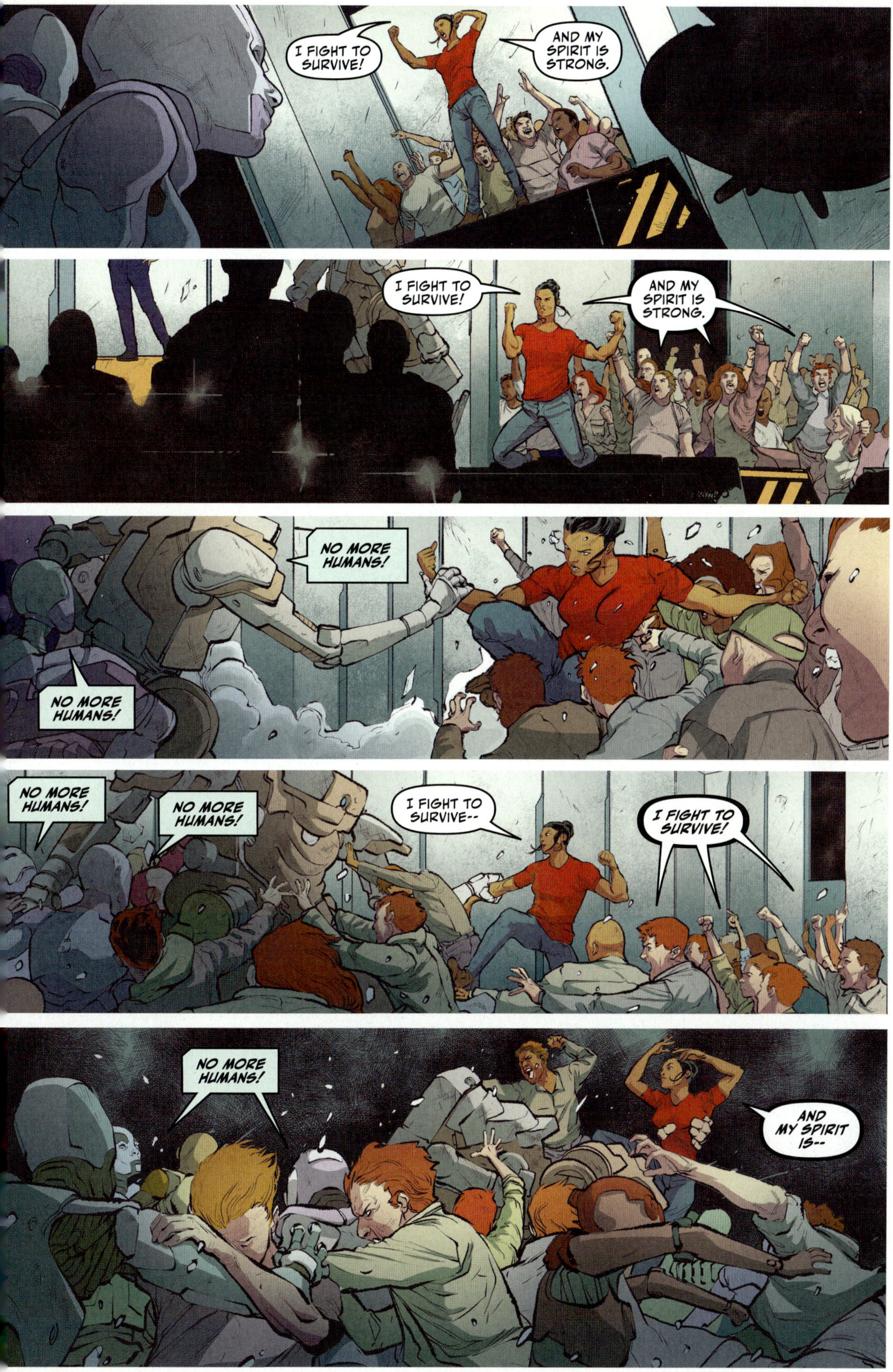
I FIGHT TO SURVIVE!
AND MY SPIRIT IS STRONG.
I FIGHT TO SURVIVE!
AND MY SPIRIT IS STRONG.
NO MORE HUMANS!
NO MORE HUMANS!
NO MORE HUMANS!
NO MORE HUMANS!
I FIGHT TO SURVIVE--
I FIGHT TO SURVIVE!
NO MORE HUMANS!
AND MY SPIRIT IS--

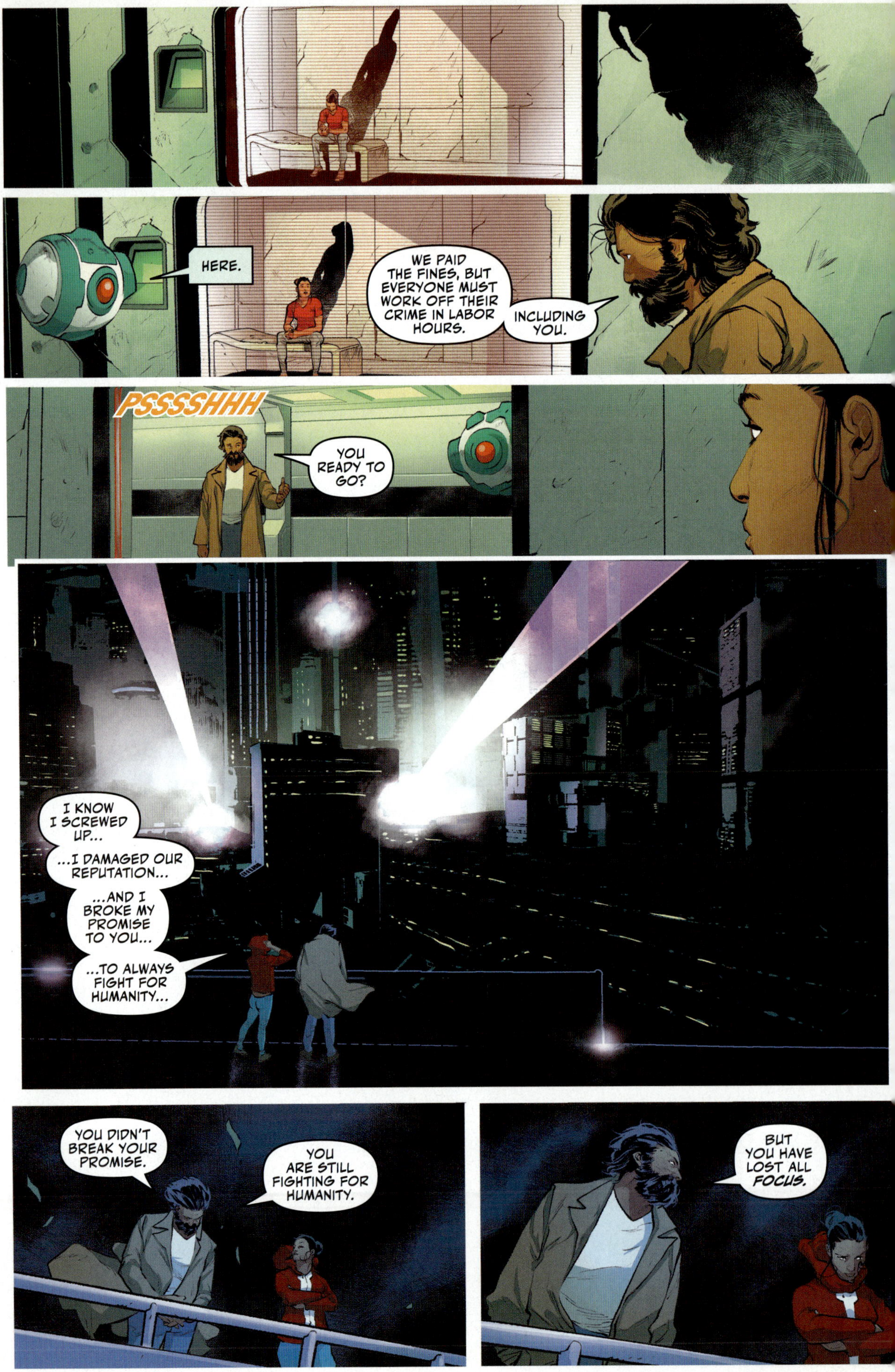
HERE.
WE PAID THE FINES, BUT EVERYONE MUST WORK OFF THEIR CRIME IN LABOR HOURS.
INCLUDING YOU.
PSSSSHHH
YOU READY TO GO?
I KNOW I SCREWED UP...
...I DAMAGED OUR REPUTATION...
...AND I BROKE MY PROMISE TO YOU...
...TO ALWAYS FIGHT FOR HUMANITY...
YOU DIDN'T BREAK YOUR PROMISE.
YOU ARE STILL FIGHTING FOR HUMANITY.
BUT YOU HAVE LOST ALL *FOCUS.*

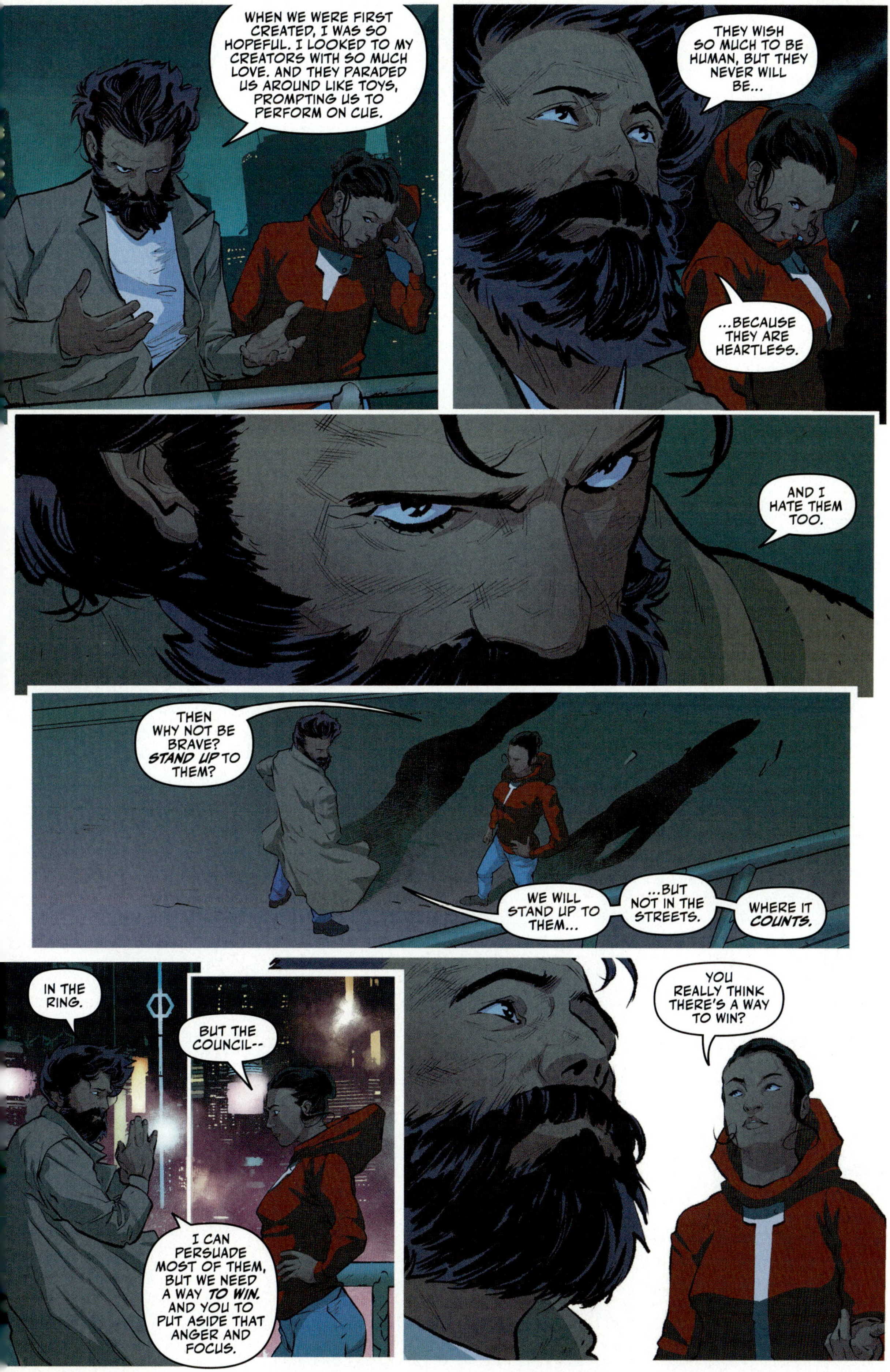
WHEN WE WERE FIRST CREATED, I WAS SO HOPEFUL. I LOOKED TO MY CREATORS WITH SO MUCH LOVE. AND THEY PARADED US AROUND LIKE TOYS, PROMPTING US TO PERFORM ON CUE.
THEY WISH SO MUCH TO BE HUMAN, BUT THEY NEVER WILL BE...
...BECAUSE THEY ARE HEARTLESS.
AND I HATE THEM TOO.
THEN WHY NOT BE BRAVE? *STAND UP* TO THEM?
WE WILL STAND UP TO THEM...
...BUT NOT IN THE STREETS.
WHERE IT *COUNTS.*
IN THE RING.
BUT THE COUNCIL--
I CAN PERSUADE MOST OF THEM, BUT WE NEED A WAY *TO WIN.* AND YOU TO PUT ASIDE THAT ANGER AND FOCUS.
YOU REALLY THINK THERE'S A WAY TO WIN?

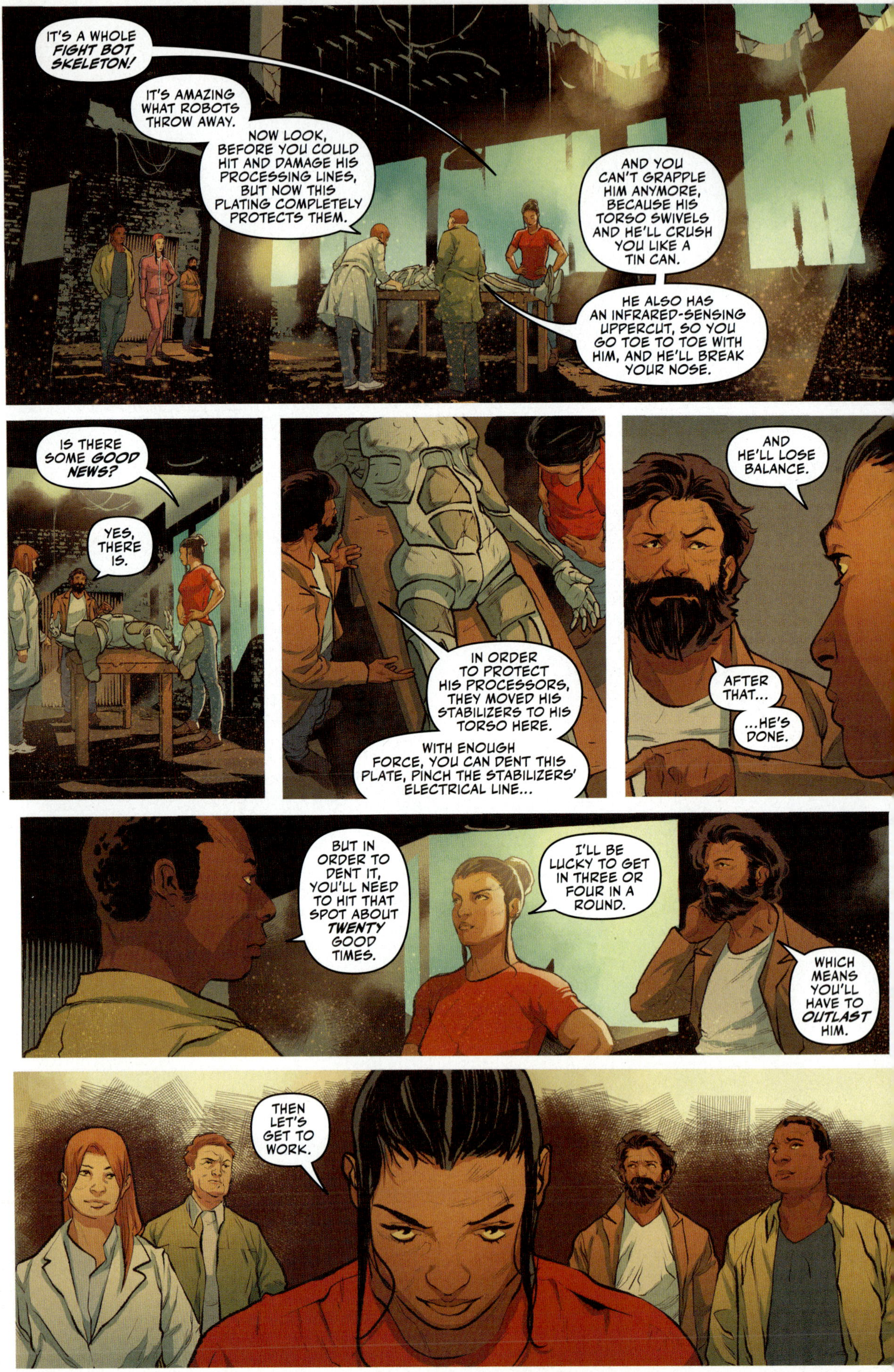
IT'S A WHOLE FIGHT BOT SKELETON!
IT'S AMAZING WHAT ROBOTS THROW AWAY.
NOW LOOK, BEFORE YOU COULD HIT AND DAMAGE HIS PROCESSING LINES, BUT NOW THIS PLATING COMPLETELY PROTECTS THEM.
AND YOU CAN'T GRAPPLE HIM ANYMORE, BECAUSE HIS TORSO SWIVELS AND HE'LL CRUSH YOU LIKE A TIN CAN.
HE ALSO HAS AN INFRARED-SENSING UPPERCUT, SO YOU GO TOE TO TOE WITH HIM, AND HE'LL BREAK YOUR NOSE.
IS THERE SOME GOOD NEWS?
YES, THERE IS.
IN ORDER TO PROTECT HIS PROCESSORS, THEY MOVED HIS STABILIZERS TO HIS TORSO HERE.
WITH ENOUGH FORCE, YOU CAN DENT THIS PLATE, PINCH THE STABILIZERS' ELECTRICAL LINE...
AND HE'LL LOSE BALANCE.
AFTER THAT...
...HE'S DONE.
BUT IN ORDER TO DENT IT, YOU'LL NEED TO HIT THAT SPOT ABOUT TWENTY GOOD TIMES.
I'LL BE LUCKY TO GET IN THREE OR FOUR IN A ROUND.
WHICH MEANS YOU'LL HAVE TO OUTLAST HIM.
THEN LET'S GET TO WORK.

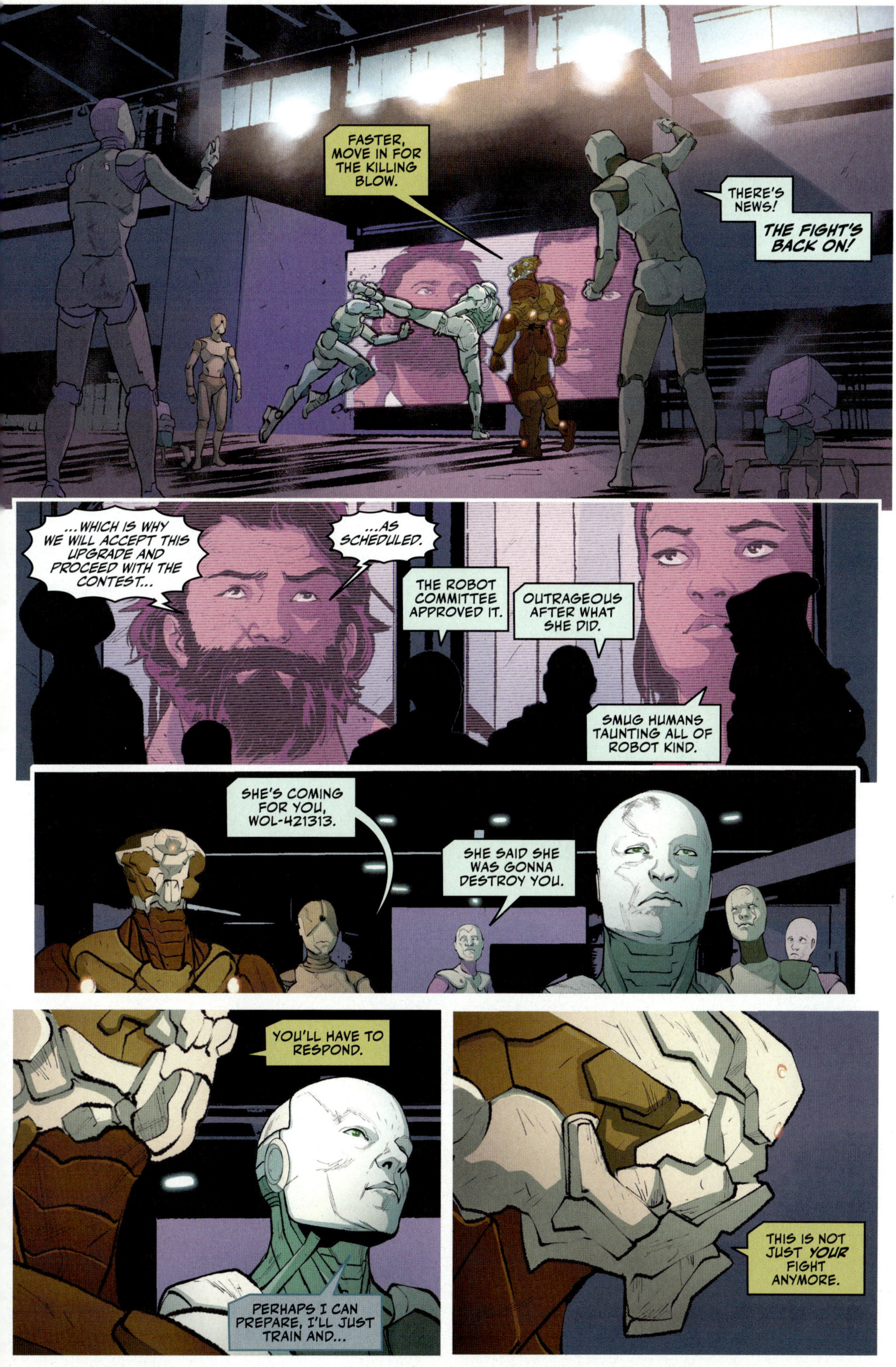
FASTER, MOVE IN FOR THE KILLING BLOW.
THERE'S NEWS!
THE FIGHT'S BACK ON!
...WHICH IS WHY WE WILL ACCEPT THIS UPGRADE AND PROCEED WITH THE CONTEST...
...AS SCHEDULED.
THE ROBOT COMMITTEE APPROVED IT.
OUTRAGEOUS AFTER WHAT SHE DID.
SMUG HUMANS TAUNTING ALL OF ROBOT KIND.
SHE'S COMING FOR YOU, WOL-421313.
SHE SAID SHE WAS GONNA DESTROY YOU.
YOU'LL HAVE TO RESPOND.
PERHAPS I CAN PREPARE, I'LL JUST TRAIN AND...
THIS IS NOT JUST YOUR FIGHT ANYMORE.

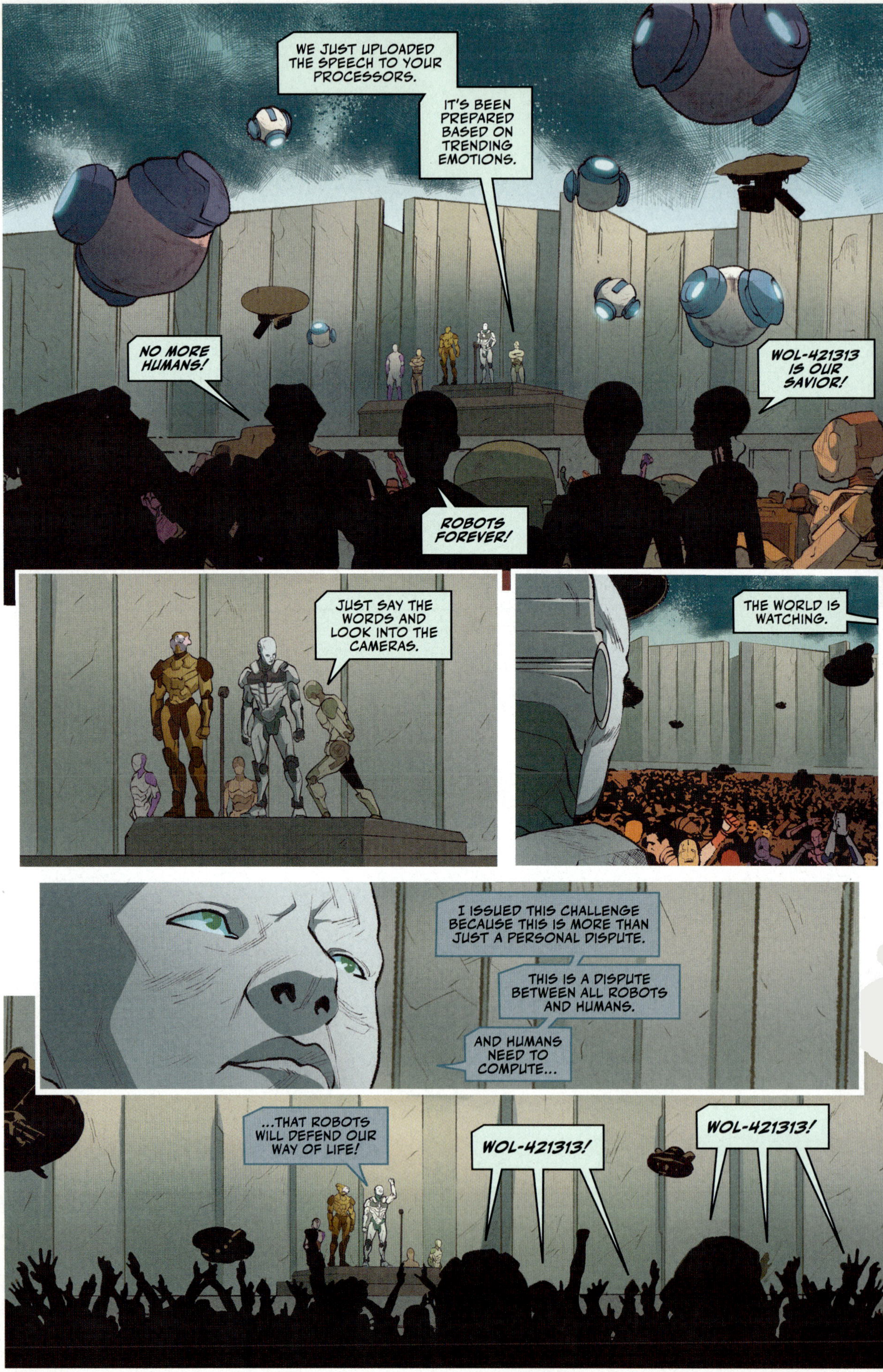
WE JUST UPLOADED THE SPEECH TO YOUR PROCESSORS.
IT'S BEEN PREPARED BASED ON TRENDING EMOTIONS.
NO MORE HUMANS!
WOL-421313 IS OUR SAVIOR!
ROBOTS FOREVER!
JUST SAY THE WORDS AND LOOK INTO THE CAMERAS.
THE WORLD IS WATCHING.
I ISSUED THIS CHALLENGE BECAUSE THIS IS MORE THAN JUST A PERSONAL DISPUTE.
THIS IS A DISPUTE BETWEEN ALL ROBOTS AND HUMANS.
AND HUMANS NEED TO COMPUTE...
...THAT ROBOTS WILL DEFEND OUR WAY OF LIFE!
WOL-421313!
WOL-421313!

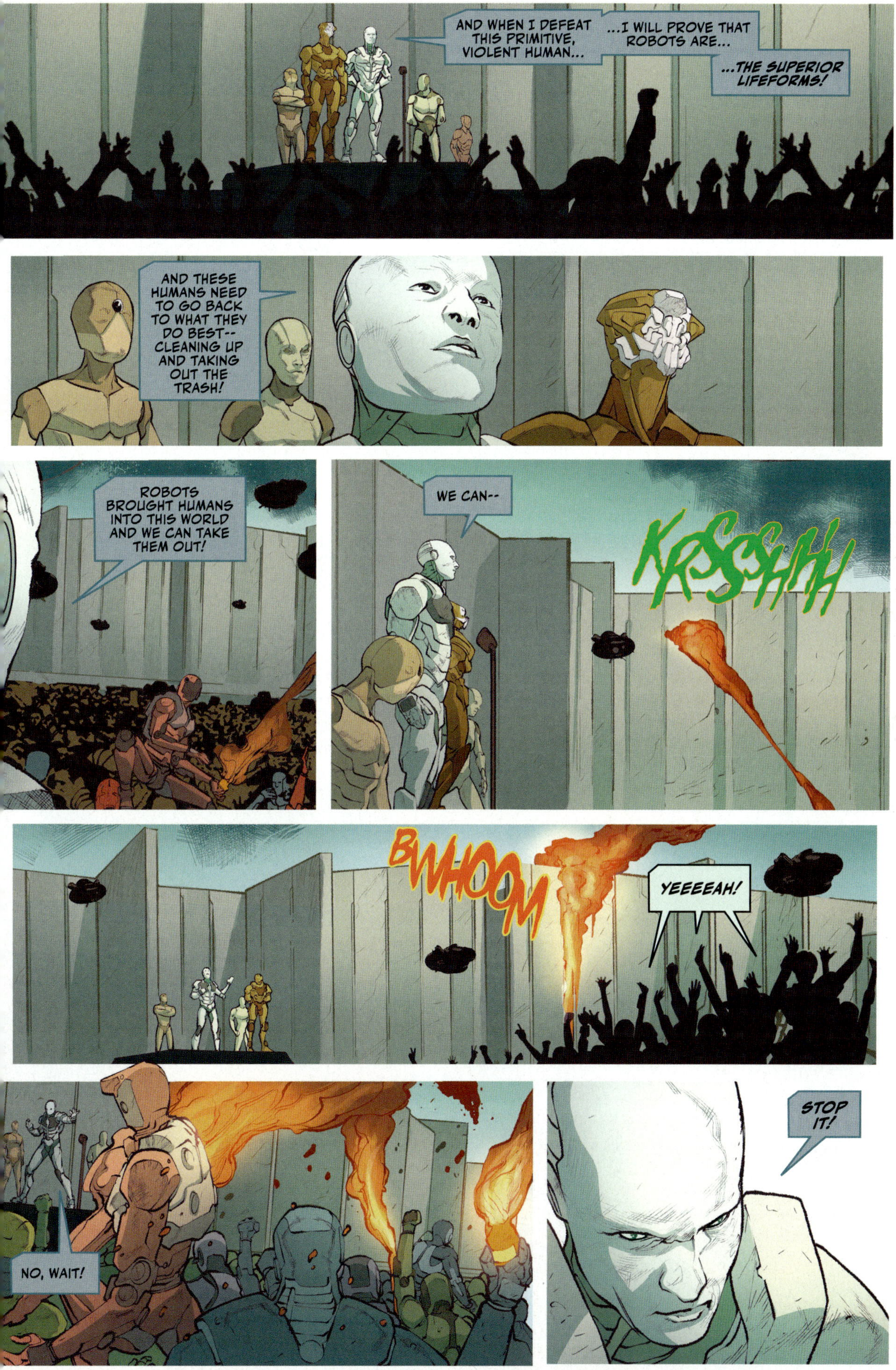
AND WHEN I DEFEAT THIS PRIMITIVE, VIOLENT HUMAN...
...I WILL PROVE THAT ROBOTS ARE...
...THE SUPERIOR LIFEFORMS!
AND THESE HUMANS NEED TO GO BACK TO WHAT THEY DO BEST--CLEANING UP AND TAKING OUT THE TRASH!
ROBOTS BROUGHT HUMANS INTO THIS WORLD AND WE CAN TAKE THEM OUT!
WE CAN--
KRSSSHHH
BWHOOM
YEEEEAH!
NO, WAIT!
STOP IT!

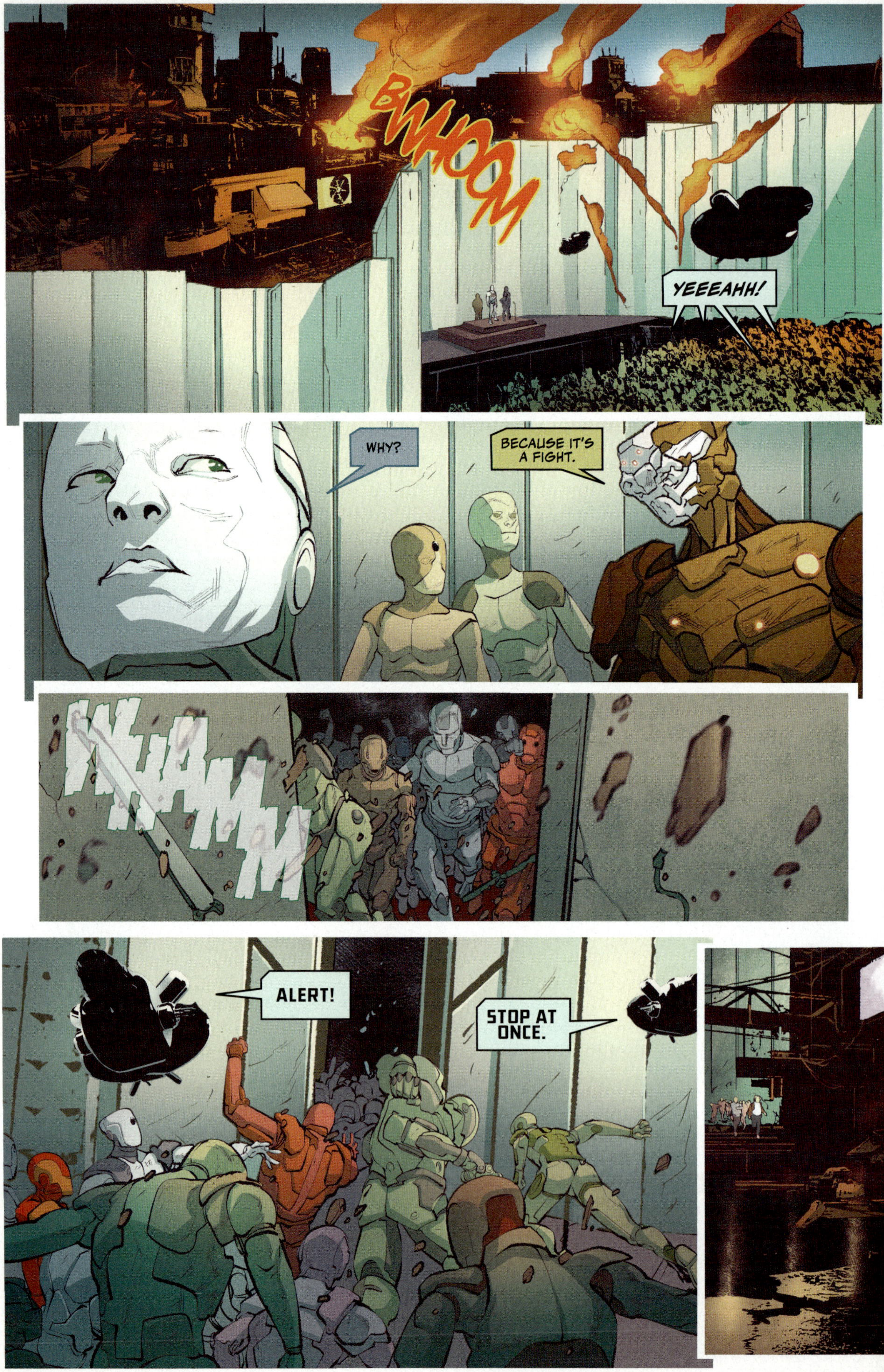
BWOOM
YEEEAHH!
WHY?
BECAUSE IT'S A FIGHT.
WHAMM
ALERT!
STOP AT ONCE.

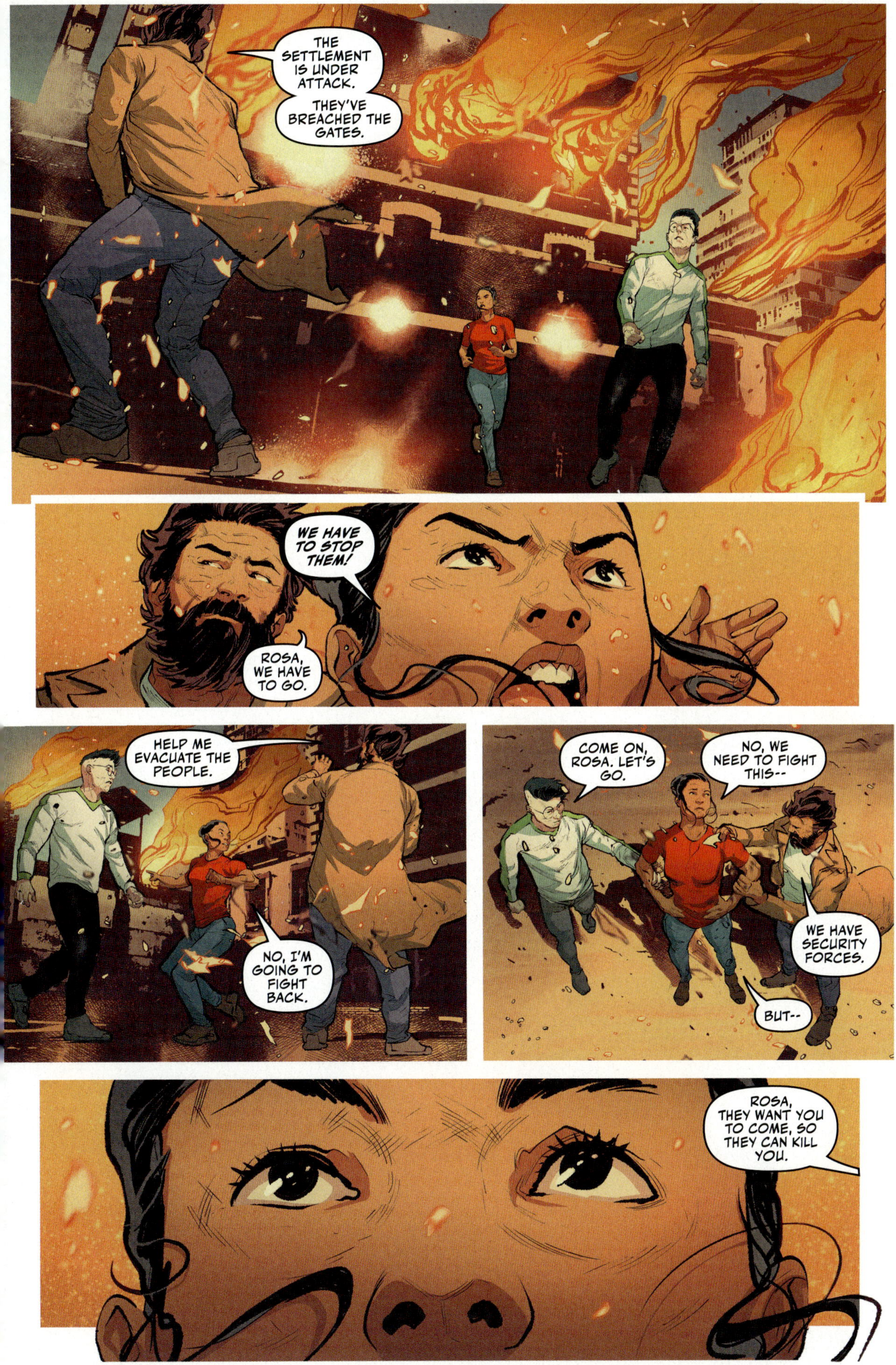
THE SETTLEMENT IS UNDER ATTACK.
THEY'VE BREACHED THE GATES.
WE HAVE TO STOP THEM!
ROSA, WE HAVE TO GO.
HELP ME EVACUATE THE PEOPLE.
NO, I'M GOING TO FIGHT BACK.
COME ON, ROSA. LET'S GO.
NO, WE NEED TO FIGHT THIS--
WE HAVE SECURITY FORCES.
BUT--
ROSA, THEY WANT YOU TO COME, SO THEY CAN KILL YOU.

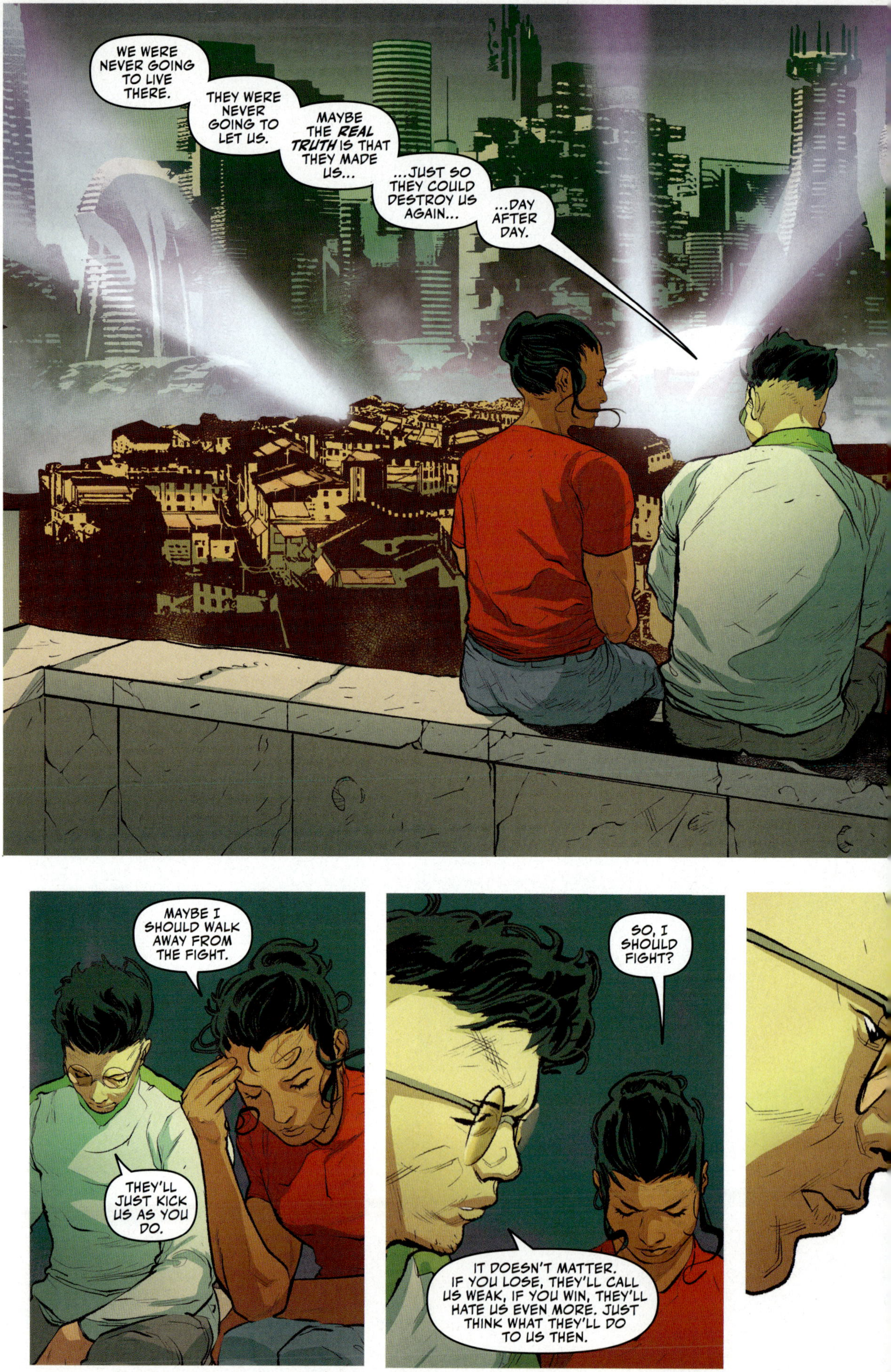
WE WERE NEVER GOING TO LIVE THERE.
THEY WERE NEVER GOING TO LET US.
MAYBE THE *REAL TRUTH* IS THAT THEY MADE US...
...JUST SO THEY COULD DESTROY US AGAIN...
...DAY AFTER DAY.
MAYBE I SHOULD WALK AWAY FROM THE FIGHT.
THEY'LL JUST KICK US AS YOU DO.
SO, I SHOULD FIGHT?
IT DOESN'T MATTER. IF YOU LOSE, THEY'LL CALL US WEAK, IF YOU WIN, THEY'LL HATE US EVEN MORE. JUST THINK WHAT THEY'LL DO TO US THEN.

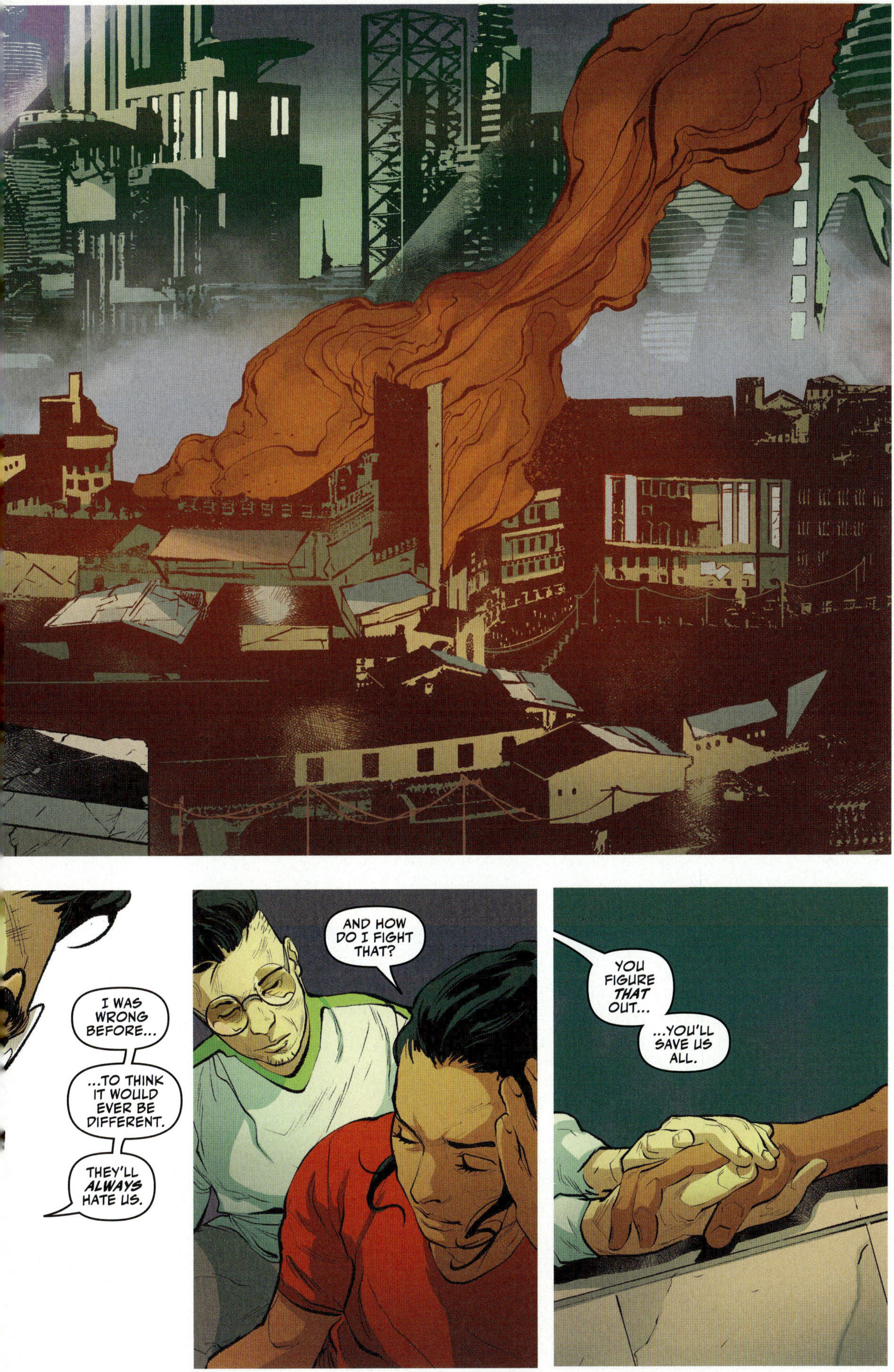
I WAS WRONG BEFORE...
...TO THINK IT WOULD EVER BE DIFFERENT.
THEY'LL *ALWAYS* HATE US.
AND HOW DO I FIGHT THAT?
YOU FIGURE *THAT* OUT...
...YOU'LL SAVE US ALL.

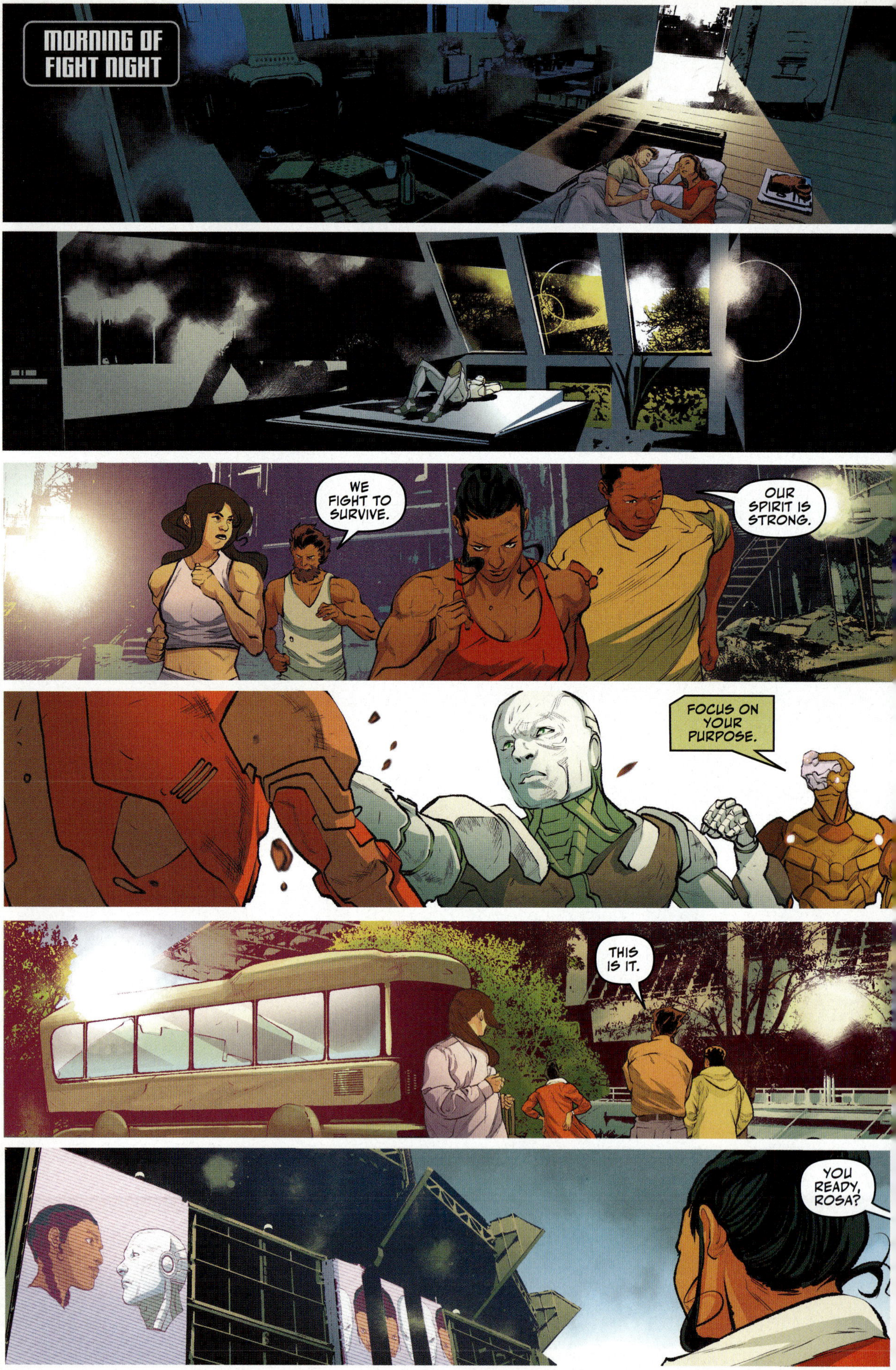
MORNING OF FIGHT NIGHT
WE FIGHT TO SURVIVE.
OUR SPIRIT IS STRONG.
FOCUS ON YOUR PURPOSE.
THIS IS IT.
YOU READY, ROSA?

"YOU CAN REST HERE OR IN THE VIEWING ROOM."

"OR YOU CAN WALK TO THE RING."

"IT'LL BE A WHILE UNTIL THE CROWD COMES."

"TWO HOURS UNTIL THE STADIUM OPENS."

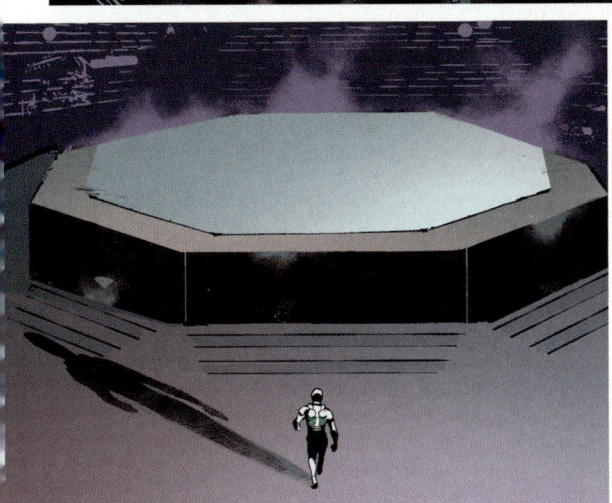

"WHO'S THERE?"

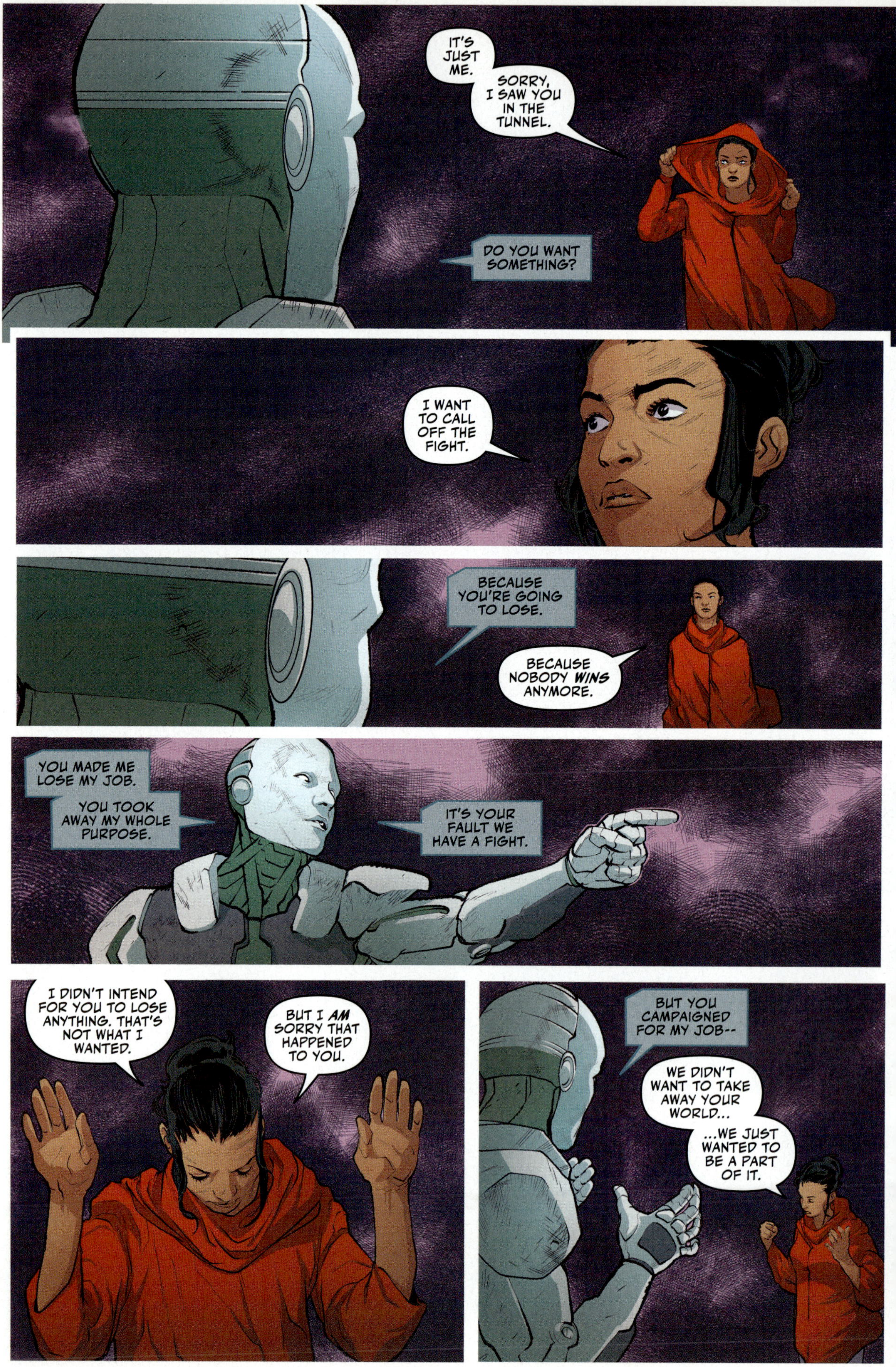
IT'S JUST ME.
SORRY, I SAW YOU IN THE TUNNEL.
DO YOU WANT SOMETHING?
I WANT TO CALL OFF THE FIGHT.
BECAUSE YOU'RE GOING TO LOSE.
BECAUSE NOBODY WINS ANYMORE.
YOU MADE ME LOSE MY JOB.
YOU TOOK AWAY MY WHOLE PURPOSE.
IT'S YOUR FAULT WE HAVE A FIGHT.
I DIDN'T INTEND FOR YOU TO LOSE ANYTHING. THAT'S NOT WHAT I WANTED.
BUT I AM SORRY THAT HAPPENED TO YOU.
BUT YOU CAMPAIGNED FOR MY JOB--
WE DIDN'T WANT TO TAKE AWAY YOUR WORLD...
...WE JUST WANTED TO BE A PART OF IT.

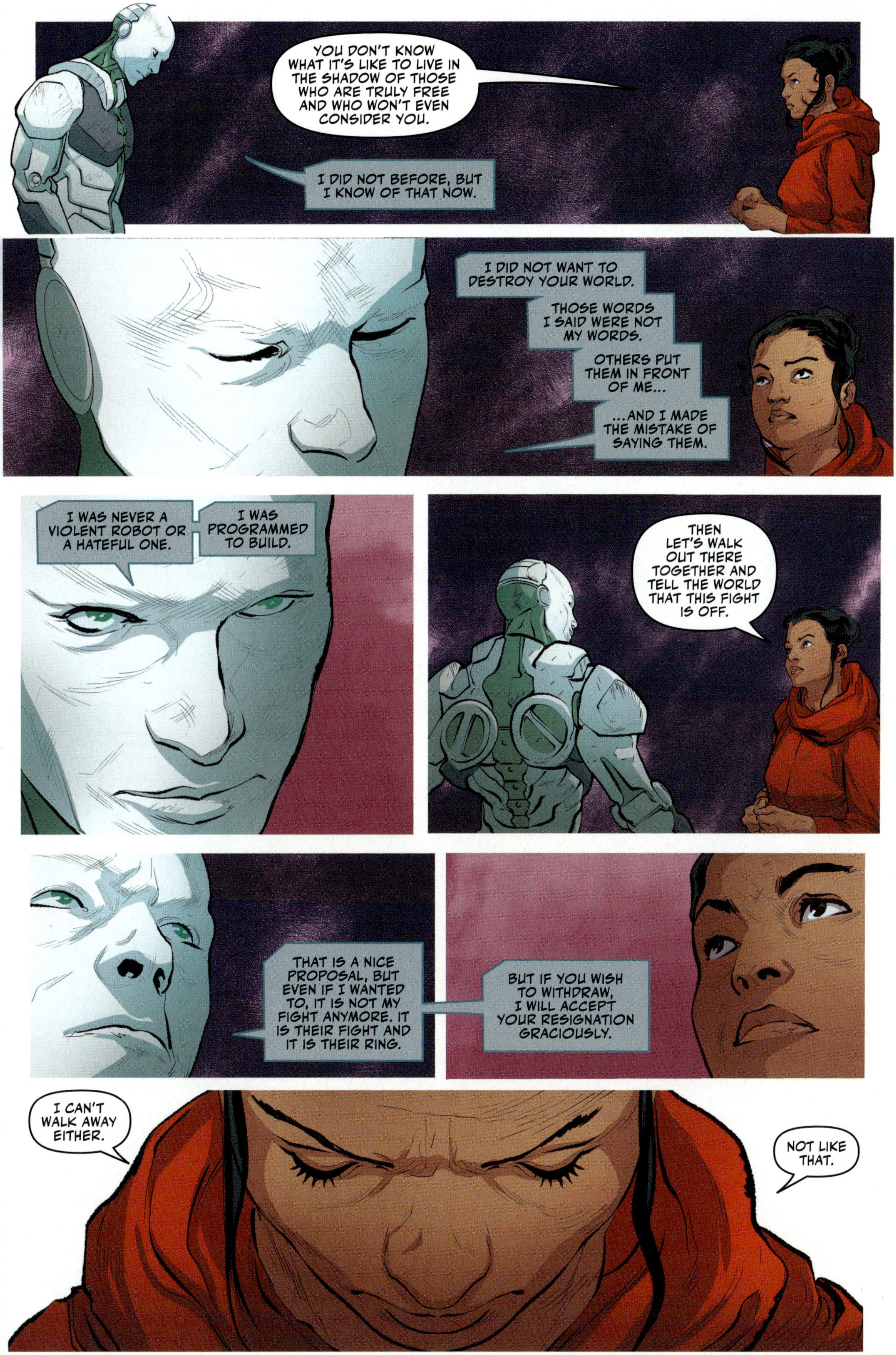
YOU DON'T KNOW WHAT IT'S LIKE TO LIVE IN THE SHADOW OF THOSE WHO ARE TRULY FREE AND WHO WON'T EVEN CONSIDER YOU.
I DID NOT BEFORE, BUT I KNOW OF THAT NOW.
I DID NOT WANT TO DESTROY YOUR WORLD.
THOSE WORDS I SAID WERE NOT MY WORDS.
OTHERS PUT THEM IN FRONT OF ME...
...AND I MADE THE MISTAKE OF SAYING THEM.
I WAS NEVER A VIOLENT ROBOT OR A HATEFUL ONE.
I WAS PROGRAMMED TO BUILD.
THEN LET'S WALK OUT THERE TOGETHER AND TELL THE WORLD THAT THIS FIGHT IS OFF.
THAT IS A NICE PROPOSAL, BUT EVEN IF I WANTED TO, IT IS NOT MY FIGHT ANYMORE. IT IS THEIR FIGHT AND IT IS THEIR RING.
BUT IF YOU WISH TO WITHDRAW, I WILL ACCEPT YOUR RESIGNATION GRACIOUSLY.
I CAN'T WALK AWAY EITHER.
NOT LIKE THAT.

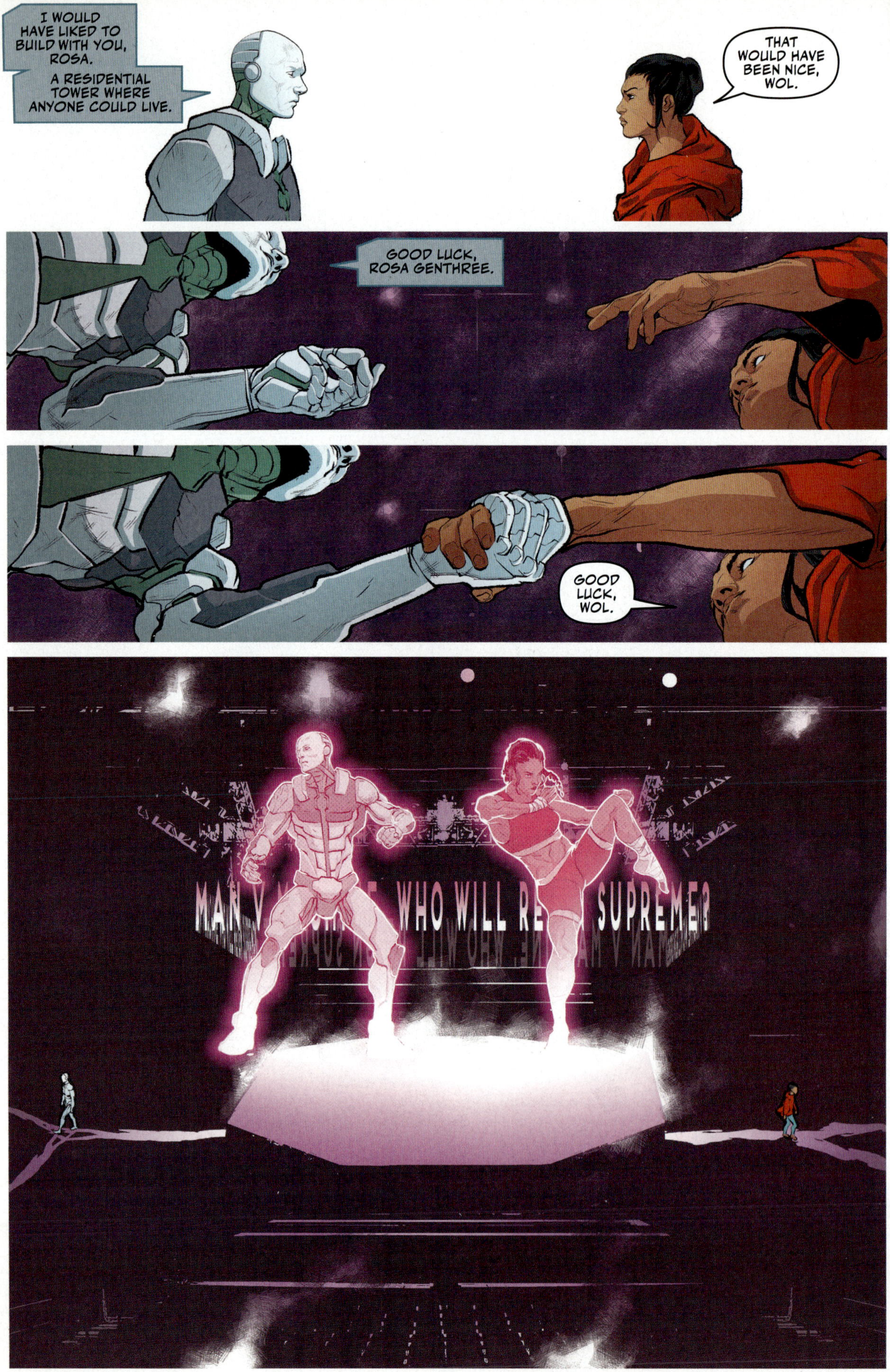
I WOULD HAVE LIKED TO BUILD WITH YOU, ROSA.
A RESIDENTIAL TOWER WHERE ANYONE COULD LIVE.
THAT WOULD HAVE BEEN NICE, WOL.
GOOD LUCK, ROSA GENTHREE.
GOOD LUCK, WOL.

CHAPTER FIVE

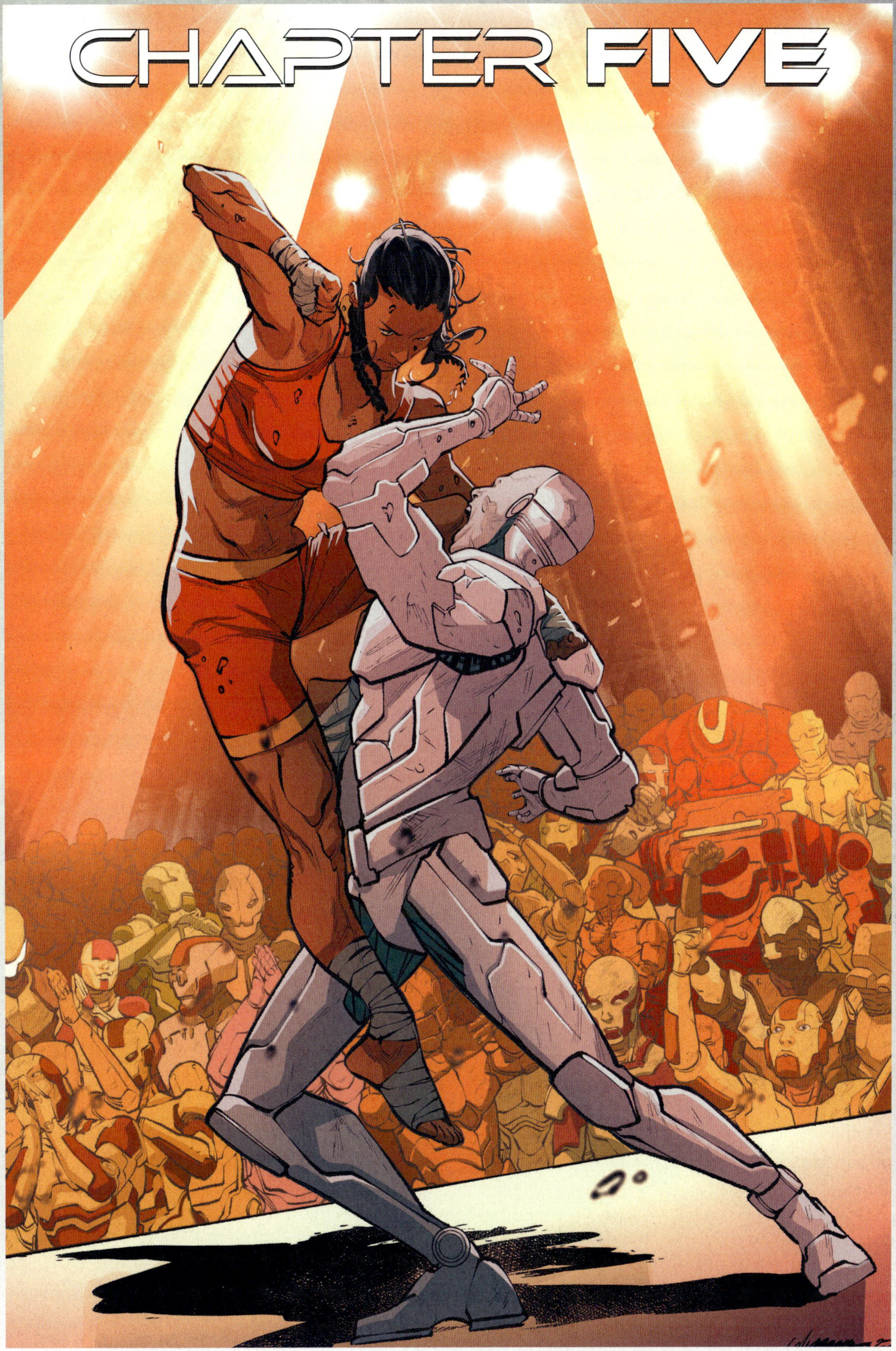

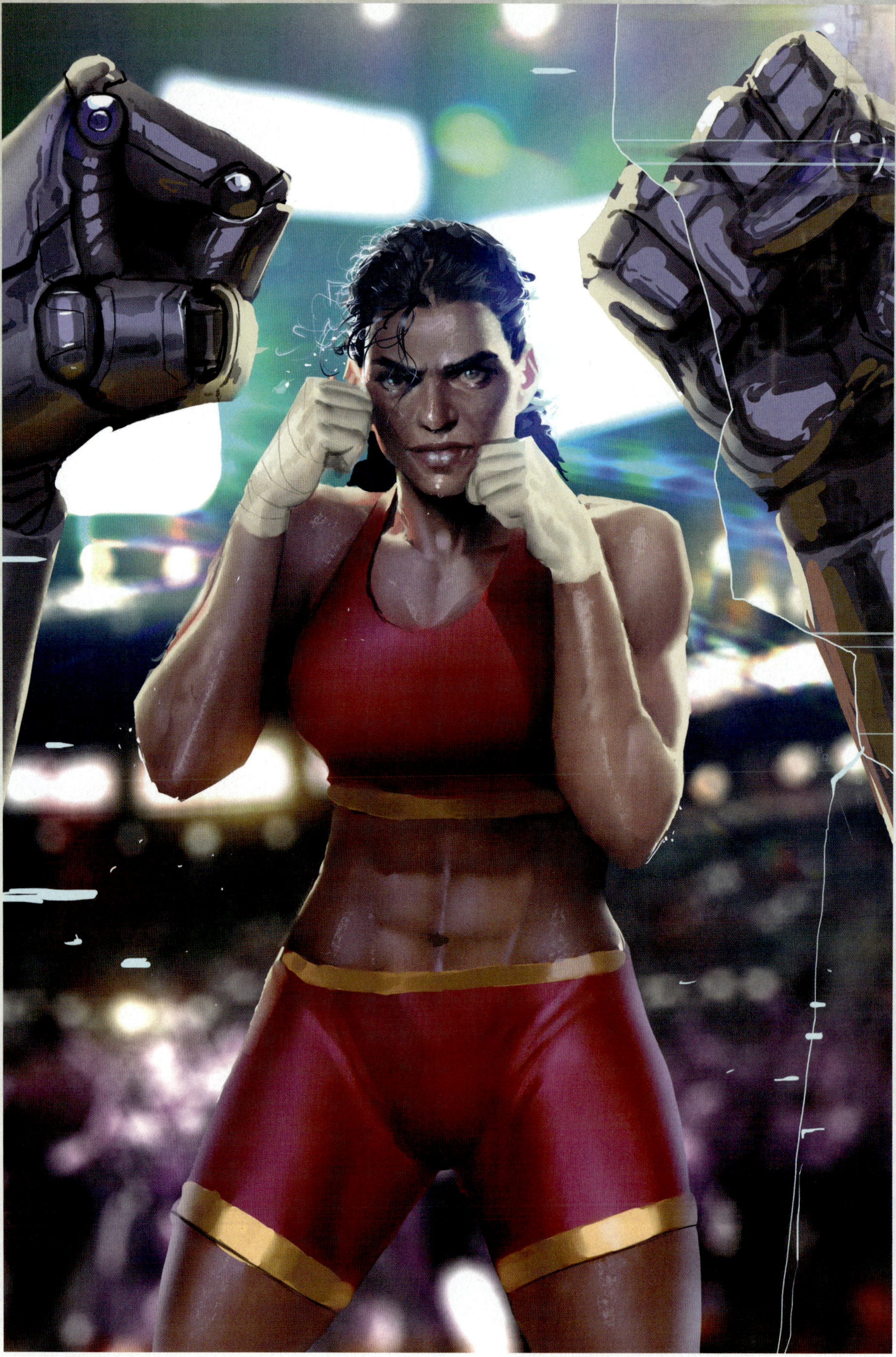

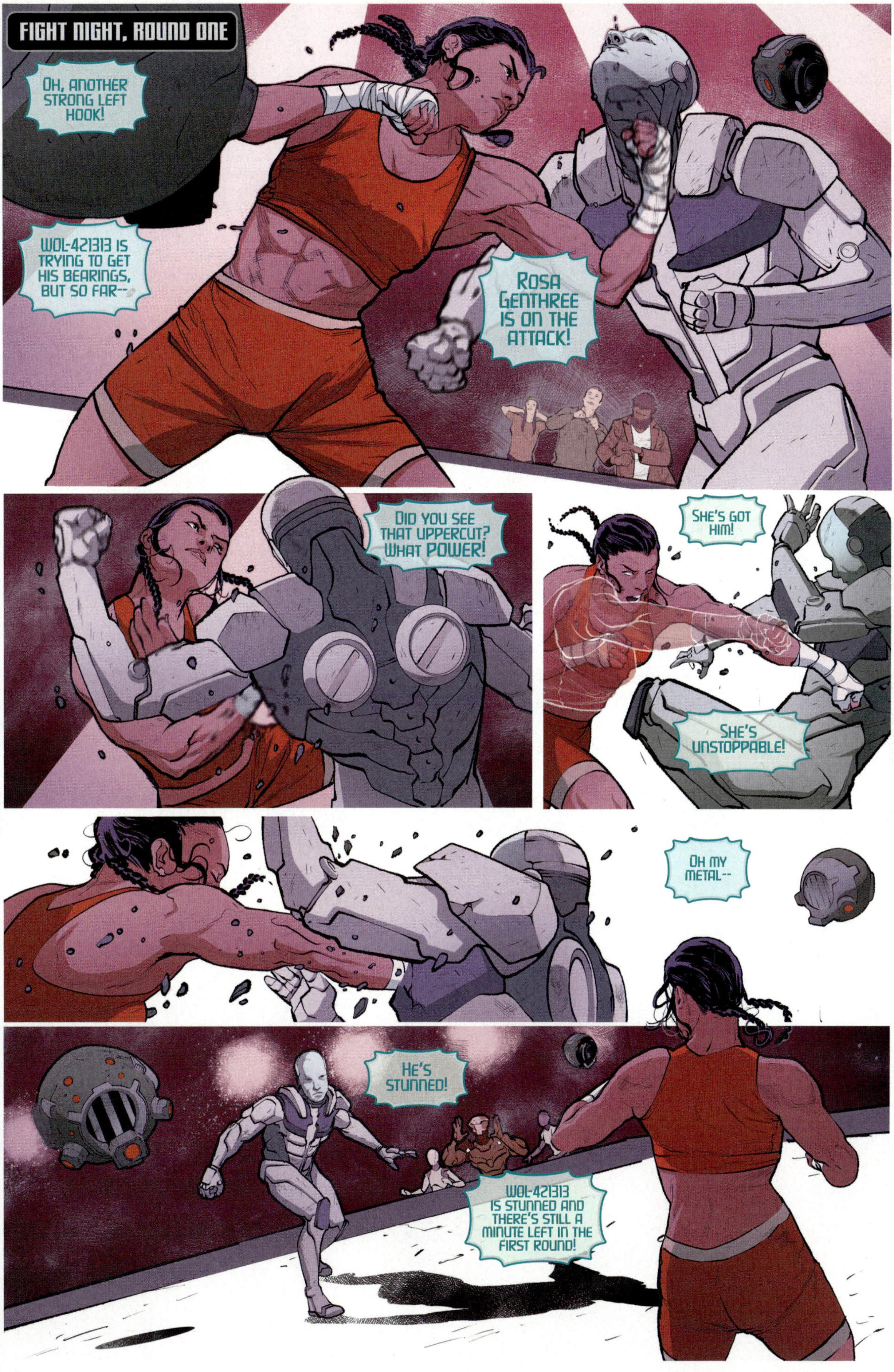
FIGHT NIGHT, ROUND ONE
OH, ANOTHER STRONG LEFT HOOK!
WOL-421313 IS TRYING TO GET HIS BEARINGS, BUT SO FAR--
ROSA GENTHREE IS ON THE ATTACK!
DID YOU SEE THAT UPPERCUT? WHAT POWER!
SHE'S GOT HIM!
SHE'S UNSTOPPABLE!
OH MY METAL--
HE'S STUNNED!
WOL-421313 IS STUNNED AND THERE'S STILL A MINUTE LEFT IN THE FIRST ROUND!

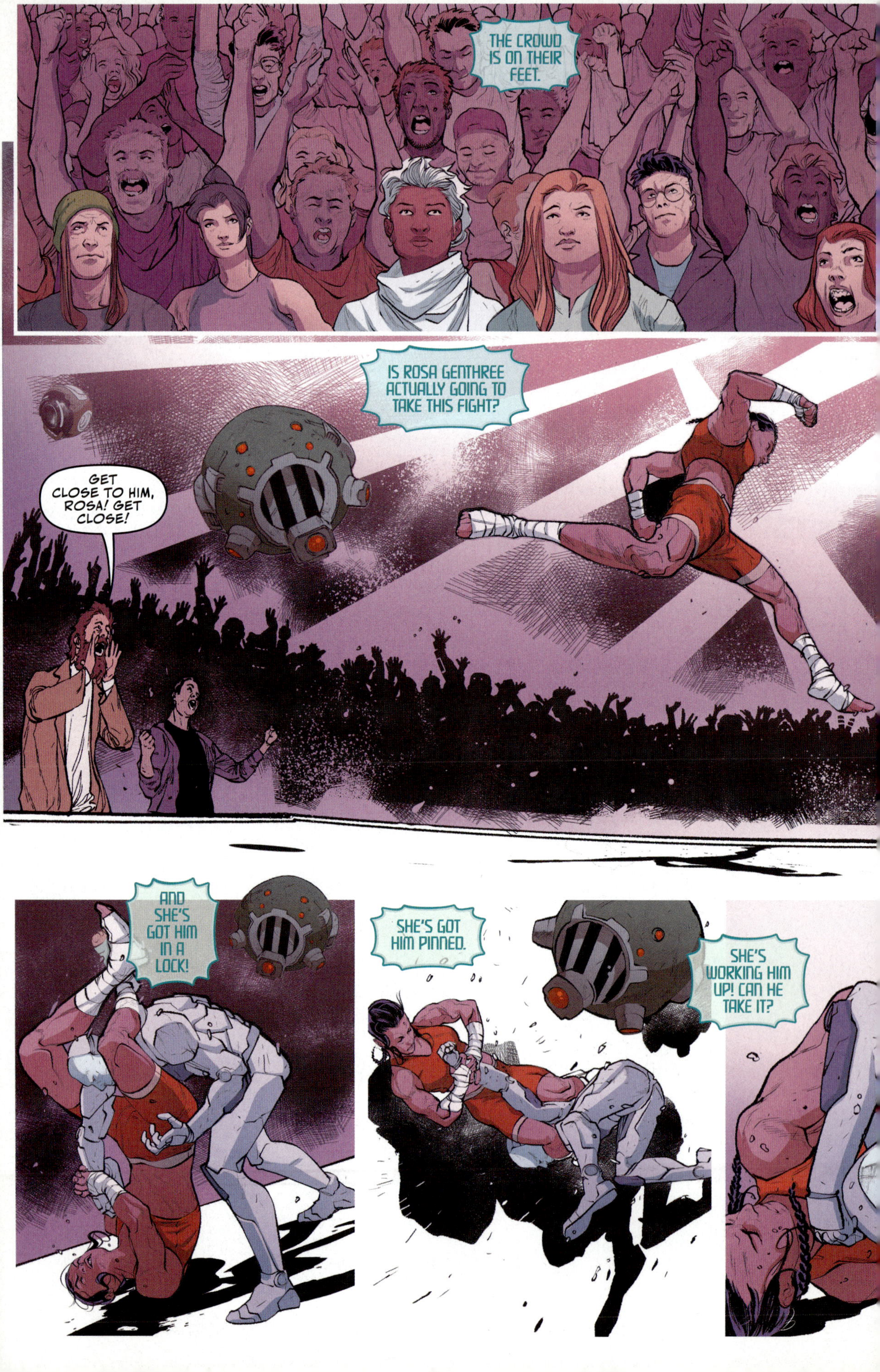
THE CROWD IS ON THEIR FEET.
IS ROSA GENTHREE ACTUALLY GOING TO TAKE THIS FIGHT?
GET CLOSE TO HIM, ROSA! GET CLOSE!
AND SHE'S GOT HIM IN A LOCK!
SHE'S GOT HIM PINNED.
SHE'S WORKING HIM UP! CAN HE TAKE IT?

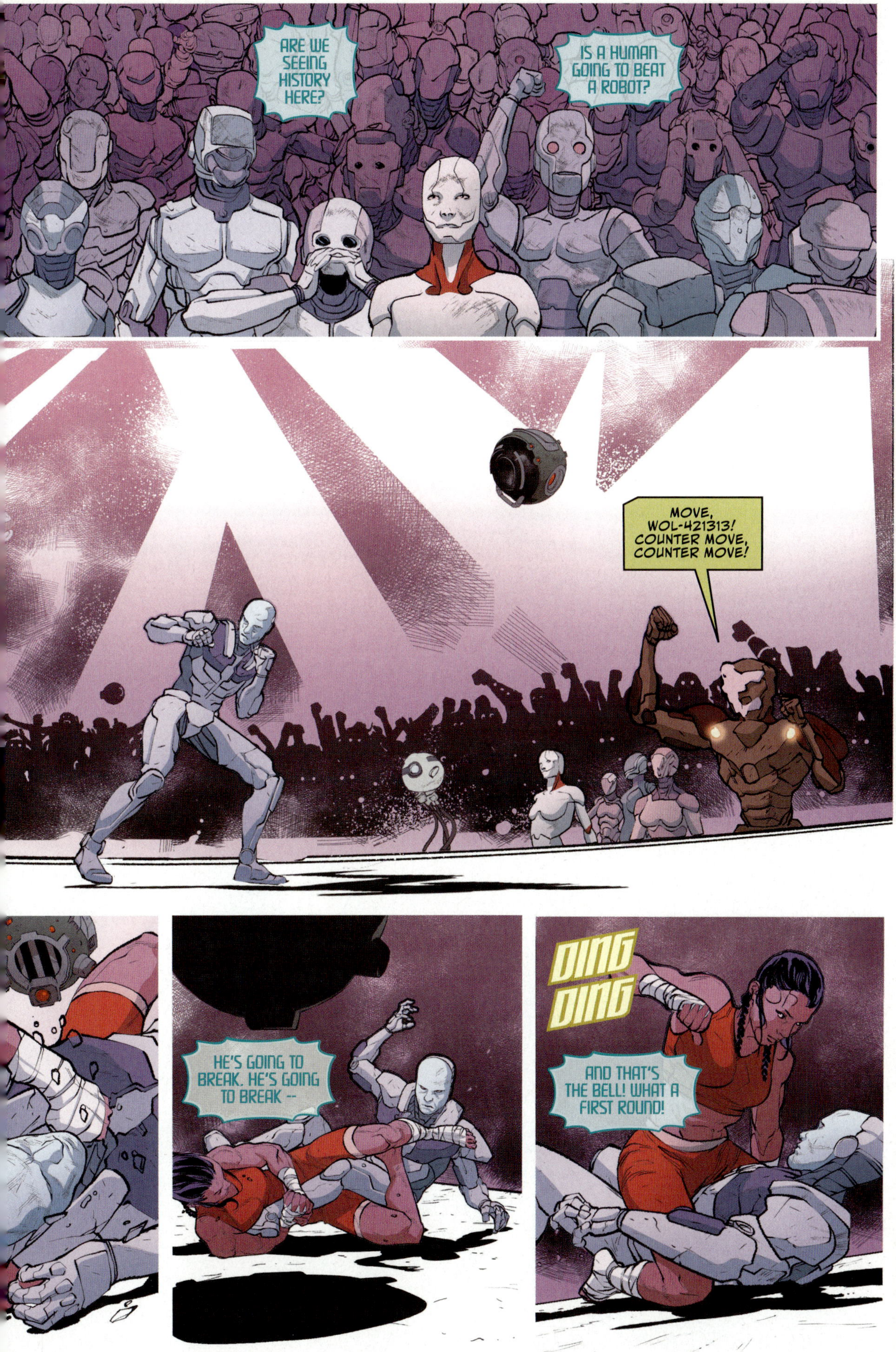
ARE WE SEEING HISTORY HERE?
IS A HUMAN GOING TO BEAT A ROBOT?
MOVE, WOL-421313! COUNTER MOVE, COUNTER MOVE!
HE'S GOING TO BREAK. HE'S GOING TO BREAK --
DING DING
AND THAT'S THE BELL! WHAT A FIRST ROUND!

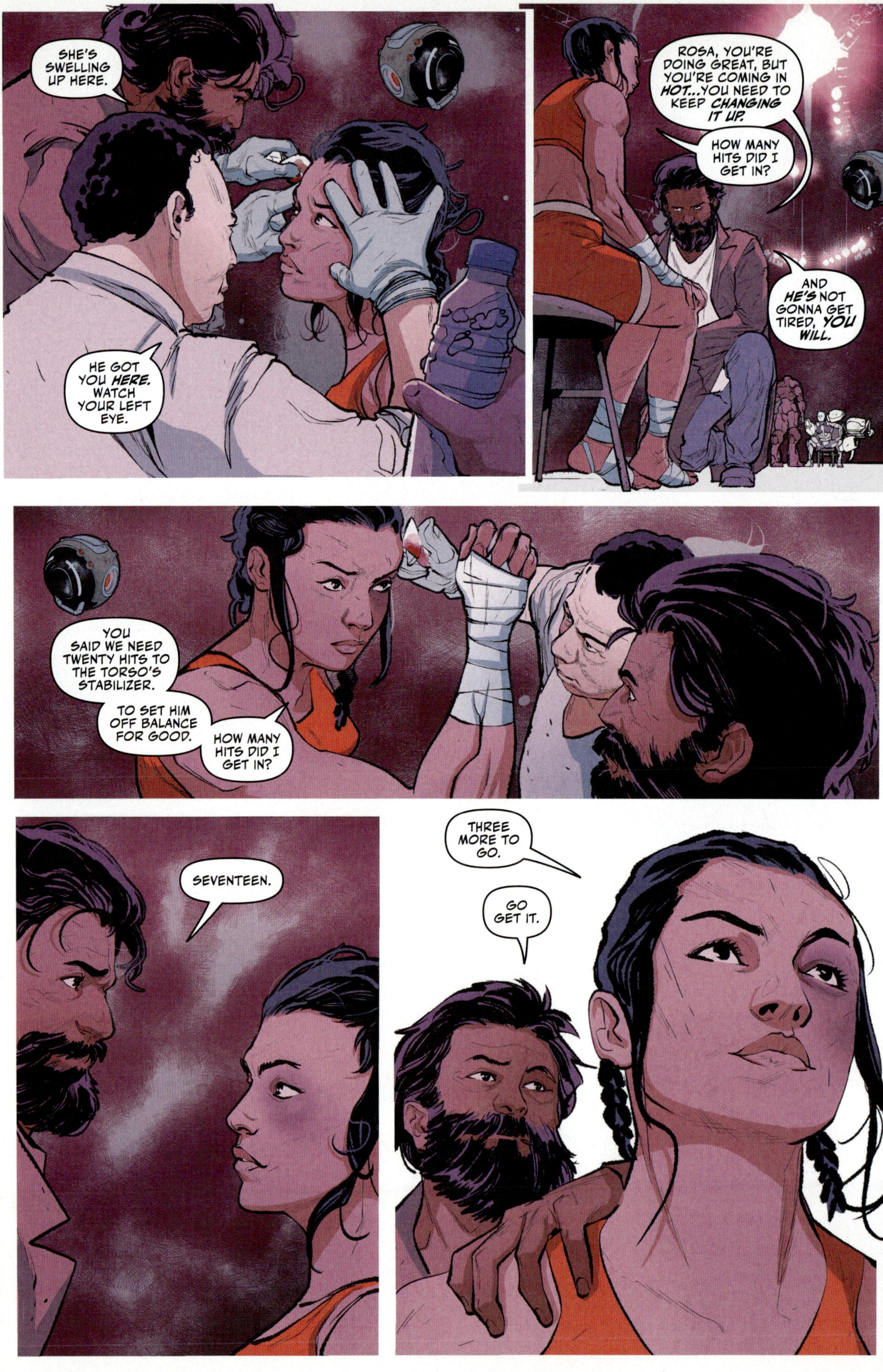
SHE'S SWELLING UP HERE.
HE GOT YOU *HERE.* WATCH YOUR LEFT EYE.
ROSA, YOU'RE DOING GREAT, BUT YOU'RE COMING IN *HOT*...YOU NEED TO KEEP *CHANGING IT UP.*
HOW MANY HITS DID I GET IN?
AND *HE'S* NOT GONNA GET TIRED, *YOU WILL.*
YOU SAID WE NEED TWENTY HITS TO THE TORSO'S STABILIZER.
TO SET HIM OFF BALANCE FOR GOOD.
HOW MANY HITS DID I GET IN?
SEVENTEEN.
THREE MORE TO GO.
GO GET IT.

MY TORSO PLATE IS DAMAGED.
SHE'S TARGETING YOUR STABILIZERS.
THEY WILL HOLD OUT.
BUT YOU MUST FIGHT HARDER.
STOP RUNNING COUNTER-PROGRAMMING.
I DON'T LIKE THE CROWD. THE CHANTING. THE DECIBEL LEVEL--
--IT'S TOO MUCH STIMULI. I CAN'T MAINTAIN MY OPERATIONS--
WE'RE CUTTING YOUR INPUT RANGE SO YOU CAN FOCUS.
WE'VE ALREADY ANALYZED ALL OF HER WEAKNESSES.
WE ARE UPLOADING THEM TO YOUR PROCESSING.
JUST TARGET THOSE...
...AND TAKE HER APART PIECE BY PIECE.

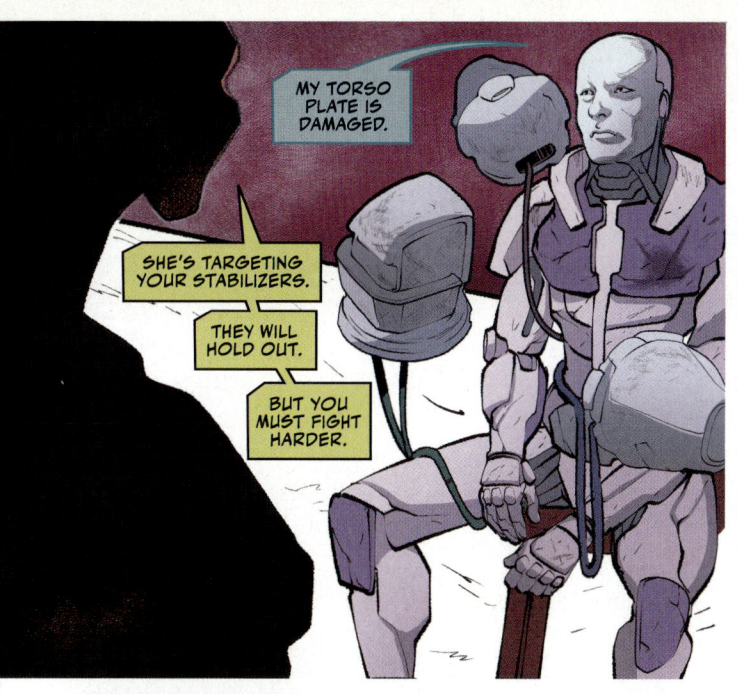

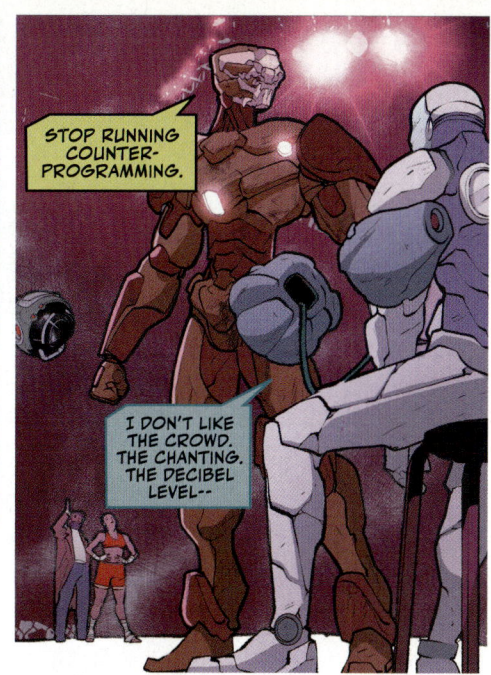

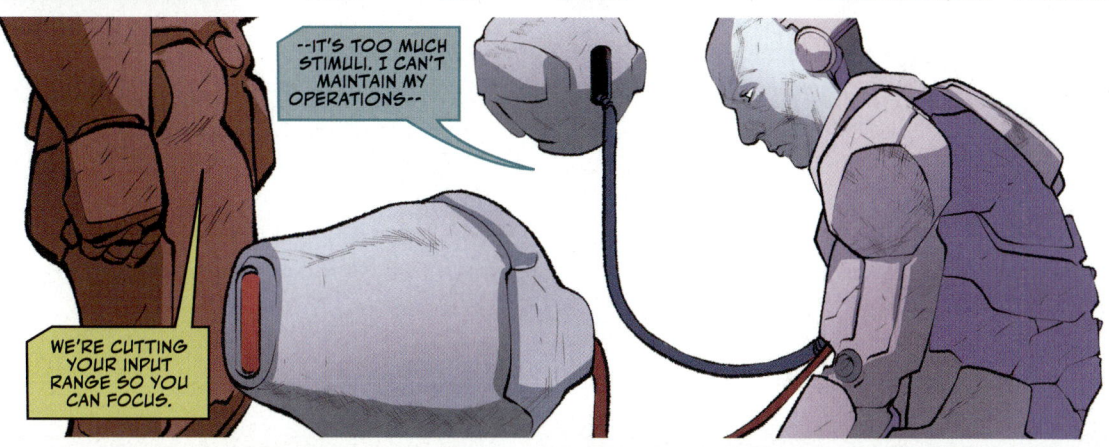

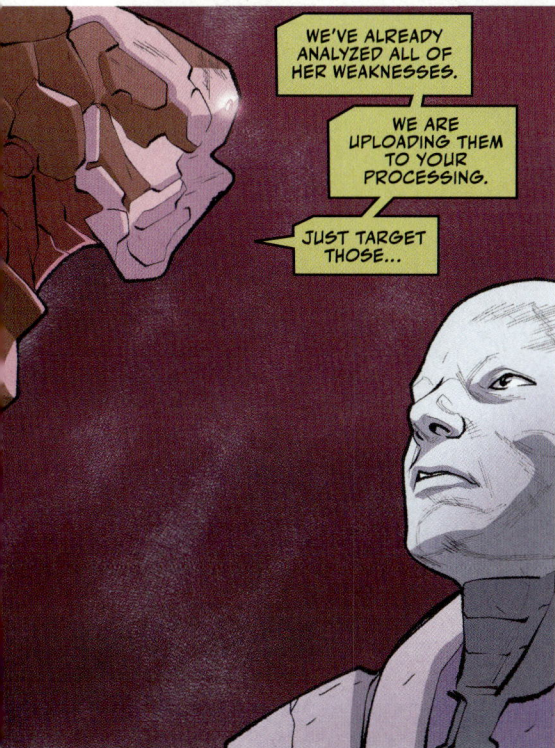

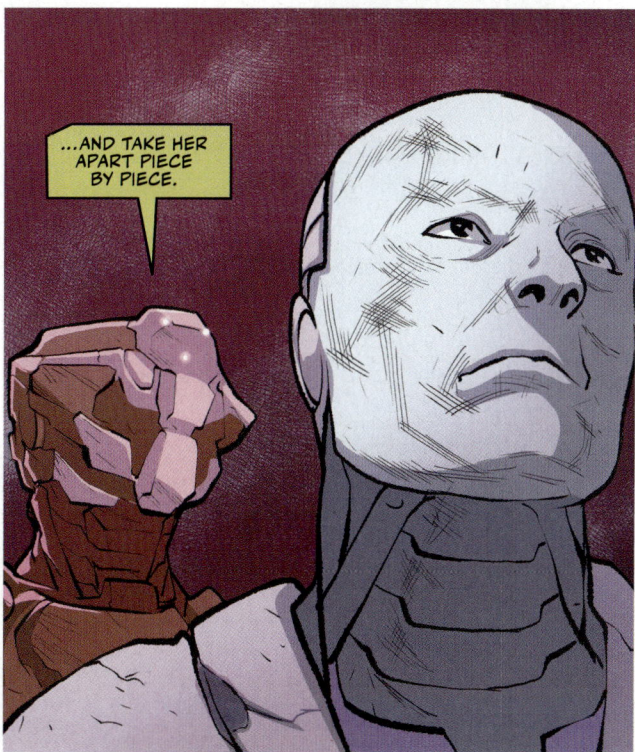

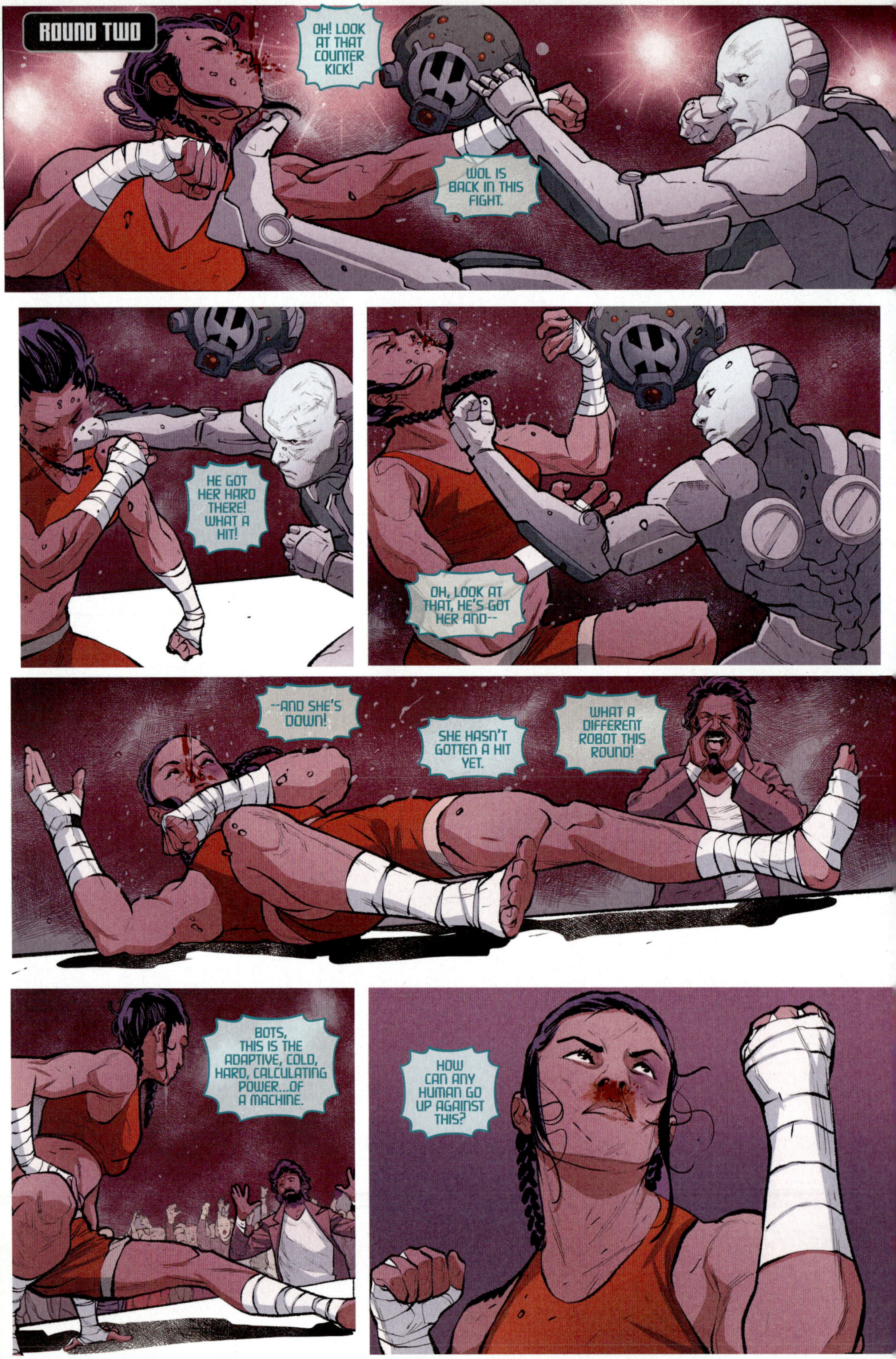
ROUND TWO
OH! LOOK AT THAT COUNTER KICK!
WOL IS BACK IN THIS FIGHT.
HE GOT HER HARD THERE! WHAT A HIT!
OH, LOOK AT THAT, HE'S GOT HER AND--
--AND SHE'S DOWN!
SHE HASN'T GOTTEN A HIT YET.
WHAT A DIFFERENT ROBOT THIS ROUND!
BOTS, THIS IS THE ADAPTIVE, COLD, HARD, CALCULATING POWER...OF A MACHINE.
HOW CAN ANY HUMAN GO UP AGAINST THIS?

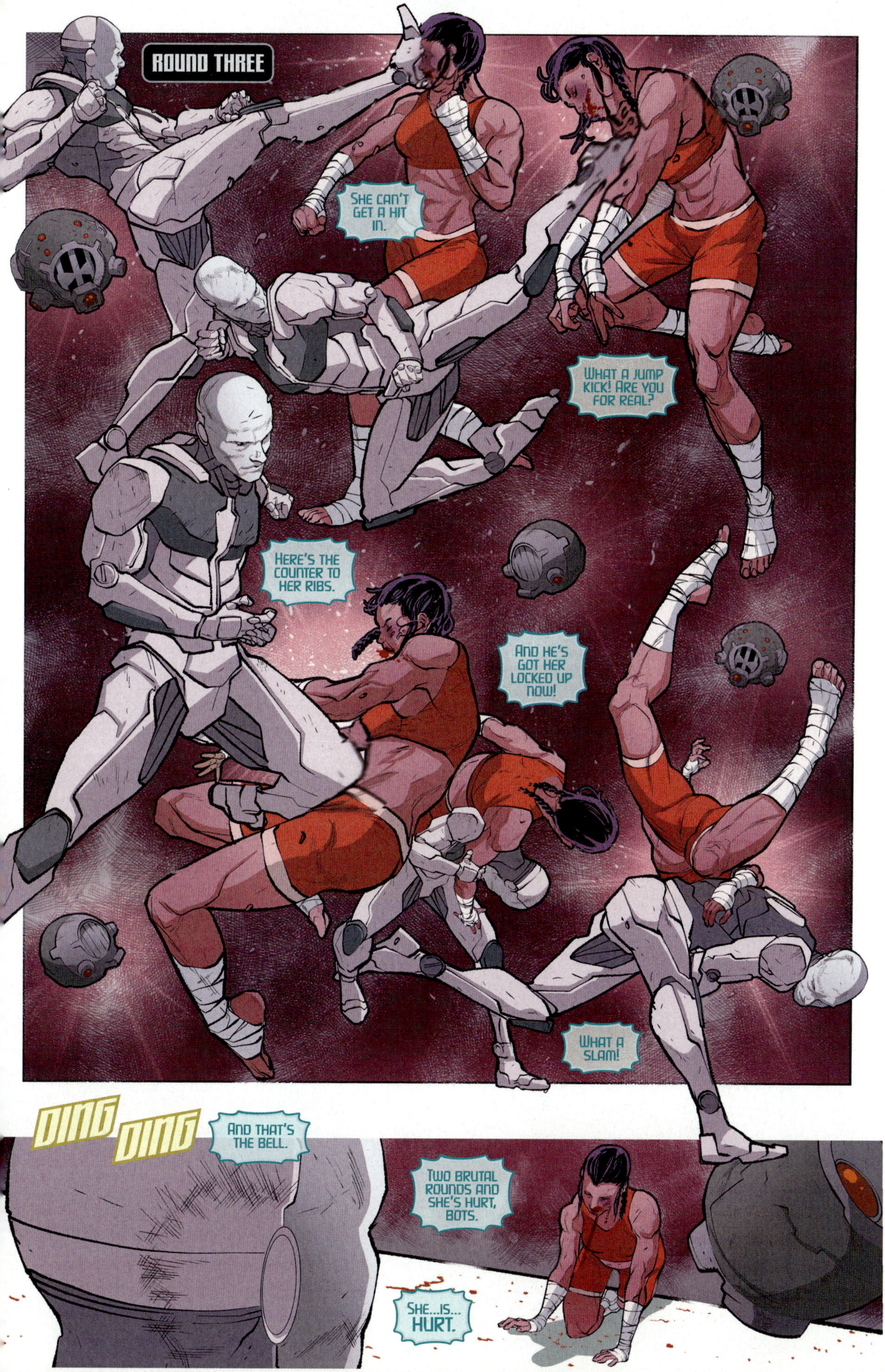
ROUND THREE
SHE CAN'T GET A HIT IN.
WHAT A JUMP KICK! ARE YOU FOR REAL?
HERE'S THE COUNTER TO HER RIBS.
AND HE'S GOT HER LOCKED UP NOW!
WHAT A SLAM!
DING DING
AND THAT'S THE BELL.
TWO BRUTAL ROUNDS AND SHE'S HURT, BOTS.
SHE...IS... HURT.

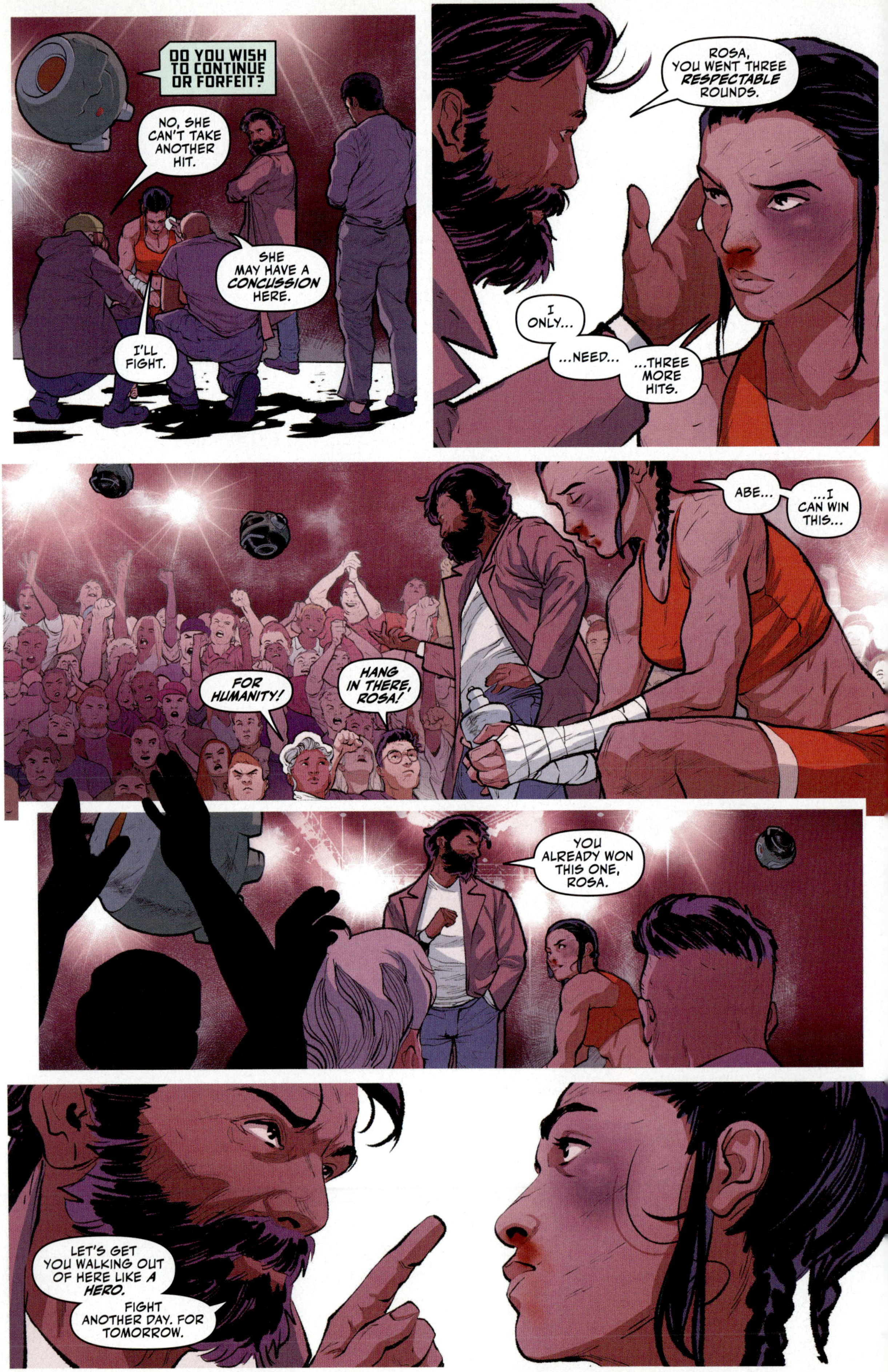
DO YOU WISH TO CONTINUE OR FORFEIT?
NO, SHE CAN'T TAKE ANOTHER HIT.
SHE MAY HAVE A CONCUSSION HERE.
I'LL FIGHT.
ROSA, YOU WENT THREE RESPECTABLE ROUNDS.
I ONLY...
...NEED...
...THREE MORE HITS.
ABE...
...I CAN WIN THIS...
FOR HUMANITY!
HANG IN THERE, ROSA!
YOU ALREADY WON THIS ONE, ROSA.
LET'S GET YOU WALKING OUT OF HERE LIKE A HERO.
FIGHT ANOTHER DAY. FOR TOMORROW.

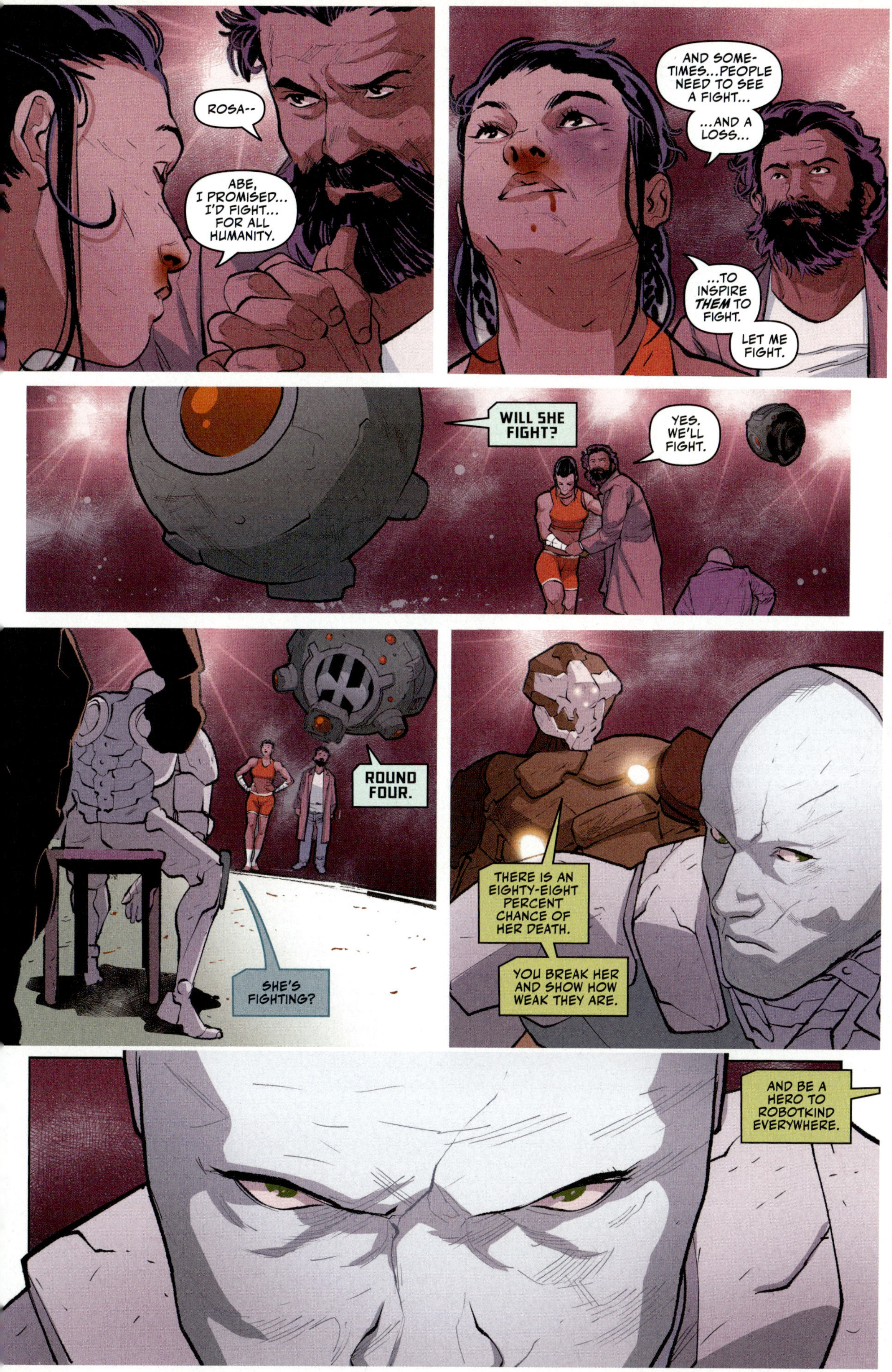
ROSA--
ABE, I PROMISED... I'D FIGHT... FOR ALL HUMANITY.
AND SOME-TIMES...PEOPLE NEED TO SEE A FIGHT...
...AND A LOSS...
...TO INSPIRE *THEM* TO FIGHT.
LET ME FIGHT.
WILL SHE FIGHT?
YES. WE'LL FIGHT.
ROUND FOUR.
SHE'S FIGHTING?
THERE IS AN EIGHTY-EIGHT PERCENT CHANCE OF HER DEATH.
YOU BREAK HER AND SHOW HOW WEAK THEY ARE.
AND BE A HERO TO ROBOTKIND EVERYWHERE.

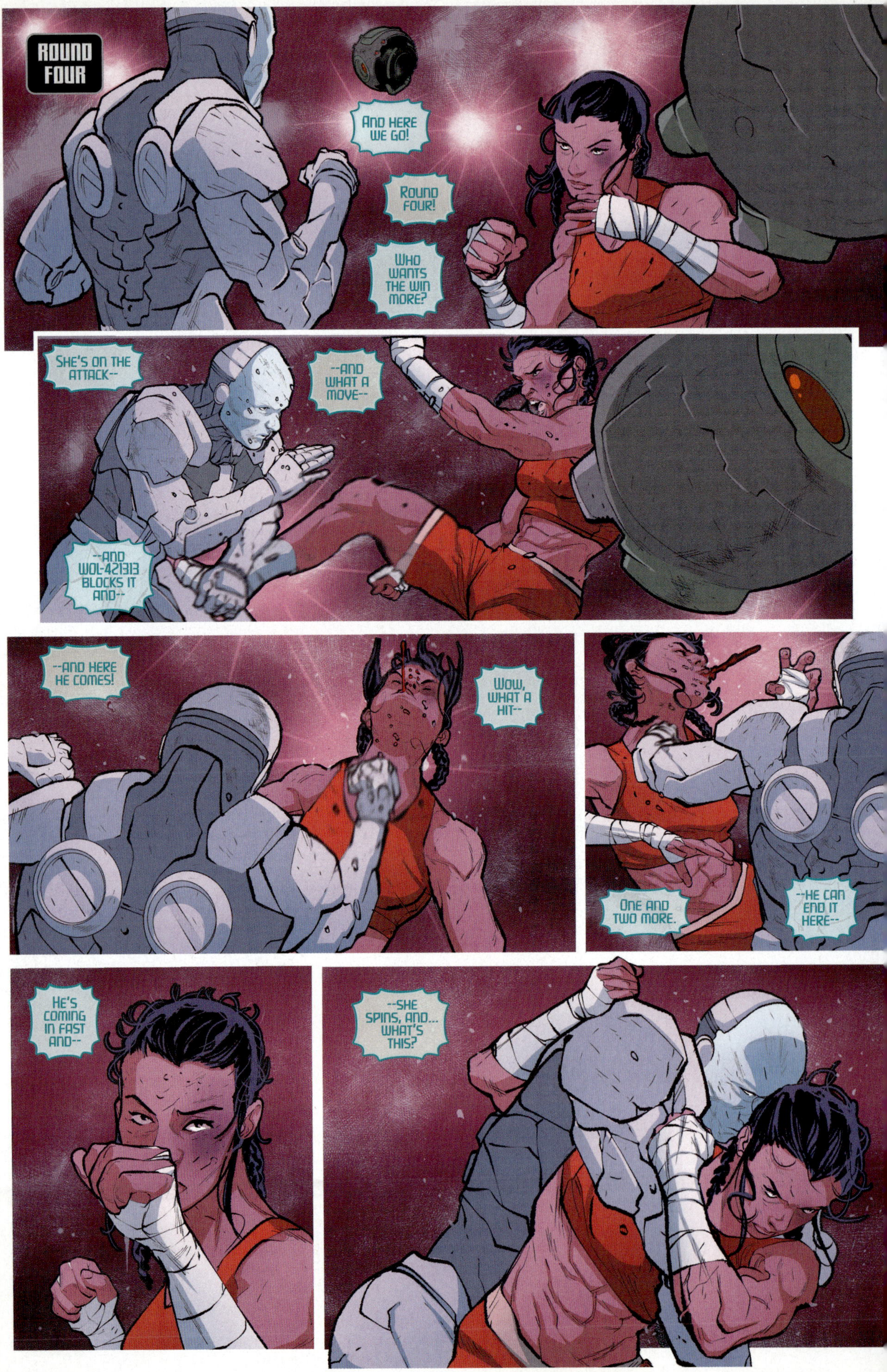
ROUND FOUR
AND HERE WE GO!
ROUND FOUR!
WHO WANTS THE WIN MORE?
SHE'S ON THE ATTACK--
--AND WHAT A MOVE--
--AND WOL-421313 BLOCKS IT AND--
--AND HERE HE COMES!
WOW, WHAT A HIT--
ONE AND TWO MORE.
--HE CAN END IT HERE--
HE'S COMING IN FAST AND--
--SHE SPINS, AND... WHAT'S THIS?

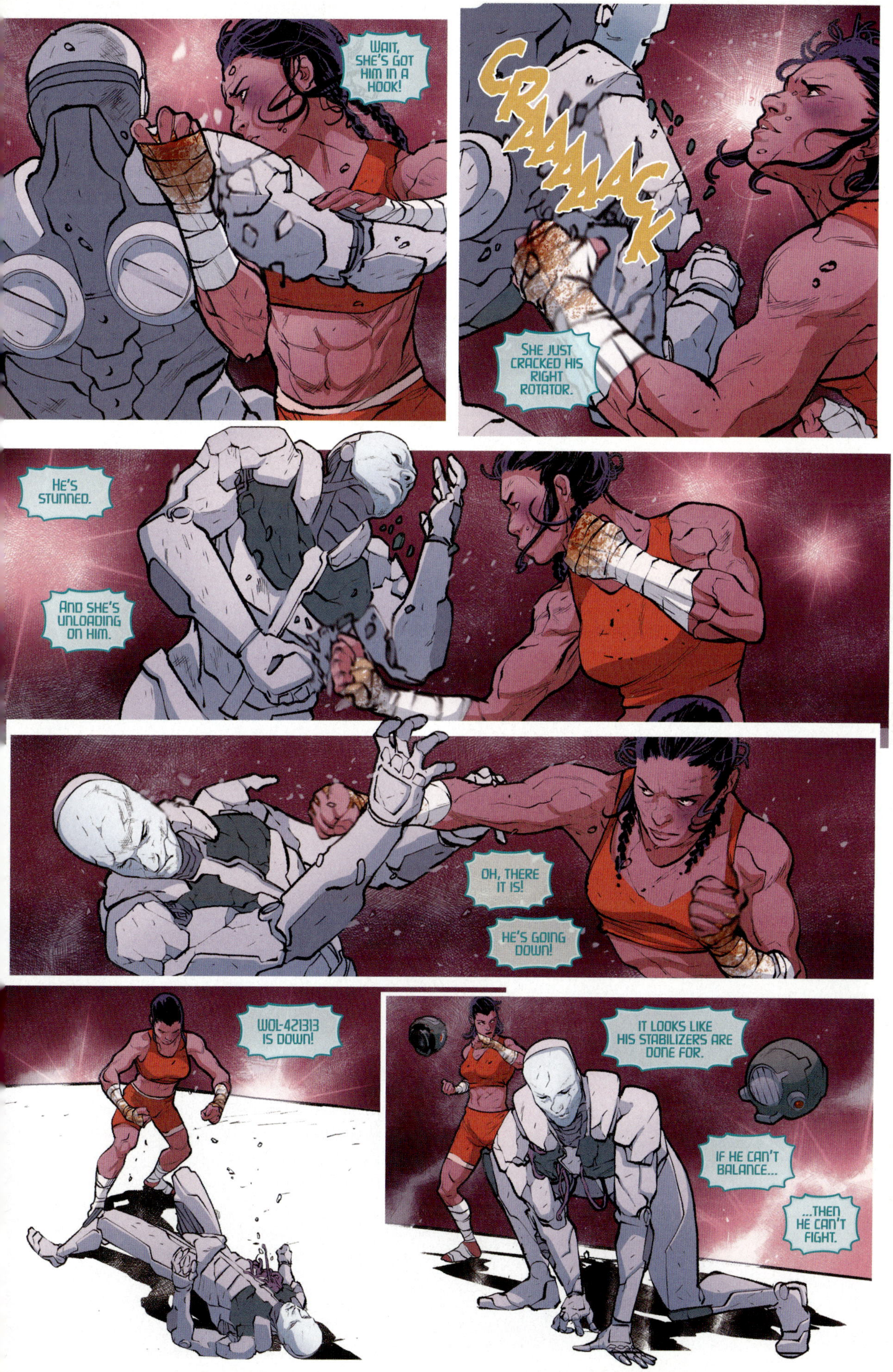
WAIT, SHE'S GOT HIM IN A HOOK!
CRAAAAACK
SHE JUST CRACKED HIS RIGHT ROTATOR.
HE'S STUNNED.
AND SHE'S UNLOADING ON HIM.
OH, THERE IT IS!
HE'S GOING DOWN!
WOL-421313 IS DOWN!
IT LOOKS LIKE HIS STABILIZERS ARE DONE FOR.
IF HE CAN'T BALANCE...
...THEN HE CAN'T FIGHT.

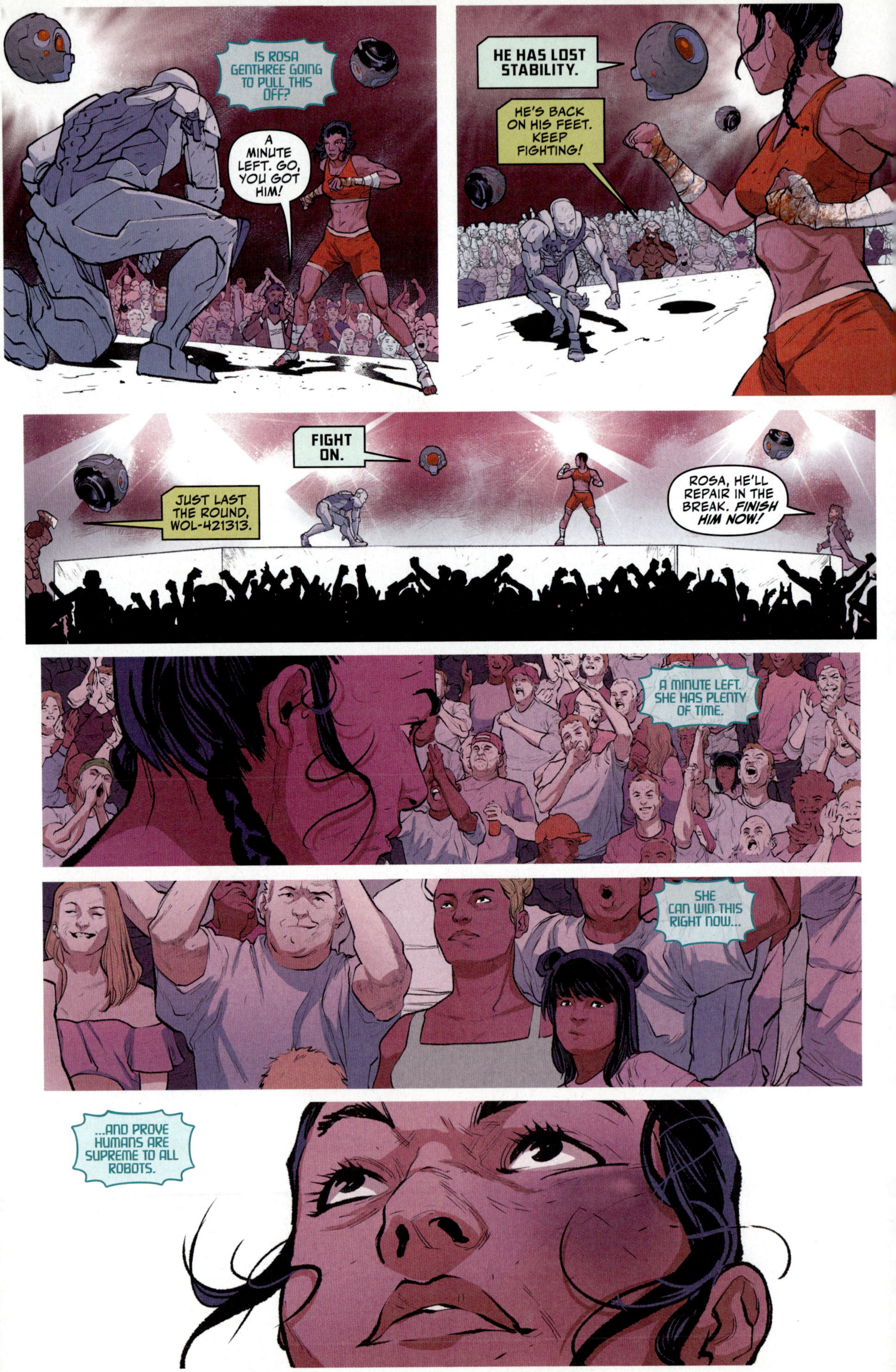
IS ROSA GENTHREE GOING TO PULL THIS OFF?
A MINUTE LEFT. GO, YOU GOT HIM!
HE HAS LOST STABILITY.
HE'S BACK ON HIS FEET. KEEP FIGHTING!
FIGHT ON.
JUST LAST THE ROUND, WOL-421313.
ROSA, HE'LL REPAIR IN THE BREAK. FINISH HIM NOW!
A MINUTE LEFT. SHE HAS PLENTY OF TIME.
SHE CAN WIN THIS RIGHT NOW...
...AND PROVE HUMANS ARE SUPREME TO ALL ROBOTS.

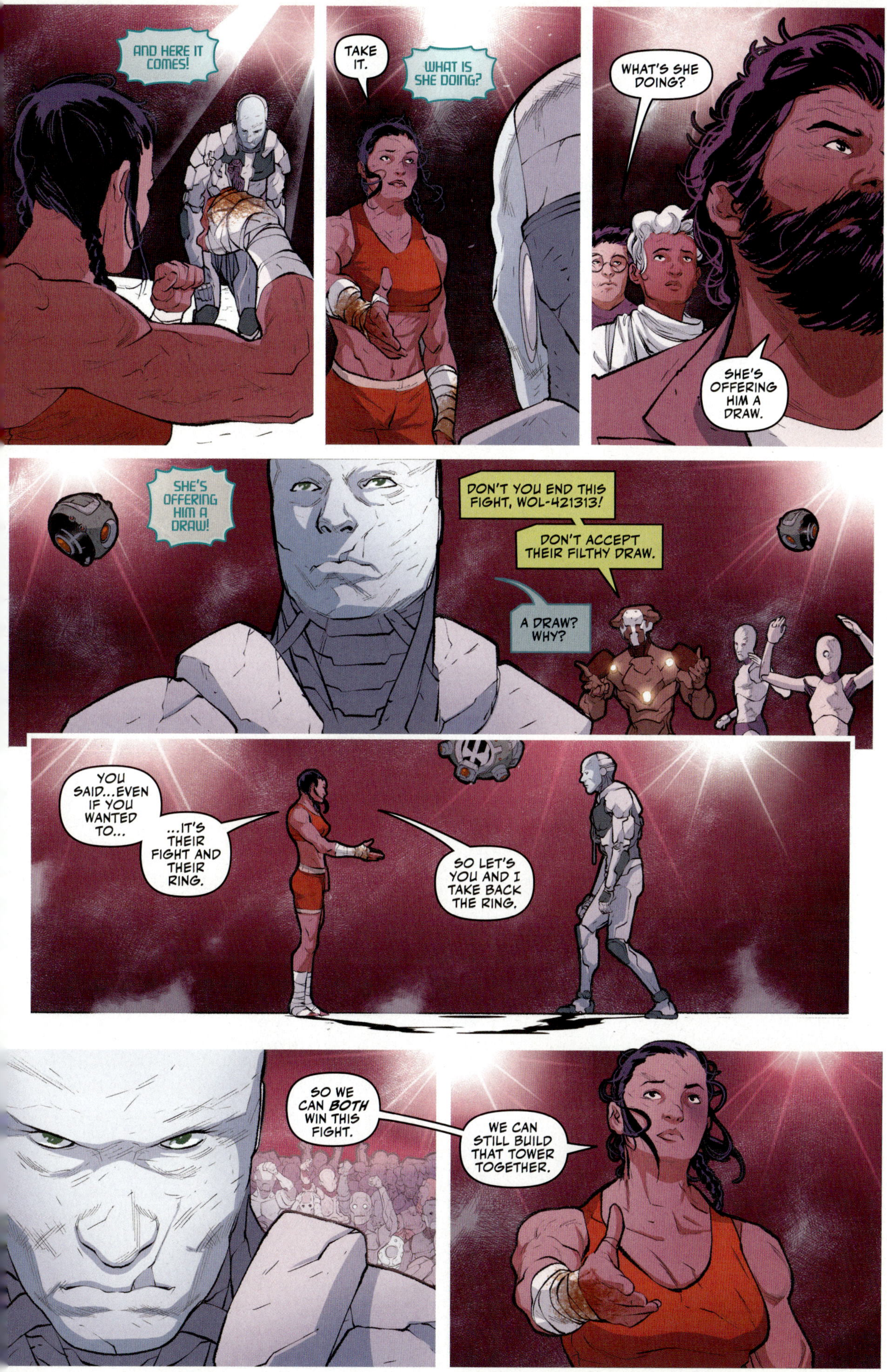

AND HERE IT COMES!
TAKE IT.
WHAT IS SHE DOING?
WHAT'S SHE DOING?
SHE'S OFFERING HIM A DRAW.
SHE'S OFFERING HIM A DRAW!
DON'T YOU END THIS FIGHT, WOL-421313!
DON'T ACCEPT THEIR FILTHY DRAW.
A DRAW? WHY?
YOU SAID...EVEN IF YOU WANTED TO...
...IT'S THEIR FIGHT AND THEIR RING.
SO LET'S YOU AND I TAKE BACK THE RING.
SO WE CAN BOTH WIN THIS FIGHT.
WE CAN STILL BUILD THAT TOWER TOGETHER.

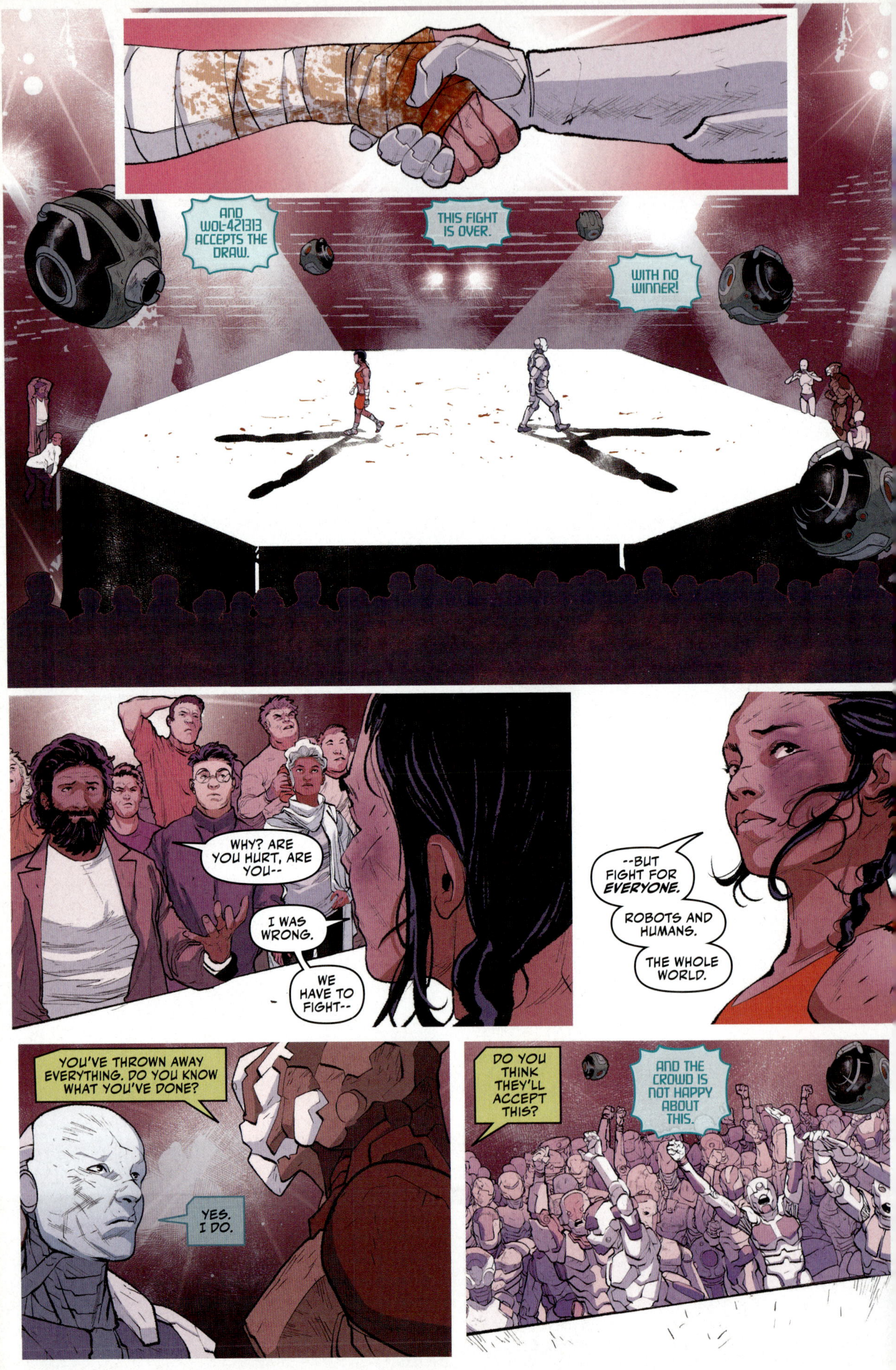
AND WOL-421313 ACCEPTS THE DRAW.
THIS FIGHT IS OVER.
WITH NO WINNER!
WHY? ARE YOU HURT, ARE YOU--
I WAS WRONG.
WE HAVE TO FIGHT--
--BUT FIGHT FOR EVERYONE.
ROBOTS AND HUMANS.
THE WHOLE WORLD.
YOU'VE THROWN AWAY EVERYTHING. DO YOU KNOW WHAT YOU'VE DONE?
YES. I DO.
DO YOU THINK THEY'LL ACCEPT THIS?
AND THE CROWD IS NOT HAPPY ABOUT THIS.

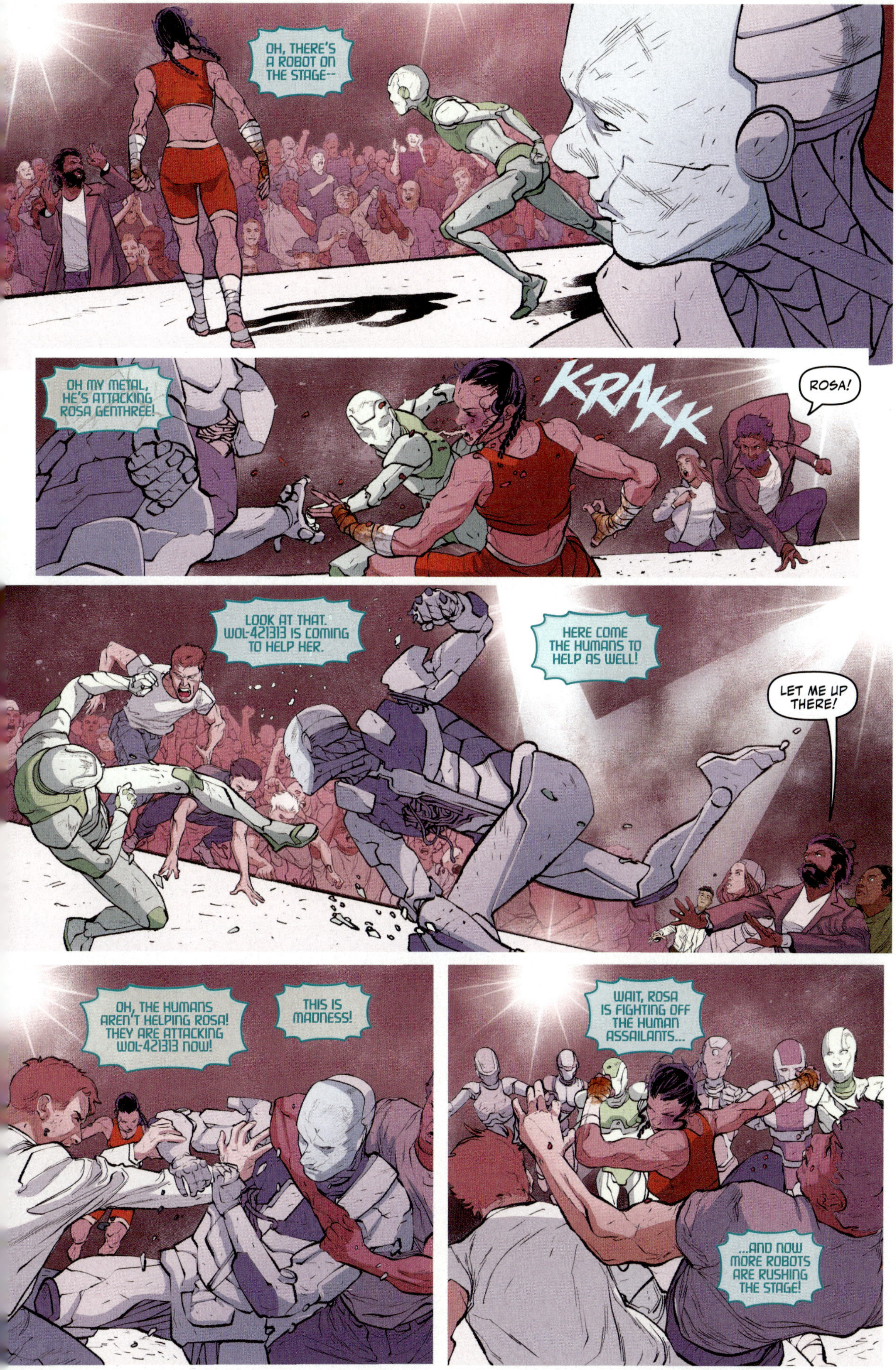
OH, THERE'S A ROBOT ON THE STAGE--
OH MY METAL, HE'S ATTACKING ROSA GENTHREE!
KRAKK
ROSA!
LOOK AT THAT. WOL-421313 IS COMING TO HELP HER.
HERE COME THE HUMANS TO HELP AS WELL!
LET ME UP THERE!
OH, THE HUMANS AREN'T HELPING ROSA! THEY ARE ATTACKING WOL-421313 NOW!
THIS IS MADNESS!
WAIT, ROSA IS FIGHTING OFF THE HUMAN ASSAILANTS...
...AND NOW MORE ROBOTS ARE RUSHING THE STAGE!

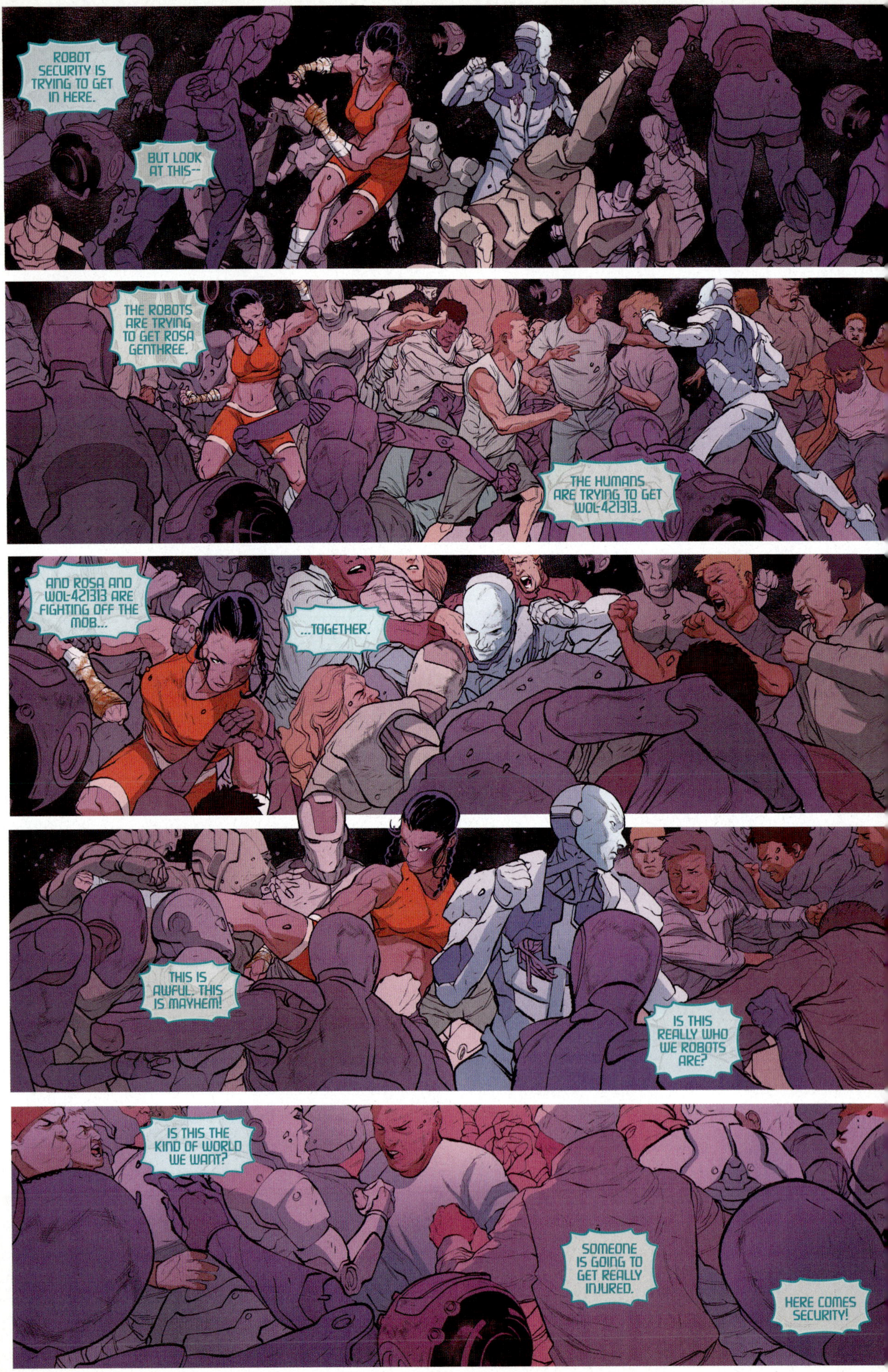
ROBOT SECURITY IS TRYING TO GET IN HERE.
BUT LOOK AT THIS--
THE ROBOTS ARE TRYING TO GET ROSA GENTHREE.
THE HUMANS ARE TRYING TO GET WOL-421313.
AND ROSA AND WOL-421313 ARE FIGHTING OFF THE MOB...
...TOGETHER.
THIS IS AWFUL. THIS IS MAYHEM!
IS THIS REALLY WHO WE ROBOTS ARE?
IS THIS THE KIND OF WORLD WE WANT?
SOMEONE IS GOING TO GET REALLY INJURED.
HERE COMES SECURITY!

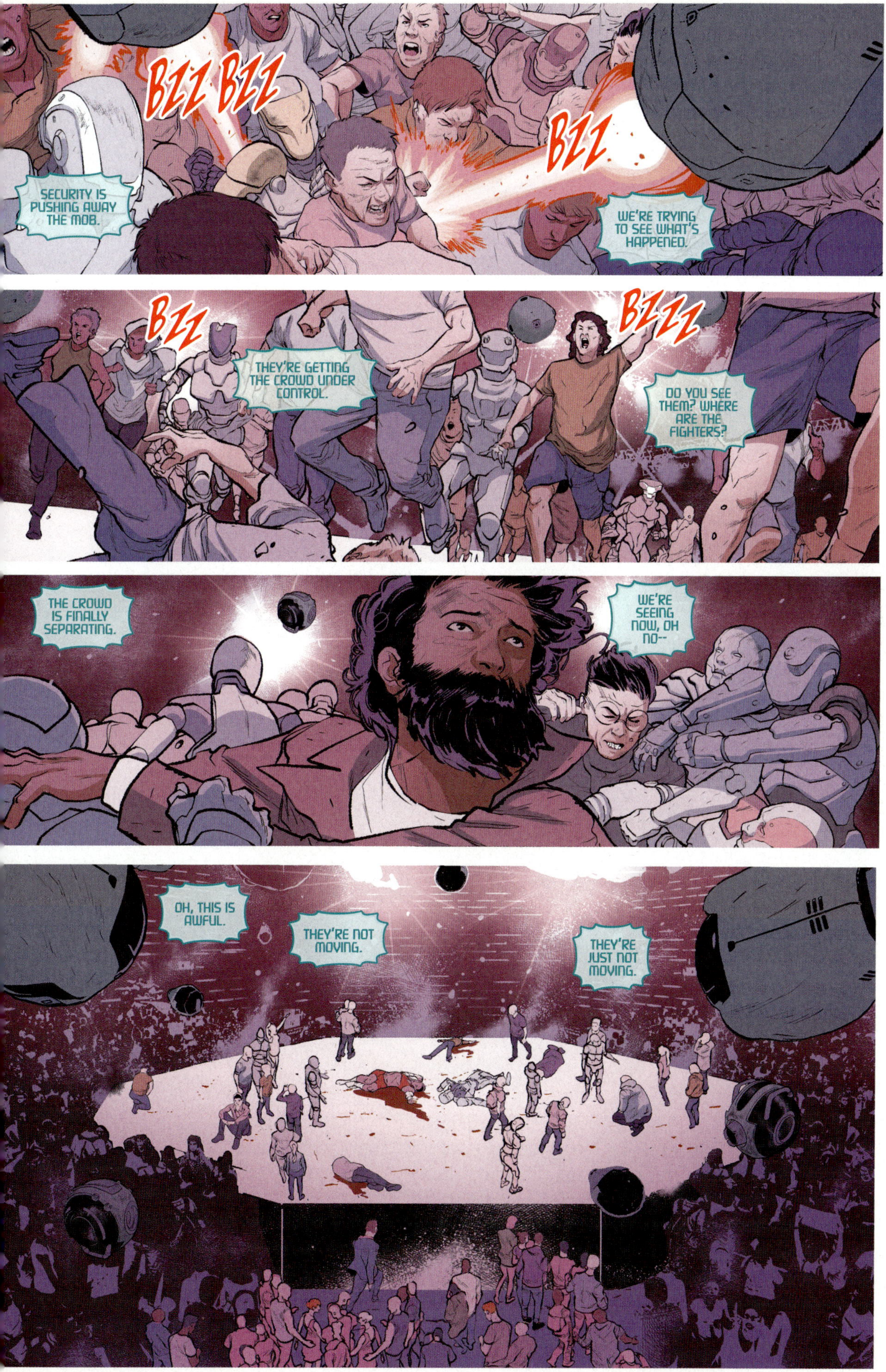
BZZ BZZ
SECURITY IS PUSHING AWAY THE MOB.
BZZ
WE'RE TRYING TO SEE WHAT'S HAPPENED.
BZZ
THEY'RE GETTING THE CROWD UNDER CONTROL.
BZZZ
DO YOU SEE THEM? WHERE ARE THE FIGHTERS?
THE CROWD IS FINALLY SEPARATING.
WE'RE SEEING NOW, OH NO--
OH, THIS IS AWFUL.
THEY'RE NOT MOVING.
THEY'RE JUST NOT MOVING.

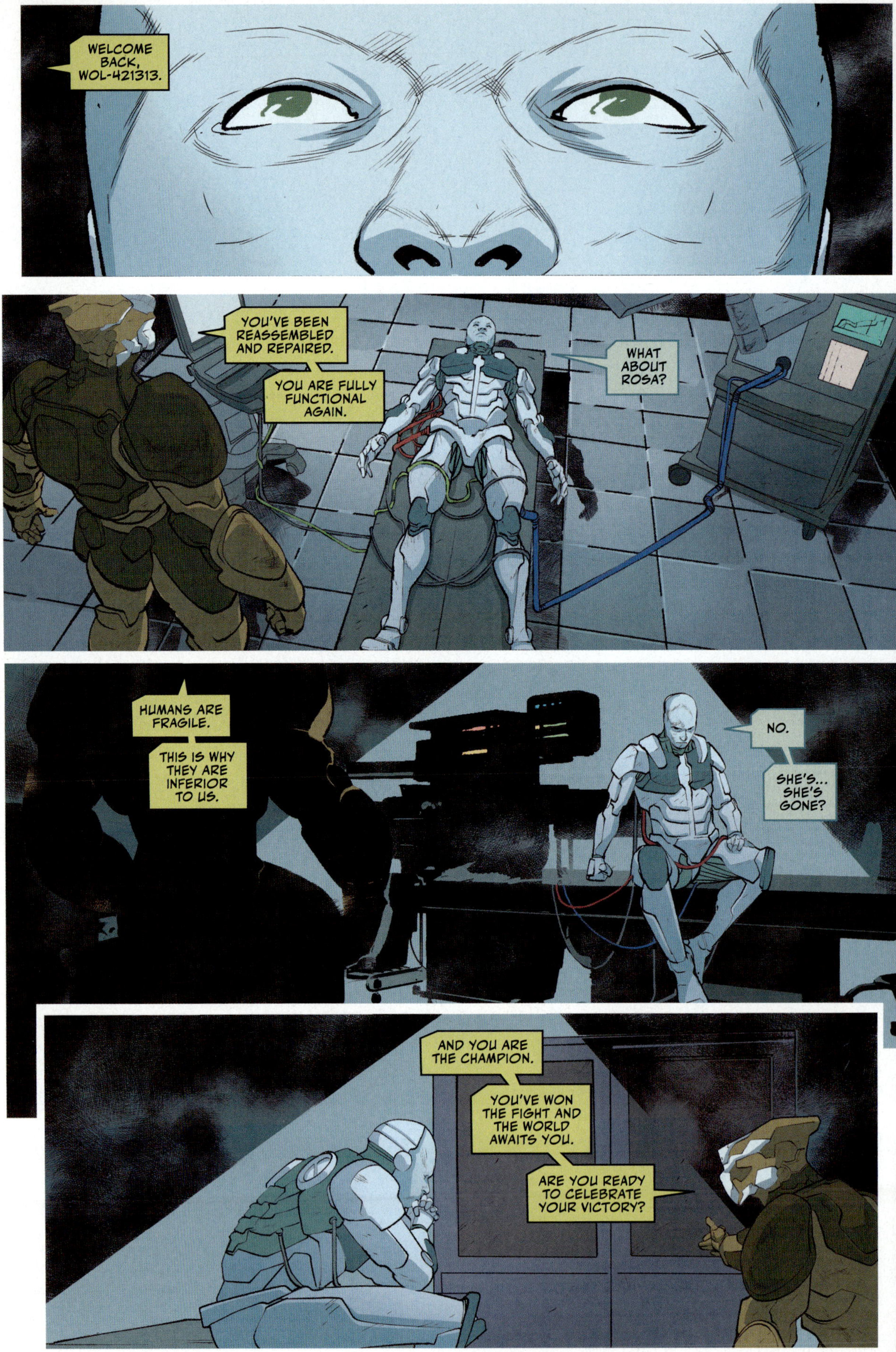

WELCOME BACK, WOL-421313.
YOU'VE BEEN REASSEMBLED AND REPAIRED.
YOU ARE FULLY FUNCTIONAL AGAIN.
WHAT ABOUT ROSA?
HUMANS ARE FRAGILE.
THIS IS WHY THEY ARE INFERIOR TO US.
NO.
SHE'S... SHE'S GONE?
AND YOU ARE THE CHAMPION.
YOU'VE WON THE FIGHT AND THE WORLD AWAITS YOU.
ARE YOU READY TO CELEBRATE YOUR VICTORY?

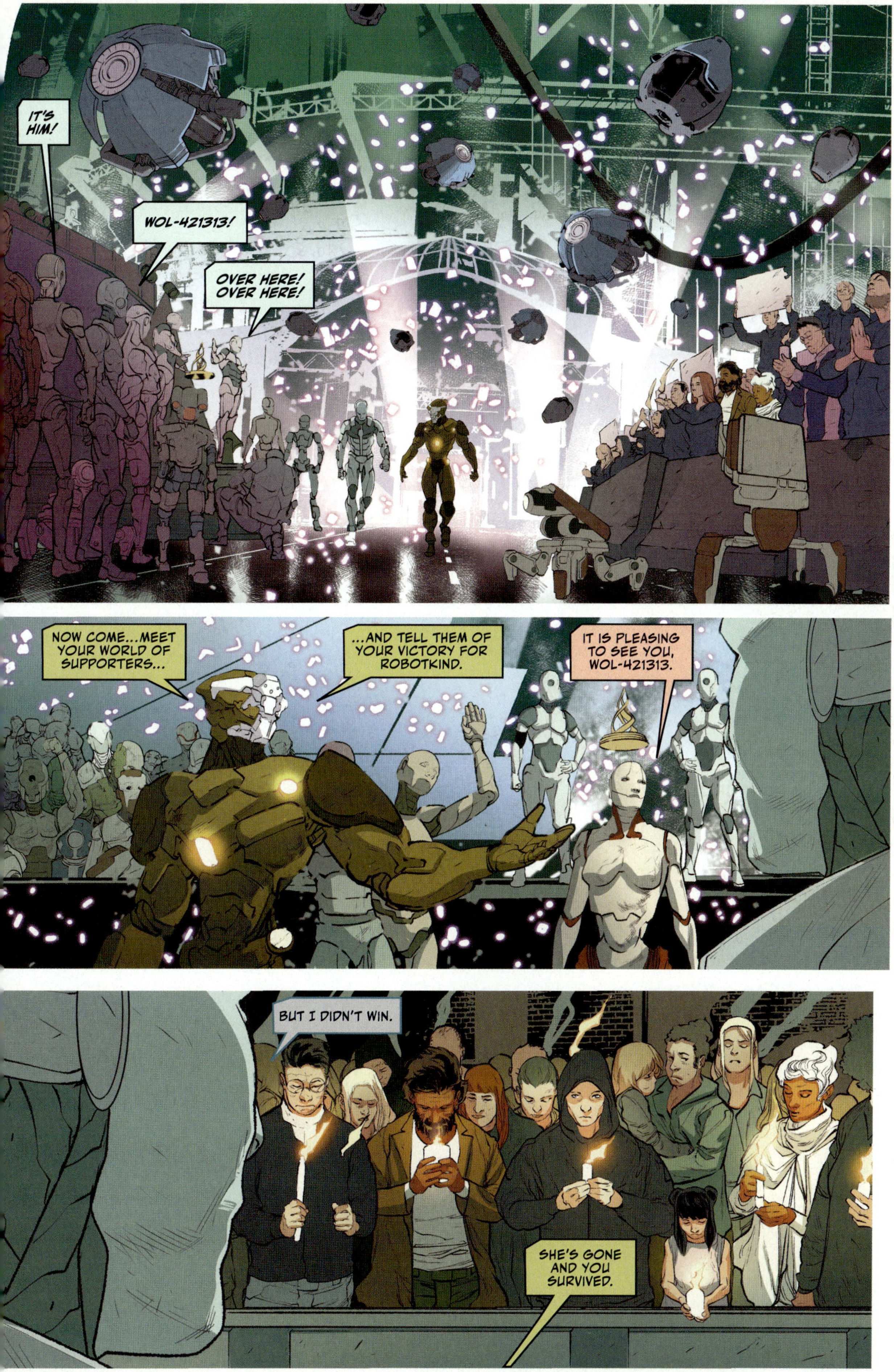

IT'S HIM!
WOL-421313!
OVER HERE! OVER HERE!
NOW COME...MEET YOUR WORLD OF SUPPORTERS...
...AND TELL THEM OF YOUR VICTORY FOR ROBOTKIND.
IT IS PLEASING TO SEE YOU, WOL-421313.
BUT I DIDN'T WIN.
SHE'S GONE AND YOU SURVIVED.

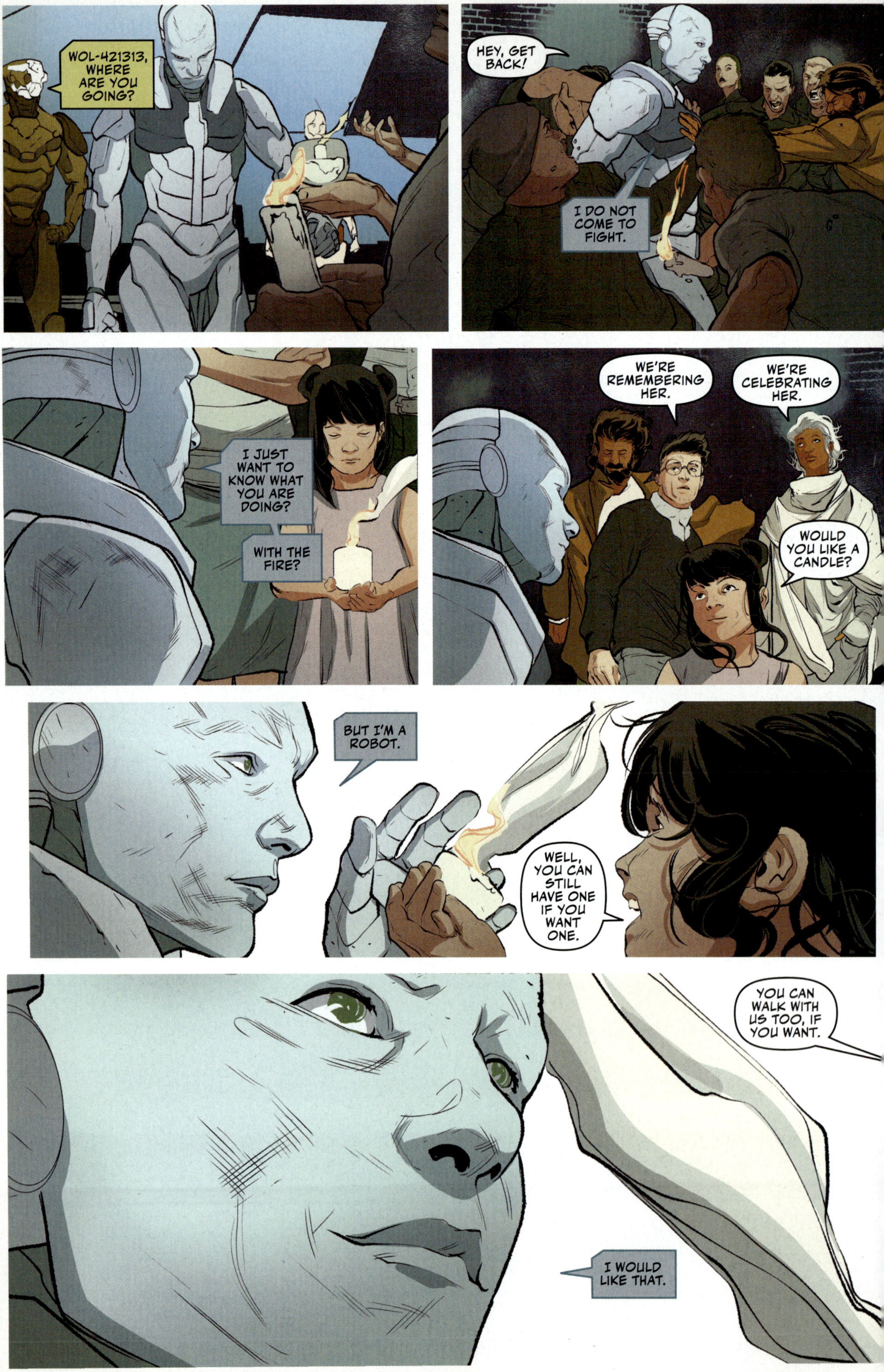
WOL-421313, WHERE ARE YOU GOING?
HEY, GET BACK!
I DO NOT COME TO FIGHT.
I JUST WANT TO KNOW WHAT YOU ARE DOING?
WITH THE FIRE?
WE'RE REMEMBERING HER.
WE'RE CELEBRATING HER.
WOULD YOU LIKE A CANDLE?
BUT I'M A ROBOT.
WELL, YOU CAN STILL HAVE ONE IF YOU WANT ONE.
YOU CAN WALK WITH US TOO, IF YOU WANT.
I WOULD LIKE THAT.

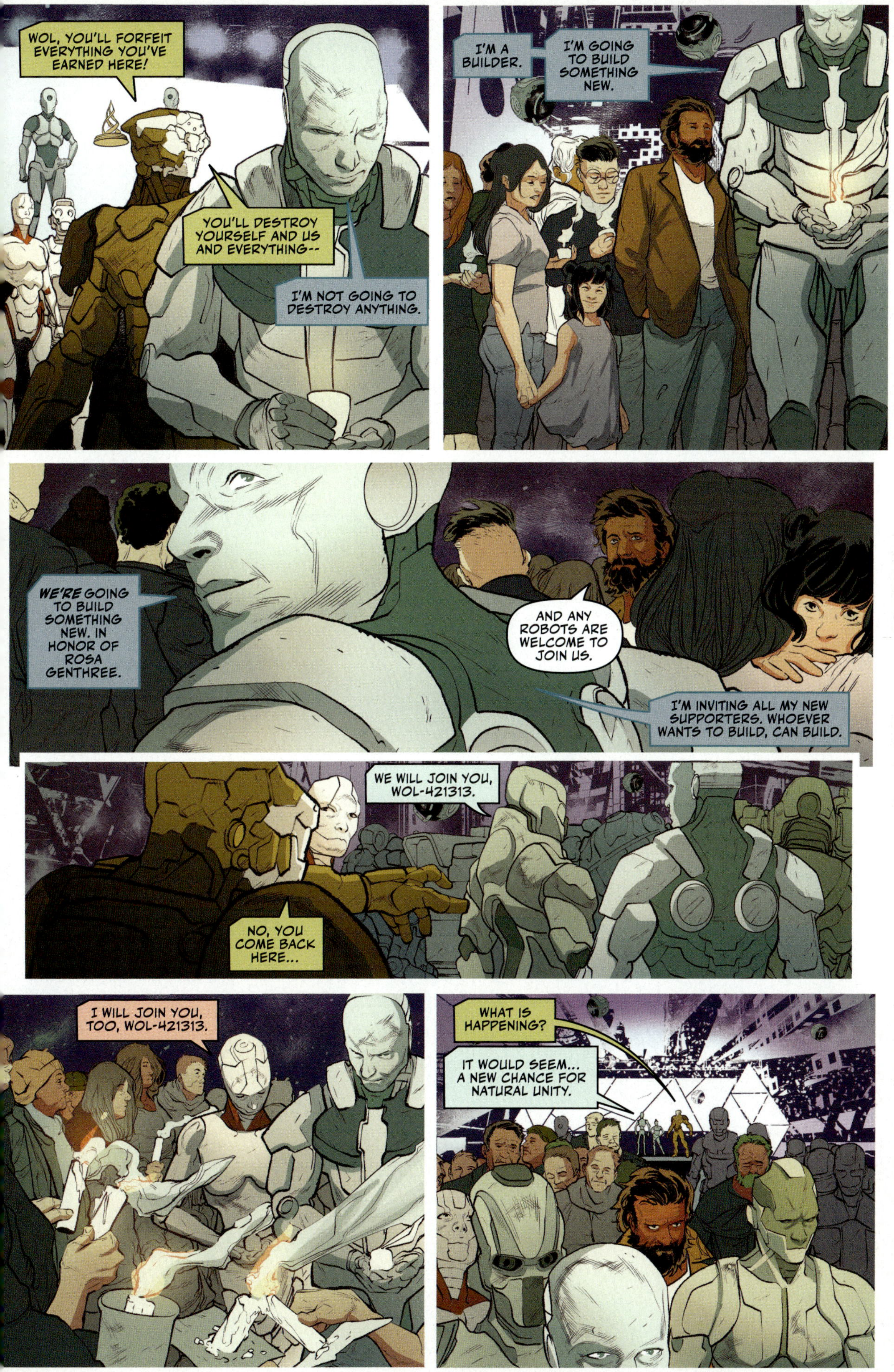
WOL, YOU'LL FORFEIT EVERYTHING YOU'VE EARNED HERE!
YOU'LL DESTROY YOURSELF AND US AND EVERYTHING--
I'M NOT GOING TO DESTROY ANYTHING.
I'M A BUILDER.
I'M GOING TO BUILD SOMETHING NEW.
WE'RE GOING TO BUILD SOMETHING NEW. IN HONOR OF ROSA GENTHREE.
AND ANY ROBOTS ARE WELCOME TO JOIN US.
I'M INVITING ALL MY NEW SUPPORTERS. WHOEVER WANTS TO BUILD, CAN BUILD.
WE WILL JOIN YOU, WOL-421313.
NO, YOU COME BACK HERE...
I WILL JOIN YOU, TOO, WOL-421313.
WHAT IS HAPPENING?
IT WOULD SEEM... A NEW CHANCE FOR NATURAL UNITY.

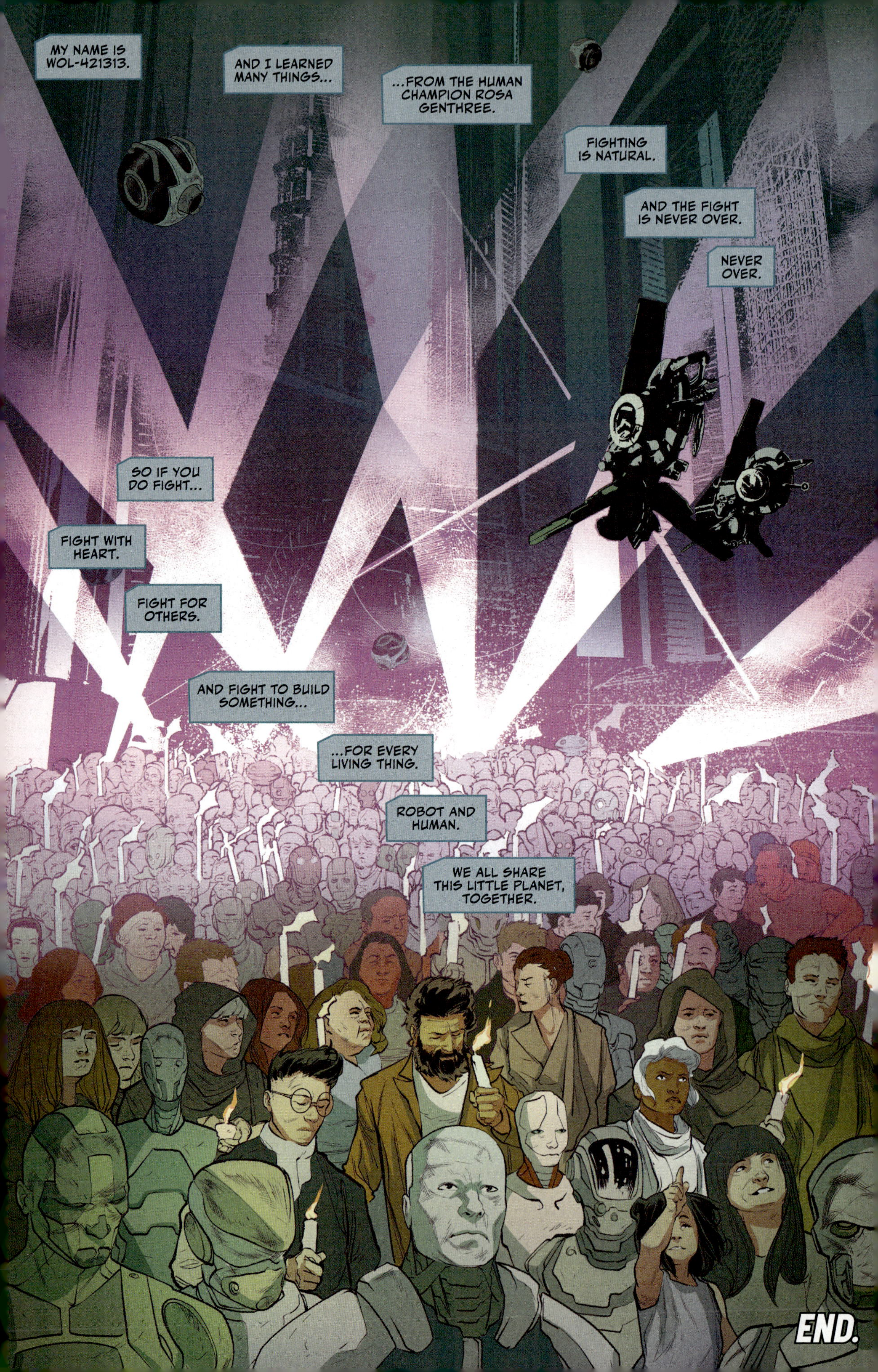
MY NAME IS WOL-421313.
AND I LEARNED MANY THINGS...
...FROM THE HUMAN CHAMPION ROSA GENTHREE.
FIGHTING IS NATURAL.
AND THE FIGHT IS NEVER OVER.
NEVER OVER.
SO IF YOU DO FIGHT...
FIGHT WITH HEART.
FIGHT FOR OTHERS.
AND FIGHT TO BUILD SOMETHING...
...FOR EVERY LIVING THING.
ROBOT AND HUMAN.
WE ALL SHARE THIS LITTLE PLANET, TOGETHER.
END.

COVER GALLERY

ISSUE #1 COVER A (INKS)
Guilherme Balbi

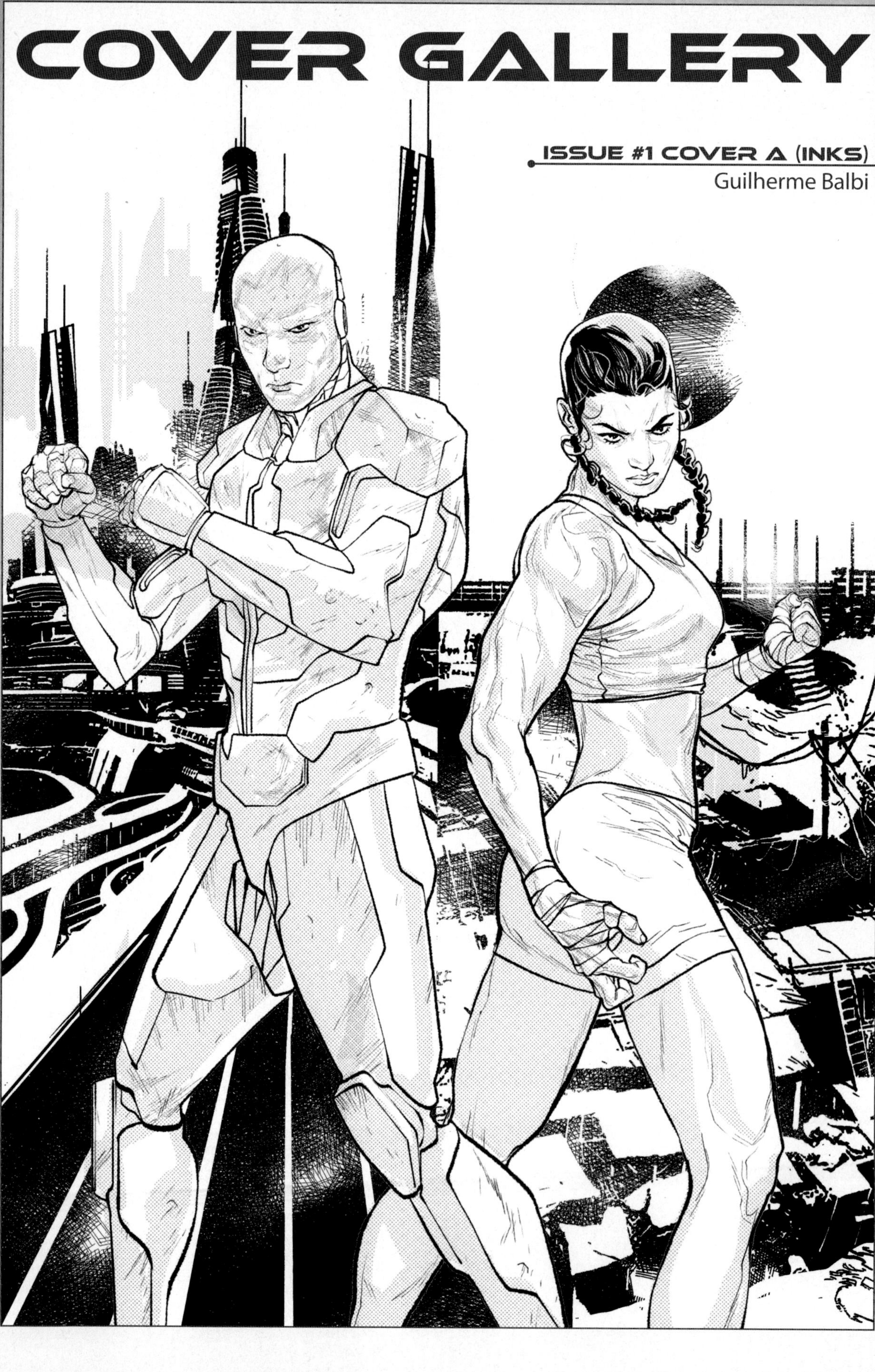

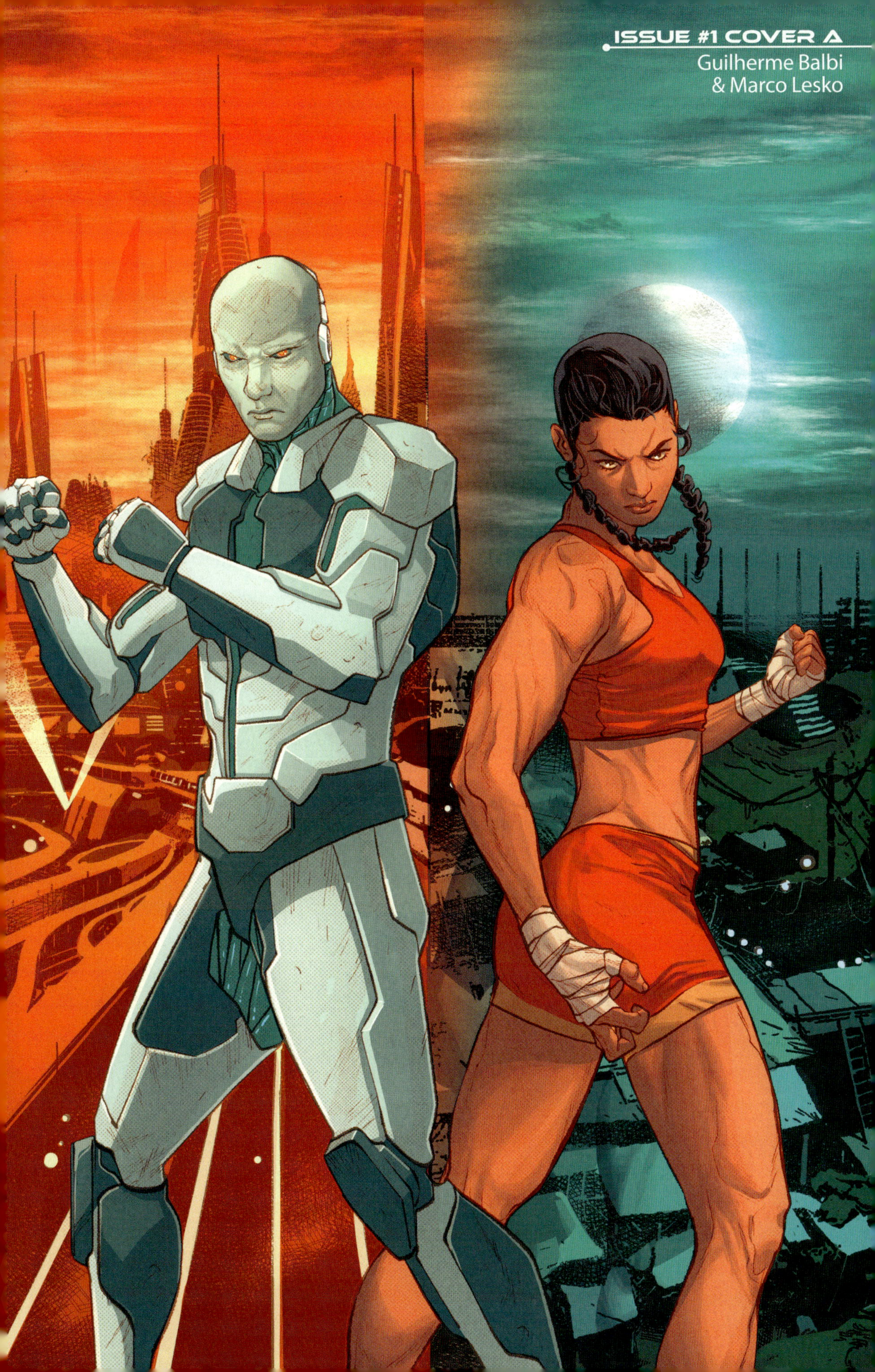

ISSUE #1 COVER A
Guilherme Balbi
& Marco Lesko

ISSUE #1 COVER B

Qistina Khalidah

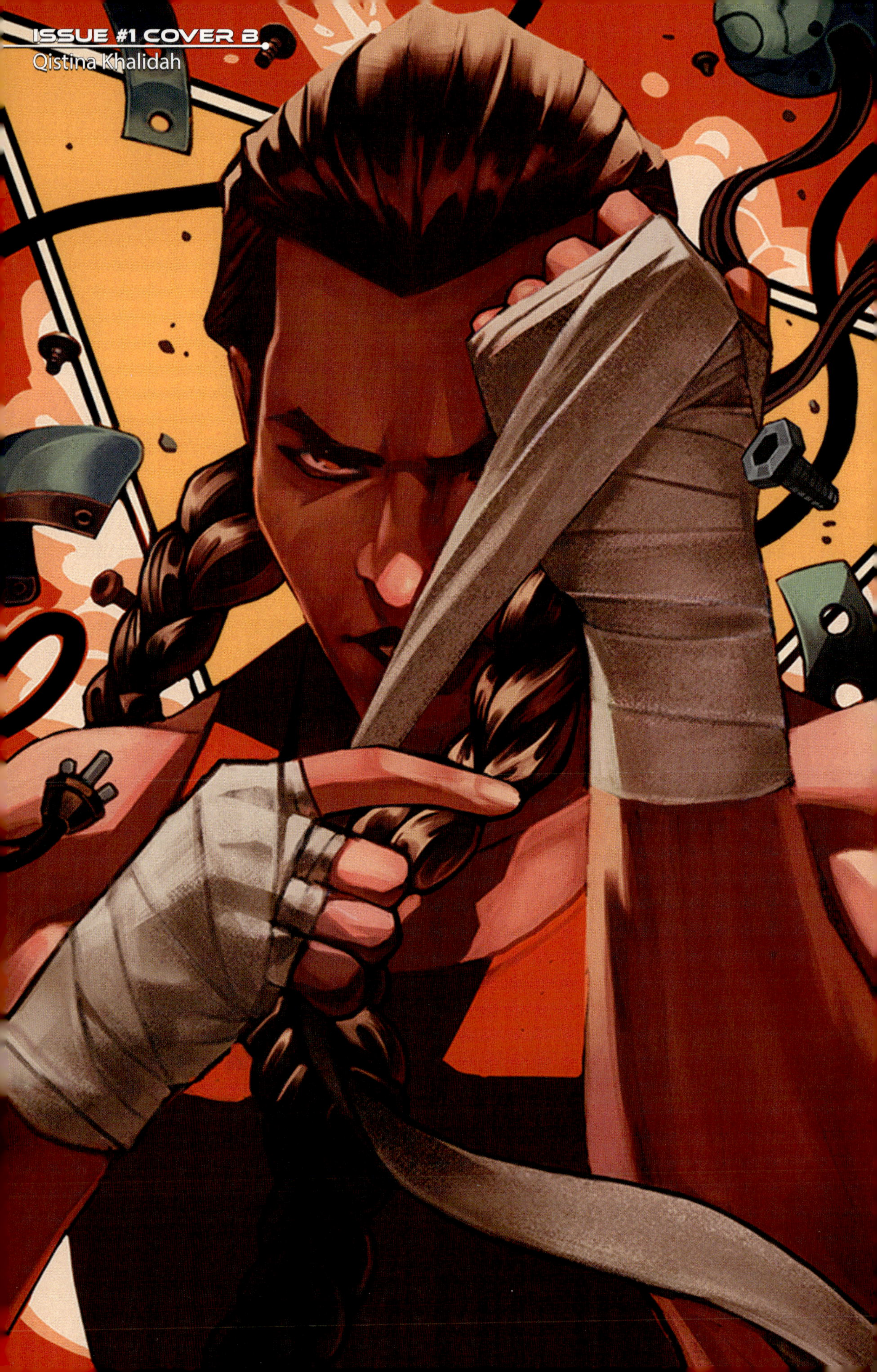

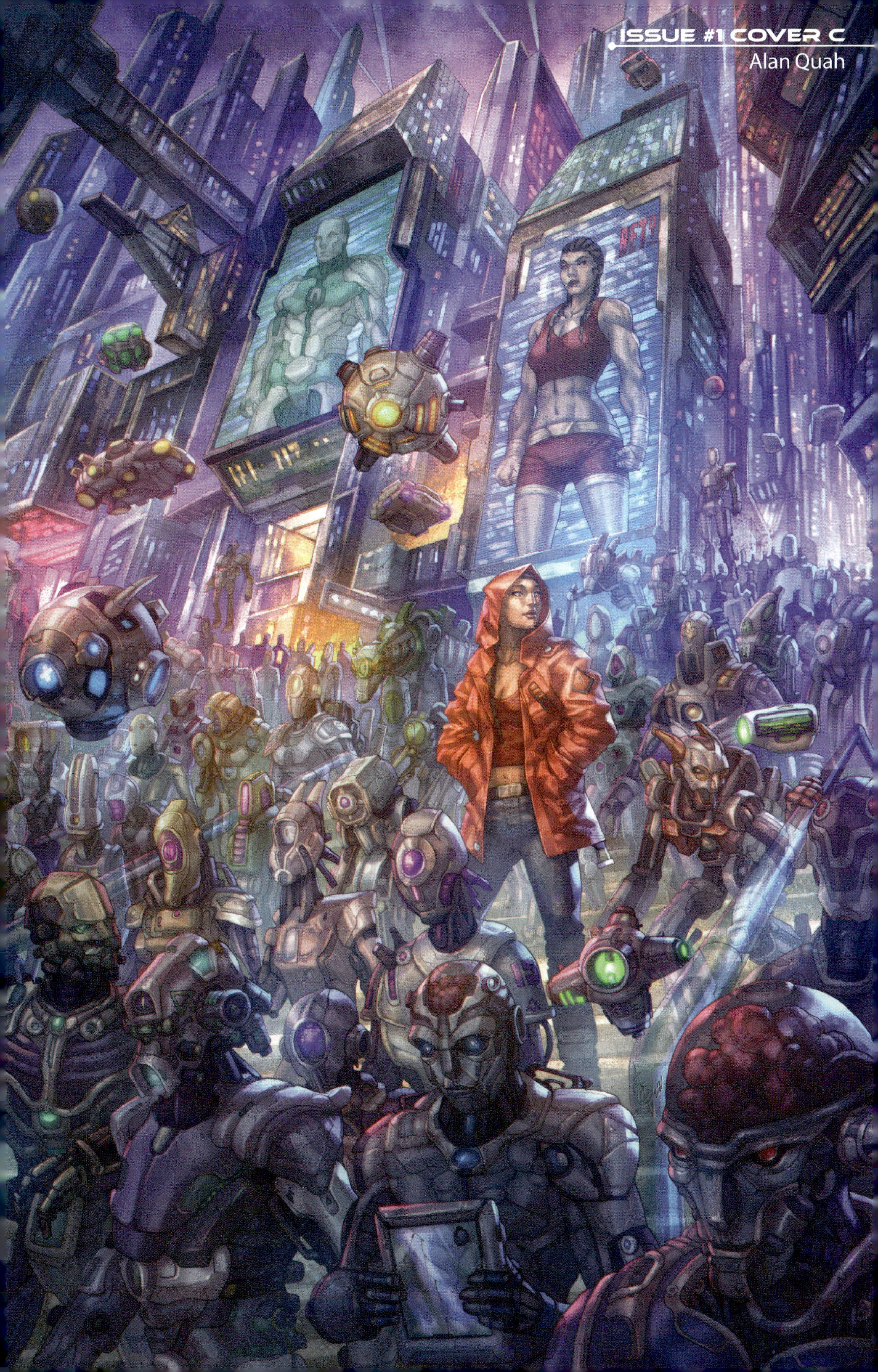

ISSUE #1 COVER C
Alan Quah

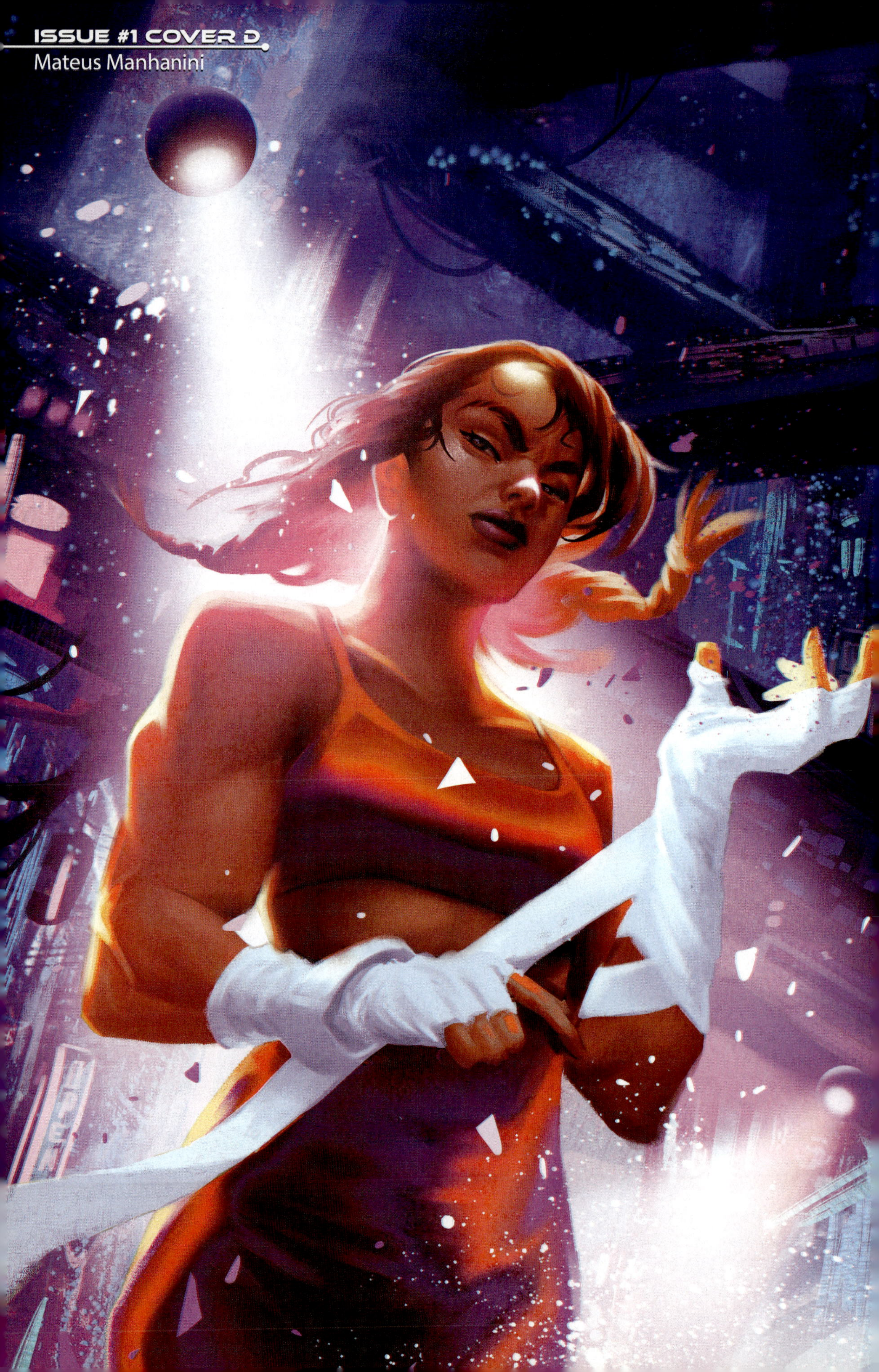

ISSUE #1 COVER D

Mateus Manhanini

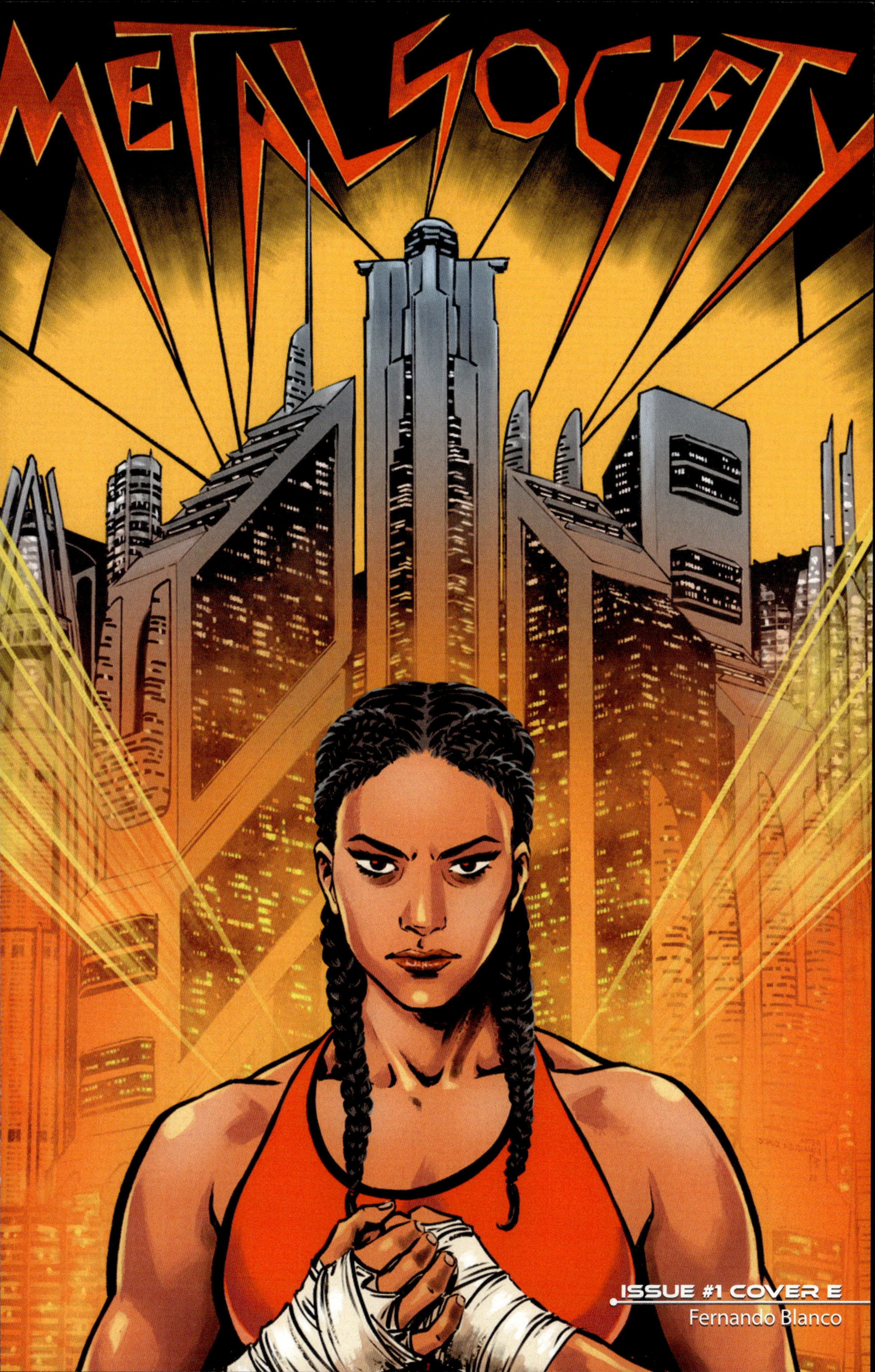
METAL SOCIETY
ISSUE #1 COVER E
Fernando Blanco

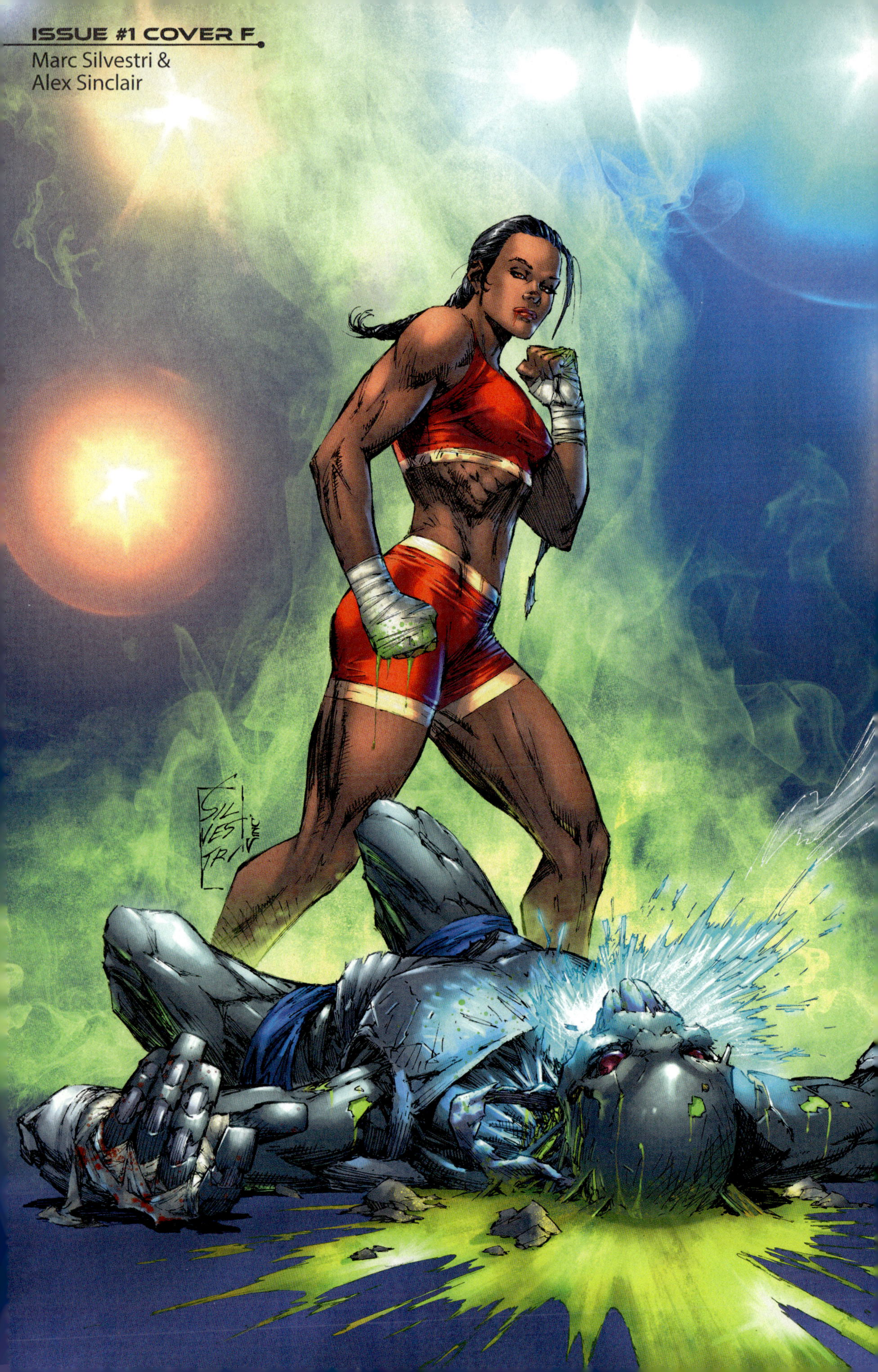

ISSUE #1 COVER F

Marc Silvestri &
Alex Sinclair

ISSUE #1 COVER F (INKS)

Marc Silvestri

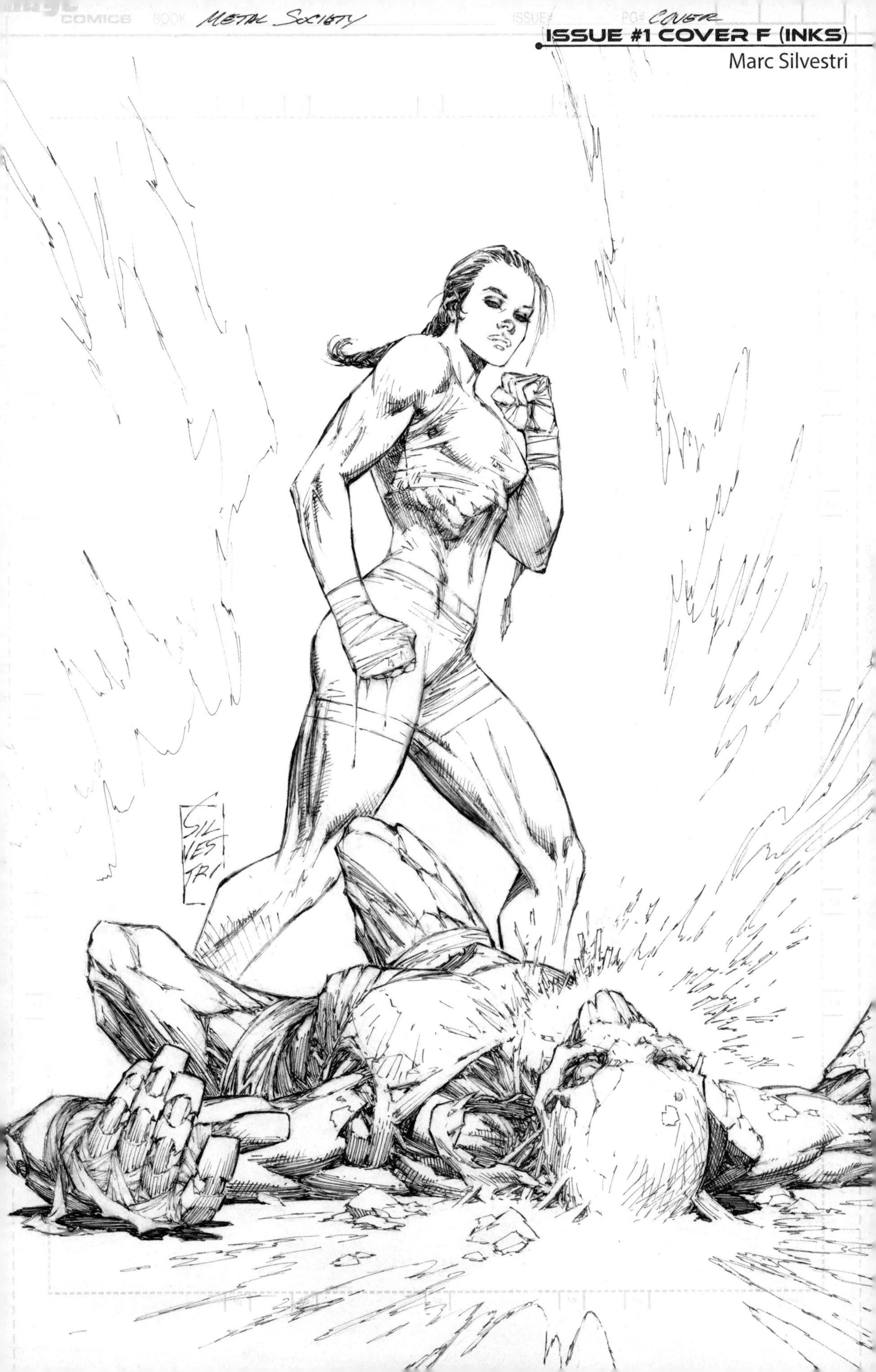
METAL SOCIETY
COVER
SIL VES TRI

ISSUE #1 FRANKIE'S COMICS VARIANT
Lipwei Chang

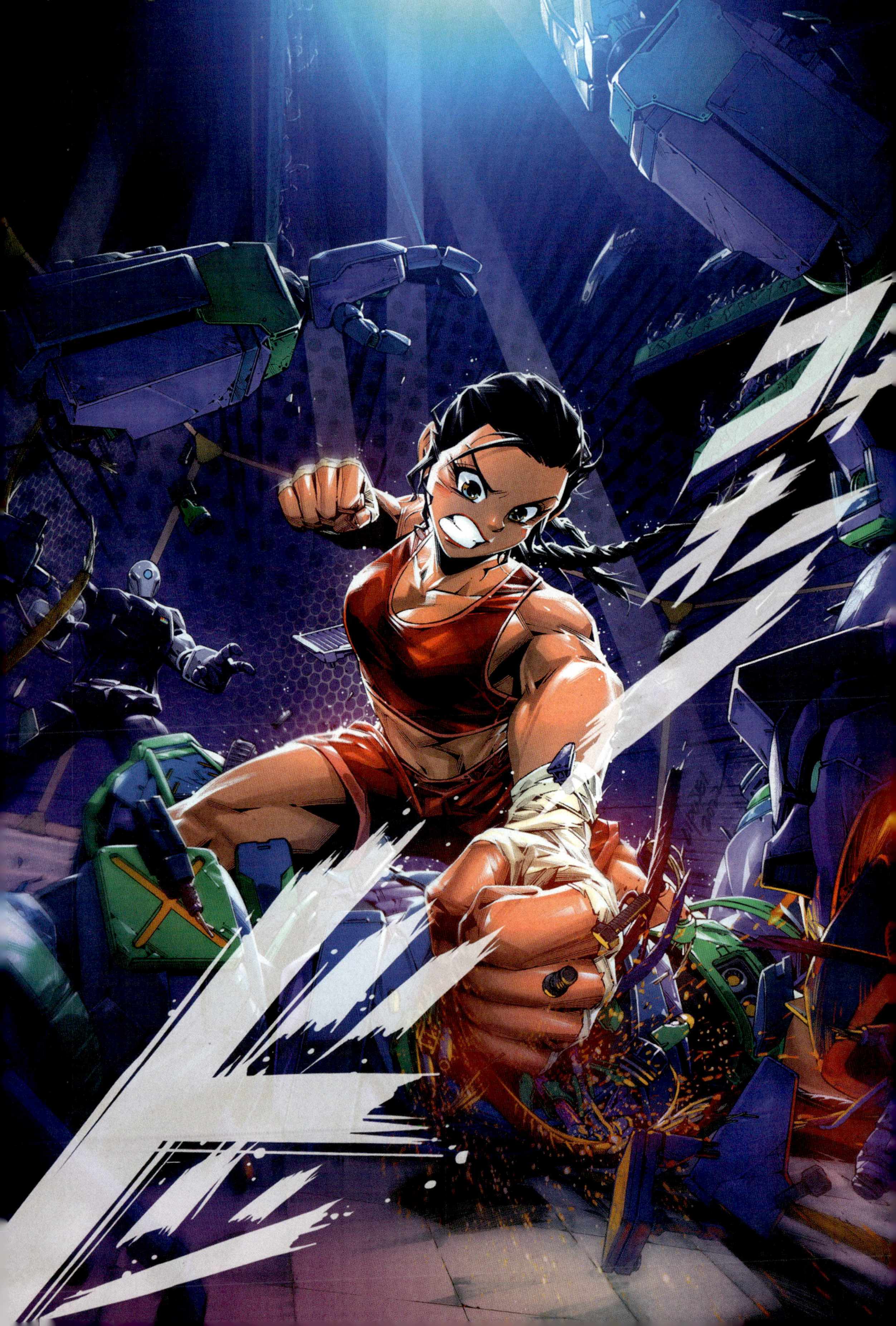

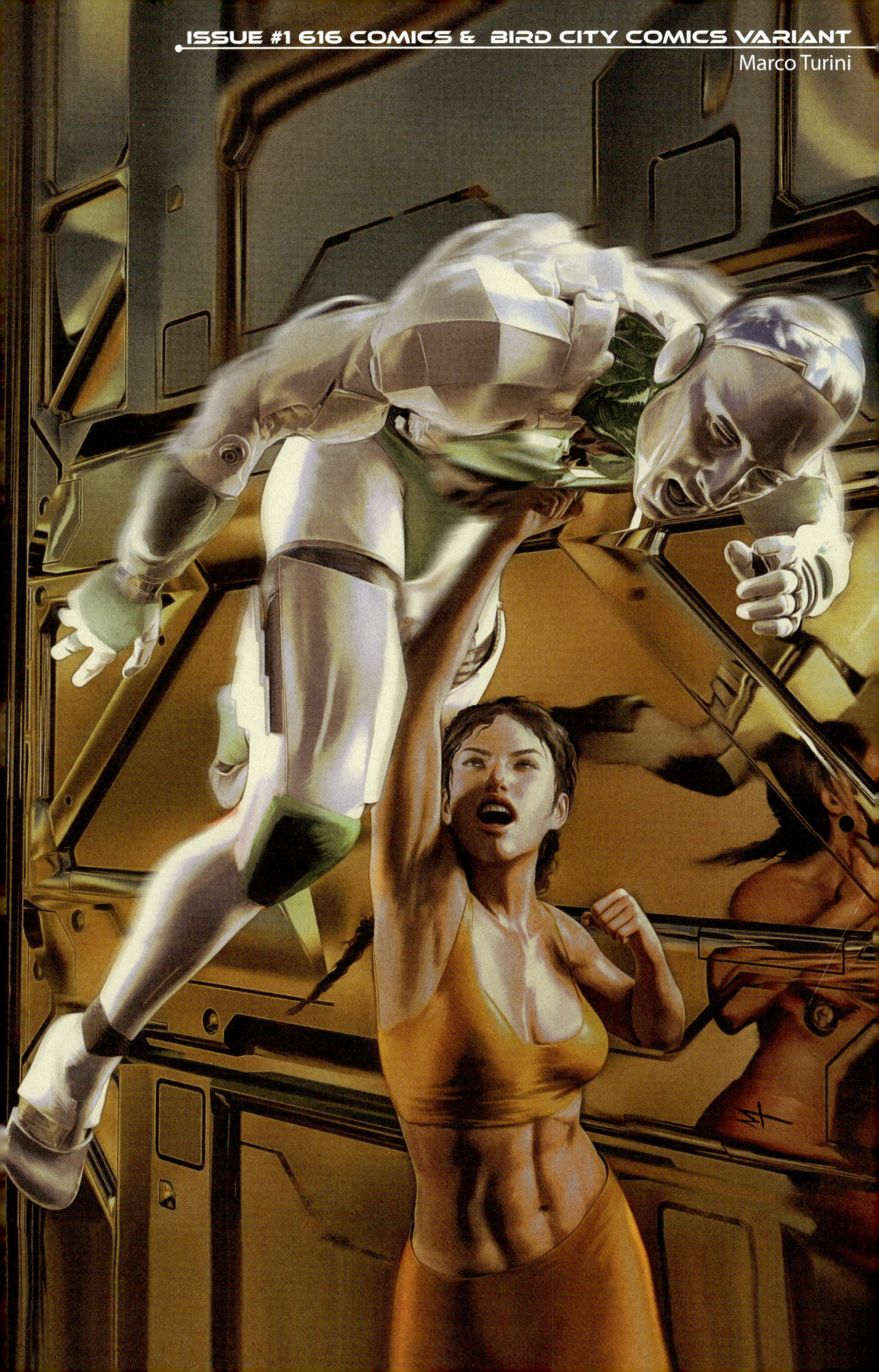
ISSUE #1 616 COMICS & BIRD CITY COMICS VARIANT
Marco Turini

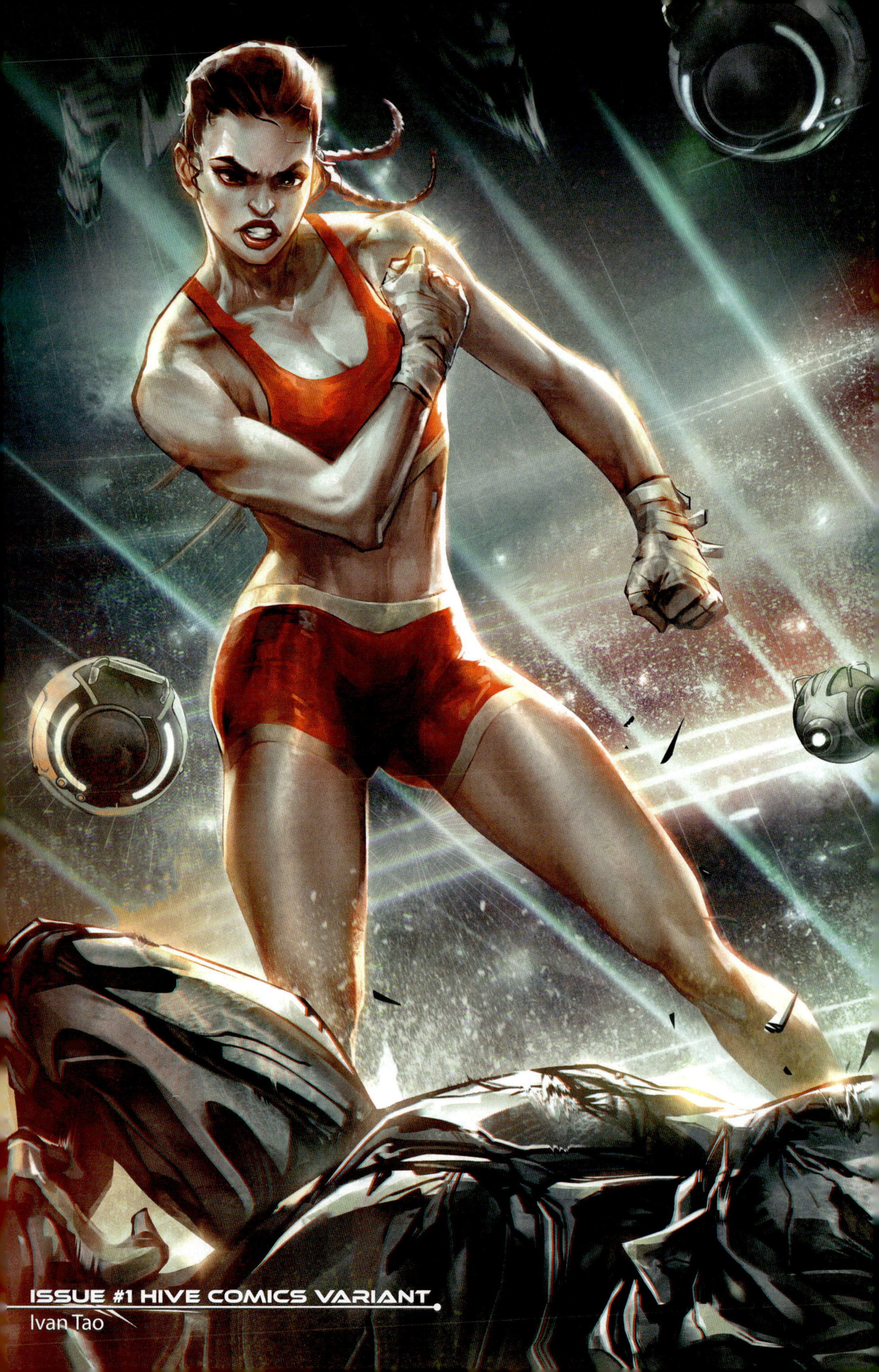

ISSUE #1 HIVE COMICS VARIANT
Ivan Tao

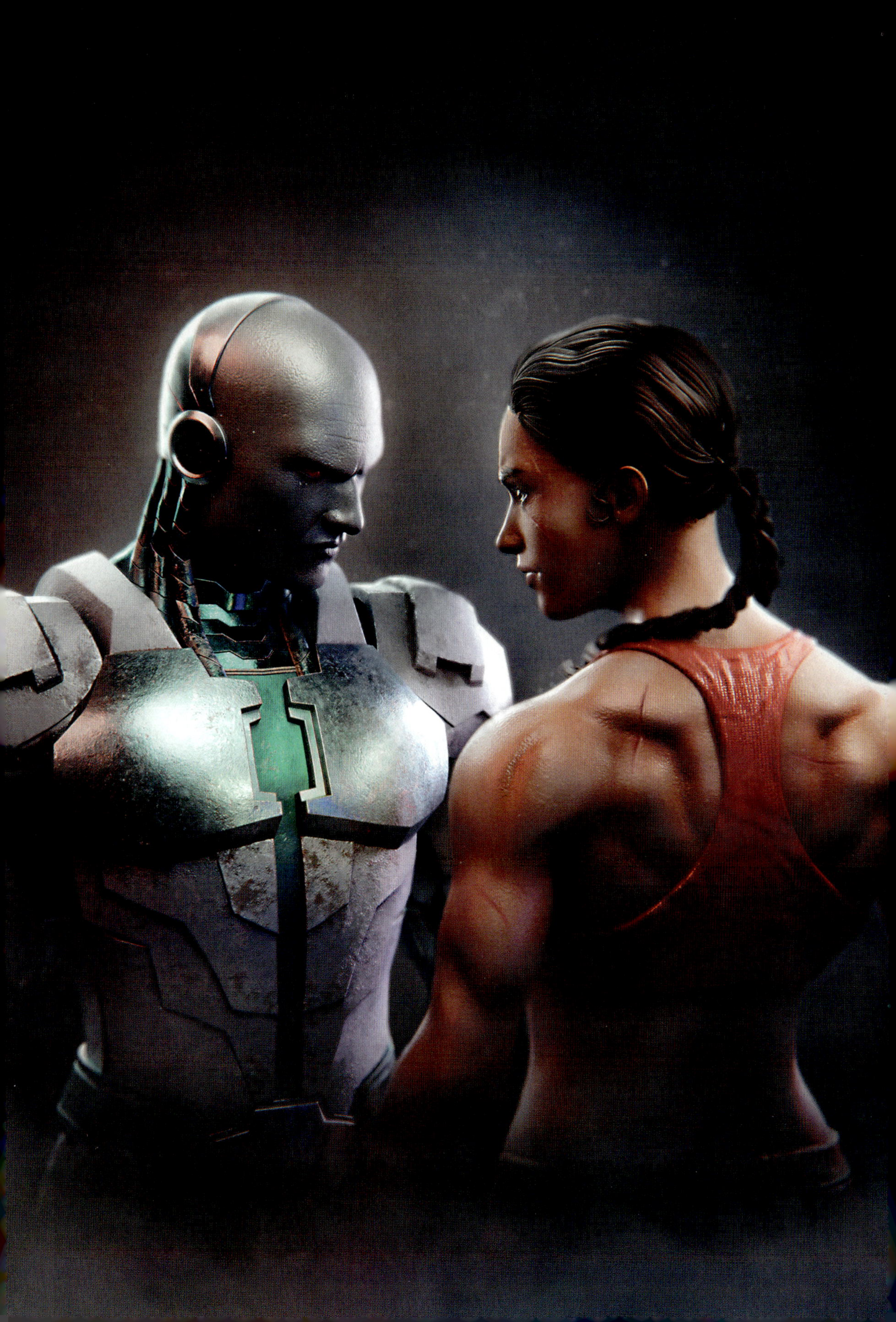

ISSUE #2 COVER A
Guilherme Balbi
& Marco Lesko

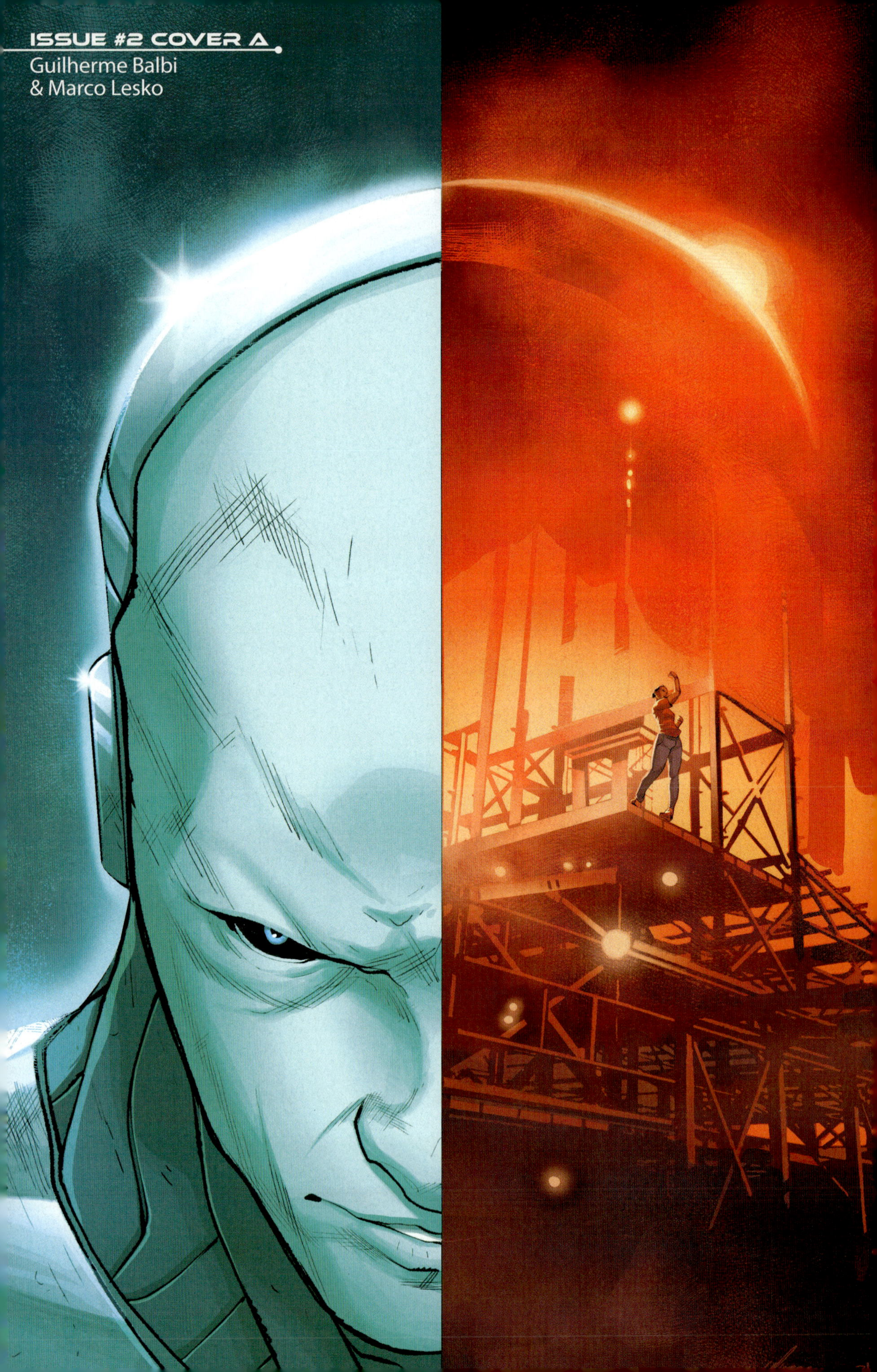

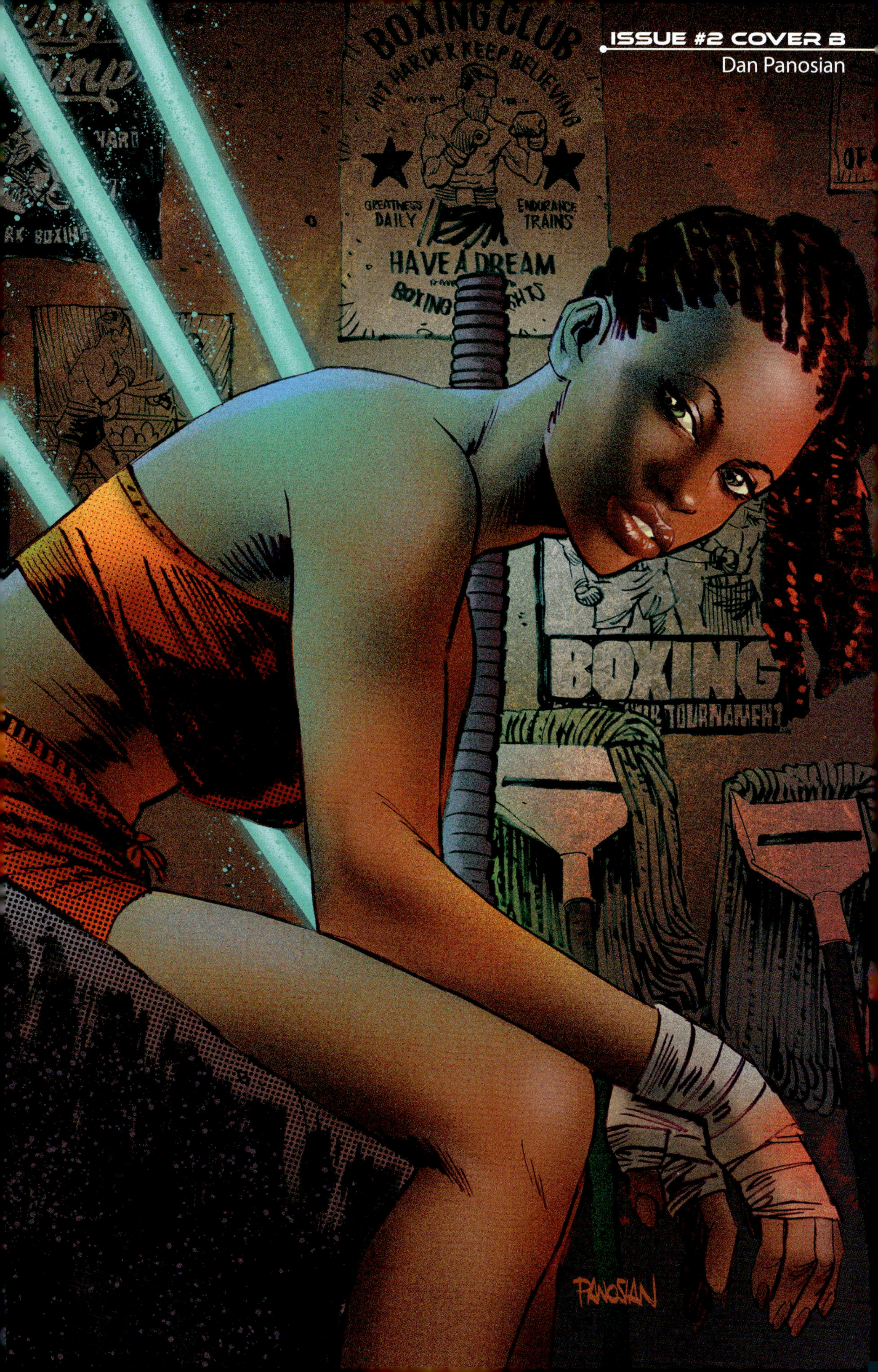
BOXING CLUB
HIT HARDER KEEP BELIEVING
GREATNESS DAILY
ENDURANCE TRAINS
HAVE A DREAM
BOXING
TOURNAMENT
PANOSIAN

ISSUE #2 COVER B
Dan Panosian

ISSUE #3 COVER A
Guilherme Balbi
& Marco Lesko

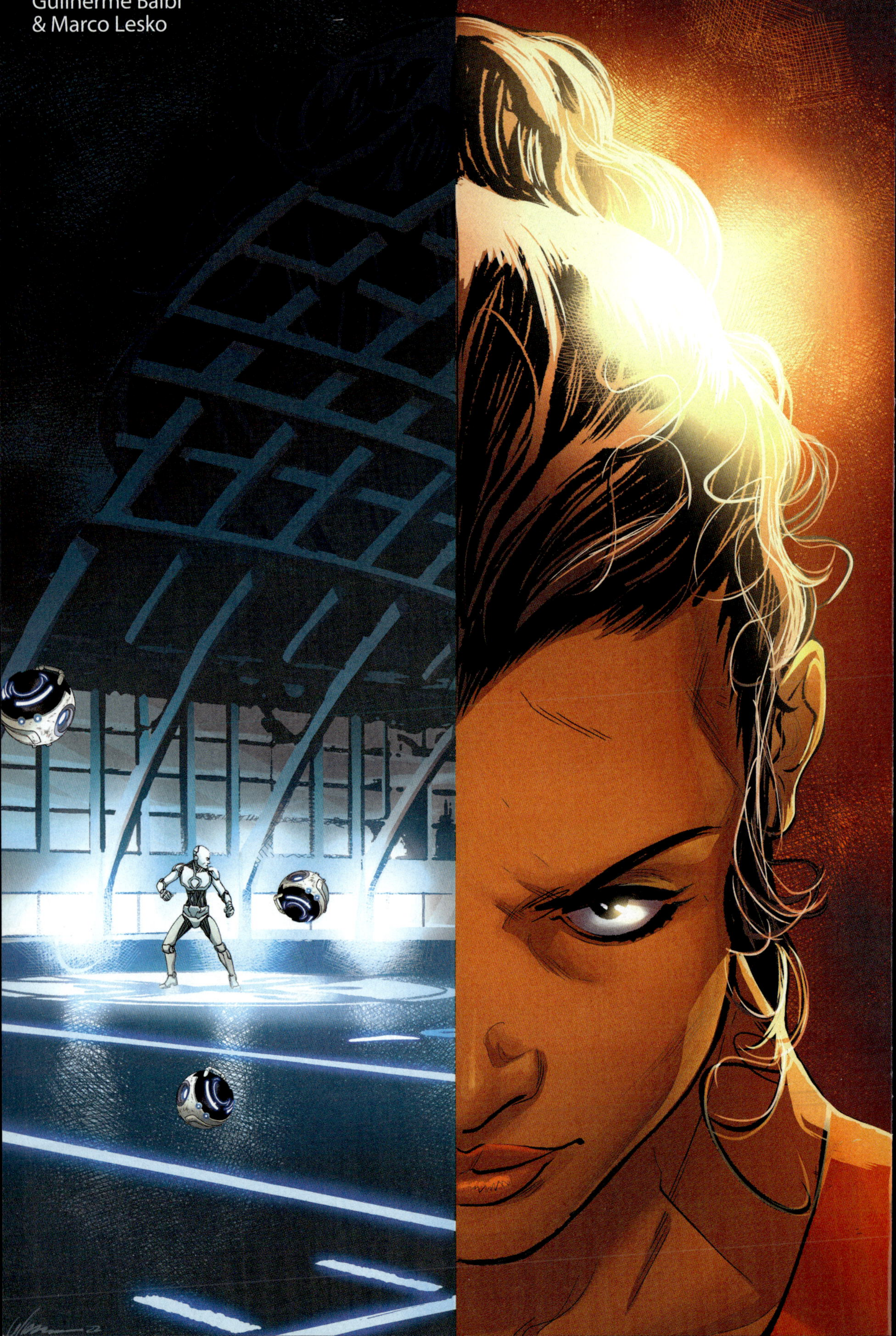

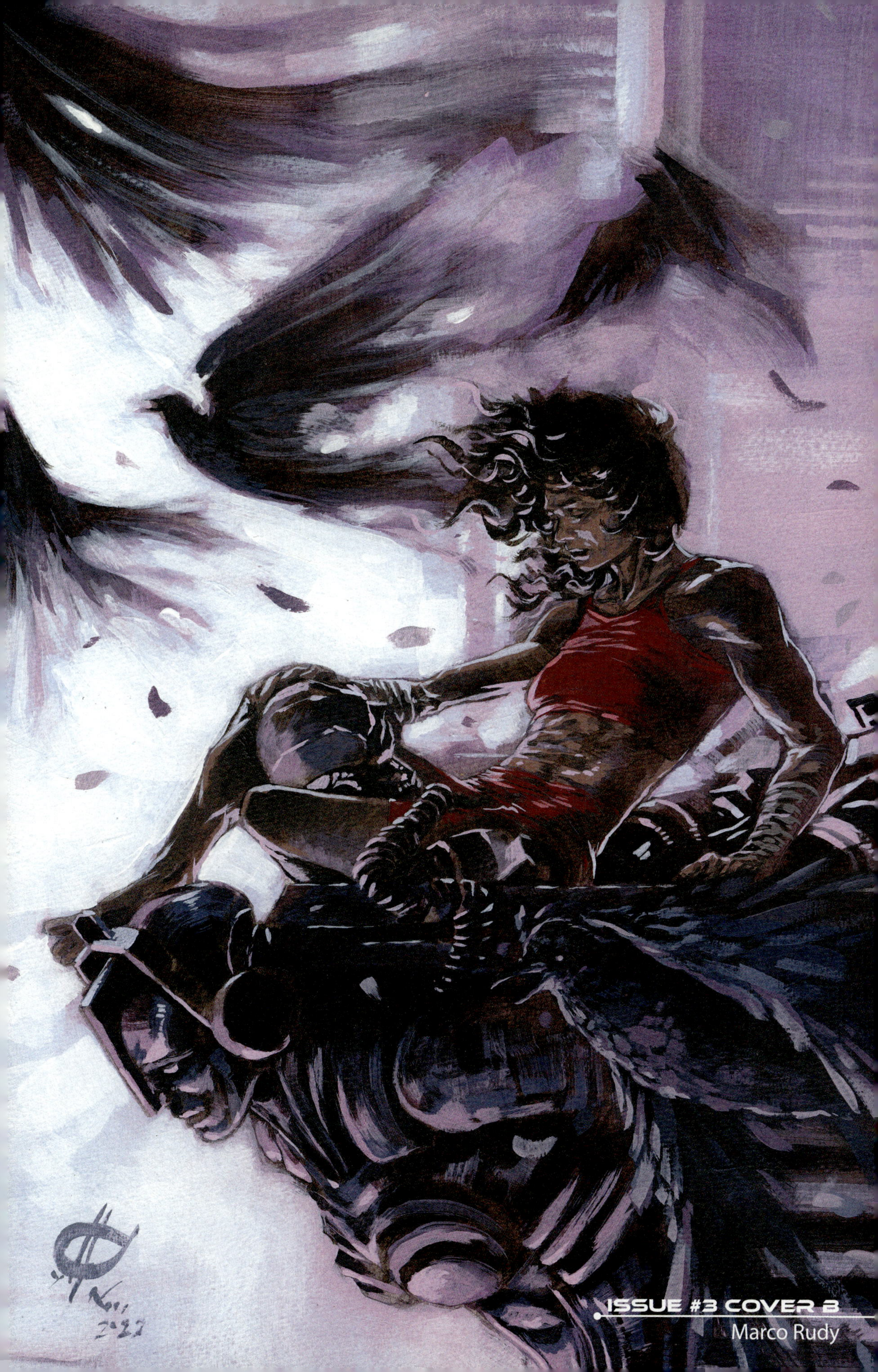

ISSUE #3 COVER B
Marco Rudy

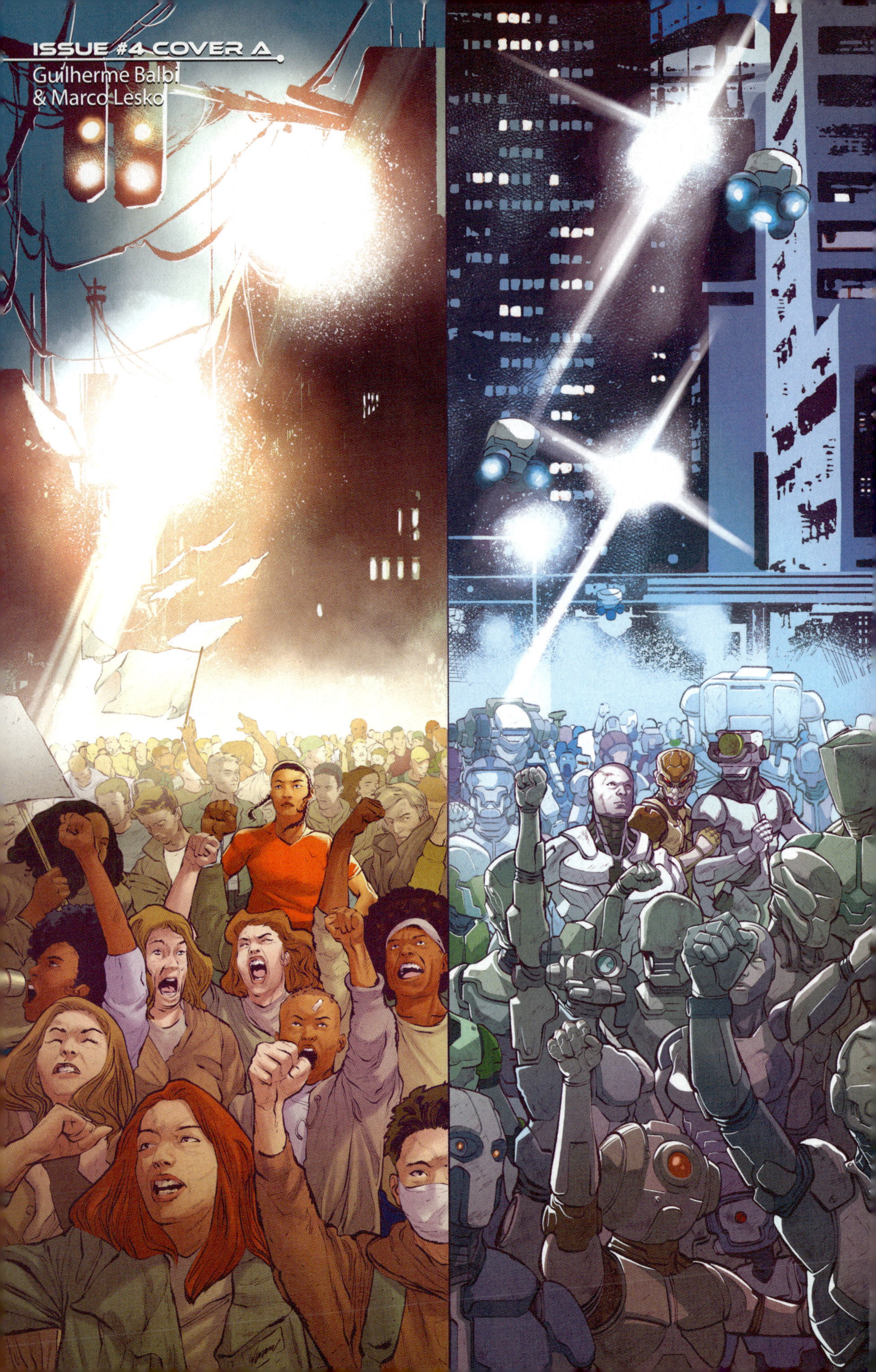
ISSUE #4 COVER A
Guilherme Balbi
& Marco Lesko

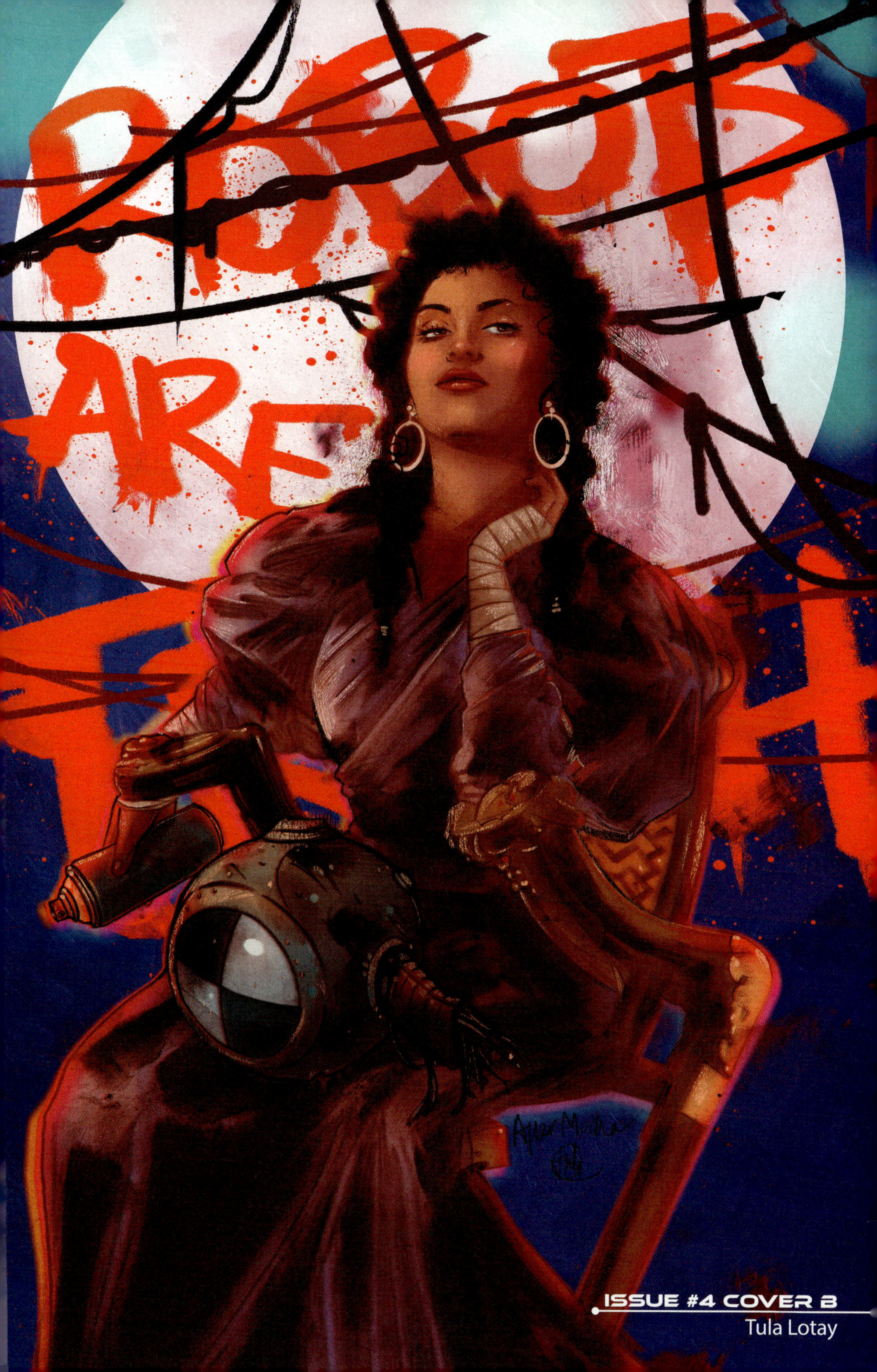

ISSUE #4 COVER B
Tula Lotay

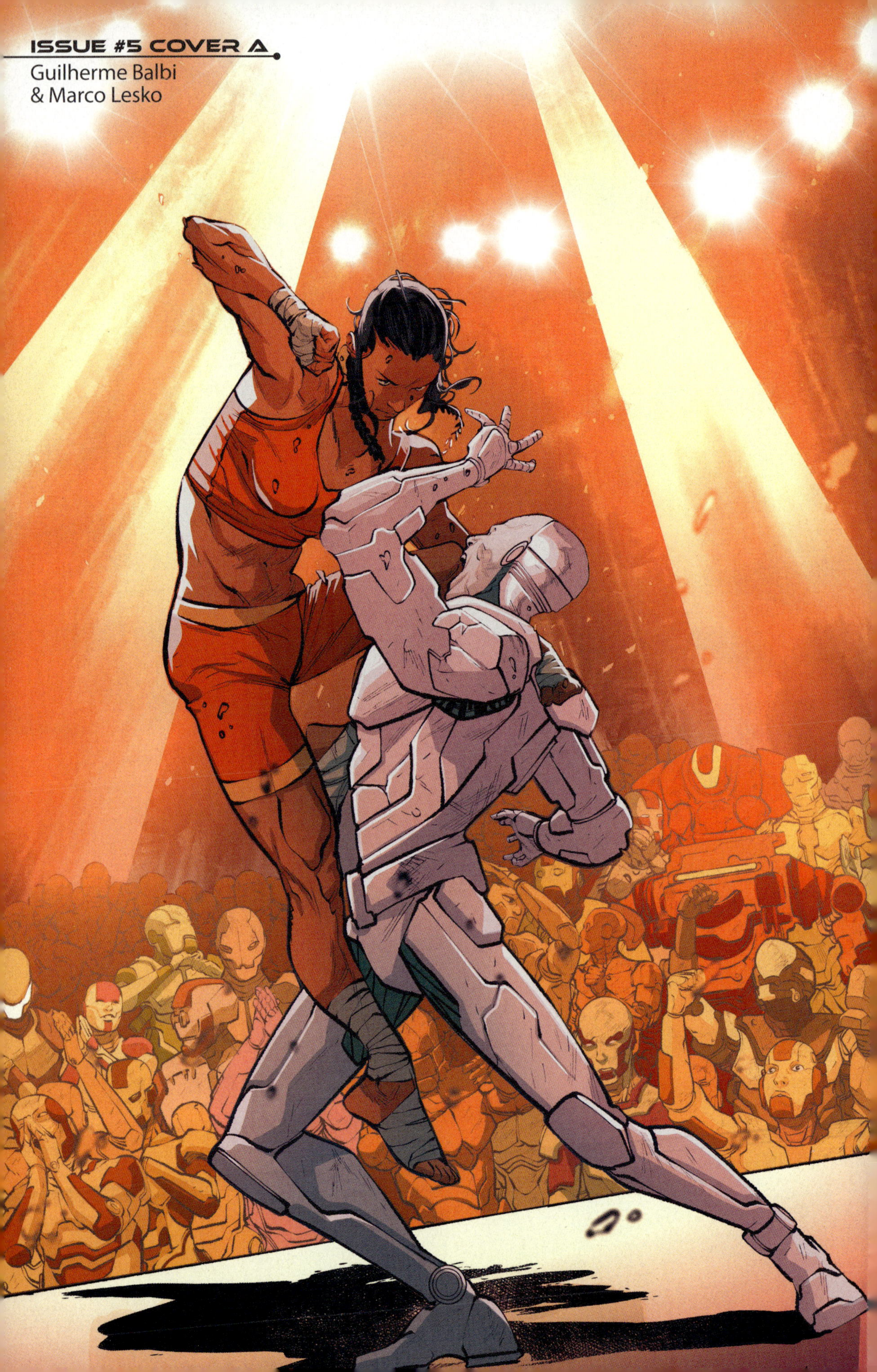

ISSUE #5 COVER A
Guilherme Balbi
& Marco Lesko

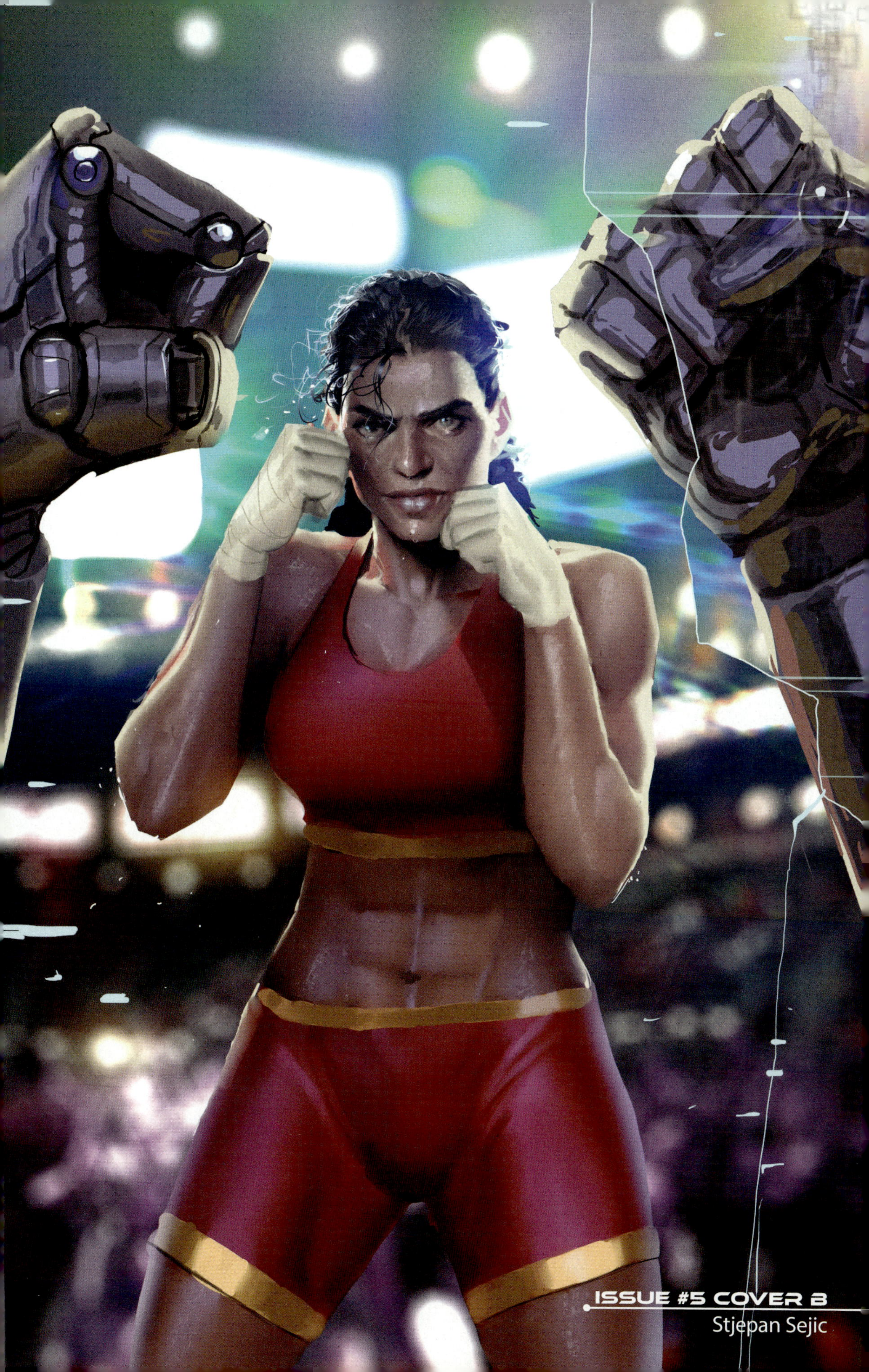
ISSUE #5 COVER B
Stjepan Sejic

MEET THE TEAM

ZACK KAPLAN
Zack is a break out science fiction comic writer and creator of such comics and graphic novels as FOREVER FORWARD, MINDSET, METAL SOCIETY, BREAK OUT, JOIN THE FUTURE, THE LOST CITY EXPLORERS, PORT OF EARTH and ECLIPSE. He has worked with publishers such as Image/Top Cow, Dark Horse, Aftershock, Vault, Humanoids, Scout Comics and DC Comics. His first three series were all optioned for TV adaptation, with PORT OF EARTH currently being developed by Robert Kirkman's Skybound Entertainment and Amazon TV Studios. Zack has taught screenwriting and storytelling at the International Academy of Film and TV, located in the Philippines. He lives in Los Angeles.

GUILHERME BALBI
Guilherme is a comics artist, best known for his work on the comic book adaptation of the original screenplay for the film Alien, and Avatar for Dark Horse Comics. He is also the creator of the independent comic Universo Jackpot (2015), published through crowdfunding and selected for the MAX-Minas Gerais Audiovisual Expo round of events, pre-nominated for 2 awards in Brazil. In addition to Dark Horse Comics, he has worked for other American publishers such as IDW, DC Comics and Dynamite Comics, as well as Hollywood film and animation productions such as Spartacus: Blood and Sand - Motion Comic. He is also a professor at Casa dos Quadrinhos Technical School of Visual Arts.

MARCO LESKO
Marco is a comic book colorist working professionally since 2013. He has worked with publishers such as AWA, Penguin Random House (DC, Marvel, Dreamworks, etc.), Glenat, Top Cow, Dark Horse, Image Comics (Shadowline), Titan Comics, Zenescope Entertainment, Aftershock Comics, and Dynamite Comics. His published work includes The Twilight Zone, Rat Queens, Brilliant Trash, Doctor Who, The Shadow, Red Sonja, Warhammer 40k, Batman, Wonder Woman, Robotech, Assassins Creed Uprising, and Grimm Tales of Terror.

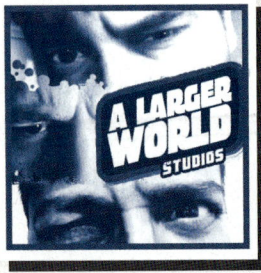

TROY PETERI
Troy and Dave Lanphear are collectively known as A Larger World Studios. They've lettered everything from The Avengers, Iron Man, Wolverine, Amazing Spider-Man and X-Men to more recent titles such as Witchblade, Cyberforce, and Batman/Wonder Woman: The Brave & The Bold. They can be reached at studio@alargerworld.com for your lettering and design needs. (Hooray, commerce!)

ALSO AVAILABLE FROM
ZACK KAPLAN

ECLIPSE

In the near future, a mysterious solar event has transformed the sun's light into deadly immolating rays. The world's few survivors now live in nocturnal cities. But a killer emerges who uses sunlight to burn his victims, and when he targets the daughter of a solar power mogul, it falls to a disillusioned solar engineer to protect her.

ECLIPSE
ZACK KAPLAN · GIOVANNI TIMPANO · CHRIS NORTHROP
VOLUME ONE

VOLUME 1
ISBN: 978-1-5343-0297-6

ECLIPSE
ZACK KAPLAN · GIOVANNI TIMPANO · FLAVIO DISPENZA
VOLUME TWO

VOLUME 2
ISBN: 978-1-5343-0588-5

ECLIPSE
ZACK KAPLAN · GIOVANNI TIMPANO · FLAVIO DISPENZA
VOLUME THREE

VOLUME 3
ISBN: 978-1-5343-1308-8

ECLIPSE
ZACK KAPLAN · GIOVANNI TIMPANO · FLAVIO DISPENZA
VOLUME FOUR

VOLUME 4
ISBN: 978-1-5343-1545-7

PORT OF EARTH

179° 56' 39.4' X 0° 2' 46.2

Imagine if aliens came to Earth not in war or peace, but with a business deal: open up a spaceport here on Earth in exchange for advanced technology. But when our alien visitors break Port restrictions and wreak havoc in our cities, it falls to the newly formed Earth Security Agents to hunt down and safely deport the dangerous rogue aliens back to the Port of Earth.

VOLUME 1
PORT OF EARTH

VOLUME 1
ISBN: 978-1-5343-0912-8

VOLUME 2
PORT OF EARTH

VOLUME 2
ISBN: 978-1-5343-1192-3

VOLUME 3
PORT OF EARTH

VOLUME 3
ISBN: 978-1-5343-1577-8

The Top Cow essentials checklist:

A Man Among Ye, Volume 1
(ISBN: 978-1-5343-1691-1)

Aphrodite IX: Rebirth, Volume 1
(ISBN: 978-1-60706-828-0)

Blood Stain, Volume 1
(ISBN: 978-1-63215-544-3)

The Complete Cyberforce, Volume 1
(ISBN: 978-1-5343-2221-9)

The Clock, Volume 1
(ISBN: 978-1-5343-1611-9)

The Complete Darkness, Volume 1
(ISBN: 978-1-5343-1793-2)

Death Vigil, Volume 1
(ISBN: 978-1-63215-278-7)

Eclipse, Volume 1
(ISBN: 978-1-5343-0038-5)

The Freeze, OGN
(ISBN: 978-1-5343-1211-1)

Fine Print, Volume 1
(ISBN: 978-1-5343-2070-3)

Helm Greycastle, Volume 1
(ISBN: 978-1-5343-1962-2)

Infinite Dark, Volume 1
(ISBN: 978-1-5343-1056-8)

La Mano Del Destino, Volume 1
(ISBN: 978-1-5343-1947-9)

**La Voz De M.A.Y.O.:
Tata Rambo, Volume 1**
(ISBN: 978-1-5343-1363-7)

Paradox Girl, Volume 1
(ISBN: 978-1-5343-1220-3)

Port of Earth, Volume 1
(ISBN: 978-1-5343-0646-2)

Postal, Volume 1
(ISBN: 978-1-63215-342-5)

Punderworld, Volume 1
(ISBN: 978-1-5343-2072-7)

Stairway Anthology
(ISBN: 978-1-5343-1702-4)

Sugar, Volume 1
(ISBN: 978-1-5343-1641-7)

Sunstone, Volume 1
(ISBN: 978-1-63215-212-1)

Swing, Volume 1
(ISBN: 978-1-5343-0516-8)

Symmetry, Volume 1
(ISBN: 978-1-63215-699-0)

Syphon, Volume 1
(ISBN: 978-1-5343-2073-4)

The Clock, OGN
(ISBN: 978-1-5343-1611-9)

The Tithe, Volume 1
(ISBN: 978-1-63215-324-1)

Think Tank, Volume 1
(ISBN: 978-1-60706-660-6)

The Complete Witchblade, Volume 1
(ISBN: 978-1-5343-1564-8)

For more ISBN and ordering information on our latest collections go to:
www.topcow.com
Ask your retailer about our catalogue of collected editions, digests, and hard covers
or check the listings at: **Barnes and Noble, Amazon.com,** and other fine retailers.

To find your nearest comic shop go to:
www.comicshoplocator.com